THE ENCOUNTER

THE ENCOUNTER

HANNA HORRELL

APEX PUBLISHING LTD

First published in 2006 by
Apex Publishing Ltd
PO Box 7086, Clacton on Sea, Essex, CO15 5WN

www.apexpublishing.co.uk

Copyright © 2006 by Hanna Horrell
The author has asserted her moral rights

British Library Cataloguing-in-Publication Data
A catalogue record for this book
is available from the British Library

ISBN 1-904444-79-2

All rights reserved. This book is sold subject to the condition, that no part of this book is to be reproduced, in any shape or form. Or by way of trade, stored in a retrieval system or transmitted in any form or by any means, electronic, mechanical, photocopying, recording, be lent, re-sold, hired out or otherwise circulated in any form of binding or cover other than that in which it is published and without a similar condition, including this condition being imposed on the subsequent purchaser, without prior permission of the copyright holder.

Typeset in 10pt Baskerville Win95BT

Production Manager: Chris Cowlin
Cover Design: "Untitled" London.

Printed and bound in Great Britain

To my wonderful daughter, Paola.

1

The house was still and quiet, apart from the gentle rhythmic sound of breathing from my fiancé, Mark, who was sleeping peacefully in bed beside me. I lay motionless, doing my best to ignore the strange voice I could hear in my head. By now I was used to hearing different voices and most of the time I paid no attention to them, but tonight the voice was very persistent, urging me to go to the open fields at the back of the house. This was strange, as until tonight I had not been asked to do anything specific.

The words kept buzzing in my head until I could no longer ignore them. Slowly, I lifted the blanket from my body and inched out of bed, being careful not to disturb Mark. Very quietly, I tiptoed from the bedroom, then downstairs through the kitchen to the back of the house. I slipped my feet into a pair of flip-flops and carefully unlocked and opened the white panelled door.

It was the middle of summer and the night was very warm. The air was fresh and smelled of newly cut grass and hot soil. The sky was illuminated by the full moon. Looking into the far distance beyond the garden, despite the moonlight, I could see nothing but a sheet of blackness. I began to feel apprehensive, but the voice in my head urged me to go forwards and not to be afraid. I hesitated, but only for a moment, as I felt that it was imperative that I go to the fields to see why I was being called. Stepping into the garden, I continued across the grass to the back iron gate. Just behind the gate, to my left, were ancient tall trees and straight ahead of me wild overgrown bushes with a narrow path running between them.

Afraid of the darkness, of being alone, I stepped onto the pathway and, feeling my way around with my hands, I carefully edged my way forwards, my hearing sharpened to any unexpected sounds. Soon my eyes adjusted to the lack of light and I could just about distinguish the path ahead of me. As I came to the end of it, I could hear a faint humming noise, and then I noticed small bright lights in the distance.

The lights appeared unusual, so I stopped to look at them more carefully. They flickered about two metres above the ground and gave an impression of moving in an oblong pattern. I realised that they were attached to a circular object, which was shaped like an upturned deep plate of about ten metres in diameter. I hesitated, unsure if it was safe to move forwards, but at the same time I was very curious and wanted to get a closer look. It appeared to be some sort of craft. As I deliberated my next move, I heard a voice asking me to come closer. Wishing that Mark were with me, I took a few steps farther, then stopped again.

Quite unexpectedly, a small door at the top of the craft began to slide to one side and rays of light escaped and illuminated the surrounding area. The door opened fully and a tall, slim figure emerged, standing in the bright light of the doorway. The figure motioned with its long arms as if inviting me to move forwards. I could not be sure if it was a man or a woman, but I assumed it to be male because its movements seemed masculine to me. However, I did not move and he made the gesture again. At the same time, I could hear a voice saying: *"Please come closer. I assure you that you are perfectly safe."*

I knew it was him speaking to me, yet he didn't make a sound. The message simply resonated in my head. I stood rooted to the spot, stunned that he could communicate with me like this. He seemed to know what I was thinking because suddenly I heard: *"This may seem very strange to you, but why should it be? We have been communicating with you through your psyche for a very long time."*

This really shocked me, as I had not known the origin of the voices in my head. It was rather bizarre that they were coming from this person who did not look much like a human being. His head was rather long and narrow, and his eyes were very large, much larger than the eyes of anyone I had ever come into contact with before. His ears were also large and looked as though they were stuck to the sides of his head. He wore what appeared to be a pale grey one-piece suit.

As I watched, I realised that I wanted to get closer and took a few more steps forwards. The craft seemed to be made of some sort of metal and yet I knew it was not of any kind I had ever encountered before. The top half had a few small indentations that looked like windows and a faint light could be seen filtering through from the interior.

The alien-like person began to descend the curved surface of the craft on a rigid, silently moving platform, which eventually came to a halt. When he stepped down in front of me I felt him say: *"Thank you for coming. We are very honoured."* There was a small pause before he continued, *"You are probably not aware that there is a cosmic plan in motion for your planet and your people. This cosmic plan is vast and is essentially the transition of your planet and your people into the new energetic structures of higher dimensions. Once this transition is complete, the inhabitants of your planet will be able to function in many different realities and the planet itself will be restored to its original purpose of becoming an intergalactic exchange centre of information. It is a huge undertaking, but without you, or rather people like you, we cannot succeed."*

"People like me?" I questioned, feeling very confused.

"Yes, Planet Earth needs evolved people like you to help with this transition. We have been calling many, but very few have responded. The cosmos cannot wait any longer. Time is running out."

I thought that a lot was being expected of me.

"It sounds like a big responsibility," I said.

"It is big, but you already know that."

"I want to help, but I am not old enough to take on such a huge responsibility," I tried to protest.

"Your body might be young, but your soul is thousands of years old," he communicated in response.

"I don't understand," I muttered to myself.

"You will, once you reach within. All the information is encoded within your being and you just need to access it."

He reached into a pocket in his suit and extracted a large crystal-like object, which he handed to me.

"This crystal contains all the information about Planet Earth. You will soon

be able to read it. This is a very powerful object and it is important that it does not get into the hands of people who are working against the cosmic plan. We know these people as 'The Manipulators'. They have been controlling your planet for centuries. Now, your planet is to be taken away from them and handed back to its rightful owners."

He had not spoken verbally and yet I heard every word and understood the great importance of the task.

"What do you need me to do?" I asked.

"*Your inner voice will guide you,*" he replied.

"Who are you?"

"*My name is Amos. You often hear me.*"

"So you are the mysterious voice I hear in my head?"

"*You hear my voice and also the voices of others. You can easily be misled, so always follow your instinct. When you are not sure of the right path to follow, ask for guidance and we'll be there to guide you.*"

It seemed that our meeting was over, as quite unexpectedly he turned and stood back on the platform, which began ascending towards the illuminated door. I looked at the crystal in my hand and could feel heat radiating from it, spreading all over my body. Suddenly, I felt very peaceful and contented.

I waited for Amos to disappear inside the craft, which was obviously a spaceship of some kind. When the door closed, the humming noise increased and it slowly started to rise skywards. Then, without warning, it rapidly accelerated, leaving a bright blue streak of light in the sky. I was alone in the field. Surprisingly, I felt very calm and any fear I had felt earlier had now completely left me. As I turned around and started walking back towards the house, I couldn't help thinking that I had been entrusted with a great responsibility and questioned whether I would be able to cope when I heard his voice once more.

"*You will not be asked to do more than you can cope with.*"

I smiled to myself, totally reassured.

When I reached the house, the back door was ajar. I could not recall if I had left it open, but everything seemed quiet, which could only mean that Mark was still asleep in bed. I climbed the stairs as quietly as I could and carefully opened the bedroom door.

"Why are you sneaking in?" Mark mumbled, startling me.

"I am not sneaking in," I replied. "I just didn't want to wake you."

"Too late, I am already awake." He reached out and switched on his bedside light. "What were you doing downstairs?"

I could not possibly tell him the truth.

"I went to the kitchen to get a drink."

"I thought I heard you outside," he remarked.

"Yes, I needed some fresh air."

"Why is it that I don't believe you?" Mark opened his eyes fully and noticed the crystal. "What on earth have you got in your hand?" he asked.

"Oh, it's just a crystal I found outside," I replied, hoping he wouldn't ask further questions.

"Let me see it," he said. "It seems to reflect the light in a very unusual way."

I opened my hand and he grabbed the stone from me.

"Shit!" he screamed, dropping it on the bed in shock. "The bloody thing burnt my hand!"

"Surely it's not that hot," I said, surprised. "I'd been holding it in my hand for some time before you snatched it."

"Take it away!" he demanded angrily, raising his hands above his head.

I picked up the crystal, carefully placing it on top of my bedside table before I climbed back into bed.

"I don't want it in the house. Get rid of it tomorrow," Mark ordered.

"But it's only a harmless stone," I protested.

"It's not harmless and if you don't get rid of it I will. I am not keeping some radioactive junk in my house."

"Don't be silly," I laughed. "It's not radioactive."

"And you know that for sure?"

"Yes, I do know," I replied simply. "Besides, the crystal is mine and you are not allowed to throw it away."

"Oh, don't give me that crap. The bloody thing burnt my hand."

"It didn't burn mine."

"It's enough that it burnt mine. Get rid of it!"

Mark could be really annoying at times.

"All right, I will," I said irritably, to end the conversation. "Now, could you please turn off your light so I can go to sleep?"

While Mark went back to sleep, oblivious to everything, I lay next to him thinking about the most amazing events of the night. The whole experience was extraordinary, and yet I had always known that I was in contact with some other beings from a different place or dimension. Deep down I had always known I was different and that I was here for a reason even if I did not understand it. Tonight that purpose had become much clearer.

Just before I fell asleep I had a very strong feeling that my life would never be the same again.

* * *

A stream of daylight falling on my face awoke me the next morning. I rubbed my eyes before I opened them. Mark had pulled the heavy cream curtains apart and was gazing outside, his broad frame cutting out most of the light.

"Hi," I muttered sleepily.

"Looks like it's going to rain again," he complained, turning away from the window. "Bloody English weather."

I did not respond. I wanted to talk about last night's experience, but Mark was not a person with whom I could discuss it. I knew he simply would not understand, for any supernatural or paranormal subject had always provoked an aggressive reaction in him. Thankfully, he seemed to be preoccupied with his thoughts and didn't notice my reluctance to speak.

As soon as he had left the room I got up, put my dressing gown on and, pulling it tightly around me, made my way to the bathroom. I brushed my teeth, rinsed my face with cold water and combed my shoulder-length dark hair, securing it together at the back with an elastic band. Looking in the mirror over the sink, I noticed that my green eyes looked unusually bright and my cheeks were flushed. I felt quite heady. I splashed some more cold water on my face, dried it with a towel and went downstairs to the kitchen.

Mark was sitting at the head of the table reading a newspaper, a half-eaten bowl of cereal in front of him.

"Would you like some coffee?" I asked casually.

"Please," he replied, without looking up from the paper.

I filled the kettle and switched it on. Gazing at Mark, with his dark hair sprinkled with grey at the temples and the creases in his brow, I suddenly felt very lonely as I knew I could not share my deepest thoughts and anxieties with him. It seemed odd that our lives were poles apart and yet we were to be married. Well, opposites attract. I quickly reminded myself to stem the unsettling thoughts.

Soon the kettle had boiled and I made two cups of coffee and put them on the table. I dropped two slices of brown bread into the toaster, and when they popped up I put them on a small plate and sat down. I spread the toast with butter and marmalade and took a bite, then realised that I was not at all hungry. I put the toast to one side and sipped my coffee.

Various fragmented thoughts were churning through my mind, which I found difficult to piece together. My life had altered irrevocably and it seemed almost impossible to carry on as normal, and yet I knew I had to do so as if nothing had happened. Trying hard to focus on my current reality, I forced myself to concentrate on the still-life painting on which I was currently working. It was difficult and my mind kept reverting to the events of the previous night and the conversation with Amos. I had many unanswered questions and I resolved to listen to the voices more carefully in future.

Mark folded his paper and quickly finished his breakfast.

"Thanks, hon," he said, taking his jacket from the back of the chair. He kissed me on the cheek. "Don't wait up for me. I'll be late tonight."

"Again?" I asked, disappointed.

"Sorry, honey. Dinner with the boss," he replied evasively, and headed for the door.

I gathered the dishes from the table and popped them into the sink, waiting until I heard Mark's car leaving the driveway before making my way back upstairs. In the bedroom, as I walked to my side of the bed, I was immediately drawn to the crystal sparkling on my bedside table. I stared at it for a moment, fascinated by the strong light inside it, which looked like a bright star emanating outwards. I was surprised I had not noticed it the previous night.

Gently, I lifted the crystal and held it in my hand. I felt warmth spreading throughout my body as if the stone wanted to convey some sort of information to me. I closed my eyes, tried to concentrate and was surprised when a disturbing thought came into my mind. I didn't understand why, but I had a distinctive feeling that Japan was going to be shaken by a gigantic earthquake within the next 24 hours. Pushing the unpleasant feeling away as something unimportant, I momentarily considered hiding the stone away, but instead placed it back on the bedside table.

I got dressed in a pair of green tracksuit bottoms and a cotton T-shirt, and made my way to the conservatory, which I used as a studio. It was the perfect room in which to paint in oils, as light streamed through three glass walls and the glass roof. Even on rainy days there was sufficient light for painting, although it would be much softer and, of course, created fewer noticeable shadows.

I looked at the still life of silk flowers, jewellery and silver arranged on a small desk on the left-hand side of the room. Two days previously I had been pleased with the composition, but now, however, I was not at all sure. The more I looked at it the more unsure I felt. Eventually, I decided to change it even though I had started painting it, so I altered the position of the silver hand-held mirror from the front of the arrangement to the side. The silk flowers were loosely laid and I tried to move them around to achieve a better balance. I also moved the jewellery, but I was still not happy with the overall effect. I spent another ten minutes trying to make changes, but could not achieve the desired result.

As I stopped for a moment, trying to decide what to move next, I heard a small voice within telling me to leave the still life and listen. I understood that I needed to relax fully before important information would be imparted to me.

I made my way to the spare room, which was located next to the living room downstairs. Apart from a bookcase and a small table, the room was practically empty and I used it for meditation. I closed the curtains to cut out the light and lowered myself onto a soft mat, arranging my body in the lotus position. Closing my eyes, I started breathing deeply into my stomach in an attempt to empty my mind. Almost immediately my body started to feel warm and a quiet voice began:

"*Many are called, but few are chosen. You have been called and now is the time when you have an opportunity to prove yourself and your commitment to the cosmos. Planet Earth is changing its energetic structure and needs highly energetic people to help with this change. You have reincarnated many times on Earth and other planets of the cosmos to learn and understand the cosmic laws. You have learnt a lot of valuable lessons: the difference between right and wrong, and that cosmic laws are absolute. The cosmic knowledge is within you. The changes that are taking place on your planet now are fully understood by your inner self. You have been preparing for this moment in history for many centuries and now is the time when the cosmos calls for your help. Through your calmness you will be able to access cosmic knowledge and know what needs to be done...*

"*Planet Earth is going through a purification process before it enters into its new energetic structure. There will be earthquakes, floods and volcanic eruptions. Planet Earth is changing - it is clearing itself of unwanted energies, purifying itself to its very core. The inhabitants of Planet Earth are part of this purification process and those who can raise their own personal body frequency will be able to move forwards and benefit from the planetary changes. The ones who are self-absorbed and not prepared to look within will be left behind. The values of the majority of people on your planet are different from the cosmic values. The self-centred attitudes and creed of greed have to go. The new energies descending on the planet will force people to learn new ways; the ways of the cosmos. As they learn, the old belief systems will be replaced with the new understanding based on cosmic knowledge ... These changes have already started and time is running out.*"

I felt I needed to ask a question. "What is my role in all this?"

The voice continued, *"You are to be a representative of the cosmos. You will act as a channel for new energies and will emanate with high frequency. This frequency will draw other people to you, people you need to educate. You will show them the right way, the way of the cosmos."*

"I am not sure I am properly equipped for the task. My knowledge is limited," I said.

"The knowledge is within you, and you know how to reach it. We will also teach you while you sleep."

I needed to ask more questions, but I felt that it was not the right time. I had to absorb what I had experienced and learnt already. As though sensing my feelings, the energy behind the voice left my body and the connection was lost.

Untangling my legs, I lay flat on the mat, trying to evaluate what I had just learnt. I was to educate people and show them the right way. I felt that it was too immense a task for one person and I would be unable to do it alone. Silently, I requested guidance.

In response I heard: *"You are not expected to do it on your own. You will be guided to the one who will help you. For now, carry on as before."*

Reassured, I left the meditation room and returned to the conservatory. I examined the still life in front of me and knew immediately how to adjust it to improve the composition. I made the necessary changes, which worked very well. Trying to return to some kind of normality, I decided to spend the rest of the day painting. As soon as I started working I felt that I would make good progress. My brush strokes were very definite and I was achieving the required result without a great deal of effort. I painted late into the night.

* * *

I stretched my arm across the bed and was surprised to find it empty. Still groggy from sleep, I half-opened my eyes and glanced at the bedside clock, noting that it was already a quarter to ten. Mark must have left for work already, I realised, immediately disappointed as it was my birthday and he had left without saying goodbye.

With a heavy heart, I lifted my body out of bed and made my way downstairs. As I walked into the kitchen my eyes were drawn to a narrow package wrapped in silver paper, which lay in the middle of the kitchen table. Propped against it was a pink envelope marked 'Carrie'.

Slowly, I opened the envelope, extracted a birthday card and read the message: 'To my darling Carrie, happy 25th birthday. Lots of love, Mark.' Putting the card to one side, I removed the wrapping paper and opened the narrow, black velvet box to find inside, on a bed of cream satin, an exquisite gold necklace. The necklace sparkled with diamonds and emeralds beautifully crafted in the shape of small flowers. I stared at the jewellery, but did not remove it from the box. I thought that it was such an extravagant present, one I certainly did not need. Mark really didn't know me at all. I would have preferred more affection from him and a tender goodbye instead of this expensive necklace. Is he ever going to realise how to really make me happy? I wondered.

As I closed the box and placed it back on the table, I couldn't help thinking that we had totally different needs - mine were very basic and had nothing to do with spending a lot of money, whereas Mark's sense of security revolved around money and luxurious items. That realisation made me question for the first time if he was the right man for me. Swiftly, I pushed such detrimental thoughts to the back of my mind. There was no point in analysing our incompatibility as our wedding was due to take place in three months.

In the corner of the kitchen, on the work surface by the window, there was a small portable radio and I switched it on. It was coming up to 10 o'clock and I felt I needed to listen to the news. I was sitting at the table, eating my cereal, when the announcement came:

"An earthquake with a magnitude of eight on the Richter scale rocked Japan's northern island of Hokkaido early this morning, injuring hundreds, cutting off electricity and water to thousands, igniting a spectacular oil tank blaze and demolishing part of an airport roof. The tremor, centred in the Pacific about 60 miles off Hokkaido's eastern shore, was followed by several strong aftershocks and a small tsunami. Three hundred and twenty-three people were confirmed injured and 24 seriously hurt ..."

I stopped listening at that point, as it suddenly occurred to me that I had known about the earthquake the day before, when I held the crystal. The realisation that the crystal was powerful enough to connect me to this kind of information was unnerving, especially when I considered that I had insight into impending disasters before they actually occurred. What was the point of my having this knowledge and not sharing it with anyone? Assuming I did share it with others, who would believe me? Most importantly, why would I need to know about upcoming disasters if I could not help anyone? The answer was simple - I had to put the crystal away and never connect to it. What I didn't know would not worry or scare me.

With that resolve I rushed upstairs and grabbed the crystal from my bedside table. I was gazing around the room looking for a place in which to hide it when suddenly I could hear a deep, loud, grinding noise that I realised was the sound of the earth's plates moving. Somehow I knew that the sounds were coming from the San Andreas Fault in California. Even more shaken, I quickly opened the drawer of the bedside cabinet and dropped the crystal into it, even more quickly slamming it shut. I took a deep breath and immediately felt better.

The unexpected sudden sound of the doorbell startled me. Taking a few more deep breaths to regain my composure, I went downstairs to answer it. I was relieved to see that it was my friend, Zoe, the closest friend I'd ever had. We'd been friends since our school days and met frequently for a chat and an exchange of the latest gossip. With a wide smile on her face, Zoe handed me a bunch of flowers and pulled a small packet out of her bag.

"Happy birthday!" she exclaimed. "Sorry for coming unannounced."

"Oh, don't be silly," I said, happy to see her. "You know you are always welcome, especially on my birthday." Leading her into the kitchen, I turned and said, "You are looking really well."

Zoe's skin was nicely suntanned, accentuating her short blonde-streaked hair and blue eyes. She was of medium height with a firm, slim body, maintained by rigorous exercise and a very strict diet.

"I should hope so, since I've just got back from the Greek islands," Zoe said saucily.

"How was it?" I asked, looking for a vase.

"It was really good. The weather was beautiful and there were a lot of very handsome men. Not that I met anyone special."

I smiled, because men had always been Zoe's favourite topic of conversation, and ever since I could remember she'd been looking for her Mr Right.

"You will meet that someone special when you least expect it," I said.

"I live in hope." Zoe picked up the narrow necklace box from Mark and opened it. "Wow, some present!"

"You know Mark, he likes to show off," I said, placing the flowers in the vase and putting it on the table. "Orange juice?"

Zoe nodded. "Orange juice is fine."

I filled two glasses with freshly squeezed orange juice and handed one to Zoe.

"Let's go into the living room."

Zoe sat on a blue armchair and I took a seat on the contrasting dark pink sofa to her left.

"So, are you planning a big celebration?" Zoe enquired, taking a sip from her glass.

"Not this year. A dinner with Mark is all I've planned so far."

"Anything exciting happened while I was away?"

I hesitated. So much had happened in the last few days that it was nothing short of overwhelming. I felt a desperate need to share my experiences with someone but, although I knew I could talk to Zoe about certain things, I also knew I would have to be very careful how much information I imparted. I did not want to frighten her.

"You know I hear voices?" I ventured.

Zoe nodded.

"Well, there is this being called Amos who communicates with me through my psyche." I was pretty sure it wasn't Amos who had communicated the last message to me, but I decided to use his name to make it more believable. "In the last few days he has told me amazing things."

"What sort of things?" Zoe sounded interested.

"He explained that the planet is going through a massive energetic change and this change will force everyone to respond. Either people have to alter their ways of thinking and accept the ways of the cosmos or they will not be able to cope. My understanding is that these new energies are to support the transition of a human being on this planet into a higher level of consciousness."

"This sounds very profound, but how are people supposed to know the ways of the cosmos?" Zoe enquired.

"Apparently, all the information is encoded within our inner self and we just need to learn how to read it."

"This is fascinating. Tell me more," Zoe demanded, shifting her body forwards in the armchair.

I was unsure what to tell her, so I just followed my intuition.

"My understanding is that the physical body is like a solid mass of energy, which is very dense with a very low frequency. To connect to our inner self, which is our true self, it is necessary to raise the frequency of the physical aspect. Within our bodies there are many encoded emotions: old traumas, old experiences. This encoding is keeping us continually on the same level and it stands in the way of our being able to access inner knowledge and connect to the higher energies of the cosmos. As the new energies hit the planet, this encoding is going to be brought to the surface and can be replaced by cosmic responses. We will be able to remove the current responses to things like fear, anger and greed from our bodies, and replace them with new ones of a much higher frequency, raising the overall body frequency at the same time."

I stopped speaking, suddenly surprised at the information that was flowing through me. As far as I knew, I had no previous knowledge of this. Was someone speaking through me or was I reaching within? I was not exactly sure.

Zoe looked at me with an absolute amazement.

"If what you are saying is true, it means that a human being on this planet has never experienced direct connection to the divine energy."

"Yes, because the density of our physical bodies does not allow us to channel high frequency energies. Emotions like fear, anger and lust, which are ever present in our bodies, are blocking the flow of divine energy."

"What about love?" Zoe asked.

"Love needs to be pure. It should be expressed unconditionally."

"Does that mean that we need to get rid of all our lower emotions?"

"No, they need to be there. They are like warning signals, however. Most of the time they will be dormant, as we will respond cosmically to various situations. For example, you might feel anger, but you would not act on it. It would just be information to you that something is not quite right and requires your attention."

Zoe seemed confused. "What I don't understand is how are we supposed to change our emotions into cosmic responses?"

"The body needs to stay calm to allow the frequency to rise," I replied. "When we express our emotions the body loses vital energy."

"It sounds simple enough, but our emotions are a big part of who we are. Controlling them would change our identity."

"It might seem that way, but isn't it much better to control our emotions instead of them controlling us? Take anger, for example. It is often expressed through violence, which frequently breeds hatred and more violence. Wouldn't the world be a better place without hatred and violence?" I asked.

"Yes, definitely," Zoe agreed. "Do you think people can change?"

"I understand that there will be many dramatic events taking place on the planet, and people will be forced to ask questions. Those who can think for themselves will find the answers within and change their ways. Those who can't will be left behind."

"I am all for it. This planet is long overdue for a change."

"I couldn't agree more."

Zoe glanced at her watch. "Gosh!" she exclaimed, rising. "I have a client in 15 minutes. I have to go."

"Put some time aside for a chat next week," I said, walking her to the door.

"Call me," she said hastily, before leaving.

I walked to the kitchen and opened Zoe's present. It was a lovely pink T-shirt with a shiny pink letter 'C' printed on the front. As I was going out to take one of my paintings to the gallery I decided to wear it. I changed my clothes quickly, grabbed the already wrapped painting and made my way to the car, which was parked outside at the front of the house. The painting was too big to fit into the boot of my Mini, so I placed it on the back seat and drove off.

Twenty minutes later I reached the outskirts of London. The gallery was located in Victoria and I took my usual route through Hyde Park. I was approaching Grosvenor Gardens when I became aware of loud sirens coming from all directions. I slowed down and pulled over to my left, allowing three police motorcycles to pass. When I reached Grosvenor Gardens the police had already cordoned off the area and the traffic was being redirected. There was a feeling of urgency in the air. The policemen began taping the place and people were hurriedly dispersing from the main station.

I slowed down by one of the bikes and lowered my window. "What's happening, officer?" I asked.

"Suspect package at the station, madam," the policeman replied shortly. "We are evacuating the area."

I had no choice but to take a different route. The traffic was snarled up in front of me and was very quickly building up behind. I ended up driving through Victoria's back streets and it took ages before I finally got to my destination. Parking had always been a problem in the area of the gallery, but on this occasion I was lucky enough to find an available space just outside the building. I glanced at my watch and realised that I was very late for my appointment with the owner, Mr Kaplowski. Urgently, I fished in my bag for some change and dropped it into the parking meter, allowing myself 20 minutes.

Grabbing the painting from the back seat, I entered the gallery where most of my paintings were sold. It was a small place with extensive front windows and light coloured walls on which various paintings were displayed, making the room colourful and warm. Directly opposite the front windows, at the back, stood a dark wooden desk covered with loose papers, behind which was a door leading to the private part of the gallery. I had an agreement with Mr Kaplowski that he would display my work and pay me as and when the paintings were sold. Fortunately, my work was selling rather well and I had never had to wait too long for the money. There was no one behind the desk, so I glanced through the half-open back door trying to locate Mr Kaplowski, but could not see him.

"Can I help you?" asked a pleasant male voice to my side.

I turned and faced a tall young man, dressed casually in jeans and a white, open-necked cotton shirt.

"I am looking for Mr Kaplowski," I said. "Is he about?"

His warm smile illuminated his face and I couldn't help thinking that he was very attractive. I noticed that he had green eyes, the same colour as mine, and as our eyes met I had the oddest sensation of feeling as though I knew him. I was certain I had never met him before, but somehow he seemed familiar.

"Unfortunately Mr Kaplowski had to go out. He left me in charge," the young man explained, and glanced at the painting I was holding in my hand.

I placed the wrapped canvas against the desk. "I would like to leave this here, if I may," I said. "I painted it for one of Mr Kaplowski's clients and I understand I can get the money for it quite quickly."

He gave me a long look and smiled again. If I didn't know any better I would have sworn he was flirting with me.

"Would you mind if I unwrap it?" he asked. "I would love to see it."

"Sure," I replied, quite surprised that he was interested in my work.

He moved some papers to one side of the desk and placed my painting on it. Carefully, he removed the wrapping, lifted the canvas and held it out at arm's length. He scrutinised the painting for a short while and then turned his gaze in my direction.

"There is a lot of sensitivity in your work. It is a beautifully painted still life," he commented.

I couldn't help feeling pleased that he liked it. "Why, thank you."

His eyes returned to the painting. "I have a feeling that painting is something you love to do. It's not something you do purely to earn money."

I was surprised he could see that just by examining my painting. "You are very perceptive," I commented.

He looked straight into my eyes and I found I could not hold his gaze as it was so penetrating.

"I study the history of art," he said.

I smiled. "That explains it."

He placed the painting on the desk and covered it with the paper wrapping. "Could I have your name, please?"

"My name?"

"Yes."

He gazed into my eyes again. I was momentarily taken aback, but then realised that he was waiting for my reply.

"Oh, it's Carrie."

He wrote my name on the corner of the wrapping paper. "Okay, Carrie. I will make sure that Mr Kaplowski gets it as soon as he comes back," he promised, giving me a sexy smile.

"Thank you, I am sure you will."

My business in the gallery was over and I was ready to leave, but something held me back. It took me a moment to realise that I was standing in front of a perfect stranger saying nothing and yet feeling as though I had so much to tell him. I wasn't sure what it was, but there was something about him - something strangely familiar.

"I suppose I'll be seeing you again?" I said at last.

"Without a doubt," he replied, smiling warmly.

As I reached the door he called cheekily, "Carrie, what does the letter 'C' across your front stand for?"

I laughed because I was sure he knew the answer to his question and was only teasing me.

"Have a guess," I said, and didn't wait for his reply.

During my journey home I could not stop thinking about the handsome young man I had just met and to whom, quite unexpectedly, I found myself very attracted. He was the most striking man I had ever seen, with his gorgeous sexy smile and beautiful, green, penetrating eyes. Despite everything I felt I simply had to see him again.

* * *

That evening, Mark was taking me to dinner to celebrate my birthday. He had booked a table for eight o'clock in an Italian eatery in Knightsbridge, which he often frequented, and had arranged to pick me up at seven. Glancing at the clock on the kitchen wall, I noted that it was already six-thirty, which meant that I had to hurry to get ready.

After a quick shower, I sat at my dressing table with a towel wrapped around my wet hair and stared at my reflection in the mirror. My skin looked smooth and healthy, my cheeks were nicely pink and my eyes were large and framed with long dark lashes. I did not need much make-up, I decided.

Pulling the towel from my hair, I roughly dried it with the hairdryer and curled strands of it around 12 large rollers. I applied dark brown mascara to my eyelashes and a warm rosy gloss to my lips. That done, I put on white lacy panties and a matching bra, then selected a sleeveless, low-cut green dress from my small assortment of evening clothes and hung it on the wardrobe door. The dress had a long zip at the back and I decided to await Mark's arrival so he could help me to fasten it.

I was taking the rollers out of my hair when I heard Mark's key in the front door.

"Carrie, are you ready?" Mark called from the hall.

"Nearly," I called back. "Can you come up? I need your help with my zip."

Mark rushed upstairs and as he entered the bedroom I was reaching for the dress, wearing nothing other than my lacy underwear.

He whistled softly, his eyes moving lustfully up and down my body. "Maybe we should stay home …"

To my utter surprise, I suddenly had an unpleasant feeling that I did not want to be intimate with him. I dismissed it quickly as something that would pass. Not responding to his suggestion in any way, I slipped into the dress and turned my back to him.

"Can you zip me up, please?"

"You've put on some weight," he criticised, struggling with the zip.

"Maybe a pound or two," I admitted. Lately, I had been spending a lot of time on my own and tended to eat more than usual.

"Pull your stomach in," he instructed, before successfully managing to close the zip. "Do you like your present?"

"I love it," I said, not quite truthfully. "It will go really nicely with my dress."

"Where is it?"

"On the dressing table."

Mark reached for the necklace and fastened it around my neck while I held my hair to one side with my right hand. When I let my hair down he turned me around and appraised my appearance.

"It looks really good on you," he decided, staring at the necklace.

"Thank you," I said, giving him a small peck on the cheek.

He checked his watch. "It's getting late. We have to go," he said impatiently. "I'll wait for you in the car," he added, leaving the room.

I slipped my feet into a pair of dark evening shoes, grabbed my bag and jacket, and followed Mark downstairs. The engine was already running when I reached the car. I did not understand the urgency, but didn't comment on it as I climbed in.

Mark seemed to be driving rather fast, as though he was in a terrible hurry, and we arrived at the restaurant well before eight o'clock. It was practically empty with only three out of 20 tables occupied. The place was divided into two areas, front and back, the latter being much darker, more intimate and lit mainly by candles. The front room, on the other hand, looked much brighter in comparison, as daylight streamed through the glass windows.

The head waiter appeared and escorted us to a small table in the far corner of the dark room, lighting the candles as soon as we were seated. He reached for a white linen, cone-shaped table napkin and with a swift movement of his hand unfolded it and placed it on my lap.

"What would you like to drink, madam?" he enquired.

"Sparkling water, please," I requested.

"Frizante, madam, of course."

The head waiter then turned to Mark, arranging his napkin. "And you, sir?"

"A bottle of your best white wine," Mark ordered.

"Very well, sir," the waiter said, and walked away.

I raised my eyebrows quizzically. "A whole bottle of wine?"

"Don't stress, Carrie. It's your birthday. Relax," Mark said, unconcerned.

I had to agree with him. I needed to relax to be able to enjoy the evening, for there were so many disturbing thoughts churning around in my mind. The last few days had been very unsettling to say the least.

"You are right," I said with a smile.

The drinks arrived and we both studied the menu for a while. Mark made his selection and signalled to the waiter to take our order. I noticed impatience in Mark for the second time that evening.

He lifted his glass. "Happy birthday!" he toasted, avoiding my eyes, and then gulped down the full glass in one go.

There was no doubt about it, Mark's behaviour was strange.

"How are things at the office?" I asked, assuming that his agitation was created by some problem at work.

"Fine," he replied, filling his glass again.

"No problems?"

"No."

"So everything is going fine?"

"Everything is going better than expected," he said, his gaze slipping away.

He was obviously not happy to talk about work, but I was sure that there was something he was not telling me.

"Mark, what's going on?"

He drained his second glass as if he needed Dutch courage to reply.

"I wasn't planning on telling you today, but it looks like you're not going to stop asking questions until I do, so here goes ... I've been promoted to the role of financial director."

I was surprised and disappointed at the same time, for we had had many discussions about his work and the commitment it required. As it was, he worked long hours and was hardly ever home, and when he was, his mind was preoccupied with office matters.

"You know I'm not happy to hear this."

He faced me and his eyes met mine at last, but only for a second, then he looked away again.

"I cannot let this opportunity pass, Carrie."

"But I will see even less of you," I complained. "What sort of future are we going to have together?"

"Bright," he replied with a confident smile. "We'll have more money to spend on things we enjoy."

I had difficulty understanding why the money was more important to him than our relationship.

"You will have no time to enjoy them."

"Wrong. With the top job I will have more assistants to help me with the work. Consequently, I will have more spare time than before."

At that moment our food was brought in and placed on the table. The waiter filled our glasses before he departed.

Mark gulped more of his wine. "Don't worry, Carrie, it's going to be okay," he said in an attempt to reassure me.

I had my doubts, but I knew it was pointless trying to persuade him to change his mind.

"So, when are you starting in your new role?" I asked, dipping into my pasta.

"After I come back from my business trip."

I looked at him even more astonished. It seemed my birthday dinner was going to be full of surprises.

"Another business trip?"

"Yeah, I'm leaving on Friday."

Friday was three days away.

"For how long?"

"A week."

"Where are you going?"

He drained his glass. "France and New York."

I couldn't help becoming irritated. "Will your new job require a lot of travelling?" I asked, feeling very uptight.

He hesitated before replying, "I am sure there will be some travelling involved."

"And what am I supposed to do while you are travelling?"

"Paint, meditate, look after the house - the things you always do," he said, reaching for the bottle.

He sounded as though he did not consider what I did important. It was becoming more and more obvious that we wanted completely different things and, try as I might, I couldn't push that thought to the back of my mind any more. I waited for him to meet my eyes, but he filled his glass with wine and drank most of it before doing so.

"This is not working, is it?" I said sadly.

"Carrie, everything will be fine, I promise."

Instinctively, I knew we were heading for problems. As I looked at him, his familiar face was suddenly transformed into a face that was ugly to say the least. His dark eyes changed into hollow spaces with little dark points surrounded by white pupils. His lips turned into a menacing snarl and the whole face had a grotesque and demonic appearance accentuated by the dark shadows created by the candlelight. It was as though his true face had pushed itself forwards in front of a mask, which was the face I had known. I shook my head to clear the horrible image and it disappeared as quickly as it had manifested itself. I was very shocked and did not fully understand what I had just experienced. The only logical explanation had to be that I had been shown the face of Mark's true soul, and I was horrified.

I grabbed my glass of water and took a few urgent sips from it, trying to calm my nerves. As realisation dawned that I had just seen the true person with whom I was planning to spend the rest of my life, I knew, without a doubt, that I had to end the relationship as soon as possible. It was painfully obvious that I could no longer marry this unpleasant human being.

Slowly, I lifted my eyes and looked at the unfamiliar person in front of me. He seemed oblivious to everything that was happening around him, eating his pasta and washing it down with wine. I noticed that the wine bottle was nearly empty.

"Do you think you will be able to drive us home?" I asked.

"Why do you ask these annoying questions when we both know that you are perfectly capable of driving?" Mark snapped, and drained the bottle into his glass, signalling the waiter for more wine.

Resigned, I lowered my head and picked at my food.

"There was a bomb scare in Victoria today," I muttered, trying to keep the conversation going.

"Unnecessary panic," Mark commented coldly.

"You can't deny that there are fanatics around who are perfectly capable of killing a lot of innocent people."

"Maybe, but panicking about it is not going to keep them alive."

"It could have been a real bomb, you know."

"It could have been, but it wasn't, was it?"

I did not respond, as there was simply no point in discussing the matter further. It was obvious that our views were miles apart. We were two completely different people, like two contrasting colours, black and white. How come I hadn't seen this earlier? I realised that I had seen a lot of things, but had been very good at pushing them to the back of my mind. Fully aware that this had to stop, I made a conscious decision never again to ignore the obvious.

Mark drained a few more glasses of wine and was becoming quite drunk. By now all the tables in the restaurant were occupied and the place was buzzing with conversation and activity. Mark spotted someone he knew, got up and stumbled over to another table for a chat, leaving me on my own. The head waiter, hovering nearby, stopped and asked if I was all right. I smiled at him graciously and assured him that I was fine.

After a while Mark staggered back and flopped into his chair, attracting the attention of the staff and pointing his index finger to the middle of our table. Swiftly, the table was cleared and a round iced cake was ceremoniously carried in with one large candle sparkling in the middle, and emitting the sound of 'Happy Birthday'.

It was one of those candles that refuses to be blown out. Luckily for me, I did not need to think about wishing for anything as I realised that my mind was in a state of total confusion. My life seemed to be changing so fast. The candle eventually stopped sparkling and the sound of 'Happy Birthday' suddenly died away. While the waiter cut the cake, Mark filled his glass with wine and saluted me.

"To Carrie," he said loudly.

I managed a weak smile in response.

The waiter served the cake, which we enjoyed in silence, and it wasn't long before we were ready to leave. Mark put his arm around me as we walked back to the car. His step was unsteady and his arm felt heavy on my shoulder. My instinct was to push him away, but I decided to bear it because I knew that would upset him and I didn't want to start an argument, especially when he was drunk and would most probably be very unreasonable.

In the car he reclined his seat and relaxed back with his eyes closed, which was quite a relief. The silent journey home took 45 minutes. I parked the car in its usual space in front of the house and went inside, leaving the door slightly ajar for Mark to follow. I was in my nightdress, ready for bed, when he eventually staggered in.

"I hope you enjoyed your birthday," he mumbled.

I did not want to disappoint him by saying that I hadn't, so I said, "It was nice." I lifted the blanket and got into bed.

Mark undressed clumsily, switched off the lights and, naked, climbed into bed beside me. As I lay motionless I could sense his hand slowly snaking in my direction under the blanket. A moment later it touched my arm and then quite suddenly was cupping one of my breasts. I went rigid all over. He did not get the message because before I knew it his lips were pressing into mine and the strong smell of alcohol engulfed my nostrils. I closed my lips tightly and practically stopped breathing.

"What's wrong?" he mumbled, puzzled.

"Let's not do it tonight," I pleaded. "I am really tired."

"Tired, tired, you are always tired," he sniggered, but he moved to his side of the bed and a short while later was snoring, fast asleep.

At last I felt I could relax. For the first time since I had met Mark I was glad he was going away on business.

2

On the day Mark left on his business trip, I decided to set up a new still life as I had finished the one with flowers the previous day. I had spent the entire morning searching through the antique shops in an attempt to find something inspiring. Eventually, I spotted a set of old porcelain plates with an attractive, blue floral print. The plates were of different sizes, but the smaller ones had ornamental edges and little stands underneath. I imagined them working well in a composition with a colourful selection of fruit.

I found some cream silk material and arranged it loosely on the small table in the studio. I positioned a dinner plate on the right side of the table, and then cut a large melon into eight portions and placed them on the plate, spreading the wedges open to show the various colours and textures. On the left-hand side I put two smaller plates one on top of the other, and filled the top one with ripe peaches. In front of those I arranged a bunch of red grapes. At the back, resting against the wall, I placed another large plate to complete the composition.

Standing back, I examined the final arrangement and made a few minor adjustments. When totally satisfied, I set up a new canvas on the easel and began marking the position of each element of the still life with light grey paint. After I had painted most of the dark background around the objects I stood back and examined it. I knew there was something wrong with the way I had painted it and yet I could not pinpoint the problem. Not wanting to dwell on it, I made the decision to start painting the fruit, as it would not stay fresh for long.

I started with the melon segments because I wanted to capture the richness of their soft textured interior. I spent two hours trying to achieve the result I had envisaged, but for some reason it wasn't working, making me more and more frustrated. Leaving the melon, I turned my attention to the peaches and soon found that I had the same problem. For some inexplicable reason, what had always been quite easy to accomplish seemed almost impossible.

Totally exasperated, I closed my eyes and took a few deep breaths to calm myself down. All of a sudden I could see a strange face, a face so unusual that I wanted to capture it on paper. Removing the still life canvas from the easel, I grabbed a piece of white drawing paper and attached it to the frame with a large metal clip. With a soft charcoal stick I began drawing the spherical face, round eyes with large orb-shaped pupils, very narrow, long nose and tiny lips. The face looked very alien, but at the same time had many human features and seemed rather pleasant.

Quite unexpectedly, I had the feeling that someone was trying to tell me something important. I left my sketch of the alien face on the easel and went to the meditation room.

"You need to write this down," I heard inwardly.

Picking up a small notebook and pencil, I sat down on the mat. I found the most comfortable position, closed my eyes and started to breathe deeply. Suddenly, I could see an intense white light and the voice continued. Opening my eyes and doing my best to hold the energy, I started writing.

"We are the Keepers of the Light and we are pleased to recognise the fact that you, who are incarnate on Planet Earth at this time, have successfully managed to raise your body frequency to such an extent that we can communicate directly with you through the path of pure white light. We are the Light Masters who work directly with those who have evolved to the level of Earth Masters. We could be described as being at the threshold of the pure white light...

"Next to us are a select group of trusted and proven helpers, some of whom you have been communicating with in the past. We are working with Earth Masters towards the energetic renewal of Planet Earth and its people. At this time there is the largest number of incarnate Masters on your planet, often very ordinary people, doing very ordinary jobs, but they have paid most, if not all, of their karma before this incarnation. Now they are learning by experience.

Some will fail and will have to be replaced, which is often a very difficult decision for us to make as we have invested some considerable energy and time in them. Please realise that we see the whole picture, not just this incarnation, so we understand all their problems. However, we cannot intervene, but can only guide their path as the cosmic law of non-interference is absolute. This law we cannot break, nor should the people of your planet, but regrettably they do constantly, often for so-called 'justifiable' reasons."

I stopped for a moment to rest my hand and began writing again when the voice continued.

"Massive amounts of cosmic energy are currently striking your planet. These energies are being transmitted to your planet to produce remarkable changes. The whole cosmos is supporting your planet at this time, as it is going through a very important transformation. Planet Earth is purifying and renewing itself. Only the strongest forms will transform and remain, which also applies to humans as they move into the higher level of consciousness. The energies are supporting everything and everyone through these difficult times. The tests are hard and only the strong and committed will be able to cope; however, the rewards are huge...

"For the next few years there will be a lot of turmoil, from which will emerge peace and tranquillity. Those who will last that long will have an opportunity beyond any other, an opportunity to inhabit a renewed planet where anger, greed, hate, fear and lack of knowledge will be the things of the past ... Your planet, Planet Earth, was originally designed as the planet of knowledge for the entire cosmos. This right was taken away, and for centuries it has been controlled and manipulated, but finally these times are coming to an end ... So, the changes have started and there is nothing that can stop them. The new beginning is but around the corner, approaching more quickly than anyone realises, but before the dawn of this new beginning the old has to go."

I couldn't concentrate any longer, and the energy went as suddenly as it had arrived. Stunned, I looked at the sheet of paper on my lap and read the first three sentences. Wow! I was a Master and I was helping with the renewal of the planet, albeit unknowingly! This was quite unexpected, but at the same time nothing short of exhilarating, and now that I was fully aware of my purpose in life it was also quite overwhelming.

My mind was still buzzing when the telephone rang, stopping my train of thought and bringing me sharply back to earthly reality. I went to the kitchen and picked up the phone.

"Can I speak to Carrie, please?" asked a male voice.

"This is Carrie," I replied, not quite sure who was calling even though the voice sounded familiar.

"Hi, this is Jason. We met the other day in the gallery."

My heart skipped a beat. "Oh, hi Jason," I said, trying to sound casual.

"I have a cheque for you and I was wondering if I could come over and hand it to you in person."

My mind was saying, yes, of course, but what I actually said was, "It's quite a long drive to my house from Victoria. Wouldn't you rather put in the post?"

"I definitely would not," he replied emphatically. "Not after all the trouble I've gone to in getting hold of it."

I smiled to myself. "Surely you didn't have to go to any trouble. Mr Kaplowski could have posted it."

"Carrie, I needed an excuse to see you again," he said decisively. "Please, can I bring the cheque over?"

"Do you know the address?" I asked.

"Yes, I found it in Mr Kaplowski's address book," he replied.

"You mean you snooped in Mr Kaplowski's private address book?"

"I wasn't exactly snooping ... Actually, on second thoughts, I think I might have been," he replied cheerfully.

I laughed. "Okay, come over, since you seem to have really gone to a lot of trouble."

"I'll see you in about half an hour."

"Okay."

As soon as I put the phone down I rushed upstairs to change my clothes. Looking into my wardrobe, I could not decide what to wear, not wanting to look too dressed up yet aiming for sexy and attractive. Eventually, I chose a pair of jeans and a white fitted shirt. I left the three top buttons undone and decorated my neck with a string of semi-precious stones in bright colours. Brushing my hair, I pulled it back into a ponytail and let a few strands fall freely around my face. Applying some gloss to my lips, I examined myself in the full-length mirror. The clothes felt slightly tighter than usual, but on the whole I was pleased with my appearance.

I made my way downstairs into the living room and sat on the sofa waiting for Jason's arrival. I felt strangely excited at the prospect of seeing him again. Having picked up a magazine from the coffee table, I found that I could not concentrate sufficiently to be able to absorb any information and ended up just nervously leafing through the pages. I tried to calm my anxiety with a few deep breaths, but only succeeded in calming my body, not my mind. For some reason, I felt like a schoolgirl going out on her first date.

At last I heard a sound of a car's engine, which seemed to come to a sudden stop in front of my house. I did not dare to look through the window, but I knew it was Jason. The expected doorbell chime sounded a moment later. Taking another deep breath, I went to open the door.

Jason was standing outside holding a 'Krispy Kreme Doughnuts' box in his hand. He was wearing blue jeans and a beige linen jacket, looking even more handsome than I had remembered. His hair was dark blond with sun-bleached golden highlights and his skin had a healthy suntanned glow. His green eyes sparkled like precious emeralds.

"Come in," I invited, when I had managed to drag my eyes away from him.

He followed me into the kitchen.

"Something sweet," he said, handing the box of doughnuts to me accompanied by a charming smile.

I opened the sugary-smelling box and looked at the 12 very fresh doughnut rings inside. "Sweet and yummy," I said. "How about coffee?"

"Sounds like a very good idea," he replied.

After placing the box on the kitchen table, I switched the kettle on.

"Your cheque," Jason said, holding out a plain white envelope.

"Thank you."

Taking the envelope from him, I dropped it into a small wicker basket that stood on the worktop and where I kept various papers requiring my attention. I reached for two mugs. Having made the coffees, I found a large plate and filled it with doughnuts.

"We can sit in the garden or living room, take your pick," I said, handing Jason his coffee.

"Garden sounds great," he decided.

"Follow me," I said, and led the way to the back of the house.

As we were crossing the conservatory Jason suddenly stopped in front of the easel.

"What is this?" he asked, pointing at the drawing of the alien face.

"A drawing of someone I've seen," I said, hoping that would answer his question.

He raised his eyebrows. "You've seen an alien?"

"It sounds unbelievable, I know."

"It sounds amazing. How did you see him or her?"

"I believe it's a him and I saw him with my inner vision," I explained, passing the plate to Jason to hold while I opened the door to the garden.

He followed me outside.

"What else have you seen?"

"I see a lot of things," I said, sitting down on a garden chair. "Why? Are you interested?"

"I've always been interested in the paranormal," Jason replied, placing the plate of doughnuts and his coffee mug on the wooden garden table and sitting down. "I believe strongly that there is more to life than that which we know. To be absolutely truthful, I don't think we understand a lot of things. For example, I believe in reincarnation, but if we do reincarnate we should have a large memory bank stored somewhere to which we have no access. As we are so unaware, we can be controlled and our minds can be manipulated to accept any explanation of the truth." He picked up a doughnut. "It's fascinating that you seem to achieve glimpses of another reality."

"I am glad you think so. Most people don't believe in the

paranormal."

"Those people are ignorant. They limit themselves by believing that we are the only civilised beings in the whole vastness of the universe."

"What do you believe?"

"I believe that there is so much more we need to understand. I believe that everything around us is changing so fast and there is some purpose behind it, the purpose we need to uncover."

I bit into a doughnut. "These are delicious," I said, but I wanted to carry on with our conversation. "What do you think is happening?" I asked.

"I don't know, but I think we have reached the point of no return. Either we change our ways or we'll destroy each other and the planet."

It was amazing to hear him saying such things. It was as though we were on the same wavelength, thinking the same thoughts. I felt I could share all my experiences with him and he would understand.

"I have to show you something," I said, and went to fetch my notebook from the meditation room. When I returned I opened the notebook at the first page and handed it to Jason. "I think you should read this. It might explain a few things."

Jason spent a few minutes reading the message.

"Did you channel this?" he asked, looking directly at me.

I nodded. "I did. Today."

"You are a Master?" He sounded bewildered.

"It seems so."

"This is unbelievable."

"Masters are ordinary people," I tried to explain.

"But this means that you are a divine being."

I did not feel that extraordinary. "My physical mind is unaware of a lot of things, just like yours."

He studied the message again. "This message feels so right," he commented thoughtfully. "It's something I believe I have known for a long time."

"This knowledge is within you."

"I don't know. There are still a lot of unanswered questions."

"I am sure that in time you will receive the answers to most of them."

"I certainly hope so."

I pushed the hair away from my face as the loose strands were being blown in all directions by a sudden gust of wind. Soon the wind intensified as the sun disappeared behind the clouds.

"Let's go inside," I said, rising to my feet.

Jason followed me into the conservatory. He stopped and picked up the unfinished canvas of still life with fruit, which was propped up against the wall.

"Are you going to finish it?"

"I would like to, but I don't seem to be able to portray the richness of colour or freshness of the fruit. I am far from happy with it," I explained honestly. "It's strange as I used to be able to do it quite easily."

"Maybe you should be painting something else," he remarked, putting the canvas back in its place.

"Maybe." I enjoyed his company and did not want him to leave. "Are you hungry?"

"I never say no to the offer of food," he said, smiling.

"It won't be anything big, just a snack," I said, leading him to the kitchen.

"Snack sounds perfect."

"Why don't you make some tea while I prepare the food," I suggested. "You'll find teabags in the cupboard above the kettle."

Jason opened the cupboard door and reached for the teabags. "Do you live here alone?" he asked unexpectedly.

I hesitated. I was afraid that if I told him I was living with my fiancé I would scare him off. "No, I share the house with a friend."

"Where is your friend?"

"Away on business," I replied, opening the fridge.

I took out butter, three different kinds of cheese, celery and various dips. I cut a French stick into diagonal slices and dropped them into a round breadbasket, then I arranged the cheeses on a wooden platter and cleaned a few stalks of celery, which I placed in a tall glass.

Jason helped me to carry the tea and food to the living room and took a seat on the blue armchair while I sat on the pink sofa to his left.

"How long have you been receiving information?" Jason asked, buttering a piece of bread.

"I have heard voices for as long as I can remember, but I've learned to ignore them. Recently, though, they have become more repetitive and persistent. It felt wrong to disregard them so I started listening more carefully. The information is coming through, but I don't exactly know what to do with it," I explained.

"That's obvious. You need to share it."

"People will think I'm crazy."

"Some will, some won't, but I don't think that matters. The information you receive is very important and needs to be passed on to others. People need to wake up."

I bit into the celery. "I don't know. Apart from today's message I haven't written anything down. The information is mostly in my head."

"Then you have to speak to people. I know one or two who would be very interested and I could bring them over. I know it's not much, but it's a start. Information can spread very quickly by word of mouth."

I was unsure. Mark was away, but he would be back in a week. My relationship with him was deteriorating very fast. It didn't seem sensible to hold meetings in our house.

"This house is not the best place for this kind of meeting," I said, digging my knife into a large cube of Cheddar.

Jason didn't pry. "It doesn't have to be here. I'll talk to my friends and see what we can come up with."

By the time we had finished eating it was dark outside.

"What do you say we go for a drive?" Jason suggested.

I smiled. "I'd like that."

In the hall I grabbed my denim jacket and the house keys, and we left. Jason opened the passenger door of his pearl grey Volkswagen Golf and I climbed in. He slid into the driver's seat and turned to me with a smile. "Would you like to go stargazing?" he asked.

Frankly I didn't mind where he was taking me. I was perfectly happy sitting next to him and being driven into the darkness of the night, but he waited for my reply.

"Sounds like fun."

Seemingly satisfied with my answer, Jason started the car and pulled away from the kerb. He drove for a long while through the main roads, then quite unexpectedly turned the car into a small country road and brought it to a halt. He opened the door on my side and took my hand in his.

"Come," he said, and led me towards a large, flat, grassy plain.

When we reached the middle of the field he let go of my hand and lowered himself onto the ground.

"Lie down next to me," he said, patting the grass.

Silently, I lay on the grass. The ground was dry and still warm from the heat of the sun. There was a slight refreshing breeze in the air and, as I looked at the clear sky above me, sprinkled with hundreds of bright stars, I felt an amazing sense of the enormity of the universe and realised that we were like two tiny dots, smaller even than two grains of sand, in the vastness of it all.

"See the stars?" Jason pointed up with his hand. "There are millions of them out there and yet most of them are a total mystery to us. How can we think that we have all the answers?"

I said nothing as I gazed upwards.

"I often look at the sky in the hope of seeing something unusual, like a spaceship. I know that there is other life out there," he continued. "Do you think there is?"

"I know there is," I replied.

He found my hand with his. "You are a very special person, Carrie," he said, squeezing my hand gently.

An electrical current shot through my body. "I think you are very special too," I said quietly.

No more words were needed, so we lay silently, holding hands and staring at the night sky. After a while the ground began to feel chilly against our bodies and we decided to go back home.

Jason parked the car outside my house. As I alighted, he rolled his window down. "Can I see you tomorrow?" he asked.

"I'm not sure," I replied, although I badly wanted to see him. "My parents are in London and I promised to have lunch with them."

"I'll come over in the evening," he declared with a charming smile, and without waiting for my response he closed the window and drove off.

I watched the fast disappearing car for a moment before I let myself into the house.

3

Whether I wanted it or not, life the following day returned to normal. In the early afternoon I drove to Barnes where my parents had a house on the green by a small lake.

My mother opened the door with a big welcoming smile. "I've missed you," she exclaimed, hugging me tightly.

She was a small woman with short, greying blonde hair and warm hazel eyes. She wore close-fitting light coloured trousers and a white silk blouse, which accentuated her suntan.

"I've missed you too, Mum," I muttered, hugging her small frame, which seemed smaller than ever. "How are you?"

"As well as can be expected at my age, dear."

I ignored my mother's reference to her unspoken old age. She was a woman who tended to see a problem in everything, often without good reason.

"How is Dad?"

"He is well. Looking forward to seeing you."

I seldom had a chance to see my parents as they lived in Spain. They still kept their old house in London as an investment because they felt a strong connection to England and hadn't totally rejected the possibility of ever returning. They came over four or five times a year to spend some time with me and to attend to their financial concerns.

"Where is he?" I enquired, noting that he had not come to greet me.

"Out in the garden, lost in his plants as usual," Mum replied.

My father was a very keen gardener who spent hours tending his plants. He maintained that the best form of relaxation was to be at one with nature. A few times I had heard him talking to his plants, but he would never admit to it openly for fear of being ridiculed.

"I hope you are hungry because lunch is ready," Mum said, leading me into the dining room. "I've got all your favourite things. You sit down, and I'll go and get your father."

Sitting at the table, I stared at the food nicely laid out in ornamental Wedgwood dishes. The aroma of fresh bread, cheeses, meats and salad was wafting throughout the whole room. I chose a small piece of roast chicken and popped it into my mouth just as my mother returned carrying a bottle of wine.

"Your father is getting cleaned up. He'll be here in a minute," she explained. "I bought this wine especially for you. It's non-alcoholic." She unscrewed the top and poured the golden liquid into a crystal glass, which stood next to my plate. "I hope you like it."

I lifted the glass and sipped some of the wine. "It's very nice. Quite sweet," I commented.

My father approached the table. "Real wine tastes much better," he said in his strong voice, kissing me softly on the top of my head. He smelled of fresh air and soap.

In contrast to my mother, my father was a big, well-built man with a full head of dark hair and gentle green eyes framed by dark eyelashes and broad dark eyebrows. Most of the time he was ensconced in his own little world, disconnected from everyday problems.

"How are you, Dad?" I asked.

"Not as energetic and flexible as I used to be," he replied, taking a seat at the head of the table. "But otherwise not too bad."

"What would you like to drink, Robert?" Mum wanted to know.

"White wine, please," he requested.

Mum handed him an unopened bottle of Chablis and a corkscrew.

"How is Mark these days?" Dad asked, removing the foil cover from the neck of the bottle.

I hesitated for a moment before I said, "Very preoccupied with his job."

"He's always been very ambitious ... Too ambitious if you ask me," Dad said.

"He earns very good money," Mum said in Mark's defence.

"I hope you don't think he's a good catch because of it," Dad countered.

Sensing an argument, my mother decided to change the subject. "How are your wedding plans going, Carrie?"

I didn't really want to talk about my forthcoming wedding or Mark. Since my birthday dinner a lot had changed between us and I knew I could never marry him.

"The wedding has been put on hold, I'm afraid," I muttered, feeling I didn't need to explain that Mark was, as yet, unaware of that fact.

Dad lifted his head from the bottle, stared straight at me and waited for my explanation. I had no choice but to give him a reason and I chose my words carefully.

"I am not sure our relationship is working. Mark is hardly ever home and now that he has accepted the promotion to financial director I will see him even less."

Mum passed me a platter with cold meats. "Have you tried to talk him out of it?" she questioned.

"Of course I have. He can be very stubborn and he hardly ever listens to me anyway. Mark always knows best."

Dad pulled out the cork and handed the bottle back to Mum to pour, and then said, "Carrie, you know I don't like to interfere in your personal life, but if Mark is not prepared to listen to your concerns you really need to think hard about marrying him."

"I agree, and that's why I've decided to put everything on hold."

My mother seemed to be more concerned about it than my father. "You are not planning to break off your engagement, are you?"

Up to that moment I hadn't thought about it, but suddenly I realised that if I was not going ahead with the marriage it was what I had to do, so I nodded. "As soon as he comes back from his business trip."

"What about the house?" Mum asked, ever the practical one.

Strangely enough I hadn't thought about that either. "I suppose we'll have to sell it."

My mother's concern was growing. "Are you sure this is wise? Is there no way you can reconcile your differences?"

"Kate, I think we should be asking if Carrie wants to be with Mark, because if she doesn't, the house won't keep them together," Dad interjected.

"I know the house won't keep them together, Robert," Mum said. "I just think it's such a shame for them to break up."

"Well, I think it's for the best. I've never really liked the guy."

I shot my father a surprised look. "You've never said anything before."

"My opinion doesn't count. I don't have to live with him."

"Of course it counts, Dad. If I married Mark he would become part of our family."

"It's just as well you are not going to marry him then, isn't it," Dad responded, filling his plate with cheese and salad.

"She might still change her mind," Mum said hopefully, "and I for one have no objections to him marrying our daughter. I actually think he would provide stability in her life."

"The man is a moron," Dad commented. "As far as I am concerned she should break off the engagement and forget about marrying him."

"I agree with Dad," I said.

Everyone decided that there was not much else to be said on the subject, so we all continued to eat in silence. When we had finished, my mother stacked up the dishes and carried them to the kitchen. I offered to help, but she insisted that I was her guest and I should not move from my chair, so I stayed put.

Within minutes Mum returned with a large pot of tea, fresh cream and a freshly baked apple strudel. She fetched white porcelain cups and dessert plates from the oak dresser, which stood proudly against a light green wall on the left-hand side of the room, and put them on the table.

"Help yourselves," she said, sitting down.

I selected a small piece of the strudel, placing it carefully on my plate and pouring cream over it.

"When are you going back to Spain?" I asked.

"At the end of next week," Dad replied.

"Your father has been commissioned to design gardens for a new development in Marbella," Mum explained. "He is starting work on it as soon as we get back."

"Sounds exciting. Still, it's disappointing that you are leaving so soon. Mum, why don't you stay a bit longer?"

"Oh no, I couldn't," Mum said, pouring the tea. "When your father works on his gardens he needs a lot of looking after."

"Now, now," Dad interjected. "I know I can get a little preoccupied with things at times, but I am quite capable of looking after myself."

"If I am not there you will be wearing the same shirt for a week and eating cereal all day," Mum complained.

I knew Dad well enough to believe he would neglect himself, as he often got so involved in his work he forgot about everything else.

"There is no argument, Dad," I said knowingly. "You'd be better off if Mum is there to look after you."

"You are both making too much of a fuss over nothing," Dad protested, stirring his tea and spilling it into the saucer. He lifted the dripping cup to his lips and the tea dribbled down his clean shirt.

My mother and I exchanged knowing looks. Dad's mind always seemed to be on other matters.

It wasn't long before we had finished our dessert and I decided it was time to make my excuses and leave. I was looking forward to seeing Jason in the evening and I wanted to go home to refresh myself and get ready for his arrival. Since I had met him my mind seemed to be constantly preoccupied with thoughts of him, while thoughts of Mark were very sporadic and mostly unpleasant. Thinking about it now it was another very good reason to break off my engagement.

I drained my cup and put it back on the saucer. "Thanks for a lovely lunch, Mum," I said.

"Are you going already?" my mother asked, disappointment in her voice.

I got up and kissed her on the cheek. "I would love to stay longer, but I've made arrangements to see someone this evening," I explained.

Mum looked at me suspiciously. "Is it a man?"

"It's just a friend."

"So it is a man?"

"Well, if she is not going to marry Mark she might as well start looking for someone else," Dad said.

Mum gave me a look as if to say that Dad did not know what he was talking about.

"Don't listen to your father," she said. "There are still three more months before the wedding, so try to work out your differences."

"I will," I promised, knowing full well that that would be impossible.

I walked over to my father and kissed him on the forehead. "Bye, Dad. I'll speak to you soon."

"Look after yourself," he said.

Mother walked me to the door and I gave her another kiss. She was watching me until I got into my car, then she waved and went back into the house.

* * *

Charged up with unusual excitement, I sped all the way home, slowing down to the allowed limit only for the speed cameras.

As soon as I got in, I rushed upstairs and flung open my wardrobe. Hastily, I slid the hangers along the rail and back again before realising I was rushing unnecessarily. Making a conscious effort to slow down, I looked through all the clothes again, pulling out two dresses, one with a pink flowery design and the other a blue and green geometrical pattern. I slipped on the pink one and struggled to pull up the side zip. I looked at myself in the mirror and gasped, for it had fitted me perfectly a few weeks previously, but was now very taut around my middle, my stomach bulging out behind the tight fabric.

Evidently I couldn't wear the pink dress, so I tried on the blue and green one, which wasn't much better. I left both dresses on the bed and rummaged through the rest of my clothes. I tried on a silk chiffon skirt and decided I looked okay in it, but the fabric was still quite tight around my waist and made me feel uncomfortable, so I took it off. I tried on a few more items before I finally settled on a pair of beige stretchy trousers and a pink T-shirt.

I looked at the pile of garments discarded on the bed and sighed. Most of my clothes didn't fit me any more, so it was obvious that I needed to lose some weight or shop for larger sizes. With that thought in mind I got dressed. Sitting in front of my dressing table mirror I brushed my dark hair back and held it together with a large clasp. That done, I applied mascara to my eyelashes and pink gloss to my lips and sprayed a few squirts of my favourite perfume around my neck.

Now that I was ready I did not know what to do with myself. Jason had not said what time he would be arriving. I thought about calling him, and then quickly abandoned that idea when I realised I did not have his private phone number. In the absence of something else to do, I began gathering up the clothes from the bed and hanging them back in the wardrobe. I had nearly finished when the doorbell sounded. Relieved, I dropped the garment I was holding back onto the bed and rushed downstairs.

Just before I opened the door I took a deep breath, trying to control my excitement, and faced Jason with what I hoped was a calm smile. He had a small folder under his arm and looked particularly handsome in his jeans, white T-shirt and beige linen jacket. He smiled back and I could not have been happier to see him.

"Come in," I invited, and led him to the kitchen. "Would like a drink?"

"A glass of water would be nice," he replied.

I poured two glasses of sparkling water and placed them on the table.

"I have brought something to show you," he said, opening the folder. "My friend, Mike, is very interested in crop circles and gave me some pictures." He spread a handful of photographs on the table. "These were taken in July and August last year. Have you seen them?"

I gazed at the pictures and shook my head. I had seen photographs of crop circles before, but nothing as intricate as these - the shapes and detail were quite amazing. All the formations looked very symmetrical and were designed in various rather complicated geometrical shapes, which reminded me of lace patterns. At the bottom of each photograph, information was printed about where and when it was taken.

I leaned on the table and pointed to one particular photograph. It was taken on 20 July at West Stowell, near Huish, in Wiltshire. The design was circular. In the centre of the main round formation was a smaller circle with 13 small triangular shapes attached to its outer edge. From each outside point of the small three-pointed shape a much bigger triangular shape was created, 13 in total. The whole design was framed by 13 very small, round shapes, divided into half-circles by two different textures of the crop.

"This one is beautiful," I said.

Jason leaned over the table and we were so close that I could feel his hair touching mine and smell his masculine scent. He gave me a quick look and smiled seductively before he pointed to another photograph and said, "I quite like this one."

The information at the bottom of the picture read 13 July, Avebury Trusloe, Wiltshire. The configuration was also in a circular design with a much smaller circle in the middle. Five double lines, running from the outer edge of the inner circle, divided the pattern into five symmetrical parts. In between the lines were large triangular shapes creating a five-pointed star. There were also five two-toned circular shapes, looking not unlike moons, crossing the outer edge of the main circle and the arms of the star.

"It's very precise."

"The real ones are always very precise," I said.

"How do you think they are they created?" he asked, facing me.

"I think there is only one explanation," I replied, trying hard to stay focused as his penetrating stare was disturbing my concentration.

"From outer space?"

I nodded.

"I totally agree," he said, and looked down at the pictures again. "Man could not possibly make them, not in the time they appear. Why do you think they're here?"

"To raise awareness in people, and show them that there is more to life than they already know and understand."

"There are a lot of people who would not accept that as an explanation," he said, lifting his head.

"I know, but that's like living in the Dark Ages. It's time to move on from our limited understanding."

"Yeah, I totally agree." Jason took a gulp from his glass. "I spoke to Mike about you and he would very much like to meet you. As it's not convenient for him to come here, what do you say we go to Swindon to meet him?"

"You mean now?" I asked, surprised.

Jason nodded. "It'll only take an hour."

"But it's getting late," I tried to protest.

"We don't need to come back tonight. We can book ourselves into a B&B and stay the night in Swindon."

I was tempted, but very unsure if spending the night with Jason was the right thing to do. After all, I had only just met him.

Sensing my uneasiness he said, "I promise we'll book two single rooms."

I was practically persuaded. However, there was something I needed to explain first.

"There is another problem though."

"What's that?"

"I need a lot of support when I speak to people. I can't do it on my own."

"Don't worry. I'll be there to give you all the support you need."

"Thank you."

"Is there anything else you need to tell me?"

"Yes, we are not supposed to talk to just anybody about what we know. Not everyone has the potential to understand. There will be people who will attach themselves to us just to cause trouble and slow down the process. I was advised by my helpers to check everyone before sharing the information with them. I was also warned that even people with potential to evolve quickly and join the cosmic co-operation can turn against us and be used by The Manipulators to create problems."

Jason looked puzzled. "What do you mean - The Manipulators?"

"They are beings who control this planet and are feeding off all the negative energy. They want to create as much confusion as possible. As you rightly said yourself, unaware people can be controlled and manipulated. The Manipulators don't want people to know the truth, and they will do anything to stop people like us educating anyone. They are putting obstacles in everyone's path, creating doubts, confusion and fear."

"How are you going to know if Mike is safe?" Jason asked.

"My helpers will tell me," I replied. "What is his full name?"

"Mike Howard."

I concentrated on the name and, even though I had never met Mike, I was beginning to formulate an idea about what sort of person he was. It seemed he was very interested in the subject of UFOs and crop circles as a worldwide phenomenon. He was totally confused, as all his information was acquired from books and articles, creating a lot of uncertainty in his mind. It seemed that he had the potential to learn more, but his mind was very inquisitive and he would have a problem reaching within for the answers. Mentally, I asked if we could speak to him and a positive answer came almost instantly.

"We can talk to him, but I think we need to concentrate on UFOs and crop circles, and see how he responds," I said to Jason. "If he responds well, we can touch on planetary changes."

Jason smiled and said, "Does that mean that you've decided to go to Swindon?"

When I nodded, Jason reached into his jacket pocket for his mobile phone and called Mike to make arrangements.

"All set. Mike is going to book a B&B for us," he confirmed a few minutes later. "He'll wait for us in his local."

"I'll go upstairs and pack a few things," I said, leaving the kitchen.

In the bedroom I pulled down a small travel bag from the top of the wardrobe and threw in a nightdress, some underwear, a T-shirt and toothbrush. That done, I quickly checked my appearance in the dressing table mirror. With a swift movement of my hand I removed the hair clasp and brushed my hair down to fall loosely around my shoulders, then I dropped the brush into the bag and, zipping it up, ran downstairs.

"I'm ready," I announced, grabbing my keys and a pair of sunglasses from a small table in the hallway.

Jason emerged from the kitchen and gave me an admiring look, which made me feel quite flushed. "You look nice with your hair down."

I managed a smile. "I am glad you like it ... Let's go," I added, opening the front door.

I locked up and we made our way to Jason's car. He held the passenger door open for me and I got in, tossing my bag on the back seat. Jason climbed behind the wheel and we set off.

We reached Swindon in a little over an hour. Jason seemed to know the town quite well and easily tracked down Mike's local pub. He parked the car opposite the main entrance and turned off the engine.

"It's time to meet Mike," he said, opening his door.

I followed him into the pub, the interior of which was dark and noisy. The smells of tobacco, alcohol, ancient furniture and soiled carpets intermingled, creating an unpleasant odour. The barmen busied themselves behind the bar pouring drinks for the customers. Clusters of people were seated around large tables or standing by the walls, talking loudly whilst getting an alcoholic buzz. I quickly decided this was not the best place for any kind of meaningful conversation.

Jason spotted Mike by the window next to the bar and we made our way towards him. He was of medium height, chubby and with a big mane of brown hair, which looked as though it had not been combed in days. His inquisitive eyes were hidden behind heavily framed glasses and he was dressed casually in jeans and a denim jacket. When we approached he removed himself from a group of friends and, after a brief greeting, asked us what we would like to drink. I requested orange juice and Jason decided to have mineral water.

"No beer?" Mike asked with a surprised look.

"Not today, I have to drive," Jason replied. "Did you manage to book us into a B&B?"

Mike nodded. "Five minutes from here." Attracting a barman's attention, he shouted over the surrounding noise, "Orange juice and mineral water please, Dave!"

The drinks were poured and Mike handed me my glass, saying with a friendly smile, "So you are the lady who has the answers to many questions."

"Depends if you are prepared to accept my answers," I replied quietly.

"I am very keen to hear what you have to say," Mike said, sipping his beer.

"That's why we are here," Jason said. "Where can we talk?"

Mike thought for a moment. "How about the B&B? There's a nice, quiet garden there, and as I know the landlady I can persuade her to make us something to eat."

"Sounds like a perfect solution," I said.

"It's getting late, so I think we should make a move," Jason added.

As soon as we had finished our drinks, Mike waved goodbye to his friends and we left the pub and climbed into Jason's car. I sat in the back, as Mike took the front seat next to Jason to direct him to the guest house.

A pleasant-looking older woman dressed in a flowery blouse and a matching skirt opened the door. Mike introduced us and thankfully we were given two separate keys for our rooms. The landlady prepared a plate of sandwiches and a large pot of tea for us and left them outside on the patio. The evening was warm with a gentle, fresh breeze as the sun sunk slowly towards the horizon, creating a wide orange glow in a distant sky. There was still about half an hour of daylight left.

We sat around a wooden table. Jason had brought his folder with him, but put it to one side unopened. I poured the tea.

"I've heard that you are very interested in crop circles," I said to

Mike.

"Yeah, I've read a lot about them," he replied. "The biggest mystery of this century. I sure would love to know how they are made."

"How do you think they are made?" I enquired.

Mike smiled knowingly. "I have a few theories, but I am not absolutely positive which one is the right one."

"Oh, come on, Mike," Jason said. "It's obvious that they are made by aliens."

"That is certainly one theory," Mike agreed, "but up to now nobody has been able to prove it and there are a lot of arguments against it."

"I don't understand why people spend so much time and energy disproving the only logical explanation," Jason countered.

Mike faced me. "What is your theory, Carrie?"

"I don't have a theory," I replied. "I know that they are made by other intelligence."

Mike laughed as though I had said something funny. "How is that supposed to answer my question?"

"You said yourself that nobody has been able to come up with any conclusive proof of how the circles are made. The truth is staring you in the face, but people don't want to accept it. They'd rather create various theories and argue about who is right or wrong. As soon as one researcher comes to the conclusion that the circles are made from outer space, another one comes along to disprove it. Researchers have been arguing about various theories for years without finding a satisfactory answer. I think the obvious conclusion is that the only way to find the truth is if you think for yourself and find your own answers."

"I've read a lot of books about the subject and the arguments both against and for are perfectly valid," Mike commented.

I wanted to be sure of what he meant, so I asked, "You mean for and against the argument that the circles are created from outer space?"

"Yes."

"As far as I am concerned they couldn't be made any other way," Jason said, opening the folder.

Jason pointed to the picture taken on 8 August in Alton Barnes, Wiltshire. The main design looked like a rounded square with five small circles within each side, surrounded by unusual curving shapes. In the middle of the square there was a circle where the same sinuous shapes were repeated, creating eight formations of three. These formations were running to the outer edge of the circle in an arc.

"How long do you think it would take you to draw this design on paper, assuming that all the shapes and distances are as perfect and symmetrical as in this formation?"

Mike studied the picture.

"You would have to decide where the middle point of each circle is going to be. This is not going to be possible without good planning. And planning takes time," Jason added.

"I am not sure. I reckon it would take maybe two hours," Mike concluded.

"Personally, I think that if you were to spend two hours recreating this on paper your picture would be very imprecise," Jason said. "Even with very good planning it would take you the better part of a day, and you would have the advantage of being able to see the whole area on which you were working.'

Mike turned to Jason. "So what are you trying to say?"

"These formations are created within minutes. How can a large field area be measured and the design planned and pressed into the crop within minutes by a human if it would take the same person hours to draw it on paper? Besides, it's impossible to create such complicated designs so accurately from ground level. You can't see what you're doing," Jason argued. "Have you seen the movie, *Signs*, with Mel Gibson?"

Mike nodded.

"It took several people three days to make the crop circle that you see in the film. And I doubt that they recreated the unusual way the crops are interlaced when they are flattened."

"There are people who claim that they have been making them," Mike pointed out. "I doubt that they spend days on each one."

"I agree, there are some hoaxes, but they are easily recognisable because they are so badly made and the designs are very simple."

"I must admit," Mike said, reaching for a sandwich, "some photographs I've seen are rather suspicious. Still, why would aliens use their technology and travel through interstellar space to arrive in Earth's orbit and communicate with us by making pretty pictures in the fields? It doesn't make a lot of sense."

"They are not communicating with us in the true sense of the word," I said. "They are simply trying to open our eyes to the fact that they are there."

"Why don't they simply land?"

"They do land."

Mike looked at me strangely. "How many people have seen them?"

"They don't land in the populated areas because they do not want to create panic," I explained. "They are very sensitive to our energies, especially to the vibration of fear. The energy behind fear is of a very low frequency and they would find that very difficult to cope with. Their physical bodies are different to ours and they do not experience as many emotions. Many of them have never experienced fear or anything like it."

Mike swallowed the last bit of his sandwich. "Okay, assuming that the crop circles are made by aliens, how do they make them?"

"They make them using energy beams that are sent down from a ship positioned a safe distance away," I replied. "There is video footage showing small bright balls of white light in and around crop circles. Many of these lights have been filmed in broad daylight."

Mike wasn't convinced. "I am not sure this proves anything. Nobody has actually filmed a circle being made by these lights."

I sensed that we needed more time for discussion with Mike for him to open up. He had not rejected our argument, but it was not fully accepted either. I decided not to pursue the matter, for, at the end of the day, our job was not to persuade anyone to accept blindly what we had to say, but to help people to reach within and teach them to think for themselves. Mike seemed to be more resistive than I had anticipated.

"Nonetheless, there were circles made where these lights

appeared," I said, closing my argument.

Mike sighed. "I don't know."

"Use your common sense, Mike," Jason pressed on. "How many theories are there? Three? They could be a natural phenomenon, man-made or made by aliens. I think we can safely reject the natural phenomenon theory, and we have more or less decided that they could not be man-made, which leaves us with the last theory that they are made by aliens. Simple."

"I do understand what you are saying, but that's like stating that the universe is round. Nobody really knows for sure."

"Have you examined the way the crop patterns form when the crop is folded over? Can you imagine how long it would take anyone to fold it like that?" Jason asked.

I ate my sandwiches in silence and left them to carry on with the discussion. I was sure it wouldn't lead anywhere as it was just an exchange of opinions. I could not understand why people needed proof for everything that was challenging for the mind and yet they believed in their own kind of God and followed their religion blindly. They were even prepared to kill and terrorise in the name of religion to expand their own particular belief system, yet they were not prepared to open their minds to the simple truths. The human mind certainly worked in a most mysterious way.

As I was not taking part in the discussion any longer, my mind would switch off every now and then. Within a short space of time I began to feel tired and decided to excuse myself and go to my room. I waited for a break in the conversation and stood up.

"I'll see you tomorrow at breakfast," I said to Jason, and extended my hand to Mike. "I am glad we've met."

Mike shook my hand. "Me too. I hope we'll see each other again."

"I'm sure we will. Goodnight," I said and went inside the house.

* * *

Even though I had spent the night in a strange bed, I had slept very well and woke up later than planned. By the time I had washed and dressed it was already well after nine o'clock and I didn't want to miss breakfast. Hurriedly, I packed my things and rushed downstairs.

The breakfast room was located at the front of the guest house and accommodated five square tables. Three of them had been cleared and covered with white tablecloths. The fourth was set with plates, cups and small containers filled with little portions of butter, honey and various jams. Jason, who was busy reading the Sunday paper, occupied the fifth table.

As I approached, Jason folded the paper and put it to one side. "Good morning, how was your night?" he asked.

"Comfortable thanks," I answered, taking the seat opposite. "It looks like you've had your breakfast already."

He nodded. "Just finished it."

The landlady appeared with a fresh pot of coffee and asked me if I wanted anything cooked from the kitchen. I requested poached eggs on brown toast.

"How did the discussion with Mike go?" I asked, pouring coffee into my cup.

"We did not agree on anything, as you might expect. Mike likes to argue for the sake of it."

"I think he needs time."

Jason raised his eyebrows. "Time for what?"

"He has an analytical mind and is not the type who accepts things easily. He needs to analyse what we've told him before he can accept it."

"I don't understand what there is to analyse. I thought we'd established that crop circles are not a natural phenomenon or man-made. There is only one other option left and one answer."

The landlady brought my eggs on toast and placed them in front of me. "If you are interested in crop circles there is a new one that has just been formed in a cornfield near Upper Upham," she informed us.

"Is it far?" Jason asked, obviously interested.

"No, not far. About 20 minutes' drive from here."

"How do we get there?"

"You turn right out of here, then right again, then left onto the main road out of Swindon. When you reach the junction with the A419 you cross over and take the road to Hungerford."

Jason seemed quite confused by the directions. "I'll get the map from the car," he said, getting up and leaving the room.

He returned pretty quickly with a folded Ordnance Survey map of the area, which he laid out in front of the landlady. "Please, can you show me the exact spot?"

The landlady studied the map for a while before she found the right place. "It's here." She pointed with her finger. "From what I've heard on the local news you need to drive up this country road," she added, showing us the road leading to Upper Upham. "It'll be on your right."

"Thank you," Jason said, folding the map.

"You're welcome," the woman responded, picking up a few dirty dishes and departing.

Jason faced me. "I think we should go and see it. What do you say?"

"I'd love to see it," I agreed readily, perfectly happy to spend more time with him.

"You finish your breakfast. I'll go and grab my things," he said urgently.

I gave him my room key. "Can you get my bag on your way down, please?" I asked, not wanting to waste any time either.

I knew that if we got to the circle early enough there wouldn't be a lot of people around. People disturbed the formations very easily. I quickly ate my eggs on toast and made my way to the front hall where Jason was chatting to the landlady. He had put his jacket on, his travel bag was slung across his shoulder and my holdall was on the floor at his feet.

Jason turned to me and smiled, and then said to the landlady, "It's time for us to leave. Thank you for all your help." He lifted my bag and handed it to me.

I muttered a quick goodbye and followed him to the car. Suddenly, I remembered that I had not paid for my accommodation.

"What about the payment for my room?" I enquired.

"It's been sorted," he replied.

I stopped in my tracks. "You mean you paid for my room?"

He nodded and unlocked the car with his remote key. It was really nice of him to pay for me, but I felt I had to say something.

"So I owe you some money?"

Jason stared at me across the roof of the car. "Carrie, I was happy to pay for you and you don't owe me anything," he said emphatically.

"If you are sure ..."

"Positive."

"Thank you. A lady likes to be taken care of," I said flippantly, and climbed into the car.

Jason got in, unfolded the map with our route and handed it to me. "I'll drive, you direct," he instructed, and started the engine.

The traffic was quite light in Swindon and it wasn't long before we left the town and were following the route to Hungerford. We had been driving for about 20 minutes when I spotted the signpost for Upper Upham.

A few minutes later Jason took a left turn and said, "It's somewhere around here."

Suddenly, I noticed a round formation in a field to my right. "Yes, it's there," I exclaimed enthusiastically, pointing to the field with my index finger.

I couldn't make out the whole pattern because it was impressed into an almost flat field and the only way it could be appreciated fully would be from the air. Jason drove to the nearest lay-by, parked the car and turned off the ignition. For a moment he gazed thoughtfully at the new formation in the distance.

"My argument stands; it is almost unthinkable that anyone could create these things from ground level because it's impossible to see the whole area. It would mean working in the dark," Jason said at last, and opened his door.

"I absolutely agree," I said, getting out.

The weather had been quite good for the previous few days and that day was no exception. There was a light, refreshing breeze, but otherwise it was warm and sunny. The sun, however, seemed very strong, so I put on my sunglasses as recently my eyes had become quite sensitive to sunlight.

Scanning the area around the crop circle, I was quite relieved to see that there were no farm buildings in the vicinity. I was fully aware that the farmer who owned the field was within his rights to object to our walking on his land. A few metres away from where Jason had parked, I caught sight of a small country lane leading in the direction of the circle.

"I suggest we take that path," I said to Jason, pointing to the lane.

The path was very narrow with no room for two people to walk side by side, so I led the way and Jason followed behind. It took us only a few minutes to reach the formation and I directed Jason to what I thought was the centre of the circle. The corn had been pressed down in some places and left upright in others, creating various shapes, but it was difficult to make out the exact pattern because we could only see a small part of the whole design at any one time.

There was an obvious circle of flattened corn in the middle and I stood there motionless for a moment with my eyes closed. I could feel a slight tingling sensation at first, and then heat slowly began to radiate throughout my body from my feet to my head, as though I were drawing it from the earth beneath me.

"Close your eyes and try to feel the energy," I said to Jason. "Can you feel it?"

He took a moment trying to decide what he was feeling before he said, "I feel a kind of heat, which seems to be generated from inside my body," he replied.

"That's good," I said, opening my eyes. "I think we'd better sit down so nobody can see us."

We sat facing each other with our legs crossed and about half a metre of flattened corn between us.

"The middle of the formation holds the strongest concentration of the residual energy," I explained. "We can benefit from it by just being here."

We sat in silence for a while. Suddenly, I had a strong feeling that I was about to receive a message. I wanted Jason to listen to it so I muttered quietly, "Listen to what is being said."

I seemed to become someone else, and my voice changed when I spoke these words:

"We are here and we mark our presence. We are what you might call extra-terrestrial beings. We come in peace and we wish for our presence to be acknowledged by the human race of Planet Earth. The time has come when the human race has to wake up and accept our existence. We have been sending symbols to your people in the form of crop formations for over 20 years of your time and it seems that people's eyes are still closed and their minds frozen. However, we will persevere. Every formation that is created by us and rejected by your people as a hoax is going to be bettered by another one more complicated in its pattern, more unusual in its geometrical symmetry until eventually there will be no arguments left and the people of Planet Earth will have to open their minds to our existence ...

"We are here to help with the transition of Planet Earth into the next stage of its development and we want to work together with the inhabitants of the planet to this end. People have been fast asleep for so long and refuse to wake up, so Planet Earth has been isolated from the cosmos by an ever-increasing energetic shield. It's up to the people of Planet Earth to open the star gate to the cosmos and we will be here as an ever-present reminder until the star gate opens again and we can work together towards the same goal ...

"We do not expect every single person to respond to our call. We are fully aware that some people are not capable of accepting the cosmic reality, as their minds are not flexible enough to allow them to change their thoughts about what they have been taught throughout their lives. Sadly, to those we have to say goodbye. The rest of you have a chance to start on an amazing journey, a journey of discovery - the discovery of the cosmic truth. We are here to guide you all the way. Farewell."

The message ended and there was a moment of silence before Jason said, "Wow! That was some message!" Then he added, "But of course this makes absolute sense. It makes you wonder though why most of these circles appear in England."

"Would it be because British people are the most sceptical?" I answered.

"Sounds like a very probable explanation. You and I recognise the importance of what is happening, but I have a feeling that it's going to be pretty difficult to make other people understand."

"I am sure that there are people out there who will understand. We just have to find them. Every single person who chooses to join us in cosmic co-operation will multiply the magnitude of the energy tenfold. The bigger the amount of energy available, the quicker the fog will lift."

"Okay, let's see ... We have to start with people we know," Jason decided. "As I said before, I have one or two friends who are very open-minded. I can organise a meeting."

I was still not sure I should be organising meetings in my house because Mark would most certainly object, and the last thing I needed was to argue with him over this issue.

"Where? My place is no good."

Jason seemed to be thinking before he said, "I live with my father, so my place is out of the question too ... Is there any chance we could use your studio?"

I shook my head negatively.

"It's because of your friend, isn't it?" Jason guessed.

I nodded.

"When is your friend coming back?"

"On Friday."

"That gives us four days," Jason reasoned.

"And then what?"

"Then we'll have to find another place."

I analysed the situation for a moment and decided that at the end of the day what Mark thought about it all was of the least importance.

"Okay," I agreed. "For the time being you can bring your friends over to my place."

I looked to my left because I could hear the sound of footsteps approaching from that direction. Sure enough, a tall man dressed in scruffy clothes appeared from behind the corn crop. He had a camera in his hand and gave the impression that he was looking for something interesting to photograph. Jason and I exchanged an understanding look and we both got up.

"Do you know when this formation was made?" the tall man asked, facing us.

"Last night," Jason answered.

"What time?"

Neither of us had a clue and we both shrugged our shoulders at the same time. The man looked down and studied the folded stalks of corn for a moment before he started clicking away. He did not seem interested in any further conversation so we moved away to another part of the formation. Carefully, so as not to damage the crop, we walked across and around the pattern trying to see and memorise as much as possible.

Fifteen minutes later, four more people appeared and we decided to leave. On our way back to the car we unexpectedly bumped into a large man with a crimson face who looked like a local farmer. He glared at me angrily.

"You people are trespassing," he said sharply.

"I am sorry," I said, realising that perhaps this was the landowner. "There is a new formation in the field and we wanted to see it."

"This bloody formation and people like you are going to destroy my crop," he bellowed. "If I catch the vandals who did it I'll break their legs. There will be a whole procession of you today, no doubt ... Vandals, bloody vandals," he complained as he marched on towards the circle.

Jason turned to me. "Vandals?" he queried mockingly, his eyes wide open.

I laughed. "If only he knew."

Jason laughed too. "Maybe it's just as well he doesn't."

Soon we were driving back to Swindon following the same route we had used to get there and then a different route out of town. It wasn't long before I realised that Jason was driving towards London. I was rather disappointed, as I would have liked to have stayed in Wiltshire longer.

"Are we going back already?" I asked, just to be sure.

Jason nodded. "I am afraid today it's my turn to do family duty. It's lunch with my sister and father," he said unenthusiastically.

"You have a sister?" I asked inquisitively.

"Yeah, a very academic sister," Jason said, his eyes fixed firmly on the road ahead. "She is studying ancient history at Oxford."

"What about your parents?"

"My father is a lawyer and my mother is a throat specialist."

"A very academic family."

"My parents and sister are all very rigid in their way of thinking. We don't communicate very well," Jason confided sadly.

I sensed the subject was upsetting for him. "Don't you like talking about your family?"

"Not particularly."

"We don't have to talk about them if you don't want to. Let's listen to the radio instead," I suggested, pressing the on/off button. I found a station playing relaxing music and leant back in my seat.

The news came on half an hour later:

"Mexican Air Force pilots filmed 11 unidentified flying objects in the skies over southern Campeche State, a defence department spokesman confirmed. A videotape made widely available to the news media yesterday shows the bright objects, some sharp points of light and others like large headlights, moving rapidly in what appears to be a late evening sky. Pilots using infrared equipment filmed the lights on 5 March. They appeared to be flying at an altitude of around 11,480 feet, and allegedly surrounded the air force jet as it conducted routine anti-drug trafficking vigilance in Campeche. Only three of the objects showed up on the plane's radar. Mr Maussan, a Mexican investigator, commented that it was historic news and that, although hundreds of videos of UFOs existed, none had the backing of the armed forces of any country, adding that the armed forces didn't perpetuate frauds. He also confirmed that Secretary of Defence, General Ricardo Vega Garcia, gave him the video on 22 April."

Jason and I exchanged knowing smiles, pleased that there seemed to be yet more proof of extraterrestrial existence.

"This should not be so easy to ignore," Jason commented.

"Humans have been successfully ignoring the facts up until now. I doubt this news will change anything," I said.

"Why is it that people can't see the most obvious things?"

"The Manipulators make sure that life's pace is fast and people are kept busy," I explained. "When they are busy, struggling for what they mistakenly think is important, their minds are never calm enough to think rationally. Besides, if people are busy and tired they don't have the time or inclination to change anything. They are more likely to accept things as they are and to resort to alcohol or drugs to feel better. When people are high on some substance they care and understand even less."

"True. It's another way of keeping control of the human mind."

"It's psychological manipulation, but people are blissfully unaware of it. For example, they are led to believe that the main goal in life is having a lot of money and all the material trappings that go with it. They rush around trying to gather as much as possible and at the same time are totally blind to the fact that everything around them is falling apart. They also lose the sense of what is really important and naively believe that they lead a very productive and successful life. The government propagates the same ideals and calls it "progress", so there is no reason to question anything."

"I've never thought of progress in quite the same terms," Jason said.

"No, because this isn't progress, it's the road to destruction," I replied.

We were approaching my house and Jason slowed down. He parked the car outside the front entrance and kept the engine running.

"I wish I did not have to leave you," he muttered, stroking my hair gently.

I turned to him, but did not say anything. I just sat completely still as though hypnotised by his touch.

Looking into my eyes, he leant over and kissed me softly on the lips. "I have to go," he muttered, reaching for my bag from the back seat.

I took the bag from him and opened the car door. I wasn't sure what to say as I still felt numb from his kiss, so I quickly said the first thing that came to my mind. "Let me know when you are bringing your friends over."

He nodded, waited for me to close the door, and with a quick wave of his hand he drove off.

Slowly, I walked to the front door and unlocked it. As I entered the empty, still house I suddenly felt very lonely. It was as if a part of me was missing and I found it very unsettling. There was a seemingly endless empty afternoon stretching out in front of me and then a monotonous uneventful evening, and I could have easily become depressed if I had allowed myself to dwell for too long on my feelings. I was fully aware that in order not to fall into the trap of negativity I had to redirect my thoughts to something else, and so I decided to finish the still life with fruit.

Decision made, I changed into my working clothes and made my way to the kitchen where I took the fruit out of the fridge. It was far from fresh, but I was determined to give it a go anyway.

In the conservatory I did my best to recreate the still life as before. When I was more or less satisfied I picked up the unfinished canvas, looked at it and for some unexplained reason felt unable to continue with it. The picture did not seem challenging enough. It was just a boring still life of fruit - fruit that was not even fresh any more. Glancing at my easel, I spotted the drawing of the alien face still clipped to it and I knew immediately what I wanted to paint.

I found a medium-sized canvas and secured it to the easel. As soon as I looked at the various tubes of oil paints I knew which colours I should use for the painting. The face was to be as green as grass, the eyes blue and yellow. I could see it so clearly in my mind as I started to paint.

4

The very next morning I spent some time in the meditation room practising various gentle yoga postures. I found that yoga was the perfect way to get in touch with oneself and achieve a certain level of tranquillity and harmony within the physical body, and at that moment I felt it was exactly what I needed.

When I had finished, I took a long, leisurely shower and washed my hair. I wrapped my hair in a large soft towel, slipped into a terry dressing gown and went to the bedroom. Opening my wardrobe, I began searching through the hangers for something suitable to wear in case Jason called and wanted to see me. With a sinking feeling I realised that, having recently put some weight on, most of my best clothes no longer fitted me and it looked as though I needed to replace them with new ones as soon as possible. I was planning where to go shopping when my thoughts were interrupted by the sound of the phone ringing.

I lifted the receiver. "Hello."

"Hi," Zoe said. "I'm glad you're home. I need to ask you about something."

"Where else would I be?" I replied shortly.

"You sound miserable," Zoe observed.

"That's because I am miserable."

"Why? What's happened?"

"Nothing much. I am just big and fat, and none of my clothes fit me any more," I complained. "Perhaps you could cheer me up by coming shopping with me for some new ones."

"Today?"

"Yes, today."

Zoe hesitated. "I'd like to, but I have a client this afternoon."

Zoe had been working as a holistic practitioner and her clients usually visited her at home.

"Please, Zoe," I begged. "I need some nice clothes and I would appreciate your advice."

"I suppose I could cancel ..." Zoe was wavering.

"Please."

"I will if we do lunch as well," Zoe bargained.

"Absolutely. Lunch is on me," I said. "You wanted to ask me something?"

"Yes, one of my clients has discovered a lump in her breast. Luckily the lump is benign, but the specialist has told her that if it does not go away in the next six months he will have to operate to prevent the possibility of it becoming malignant. The woman is desperate to get rid of it any way she can to avoid the operation and I thought I could try energetic healing on her. Who knows, it might help."

"It might. Have you done it before?"

"No. I was hoping you could explain it to me."

"To be honest I haven't done it myself, but the principle is quite simple. I'll explain it to you when I see you."

"Could you explain it to me now over the phone, please? The woman concerned is here and I would like to do the healing straight away."

"Sure, no problem. Your aim is to try to restore the energy flow to her body by recharging and rebalancing the meridian channels around the affected area. To do this you pull the tips of your fingers and thumb of your left hand together and place them on the consciousness chakra or third eye. Next, you do the same with your right hand and place it at the top of the first of the five meridian channels running from the collarbone to the pelvis, creating a closed circuit of energy. You recharge them by moving your right hand down the channel and stopping for about ten seconds every time you change the position. When you reach the end, you start on the next channel and continue until you have recharged them all."

"Thanks, I understand," Zoe said when I had finished. "I hope it works."

"I hope so too."

There was a moment of silence.

"Zoe, are you still there?"

"Yes, I'm trying to think where we can go shopping."

"How about central London?" I suggested.

"Why not? Let's go to Oxford Street."

"Okay," I agreed readily. "We'll go in my car. When do you think you'll be ready?"

"In about an hour."

"Cool. I'll pick you up in an hour," I said, and hung up.

I dried my hair, put on a pair of baggy jeans and a T-shirt, and went downstairs. Checking my watch, I discovered that I had about 15 minutes to spare, so I used that time to tidy up the kitchen and living room.

I was on my way out when the phone rang. Expecting Mark to call, I didn't rush to answer it and just waited for the answering service to pick it up. After six rings the machine clicked to the answering mode and Mark's voice came on the line. He explained briefly that he was leaving Germany the following day and would be flying to Paris where I could reach him at the Hilton Hotel. As soon as the message had ended I closed the door and made my way to the car.

Driving to Zoe's house, I thought about Mark and our falling-to-pieces relationship. As far as I was concerned, the relationship was doomed and there was no turning back, but somehow I had to find enough courage to tell him. I knew it would be nearly impossible to explain to Mark that it was over between us without upsetting him. To be perfectly honest, I was dreading the inevitable confrontation, as Mark tended to become angry easily and when he was angry he was usually very unreasonable. The whole situation could present other problems as well. If we were to go our own separate ways, which I felt was unavoidable, it could mean that the house would have to be sold and I would be searching for another place in which to live. Also, it would mean that my financial situation would change drastically and I would have to support myself from my paintings, which might not be an easy thing to do now that I didn't feel at all inclined to paint commercial pictures. I had some savings, but it wasn't much and the money wouldn't last long if I didn't supplement it with some extra income, an idea that at that point seemed quite remote.

With all these thoughts churning around in my mind, I pulled up outside Zoe's house and blew the horn. Zoe peered out of her kitchen window and a moment later rushed out and climbed into my car.

"Hiya!" she exclaimed in greeting.

I didn't reply and she gave me a concerned look.

"You look terribly worried."

I put the car into gear. "It's just one of those days."

Zoe gave me another look. "Don't worry. You don't look at all fat."

"It's not just that. I've got other problems as well."

"What other problems?"

"You don't want to know," I said, pulling away from the kerb.

"I do, especially if I can help."

"Sorry, Zoe, but I don't think you can."

"Carrie, hasn't anyone told you that a problem shared is a problem halved?"

"Can we talk about it later, please?" I said, and checked the road for traffic before turning.

"Sure. We'll talk over lunch."

During our journey to central London, Zoe did her best to cheer me up with some light conversation about clothes, men and her never-ending diet, so by the time we reached Oxford Street I had managed to push most of my worries to the back of my mind, even if only temporarily.

I left the car in an NCP car park and for the next three hours we walked from shop to shop, from department store to department store, looking for various items to purchase. To my surprise, I discovered that shopping for larger sizes wasn't much fun. It took a long time to find something nice that would fit me as my now bigger, fuller figure was between a size 12 and 14 and most of the fashionable, sexy-looking clothes seemed to have been designed for very skinny, flat-chested women. It was as though the current designers conspired not to design any clothes for 'obese' people who were size ten and above. While I had a problem finding anything remotely sexy and appealing, Zoe, a size ten, managed to find some really nice clothes for herself. She definitely enjoyed our shopping expedition more than I did.

Three hours of the torture of having to look at myself in large mirrors under harsh fluorescent lights while trying on clothes that were either too small, ill-fitting or simply too plain had done nothing to improve my self-confidence. I felt exhausted and hungry.

"I think it's time for lunch. What do you fancy to eat?" I asked Zoe.

"Pizza," Zoe replied, without hesitation, "but you know me, I will most probably end up having salad."

"I hope you won't because I quite fancy pizza myself. Why don't we go to Pizza Express? One pizza won't make us any fatter."

Zoe laughed. "So we live in hope."

"Is that a yes or a no?"

"It's a yes. Let's go and have pizza."

With our hands full of carrier bags, we entered Pizza Express, which was located in one of the side streets at the back of Oxford Street. The place was buzzing with activity, which was to be expected during lunchtime, and all the tables were occupied, so we decided to wait until one became available. Fortunately, a small table was vacated within minutes and we rushed for it, grateful that we could at last sit down and rest our legs.

It wasn't long before a young, attractive-looking waiter appeared. Zoe gave him one of her sweet, sexy smiles and ordered vegetarian pizza and a bottle of Perrier. I said I would have the same.

As soon as the waiter had departed, Zoe said, "While we are waiting for our food, why don't you tell me what's been bothering you?"

"It's Mark ..." I hesitated for a moment before adding, "I've decided not to marry him."

Zoe gave me a puzzled look. "Why?"

"Because I don't love him any more." The answer was simple.

"You don't?"

"No, I don't," I replied. "Why do you look so surprised? You know it's been far from a perfect relationship."

"That's true, but in so many ways you seemed really committed to each other."

"We were never that committed," I protested.

"But you have bought a house together and you have been engaged for months," Zoe reasoned.

"We have been engaged and we have bought a house together, but you know as well as I do that if it came to the crunch Mark would always choose his work over our relationship. I wouldn't call that commitment."

"So what does Mark have to say about it?"

"He doesn't know. I haven't told him yet."

At that moment the waiter approached the table with our food and drinks.

Zoe waited for him to depart before she said, "I have a bad feeling about this. Mark can be very nasty when he wants to be."

I looked at her in surprise, as I could not recall Zoe ever arguing with Mark or even having an unpleasant conversation with him.

"Has he ever been nasty to you?"

She nodded. "Yes, he has."

"When? I don't know anything about it."

"It wasn't that long ago, probably a month or so. I rang your house, but you were out and he answered the phone. He was really in a foul mood," Zoe said, pouring Perrier into her glass. "We talked for a few minutes and before I knew it we were arguing about my work. He called me stupid and naive for thinking that I was helping people." Zoe sipped some water. "It was a very unpleasant conversation, to say the least."

"Why have you never told me about it?" I asked.

"I wanted to, but it was never the right time and after a few days it didn't seem important enough." She shrugged her shoulders. "Everyone gets in a bad mood from time to time."

I felt strangely apprehensive as I cut into my pizza.

"I suspect Mark and I will have quite a few arguments before we can go our own separate ways. Knowing him, there will be arguments about the house, about who takes what, and who is right and who is wrong - the usual stuff when people separate, but with Mark it will probably turn rather unpleasant."

"As long as it's not too unpleasant," Zoe said, reaching for her glass of water.

I couldn't help recalling the 'other' Mark I had seen that day at the restaurant during my birthday dinner. The image was horrifying and I shivered slightly from the memory.

"So do I," I said resignedly.

"For what it's worth, I think you are doing the right thing," Zoe admitted, "but let's not talk about him any more. Now that we've decided to eat all this naughty food, let's enjoy it!"

Zoe was right. There was no point in talking about Mark and allowing him to spoil our day. I tucked into my pizza and enjoyed every little bite before I picked up the dessert menu.

"I am going to have cheesecake with cream. How about you?"

Zoe smiled mischievously. "To hell with the diet, I'll have one too."

I smiled back, suddenly feeling much better. There was a lot to be said for comfort food.

* * *

It was nearly 7 o'clock when I eventually arrived home. I unpacked all my shopping, made myself a cup of coffee and sat in front of the television to relax and watch the news. The news always seemed grim and today was no exception.

I began to listen more carefully to an unsettling item about contingency plans for the mass evacuation of London in the event of a terror attack, revealing how the huge transit operation would work in the wake of a chemical, biological or conventional strike. The plans did not relate to the evacuation of the entire capital, as moving eight million people at once would be impractical, but it did cater for the mass evacuation of a whole area such as the City or West End, with 300,000 residents and workers. Many people were expected to leave the City by private car, and the main road arteries were going to be cleared to help them. Trains, coaches and buses were to move others. If the tube was not affected by the attack, it was going to be used as well. Council staff were to be posted to railway stations and other locations outside London to pick up passengers and give them accommodation. Additionally, there was going to be guidance on how to decontaminate buildings from chemical or biological damage.

I was contemplating the futility of it all when a sudden ringing of the telephone jolted me back to the present. I listened to it ring a few times before I finally picked it up. My spirits lifted when I heard Jason's voice.

"I couldn't stay away," he said lightly.

I laughed. "Where are you?"

"In my car outside your front door."

"Why didn't you just ring the doorbell?"

"I was thinking about it, but decided it would be better if I called first. Will you let me in?"

"What a question. Of course I'll let you in."

"Are you hungry?"

"Not really. I've had a very big and naughty lunch."

"Well, I am," Jason said. "I passed a takeaway on my way here, so I'll go back and get some food. Get the plates ready."

The phone went dead, and then after a moment it rang again.

When I answered, Jason said, "Do you like Chinese?"

"I do," I replied, and the phone went dead again.

I hung up and ran upstairs to change my clothes. I was more than thrilled at the thought of seeing Jason again and, like a schoolgirl going on her first date, I wanted to look my best, and baggy jeans and a T-shirt simply wouldn't do. Quickly, I changed into beige cotton, stretchy trousers and a pink and brown floral chiffon blouse. I brushed my hair back and secured it with shiny clips on both sides above my ears. Finally I applied some pink gloss to my lips. Assessing myself in a full-length mirror I was pleasantly surprised with the way I looked in my new clothes. I thought I looked voluptuous and feminine, and not at all fat.

I was on my way down the stairs when the doorbell rang. Heading straight for the door, I flung it open to face Jason, and for a moment I just stood there and stared at him. He looked gorgeous in his light blue jeans, white shirt and caramel suede jacket. I realised I had nearly forgotten how dashingly handsome he really was and looking at him then it felt as though I were reminded again.

"Hi," he said, smiling.

His smile was warm and captivating, and I couldn't help smiling back.

"Hi."

"You look radiant."

"Thank you." I opened the door wider. "Come in."

He stepped inside.

"Food and drink," he said, raising the large white carrier bag in his hand. "Where shall I put it?"

"Why don't you take it to the living room and I'll get plates and glasses," I said, and headed for the kitchen.

Quickly, I grabbed plates, glasses and cutlery, and made my way back to the living room where Jason had already unpacked an assortment of Chinese dishes that were arrayed on the coffee table. There were eight takeaway boxes altogether and it seemed much too much food for two people.

"Gosh, who is going to eat all this food?" I questioned lightly.

"I forgot to ask what you'd like and ended up getting a selection of different things," Jason replied.

"I eat most foods apart from red meat," I said, thinking it was better to clarify that straight away.

"Why don't you eat red meat?" Jason asked.

"Because red meat is difficult to digest and the body uses a lot of energy to break it down. I prefer to use that energy to keep my body healthy," I explained, while setting the table.

"A good reason not to eat it, I suppose," Jason said, and then he asked, "You aren't a vegetarian are you?"

I smiled. "No, I do eat chicken and fish. The body needs certain proteins, and chicken and fish are a good source of them."

When the table was set, Jason sat on the sofa and I took a seat on the armchair to his left.

"You are much too far away," he said, and patted the place next to him. "Come, sit here."

"Okay."

I moved to sit beside him and quickly grabbed a plate, as suddenly I needed to distract myself from being so close to him.

"Which dishes have red meat in them?" I asked.

Jason smiled. "None of them. I don't eat red meat either, although for different reasons."

I faced him. "Why don't you eat it?"

"I don't eat it because I am wary of all the diseases that are associated with eating animal meat. It concerns me that animals get these awful diseases and can pass them on to humans." Jason reached for a big plastic bottle of water and filled our glasses. "It seems to me that either we don't look after them properly or we should not be killing them for food," he explained.

"Both I think," I said, helping myself to some sweet and sour chicken and egg noodles.

Jason reached for the box of egg noodles.

"What did you do today?" he asked, spooning some noodles onto his plate.

"I went shopping with my friend, Zoe," I replied, tucking into my food.

Jason put the box back on the table and grabbed another one.

"Did you buy anything nice?"

"Yes, I bought the clothes I am wearing and a few other things."

Jason scrutinised me carefully, his eyes stopping on my well-defined breasts for just a moment too long.

"Nice."

I smiled. "You like my new top or you like my breasts?"

Jason looked straight into my eyes. "I like everything about you," he muttered seriously.

I stared at him and marvelled at being so lucky. He was everything I had ever wanted in a man. He was attractive, generous and considerate, and he knew how to make me feel appreciated. When I was in his company it did not seem to matter if I was a size 10 or a size 14 because he liked me as I was. He understood that there was more to a person than looks and size alone, and that judging people on that basis was very shallow and limiting. After all, the true person is always hidden behind the physical body irrespective of its size and looks. Mark had been a perfect example of how easy it was to like someone for all the wrong reasons and I was grateful that Jason was there to help me understand the difference.

"I like quite a lot about you too," I said to him.

We gazed at each other as though under a spell, our eyes full of desire. I desperately wanted to put my hand on Jason's face and stroke his soft, beautiful skin, to touch his silky hair and kiss his sexy lips, but I looked away instead. The spell was momentarily broken and distractedly we returned to our food.

By the time we had finished eating it had become dark in the room. I switched on the tall floor lamp, gathered the half-empty plastic food boxes and dirty plates, and deposited them in the kitchen. When I returned to the living room Jason was looking through the TV guide.

"Anything worth watching?" I asked, getting back to my place on the sofa.

"Nothing really, unless you want to watch *Cabaret*. It starts in five minutes."

"*Cabaret* the film?"

He nodded.

"I've seen it, but I don't mind watching it again."

The film started and Jason pulled me close. I cuddled into him, wrapping my arm around him and resting my head on his shoulder, and it felt really good being that close to him and breathing his wonderful scent, which reminded me of a mixture of rice flower, vanilla and soft masculine cologne. Neither of us wanted to move away and we stayed in that position for most of the film.

Just as the film was coming to the end, Jason gently lifted my chin with his index finger and kissed me tenderly on the lips. His kiss was very erotic and all of a sudden I felt hot all over as my body responded with a strong desire for him. Placing my hand on the nape of his neck, I pulled his head even closer to mine and kissed him back. Very soon our kisses turned into many other kisses, which became more urgent and passionate, while our hands became more probing and our bodies more and more aroused and demanding.

"Where is the bedroom?" Jason asked hotly.

"Upstairs, first door on the right," I answered urgently.

Jason pulled away from me and in one quick movement lifted me up from the sofa. He carried me across the room into the hall. I knew I was rather heavy and in any other circumstances I would have felt really uncomfortable being carried by a man, but Jason's body felt strong and he was holding me firmly, so I allowed myself to relax. I put my arms around his neck.

"How far are you going to carry me?"

"As far as the bedroom."

"You can't carry me all the way to the bedroom, I am way too heavy," I laughed, as he carried me towards the stairs.

"Try me. I haven't done all that weightlifting for nothing," he said, climbing upwards.

"A giant of a man, not at all fazed by the weight of a big girl like me," I joked, kissing him on the cheek.

"You are not big. You are sexy and gorgeous."

"You are such a flatterer."

There were no lights on the first floor and there was hardly any light on the stairway. For a split second I was worried that he might trip and we would both end up falling down the stairs, but at the same time I felt too happy and carefree to care.

Reaching the first floor landing, Jason stopped in front of the first door on the right.

"Is this the bedroom?"

"Yes, and there should be a double bed somewhere in the middle."

"You can't imagine how glad I am to hear it."

He kicked the door open and carried me into my bedroom, which was gently illuminated by the moonlight. He put me down on the bed, lay next to me and we kissed passionately. Our lips were still moulded together as he unbuttoned my blouse, exposing my flesh, and then began placing gentle featherweight kisses from my neck all the way down to my breasts.

"Don't move," he whispered, swiftly undoing the bow on my front-fastening bra.

As it opened up he lowered his head and continued with more deliberate kisses on my breasts and nipples, making me hot with desire. Silently, I was yearning to feel his naked body close to mine and to touch his bare skin. I reached for him, but he stopped my hand.

"Wait, not yet."

"You are torturing me," I complained.

"That's the whole idea," he muttered, kissing me all over and driving me totally crazy.

Eventually, I could stand it no longer. I grabbed his shirt and urgently began undoing the buttons and as soon as they were all undone I pulled it off him then quickly unzipped his trousers. I tugged at the fabric trying to pull them off, but it seemed impossible.

"I can't do it. You have to get up."

He lifted himself up and got off the bed.

"Shit! That hurt!" he exclaimed as he stepped on something. He fumbled for the bedside light switch and as the light came on he looked down at the floor.

"A man's shoes? What are they doing in your bedroom?"

It only took a split second for me to come back down to earth. What was I going to say? If I told him the truth he would just leave and I couldn't allow that to happen, but at the same time I knew that lying wasn't an option either. Stalling for time, I pulled my blouse tightly around me and sat up.

"Are you going to tell me?" Jason asked, looking at me with his disappointed eyes.

"I was going to tell you ... It's complicated ..."

He sounded upset when he asked, "Is this the same friend who shares this house with you?"

I decided it was time to come clean. "It's my fiancé actually," I muttered.

Jason raised his eyebrows in shock. "Fiancé? You are engaged and you didn't feel it was important enough to tell me? That's bloody great!"

I lifted myself up to my knees, moved closer to him and looked into his eyes.

"Jason, listen to me," I said firmly. "I decided to break off the engagement some time ago. Soon there won't be any fiancé and there certainly won't be any wedding."

"What difference does it make? The man still sleeps in this bed with you," he said much more calmly, and then he added, "How stupid of me. I had noticed that you were wearing a ring, but I didn't like to ask. Now I wish I had."

"You don't understand. The relationship is over." I grasped his hand and tried to pull him towards me. "Please can we kiss and make up."

"No, I don't think we can."

"Why? I thought you wanted to make love to me."

He looked straight into my eyes. "I do want to make love to you, but I can't, not now, and not for as long as this man shares your bed."

"Can you at least sit next to me so we can talk?" I asked, resigned to the situation.

He sat down and faced me. With both hands he gently removed the hair clips and tidied my hair behind my ears, then he traced my cheek with the back of his hand and said tenderly, "You are very special to me and I don't want to lose you."

I realised I was falling badly for him and there was absolutely nothing I could do about it.

"You won't. We need to educate people, remember?" I said with a smile, in an attempt to lighten up the mood.

He helped me to fasten my bra and button up my top.

"Is your fiancé coming back on Friday?"

"He is no longer my fiancé!" I snapped, and to make the point I pulled my engagement ring off my finger, opened the drawer of my bedside cabinet and dropped it into it.

Jason noticed the light emanating from inside the drawer. "What's that light?" he asked.

Pulling out the drawer as far as it would go, I reached for the crystal, which was hidden at the back.

"It's a very special crystal. If I concentrate while I'm holding it I can connect to all sorts of things taking place on the planet," I explained. The crystal was even brighter than I had remembered and for some strange reason holding it did not frighten me any more. "Open your hand." I placed the stone in Jason's palm. "Now, try to concentrate and see if you can feel anything."

Jason was staring at the crystal as though hypnotised by it.

"How strange ... I can feel volcanic lava flowing and falling into water, breaking into pieces and being carried away by waves ... A few small, low-frequency earthquakes are coming from the summit ... A new, black sandy beach is forming and is adding to a pre-existing beach below a sea cliff ... I am pretty sure this is happening somewhere close to the Pacific coast."

"It could be Kilauea in Hawaii," I suggested.

"Yes, that seems right. How did you guess?"

"Kilauea has been active for the past 19 years and often throws lava into the Pacific."

Jason turned the crystal around in his hand and the brightness was quite exquisite.

"This is a very powerful rock," he commented, totally stunned by its power.

"I know, it used to scare me," I confided. "When I hold it I connect to all sorts of information I would rather not know. If I know that somewhere on the planet tectonic plates are shifting and there is going to be a massive earthquake, how is that going to help all the people who live there and end up being affected by it? It distresses me that there is nothing I can do. I can't even talk to anyone about it because no one would take me seriously."

"Surely other people can connect to the information in exactly the same way we can," Jason reasoned.

"It's not that simple as not everyone can connect to the power of this crystal. Some people will only feel an intense heat when they hold it."

"Why is that?"

"Everyone operates at a different frequency. This crystal sends signals on very high frequency waves. People whose overall body frequency is very low cannot read these waves. They simply cannot channel the necessary frequency."

Carefully, Jason placed the crystal back into the drawer.

"Where did you get it?"

I hesitated, not sure if I should tell him the truth or make up some plausible story. I opted for the truth.

"It was given to me by Amos."

"Who is Amos?" he asked.

"He is an alien," I replied unsurely.

Jason stared at me for a long moment.

"You mean you have actually met an alien?"

I nodded.

"Where?"

"In the fields behind my house."

"No kidding?" he asked, with a smile.

"Why are you smiling?"

"Because I have wasted so much time trying to spot a spaceship up in the sky and it's pretty obvious that if they want to show themselves they simply land in your back garden."

"Shush!"

I stopped him, as quite unexpectedly a voice came through to me:

"This is Amos speaking from the mother ship, which is in stationary orbit around your planet at a constant computed distance of 1,177 million kilometres. We are about to commence our descent to a distance of 500,000 kilometres. This will be completed in 17.33 minutes earth time span. The star gate will open for a short time tonight and we are considering the possibility of landing a small craft close to you to enable us to meet both of you. We will not give you prior warning, but estimate the landing time to be around midnight your time. Follow the same instructions as before. We will land after we adjust our frequencies to be within the range of your visible spectrum. Your ability to remain calm as we land is of the utmost importance. I bid you farewell for now."

As I listened to the message, Jason was looking at me curiously.

"That was Amos," I explained carefully. "He told me that he will be landing a ship at midnight our time in the field behind the house, and he would like to meet both of us."

Jason stood up and ran his hand through his hair. "Unbelievable," he muttered, as though shocked by the news, and then he looked directly at me and laughed. "You mean we are going to meet Amos, the alien?"

I nodded. "That's what I was told."

Jason laughed louder. "This is absolutely, totally unbelievable."

He seemed very excited.

"You mustn't get too excited," I said, trying to calm him down.

"How can I not be excited? This is nothing short of a miracle. It's something I have always dreamed about and never in a million years thought would actually happen."

Glancing at the bedside clock, I noted that it was nearly twenty to eleven.

"We have a long wait before anything happens, so let's go downstairs and have some coffee to help us stay awake."

"Stay awake? You must be kidding. There is no way I could fall asleep even if I tried."

"Let's have some coffee anyway."

"No, I have a better idea," Jason said, buttoning up his shirt. "Let's go to the field and wait there."

"I am not sure that is such a good idea," I said hesitantly.

"Please, Carrie."

He looked at me with his beautiful pleading eyes and I couldn't say no.

"All right, we'll go, but promise me you will calm down, otherwise they will not land at all."

I suspected it would be cool out in the field, so I found two large jumpers, threw one on and handed the other one to Jason.

"You'll be more comfortable in this," I said, heading for the door.

Jason put on the jumper and followed me downstairs. In the kitchen, I filled a small thermos with the hot black coffee and put it in a carrier bag together with two plastic cups. I searched through the kitchen drawers for a torch, and as soon as I had found one we left the house through the back door. Once we had crossed the garden we had to go down a narrow path and, as I knew the way very well, it made sense that I would go first with Jason following. We walked slowly, illuminating the path with the torch. When we reached the end we found a nice piece of grass under the trees on the edge of the field and sat down on the ground. The sky was clear and the moon was providing enough light for us to see into the distance reasonably clearly.

I gave Jason the torch to hold while I poured coffee into the cups and then we just sat there silently sipping the hot liquid and staring into the sky, feeling apprehensive yet knowing we had to remain calm if we wanted the ship to land. After what seemed like a rather long wait, I spotted some small lights flashing every second or so in the far distance.

"Can you see the little lights flashing?" I asked.

"No," Jason replied. "Can you see them?"

"Yes, over there." I pointed at the sky. "Look carefully, they flash quickly and it's easy to miss them."

"Oh, yes, I can see them!" he exclaimed.

At that point I heard a distinctive humming noise.

"I can hear humming."

The noise was getting louder.

"So can I," Jason said, and then added, "and it seems to be intensifying. I think it's time to get ready for our encounter."

He got to his feet and helped me up. Hand in hand we walked a few steps forwards, then stopped and waited. Quite unexpectedly an indistinct large shape resembling a heavy cloud appeared directly in front of us. This quickly changed into a saucer-like spacecraft, which was hovering about ten metres above the ground. Small circular lights surrounding the whole structure came on, then four small legs extended from underneath the craft before it gently landed on the ground and the humming noise ceased.

Jason squeezed my hand as we stood in front of it in anticipation. Slowly, a small door on the side of the craft opened and two slim figures dressed in pale blue suits stepped down onto a small platform in front of the door. They stood there for a moment, then the platform began to move and they slowly started to descend. It nearly reached the end of the sloping surface before it came to a stop. A set of steps unfolded and the two figures stepped down and walked towards us. I recognised one of them as Amos. The other figure looked very similar to Amos, but was smaller and I suspected it was female. They stopped about five metres in front of us.

Inwardly, I could hear a greeting, but realised that Jason could not hear it.

"They are greeting us," I said. He looked at me in surprise and so I explained, "They communicate with me through my psyche. I will speak their words as I hear them. If you have a question say it aloud so I can follow the conversation."

Jason nodded in agreement.

"This is Elia." Amos introduced the smaller figure as I spoke his words for him. *"We can't stay long on your planet as your energies are not compatible with ours, but we are very pleased to have a chance to speak to both of you today. We have waited a long time for this moment and we rejoice that at last we can communicate with earthlings in this way. Both of you are unique. Your progress has been remarkable and the cosmos feels that it is time for you to form a partnership with Elia and myself as your cosmic partners. Together we will work as one unit towards the restoration of the Planet Earth. We will be supporting you energetically and assisting you both in achieving the ultimate fusion of energies. This will lift the level of your consciousness and allow you to experience higher realms of existence. You will learn a lot of new aspects of yourselves by being together. You will learn patience, understanding, tolerance and the true meaning of unconditional love. The key is to let go of your past and embrace the simplicity of the future."*

Amos gave Elia a signal to continue. I could feel Elia's energy, which was gentle and very calming. The words began to form in my mind as she tried to communicate the rest of the message. Again, I spoke the words for Jason's benefit.

"The cosmos never forces anyone into cosmic co-operation. You need to think about what Amos has said to you and decide if you want to commit yourselves

to this partnership. The commitment carries certain responsibilities because as soon as you commit yourselves the cosmos will start to invest a lot of energy in you to help you evolve and grow. However, even though the energy is never wasted it would be a great loss if you were to decide not to continue later on. This energy, given to you freely, should nourish you and assist you in the understanding of what is required of you. You will always be linked to us through consciousness and we will help you in every way we can." She lifted her arm in a kind of goodbye gesture. "It's time for us to depart, so we'll leave you now. When you have made your decision just use our names to call us and transmit the message to us through thought waves. Farewell for now."

The short meeting was over, and Amos and Elia began walking back towards the platform.

"I have a question," Jason called. He waited until they both turned to face him. "Why did you give Carrie the crystal?"

"The crystal is for your protection," Amos communicated. "There will be a lot of upheavals on your planet, and many places will become unsafe. If you choose to, you can connect to these places through the crystal."

They turned again and carried on towards the platform. They walked slowly, putting a lot of effort into lifting their legs as if the gravitational pull of the Earth affected them.

Eventually, they reached the steps leading to the platform, climbed onto it and the platform began ascending until it arrived at the door and stopped. They entered the ship and the door closed. The humming sound commenced and we watched as the ship started to rise very slowly. The four small legs retracted underneath the craft and it slowly lifted to about 100 metres above the ground. Quite suddenly it shot almost vertically into the sky at a phenomenal speed, and moments later it had disappeared completely leaving a faint cloud behind.

* * *

We were sitting on the sofa in a semi-dark living room talking and drinking hot tea with only a small table lamp providing the light. We were both quite energised by the whole experience and neither of us was ready to go to sleep.

Jason put his empty mug on the table, and said, "I am very unsure about this partnership we have been asked to start. What exactly does it mean in practical terms?"

"I am not sure either."

The moment I uttered those words I saw a six-pointed star in front of me. The star looked very much like the Star of David, but the two triangles were not interlaced. They were very clearly separate and one lay on top of the other.

"I can see a six-pointed star," I said.

"It must be a symbol of some sort," Jason reasoned.

"It definitely means something. Let me ask."

I asked inwardly and the answer came almost instantly. I spoke the words as I heard them.

"The six-pointed star, or should we say two equal triangles or halves fused into one six-pointed star, is the symbol of unity and oneness - the perfect union of male and female. The triangle pointing up represents male and the one pointing down represents female, and the two are totally equal and dependent on each other to reach balance, harmony and spiritual wholeness. This is achieved through energetic interaction between male and female on both physical and spiritual levels. The deepest and most important interaction is through the sexual experience. This, however, should reach far beyond the physical level in order to achieve the total fusion of energies between the two halves and experience the divine. The divine experience itself is the ultimate connection to the Creator."

"Very interesting," Jason remarked, thoughtfully. "So let's discuss our partnership and make a decision."

"Okay, I'll tell you how I see it. I haven't known you for long, but at the same time I feel like I've known you for ages, which would suggest that we have met before."

"You mean like in previous lives?"

I nodded and continued, "Also, the fact that I am very attracted to you would suggest that in one of our previous lives we had a very close relationship and that there is still a strong connection between us. All this leads me to believe that our paths have crossed this time around for a purpose, almost as if we planned it all before we incarnated. This purpose is slowly becoming clear and now we just have to decide if we are going to take on the assignment we have most probably come here to fulfil."

"Which assignment do you have in mind?" Jason asked.

"To help with the energetic restoration of the planet," I replied. "And since every person who works for the cosmic good needs a compatible partner to learn, grow and help them carry out the task most effectively, we have been asked to become partners."

"I guess this answers the question of partnership." Jason pulled me towards him and kissed my lips gently. "I'd love you to be my partner …"

I had a feeling that he wanted to add something. "There is a but isn't there?"

Jason nodded. 'We are expected to become lovers, and there is nothing I would like more than to make love to you, but there is still a small matter of your fiancé standing in the way."

"Does that mean no sex?"

He shook his head. "No sex."

"Okay, no sex for now," I agreed, "but this should not stop us from making a decision about becoming partners. You said you wanted me to be your partner and I want you to be mine."

"Then the decision has been made," Jason concluded with a smile. "From now on we are partners."

"Yes," I said, snuggling up to him. "From now on I belong to you."

He pressed his face into my hair and kissed it with soft brushes of his lips.

"And I belong to you," he murmured.

I snuggled closer to him and closed my eyes, revelling in his closeness and his tender kisses. After a while we stretched out on the sofa, and cuddled together until eventually we fell into a calm and contented sleep.

5

Jason moved and I awoke. I glanced at the clock, which stood on the shelf next to the sofa, and I was surprised to find that it was already close to midday.

Jason opened his eyes. "Good morning," he mumbled sleepily.

Lifting myself up, I kissed his stubbly cheek. "It's time to get up, sleepy head. It's nearly afternoon."

"Don't go," he murmured, grabbing my hand.

"I'll be back soon," I promised, gently pulling away.

I headed upstairs where I washed, brushed my hair and changed into some clean clothes. Fully refreshed, I returned to the living room. Jason hadn't moved and was still sprawled on the sofa.

"Aren't you getting up?" I asked, walking to the window and pulling the curtains apart, allowing the strong sunshine to flood the room.

Jason squinted, his eyes reacting to the unexpected bright light. "Come here," he said, reaching out.

I went over and lay down next to him. Jason wrapped me in his arms.

"You smell lovely," he muttered. "I doubt that the same could be said about me."

His body was slightly sweaty from sleep, but in spite of it I found his smell masculine and pleasant.

"I like the way you smell. It's sort of ... sweaty, but nice at the same time."

He gave me a lopsided look. "Sweaty, but nice?"

"Mmm."

"Nice I can cope with; sweaty I'm not too sure." He gave me a kiss and lifted himself up. "Where is the bathroom?"

"On the first floor next to the bedroom," I instructed. "You'll find a new toothbrush and a disposable razor in the cabinet above the sink."

While Jason washed I went to the kitchen and checked the contents of the fridge. There was half a carton of milk, a few eggs, a small piece of cheese plus leftovers from the previous night's takeaway. Hardly inspiring, and unless I heated up the leftovers there definitely wasn't enough for a substantial meal for two people. Resignedly, I closed the fridge and busied myself brewing some fresh coffee. By the time Jason came downstairs the coffee was ready and I poured it into two mugs and handed one to him.

"There's not much food in the house. You can have a choice of yesterday's Chinese, cheese omelette or scrambled eggs for lunch."

Jason sipped his coffee. "Why don't we go out to eat?" he suggested, not very impressed with the choice on offer.

"Or why don't we drive to the nearest supermarket and buy some fresh food, and prepare it here?" I proposed instead.

"Excellent idea."

We finished our coffee hurriedly. Jason found his jacket while I grabbed my bag and we left the house.

"My car?" I asked.

"Why not. Which is your car?" Jason enquired.

I pointed to the silver Mini, parked by the kerb in front of the house. "That one."

"Nice car. Suits you," Jason commented.

"I like it," I said, searching in my handbag for the keys.

I pulled them out and flicked the remote control fob. The sidelights flashed to indicate that the doors were unlocked and we climbed in. The drive to the nearest supermarket took roughly ten minutes.

"This place is huge," I said as soon as we entered the store. "It will take ages to find anything here, so let's make a shopping plan. Before we do, I think I should confess that I am an absolutely lousy cook." I smiled before I added, "I get the best results with food that is very easy to prepare, like ready-made or at least half-prepared meals."

"How does freshly cooked pasta sound?" Jason suggested, reaching for a small shopping basket.

I was beginning to feel hungry and freshly cooked pasta certainly appealed to me.

"It sounds like something that shouldn't be too difficult to rustle together."

"Pasta it is then. With chicken and mushroom sauce - my favourite."

"Cool. Let's grab some fresh pasta and a pack of ready-made chicken and mushroom sauce then."

"I was thinking more of freshly made."

"I promise you if I am the cook it won't be nearly as good as the ready-made one."

"I'll cook it," Jason offered.

I smiled gratefully. "You can't imagine how relieved I am you said that."

For the next 20 minutes we walked around the big food hall choosing fresh produce. Jason dropped chicken breast, mushrooms, spinach, Parmesan cheese, cream and a packet of tagliatelle into the basket. I added an apple cake, four different packets of biscuits and a jar of freeze-dried coffee, and the shopping was done.

Back at the house, we unpacked our purchases and divided our roles in the kitchen. Jason was doing all the cooking while I was happy just helping with the preparation of the ingredients.

"I hope you are hungry because there's a lot of food," Jason said when the meal was ready.

"Famished," I replied, and it was true, for I was so hungry that I could have eaten anything.

I set the table while Jason filled two plates with hot pasta and white creamy sauce, and we sat down to eat. The food was delicious.

"Compliments to the chef," I said with a smile.

Jason smiled back. "And compliments to the chef's multi-talented assistant."

"Multi-talented," I mused. "I like the sound of that."

"Well, you are."

"You think I am?"

Jason tucked into his pasta.

"Definitely. You paint great pictures, you channel-"

"Channelling doesn't count," I interrupted, "because channelling is not a talent."

"I think it is. Not everyone can do it."

"Maybe, but nearly everyone can learn to do it."

"Everyone?" Jason asked, as though surprised.

"All the sensitive people can," I replied, twisting some pasta around my fork.

"How?"

"By trying to connect to different frequencies and learning to use the brain as the transmitter."

Jason sipped some water.

"What about trance channelling?"

"Trance channelling is different. It's done in a hypnotic state and the vocal cords of the medium are used by another being to pass on the message. As the medium is not fully aware, this is probably the best way of receiving information because it prevents any distortion of the message. Channelling is different. It's an ability to recognise different frequencies of energy and translate them into a language that is understood. It is done through consciousness, and thought waves are used to pass on the message. These messages could be coming from different levels of existence and the trick is to be able to differentiate between the message that is coming from the masters and the one that is coming from lower astral plains, for instance. There is a lot of responsibility attached to channelling because it's open to misinterpretation, especially when the person receiving the information becomes emotionally involved in what is being said."

"How do you recognise a message from another being though?"

"I recognise the frequency of energy and then my thoughts begin to formulate outside my control," I explained. "It's like I switch off my emotional body and allow the energy to flow freely through my brain. My body has to be totally calm and still for me to be able to connect to different frequencies, and then my mind starts to work like a radio and I can tune into the station of my choice as it were."

"So calmness is the key?" Jason said, finishing his pasta.

"Yes, calmness is the key to everything."

At this point the kitchen telephone rang and I got up to answer it.

It was Zoe.

"You remember my client who had a lump in her breast?" she asked eagerly.

"Of course I remember. We only spoke about her yesterday."

"You'll never guess. The lump has completely gone - and I mean completely. She is so grateful that she arrived here today with two presents, one for you and one for me. When she found out that you live only a short distance away she insisted I call you and arrange a meeting so she can thank you in person."

"Thank me for what?" I asked, confused.

"For healing her."

I was even more confused.

"You are the person who healed her, not me."

"That's true, but I wouldn't have known what to do without your help," Zoe said, adding, "I told her quite a bit about you and she is very interested in your channelling and would love to talk to you about it."

"Sure. Why don't we meet some time next week?"

"Can we meet today?" Zoe asked tentatively.

Today was probably the worst time.

"Today?"

"Now, to be more precise."

"Can't we arrange it some other time? My friend is here and it's really awkward."

"Do I know her?" Zoe asked.

"It's a him actually," I corrected, "and no, you don't know him."

"Is he good looking?"

"Very. Can I meet with your client another time?"

"Please, Carrie," Zoe urged. "She is so excited about meeting you, and I don't really know how to say no to her."

"Oh, Zoe, you can never say no to anyone."

"I know, but I can promise it'll only be a short visit."

"I am not going to be able to get out of this, am I?" I asked lightly.

"Probably not," Zoe admitted.

"All right," I relented. "Bring her over and make sure it is a short visit."

"Thanks, we'll be there in 15 minutes," Zoe said, and then added before she hung up, "By the way, her name is Victoria, but she likes to be called Vicky."

I turned to Jason. "I'm sorry, but my friend Zoe has just invited herself over with one of her clients," I explained, clearing the kitchen table.

"Let me help you," Jason said, getting up. He opened the dishwasher and began stacking it with dirty plates and pans.

I flicked the kettle on. "I'll make some tea."

I had just finished making tea when the doorbell sounded. I went to open the door.

"Carrie, darling," Vicky exclaimed, hugging me as soon as she walked into the hall. "Zoe told me so much about you. I simply insisted I come to see you."

Zoe made a resigned face. "Vicky brought a present for you."

"Oh, of course, the present," Vicky said, as if she had forgotten about it already. She extracted a small box wrapped in silver paper out of her large Louis Vuitton handbag and handed it to me. "It's only a little something to say thank you for helping with my healing."

Vicky was a tall and slender woman with medium length, blonde streaked hair and blue eyes. Her skin looked fresh and suntanned as though she had just returned from an exotic holiday. Her face was heavily made up, and her fingernails were long and painted scarlet red. She was dressed in expensive designer clothes and smelled strongly of expensive perfume.

"Thank you, Vicky. I hope you don't mind if we go into the kitchen?"

"Not at all, the kitchen is usually the warmest place in the house," Vicky said approvingly, following me into the kitchen.

Zoe followed close behind. As we entered, Jason was leaning casually against the worktop, his arms folded across his chest. I introduced everyone. Vicky gave Jason a disarming smile.

"Carrie's friend? How charming," she remarked.

"Yes, we are working together ..." Jason said, and then hesitated and added, "... on a project."

Zoe raised her eyebrows at me. "A project?" she mouthed.

I shrugged my shoulders, feigning ignorance.

Vicky seemed oblivious to our exchange. "Oh? What sort of project?"

Jason seemed to be caught off guard and took a moment to answer. "I suppose you could call it, 'the energetic nature of humans'," he improvised.

Zoe shot me a questioning look.

I shrugged my shoulders again and said, "Please, sit down."

"How very fascinating," Vicky declared, pulling out a chair and sitting down. "I would love to know more about the subject, as I was healed with some kind of energy only yesterday."

"Oh really?" responded Jason, as he pulled a chair out for Zoe and waited for me to take my seat before he sat down next to Vicky.

"Yes," Vicky said. "Six months ago I discovered a lump in one of my breasts. My doctor told me that there was no treatment available, so I had no choice but to seek an alternative route. I had tried every possible treatment there was and it didn't make the slightest bit of difference until yesterday when Zoe did some kind of cosmic energy healing. To my utter amazement when I checked for the lump this morning it had gone." Vicky turned to me. "Carrie, dear, please do explain to us how it works. I am totally fascinated by this."

"The healing works on the principle that the physical body is an energetic mass of different frequencies," I explained. "When the body is healthy the energy flows smoothly through its normal channels, energising the whole body equally. Sometimes these frequencies are disturbed and the flow of energy is altered, thus creating an energetic imbalance, which can manifest itself in the form of pain or other physical symptoms like tumours, for example. A healthy body usually compensates for this change by automatically adjusting the frequencies, and the natural healing process takes place. Often, though, the body can't cope on its own to correct this imbalance. When that happens the energetic flow needs to be corrected from outside or the body will slowly deteriorate."

"I have been rather stressed in recent months," Vicky said, lifting her teacup, her fingernails looking even longer and more crimson against the white ceramic. "I'm sure this contributed to my body not being able to heal itself." She turned to Jason. "Would you agree, Jason?"

Jason smiled politely. "I am sorry, but I am not the best person to ask."

Vicky decided to ask me instead. "Carrie, dear, what do you think?"

"It's possible," I replied, pouring tea into my cup. "Stress definitely contributes to the weakening and ageing of the body," I said, reaching for a biscuit.

Vicky filled her cup. "Are you saying that we can slow down the ageing process by avoiding stress?"

"Yes, I believe that stress and every negative emotion amount to the wastage of precious energy that could be used for maintaining and regenerating the body."

"I suppose that makes sense," Vicky agreed. "But, going back to healing, if it's only a matter of channelling some corrective energy from outside, why is it that not everyone can be healed? I've heard of people who were terminally ill and tried various alternative treatments without any success whatsoever."

"This is a karmic planet and everyone incarnated here carries some karmic debt," I explained. "Sometimes this karmic debt manifests itself as an incurable illness that serves as a learning experience for the person concerned. If, for example, the illness is designed to bring to the surface patience, tolerance and humility, and instead it brings up bitterness, intolerance and arrogance, these negative emotions alone will ensure that the condition remains."

"There is so much we don't understand," Vicky said, sipping her tea.

"That's very true," I agreed.

"Zoe told me that you channel information from other dimensions," Vicky continued.

"Yes, I do."

Vicky put her cup down. "Well, I've come across some channelling from the Pleiadians and it's rather interesting. From what I understand, our planet is coming to some kind of completion and the Pleiadians are here to help us. Apparently this completion or transformation has been heralded for eons and now it's a very important time on Earth because what happens here will affect the whole universe."

"How exciting," Zoe said.

"It is, isn't it?" Vicky reached for her handbag and pulled out a pack of cigarettes. "Do you mind if I smoke?"

Before I had a chance to reply Zoe chipped in, "This is a non-smoking household, Vicky."

"That's all right, I'll go outside," Vicky said, rising to her feet. "Jason, dear, would you mind showing me the door to the garden, please."

"Not at all," Jason said, getting up.

As soon as they were out of the earshot Zoe asked, "Who is this utterly gorgeous man?"

"I told you. He's a friend."

Zoe gave me a suspicious look. "A friend who knows the way around your house? Does he know upstairs as well as downstairs?"

"Zoe, what naughty thoughts you have," I said, smiling.

"He's not the reason why you are splitting up with Mark, is he?"

"Of course not."

"I wouldn't blame you even if he was," Zoe admitted, with a well-wishing smile. "He is drop-dead gorgeous."

"Yes," I agreed readily. "He is rather handsome."

We didn't say any more on the subject because Vicky and Jason returned.

As soon as they both sat down, Zoe asked, "Vicky, what else have you learned from the Pleiadian channellings?"

"Let me think." Vicky contemplated the answer for a moment, and then said, "It seems that we are being steadily beamed with energy from the outer cosmos and this energy is constantly being increased as and when we are able to handle it. People are evolving now at an extremely accelerated rate. It's like one year of this decade corresponds to ten years from the previous century." She turned to face me. "Carrie, darling, is that the sort of thing you are getting?"

"Yes, very much so," I replied.

"Do you believe that's true?"

"Yes, I believe there is a lot of truth in it."

"It's such a vast subject and I regret that there is not enough time to talk about it today as I know Zoe has to get back," Vicky said. "We must meet again soon."

"Yes, we have to be going," Zoe confirmed, and as she rose to her feet, everyone followed suit.

Vicky extended her hand to me. "I enjoyed our conversation. We definitely must stay in touch."

"Absolutely," I replied.

We said our final goodbyes in the hall and Zoe and Vicky left.

"There is something that bothers me about Vicky," I said to Jason as soon as I closed the door behind them. "Did you get her second name by any chance?"

He shook his head. "No, I didn't."

"I must ask Zoe. I would like to find out more about her. Do you think she might be willing to help us in our cosmic work?"

"Maybe, I am not sure."

"Me neither. I've got a feeling that she is very attached to her material possessions and might find it difficult to distance herself from them."

"Does she need to give them up?"

"No, but she needs to be completely detached from them. That means it should not matter to her one way or another whether she has them or not, or whether or not she dresses in expensive designer clothes and has expensive designer accessories."

"Speaking of which," Jason said, "I haven't changed my clothes since yesterday."

I knew it meant that he'd decided it was time for him to leave.

"I can give you a clean shirt," I offered, not wanting him to go.

"Thanks, but I wouldn't want to overstay my welcome."

He pulled me towards him and gently kissed my forehead. I knew

I should let him go, but it wasn't easy.

"Stay until tomorrow."

"You know I would love to, but it's better if I go," he said, stroking my hair.

"When will I see you again?" I asked, slowly moving away from him.

"I'll talk to my friends and arrange a meeting as soon as they are free."

"What are their names?" I asked, wanting to make a connection.

"Anna Kozniewska."

"Her name sounds Eastern European."

"It is Eastern European. Her parents come from Poland."

I concentrated on the name. "I feel warm, positive energy around her. Who else?"

"Martin Grimley."

I connected to the name. "I get a positive feeling about him as well."

"I am sure you'll like them both." Jason opened the front door. "I'll call you tomorrow," he said, and then drew me to him again and held me tight for a moment before finally leaving.

I stood in the doorway, hugging myself as I watched him drive away. When his car disappeared around the corner and I could see it no longer I suddenly felt a strong sense of emptiness and desolation, and I knew that I would miss him terribly. Slowly, I closed the door and went into the empty house, which felt more empty than ever.

6

The following day I felt very restless. Painting was out of the question as I could not focus my mind on it. I missed Jason badly and could not stop thinking about him.

Trying to pass the time until he called, I did an hour of yoga, which managed to calm me somewhat. After yoga, I picked up a romantic novel and settled on the sofa in the living room. I tried to read a few pages, but found I could not concentrate on the story, so I closed the book and put it down. Utterly bored, I switched the television on, but again I could not concentrate on anything, so I gave up. With nothing much else to do, I decided to have a soak in the bath with scented, calming oils.

Feeling much more settled after my bath, I spent some time in front of a mirror absent-mindedly curling my hair with hot curling irons and then applying make-up. When I had finished I couldn't think of anything else to do so I called my parents' house. My mother answered the phone on the third ring.

"Hi, Mum. How are you?" I asked cheerily.

"Tired," Mum replied miserably. "This city seems so crowded and busy it wears me out."

"I know, London can be a nightmare," I sympathised, and then quickly changed the subject. "How is Dad?"

"He is fine. He is always content so long as he has a garden to weed," my mother continued in her miserable tone. "I just hope he can finish all the weeding before we leave."

"If he doesn't he can always finish it next time you come," I said, trying to be positive.

"We are not planning to come back in the near future. I think the next time we'll be here will be for your wedding in September."

"Mum, I told you, there won't be any wedding in September," I said firmly, making sure she understood.

"I thought you might have changed your mind, or at least I hoped so."

"No, I haven't, and it's very, very unlikely that I ever will because I don't love Mark any more, so stop hoping. The wedding is very definitely off."

Mum sighed resignedly. "Oh, Carrie, what are you going to do? You share a house with him."

"It's not the end of the world," I said, trying to reassure her. "We'll sell the house and I'll buy something smaller for myself."

"Will you be able to support yourself from your paintings?"

At that precise moment it was rather doubtful as I had completely lost interest in painting commercial pictures, but I did not want to worry my mother unnecessarily and so I replied, "I am sure I will."

"You know we are only a phone call away if you need any help and you can always stay in our house if you need to."

"Thanks, Mum."

"Come and see us again before we leave."

"I'll try," I said. "Give Dad my love."

"I will."

The moment I hung up, the phone rang again. My heart leapt with joy when I heard Jason's voice.

"I've missed you," he said tenderly.

"I've missed you too," I replied quietly.

"I want to see you."

"Me too."

"How about this for a plan? Anna is very keen to meet with us, so we can see her sometime this evening and spend the whole afternoon together, just you and me."

"What about your collage?" I asked, even though I wanted nothing more than to spend the rest of the day with him.

"I've decided to take the afternoon off. Somehow learning art history doesn't seem all that important any more."

I knew exactly how he felt. It was difficult to focus on everyday matters when we had much bigger and more important tasks on which to concentrate.

"I suppose it doesn't."

"What do you say we meet Anna around seven?"

"Yes, that's absolutely fine."

"I'll call her and confirm."

"Where does she live?" I asked.

"Richmond," Jason replied. "We could spend the afternoon in Richmond Park."

It didn't sound like a great idea to me. "What will we do in Richmond Park all afternoon?"

"Leave it to me. Just wear comfortable trousers and boots with small heels. Get ready. See you in half an hour," he said, and then hung up.

I was dressed and ready before the 30 minutes were up. Following Jason's instructions, I wore tight stretchy jeans and brown boots with flat heels. For the top I had chosen a pale yellow cotton shirt.

When I heard the distinctive sound of Jason's car, I grabbed my jacket and house keys, and hurried out, locking the door behind me. Climbing into his car, I leant over and pecked him on the cheek.

"Hi."

He put his arm around me and pulled me close. "Have I told you how much I missed you?" He kissed the top of my head. "Lots."

I looked up into his eyes. "I missed you lots, too."

Gently, he touched my curls. "I like your hair." Then he touched my face. "You look really nice today."

"You always say the nicest things," I muttered with a happy smile.

"And I mean every word," Jason said, moving away from me and putting the car into gear.

"So where are we going?" I asked, as soon as the car began moving.

"Horse riding."

I gave him a bemused look. "You are joking?"

"I promise you, it's going to be fun."

Yes, maybe for someone who knew how to ride a horse. I, on the other hand, didn't have a clue.

"I've never ridden a horse in my life," I confessed.

"I know all the horses at Richmond stables and I have booked a very quiet one for you. You'll be perfectly safe," Jason tried to reassure me.

I was far from reassured.

"We'll need proper riding hats," I said, because that was the first thing that came to mind.

"We'll hire them from the stables." Jason glanced at me. "Don't look so worried."

"But I am worried. What if my horse gets scared and decides to bolt with me on its back? There's no way I am going to be able to halt it."

"These horses are very placid and they are used to inexperienced riders. They never canter, they walk or trot." I must have still looked unconvinced because he added, "I'm sorry. I should have spoken to you before I went ahead with the booking. Would you like me to cancel?"

I thought about it for a moment and decided that if so many other people could do it I would certainly give it a try.

"No, I'll give it a go."

"Are you sure?"

"Absolutely."

Half an hour later we approached Richmond Gate and Jason followed the signs towards Robin Hood Gate where he parked the car in a small car park by the road. As we got out he walked to the back of the car, opened the boot and reached for a large sports bag. He swung it across his shoulder, took my hand in his and we walked to the stables.

The stables proper, which were located at the back of a small two-storey building, housed around 30 horses. From the outside the place looked very inconspicuous and it seemed there was hardly any activity there. We entered the building and stepped into the tiny reception area where a middle-aged woman sat behind a dark wooden desk. She confirmed our booking and, after we had chosen riding hats from a large pile by the wall, she handed Jason a key to a locker.

"I'll see you at the stables," Jason said, disappearing through the back door to the changing room.

I left the reception and found my way to the stables at the back where two horses were already saddled up and waiting. A tall, well-built groom was standing next to the horses, holding two sets of reins.

Noticing a riding hat in my hand, he asked, "Are you one of the riders?"

I nodded and then enquired, "Which one is the most placid?", stroking the cheek of a golden brown horse with black mane and tail.

The groom pointed to the older-looking chestnut horse. "This one."

"Then that's the one I'm going to ride."

"Are you ready to mount him?"

"As ready as I'll ever be," I replied, putting on my riding hat.

The groom kicked the mounting block into position and I stepped onto it. While he was holding the reins I grabbed the stirrup with my right hand and directed my left foot into it. After that I wasn't quite sure what to do.

"What do I do now?"

"Hold on to the saddle and jump up," he instructed.

I grabbed the saddle with both hands and jumped, throwing my right leg over the back of the horse. It wasn't a very good jump and my leg ended up sliding down the horse's back. The animal moved away, dragging my other leg with it. I had to balance myself by skipping on one leg while the groom pulled the horse back into position. I grabbed the saddle again and managed to steady myself before I attempted another jump. This time I put a lot more energy into it and ended up on the horse's back. I found the other stirrup with my right foot and slid the foot into it.

Once settled, I looked down and the ground seemed a long way away. I faced the groom. "Are you sure I am safe on this animal?"

"Perfectly safe, as this is the calmest horse we have," the groom assured me. "You might even find him a little slow at times."

I bent forwards and patted the horse's neck. The animal reacted by blowing air through its nostrils.

"He likes you," the groom said with a reassuring smile.

I patted the horse again. "Does blowing air through his nostrils mean he likes me?" I asked.

"It means he's friendly," the groom replied.

At this point Jason appeared clad very appropriately in beige breeches, black horse-riding boots and a white polo shirt, hard hat in hand. He put on his hat, fastened the leather strap under his chin and swiftly mounted his horse. The groom handed him the reins.

"Look after the lady," he said, moving the mounting block away.

"Thanks, John, I will," Jason replied, and walked his horse towards mine. "You need to remember a few simple rules. When you squeeze gently with your legs and pull the reins towards you, the horse will slow down or halt, depending on how tightly you are squeezing and pulling. If you want him to move forwards, squeeze gently with your lower legs or just give him a gentle tap with both your heels. If you want him to turn left, pull the left rein as if trying to make the horse bend his neck to the left. To the right, do the same with the right one, and hold the reins tightly at all times." Then he asked, "Can you remember all this?"

"I think so."

"Okay, let's go!"

Jason tapped his horse's flanks with his heels and the animal shifted its legs and started walking. I followed Jason's instructions and tapped my heels against my horse's sides, and the elderly animal moved forwards. We walked the horses out of the stables and carried on into the park.

Jason halted his horse and mine followed suit.

"I suggest we take the path through the woodland. This way we don't need to cross the main road," he said, and pulled on his left rein to direct his horse towards the small woodland to our left.

I squeezed my legs and tapped my heels against my horse's flanks, but the animal wouldn't shift and stubbornly stood rooted to the spot.

"Jason," I called, "this damned animal won't move."

Jason turned his horse around.

"He has a tendency to be lazy. You need to give him a good nudge," he advised.

I gave the horse a harder tap and it slowly lifted its legs. Once it started walking, I found it quite easy to navigate with the reins. I followed Jason down the horse's trail through the small woodland, and then into the open fields. Eventually the trail widened and we could walk the horses side by side.

It was an absolutely idyllic afternoon. The temperature was a perfect 25 degrees, the humidity was low and the sky clear and blue. The scenery around us was very beautiful, with large open fields spreading across the park, ancient, majestic-looking trees and herds of red and fallow deer grazing in the distance.

"These animals need exercise. I think we should make them trot for a bit," Jason said, putting his horse into a trot.

Mine immediately went into the trot as well and I started jumping up and down in the saddle.

"What do I do?" I cried, panicking.

"Push your hips upwards and forwards in a gentle thrusting movement," Jason instructed.

I followed his instruction and soon got the rhythm right.

We trotted for a while before Jason asked, "How are you doing?"

"Quite well, I think," I responded, automatically lifting my body up and down to the rhythm of the horse. "I feel as though this horse is perfectly happy to take me wherever I want to go."

"He probably is."

After ten more minutes of trotting I began to ache.

"I have to slow down, otherwise I won't be able to move tomorrow," I said, gently pulling on the reins.

The horse obediently changed from a trot to a walk. Jason slowed down his horse and we walked side by side again.

I bent forwards and patted my horse's neck. "Clever animal," I said affectionately. "Even if a little lazy at times."

As if understanding the word 'lazy', the horse suddenly halted.

"It seems 'lazy' is one word I definitely shouldn't use," I observed laughingly, and then tried to make him move by tapping my heels against his flanks. It didn't seem to be working, for the animal stood rooted to the spot and would not move.

Jason checked his watch. "I think he is cleverly letting us know that it's time to go back to the stables."

"He can't go back if he's not prepared to walk," I commented, stating the obvious. I shook the reins and tapped his sides again. "Move, you lazy thing!" Nothing. "Are you going to walk or not you stubborn animal?" I demanded, shaking the reins harder. "Walk!"

Magically, the horse reacted to the command 'walk' and began to move again. Jason brought his horse next to mine.

"We need to turn back," Jason said, slowing down his horse so I had more room to manoeuvre.

"Which way should I turn him?" I called.

"Left," he called back.

I pulled back on the left rein and once the animal had turned I stayed on the trail and continued back towards the stables. Jason turned his horse and trotted forwards to catch up with me.

"Does Anna come horse riding?" I asked, as we walked side by side.

"Yes, as a matter of fact that's how we met," Jason replied.

"What does she do?"

"She has a shop with New Age stuff. You know, books, music, crystals, jewellery."

"Is she involved in the New Age movement?"

"She used to be. I think many people thought they would find answers through it, but ended up being disillusioned and the movement all but died down."

"A lot of people were in it for the money, and when that is the main motivation for doing things the truth easily becomes distorted. People don't realise that distorting the truth for financial or personal gain is against the cosmic laws and creates a big karmic debt."

"But a lot of people don't believe in karma," Jason pointed out.

"No, they don't, and yet they want to understand why there is so much suffering in their lives, "I replied.

"Our world seems very unjust, so it's reassuring to know that there is some cosmic justice in place," Jason said.

"I agree."

As we approached the stables, Jason speeded up his horse and we entered in single file. Jason promptly dismounted and helped me off my horse. The groom appeared and took the reins, leading the horses inside to be unsaddled, and we split up. Jason went inside the building through the back door to the changing room and I headed to the reception to return our riding hats. A few minutes later we met outside and made our way back to Jason's car together.

"Have you been to the famous spot from which you can see St Paul's Cathedral?" Jason asked, starting the car.

I glanced at him not quite sure what he meant. "St Paul's Cathedral, the one in central London?"

Jason nodded. "The exact one."

"And you can see it from here?"

Jason nodded again.

"But it's miles away from here."

"Ten miles, to be exact."

"Well, that I would definitely like to see."

Jason drove into the car park that was located close to Richmond Gate and parked up.

"Come on, I'll take you to the spot from where you can see it."

We walked through Pembroke Lodge Gardens and followed the path to the summit of King Henry's Mound where Jason pointed to a small clearing between the trees. "Look through there," he instructed.

As I looked through a small metal arch, I could see a long alley of trees running through a built-up cityscape at the end of which was a completely uninterrupted view of St Paul's Cathedral.

"This is absolutely incredible!" I said excitedly.

"It's even more incredible that this view has never been obstructed since the beginning of the eighteenth century," Jason commented.

"Amazing, and I thought there was not much to do or see in Richmond Park," I said, and kissed him on the cheek. "Thank you for proving me wrong."

"My pleasure," he responded with a smile, and then he grabbed my hand and led me back down the mound. "We still have some time before we go to see Anna, so let's go to Pembroke Lodge for tea. We can sit outside and enjoy the fantastic views across the Thames Valley.

If you haven't done it before, it is definitely something worth doing."

* * *

At exactly 7 o'clock, Jason pressed the doorbell to the side of a large, purple painted door. The door was opened by a middle-aged woman of medium height with short brown hair and penetrating green eyes. She had a friendly, motherly look about her and I liked her straight away. A small white dog with brown patches and long floppy ears fussed excitedly about her feet.

"Come in, come in," she invited warmly, and as we stepped inside she extended her hand to me. "Hi, I am Anna," she introduced herself, "and you must be, Carrie, the woman Jason can't stop talking about."

I smiled at Jason. "I hope you were not boring Anna with stories about me?"

"Quite the contrary," Anna interjected before Jason had a chance to respond. "Let's go to the living room." She glanced down at the dog. "Harry, move over!" she commanded, and then led us to a small room at the back of the flat.

The living room was tastefully decorated in a contemporary style. On the left of the room, against the wall, there was a combination of oak storage units with a number of open shelves. On one of the lower shelves was a television set and a state-of-the-art stereo. The higher shelves were mostly filled with books, a lot of them of spiritual interest. In the middle of the room was a small oak coffee table that stood proudly on a richly coloured Persian rug and was surrounded by two armchairs covered in white fabric and a matching sofa. There were quite a few plants in the room and the lighting was dimmed, which created a warm relaxing atmosphere.

"Please sit down," said Anna, indicating towards the sofa. "Would you like something to drink?" she enquired as soon as we had seated ourselves.

"Just some water for me," Jason requested.

Anna turned to me. "Carrie?"

"Water for me as well, please."

Anna went to the kitchen and returned with three glasses and a large bottle of Perrier. Unscrewing the bottle, she poured the sparkling liquid into the glasses and then sat in one of the armchairs. The little dog came over and stood fixed to the spot staring up at me. I leant forwards and stroked him and he wagged his tail.

"He seems very friendly," I said.

"He can be too friendly. Harry, come over here!" Anna ordered. The dog padded over to her and she picked him up and placed him on her lap. "Did you go horse riding?" she enquired.

"Yes, we did," Jason answered, reaching for his glass. "Carrie had never ridden before, so it was quite an adventure for her."

Anna smiled in my direction. "I hope it was a pleasant one."

I smiled back. "There were a few moments when I wasn't quite sure what to do, but on the whole I enjoyed it very much."

"I think horses are the most gracious of animals and I love being around them as well as riding them," Anna said, stroking her dog. "I try to get my horse-riding fix every week."

"You are lucky to live so close to the stables," I commented.

"That's true," Anna agreed.

"Jason told me that you are running a New Age shop," I said, changing the subject.

"Yes," Anna replied. "I opened it years ago just after the New Age movement started and there was a lot of hunger for anything spiritual. The business has been quite successful. Of course it helped that I am interested in spiritual development myself and that it is something close to my heart. I've been searching for answers to our existence, to our past and our purpose on this planet for as long as I can remember. I've read a great number of books on the subject, but to be quite honest I feel that much of the information is contradictory and confusing. I found some answers, but I still have many questions."

"I am sure Carrie can answer some of your questions," Jason stated.

"I will certainly try," I said.

"Thanks, Carrie," Anna responded gratefully. "Do you mind if we start with past lives? This is something I feel very strongly about."

"Not at all."

"There is a lot of controversy about reincarnation, but I personally believe that after death the soul is reborn again in another body. So, assuming that we accept reincarnation as a fact, why is it that we have no conscious memory of our past lives?"

I took a sip of water and began to explain.

"Long ago, beings on this planet had full memory and access to all the cosmic knowledge, but other entities from the cosmos started experimenting with the species of this planet and genetically modified them in order to create beings for their own needs. Our DNA was scattered and our memory was lost. Since then, people have been kept in ignorance, and because of their memory loss they have been very easy to manipulate and control. The good news is that now is the time to put it right. With the energies currently hitting the planet, the scattered DNA can be pulled together and the original strands can be reformed. As this rebuilding takes place, our nervous system will evolve and allow more data to be moved into our consciousness. The 90 per cent of cells in our brain that have been lying dormant will start to awaken and function again, and this in turn will allow the regeneration of the physical body that will no longer need to die."

Anna looked at me with uncertainty. "Are you saying that we can keep our physical bodies?"

"Yes," I confirmed. "The physical body is nothing more than a dense mass of energy. As the frequency of the body rises and the full function of the brain is restored, the body will be able to use the knowledge that has lain dormant for centuries to regenerate itself and sustain life for as long as is needed."

"So the key is to raise the frequency of the physical body?" Anna concluded.

I nodded. "It's the only way. The higher the body frequency, the better the connection to the cosmos and the living library."

"Why has it been so difficult to access this information before?"

"Because our super senses have been shut down and we can't

connect to the cosmic knowledge. People receive glimpses but, in most cases, people who do have used their insight to make money, to gain power or to control. As this is against the cosmic laws they end up being discredited by the cosmos and their connection is severed, so the information they pass on is nothing more than their interpretation of the truth contaminated by their greed or ego. True cosmic knowledge is absolutely free and the only way to connect to the information is from within or through your own connection to the living library."

"This all feels very right to me," Anna said, stroking her dog. "But how can I raise the frequency of my body?"

"Through calmness and tranquillity. The inner consciousness, which is the divine part of a human being, is going to prompt you in the right direction. Often there will be a conflict between your inner self and your physical body, and this conflict will manifest itself as an emotional response. This emotional response is a sign that your understanding or the direction in which you are going needs to be changed. Once you allow for this change to take place, your earthly responses will start to change into cosmic ones and your inner and outer consciousness will synchronise a little bit more, and this in turn will raise the frequency of the body."

"What if you don't know how to change your understanding or direction?"

"Sometimes it won't be easy to understand the lesson straight away, but you will be taught and guided during your sleep."

"You mean through dreams?"

The dog stirred, giving an impression that he wanted to get down off Anna's lap, so she lifted him up and put him on the floor. He flopped next to her feet.

"Mostly through the direct connection to your consciousness, which sometimes manifests itself in the form of a dream."

"I never analyse my dreams, but I connect to the mood and intensity of the images," Anna said. "I noticed that my dreams become very vivid whenever I visit my parents in Poland. Do you know why that is?"

"I am not sure, but I do know that the energetic nature of Poland is different to any other part of the planet because two of the main planetary chakras are located there."

"I did not know that there were chakras in Poland," Anna declared, surprised.

"Not many people are aware of this and as far as I know nothing has been published on the subject," I said, adding, "A lot of information has been published about human chakras, but different philosophies follow different teachings, so the information is inconsistent."

"Well, according to Buddhists, human chakras are the energy centres and there are seven of them: crown chakra located at the top of the head; brow chakra or third eye; throat chakra; heart chakra; sacral chakra located in the spleen area; root chakra located at the base of the spine; and solar plexus chakra." Anna counted them on her fingers. "I hope I've got it right."

"Not quite," I said, smiling. "Altogether there are 12 energetic centres in a human, seven with positive-going energy and five with negative. The ones you listed are positive going."

Anna raised her eyebrows. "I've never heard about negative-going energy chakras before."

"That's because they have been switched off and can't be detected. This is going to change soon as the energies that are being beamed from the cosmos to our planet begin to activate them."

"Do you know where they are located?" Jason asked.

I nodded. "All of them are located deep in the brain, and once they are activated they will open the super senses of sight, hearing, smell, taste and touch. The expected leap in human consciousness simply means the opening of these super senses."

"This is very exciting," Anna said. "Are we talking about the opening up of abilities like clairvoyance or clairaudience?"

"Yes," I replied simply.

"Some people have these super senses already open," Anna pointed out.

"A very small number of people have one or two super senses

partially open. At the moment there is so much negative energy on this planet that no one would be able to cope if all their super senses were fully activated."

"It's a fair point," Anna agreed, "but going back to the planet itself, you said that there were also planetary chakras."

"The planet is a living organism with an energetic structure similar to a human's and similarly it has energetic centres or chakras," I explained. "There are seven positive-going ones. Two of them are located in Wroclaw and Krakow in Poland. The other five are located in India, Tasmania, Tibet, Lake Titicaca in Peru and Lake Bajkal in Russia. The five negative ones have been sealed and are temporarily located at Kinder Scout in England. Eventually they will have to be moved to Poland as they need to be close to the chakra of consciousness, which is the one located in Wroclaw."

"Have you channelled all this information yourself?" Anna queried.

"Some of it has been channelled and some of it I simply know from within," I replied, "but it does not make any difference as there is only one source of information and it can be accessed by anyone through consciousness. Consciousness is the divine energy that spreads throughout the whole universe connecting everything together. If you know how to tap into it you can communicate with other beings or connect to the living library where you'll find answers to all your questions."

Harry lifted himself up and stood in front of Anna, staring at her with his big eyes.

"This is quite fascinating and it does make a lot of sense," Anna said, ignoring the dog. "We take so much for granted, but when you look at the beautiful things that have been created on this planet, like animals and plants, it makes you wonder how they were created in the first place."

"They are the manifestation of consciousness," I said. "Consciousness expresses itself in different ways and it constantly creates and expands."

"If that's the case, it's really naive to think that we are the only intelligent beings in the whole universe."

"We are not that intelligent if we can't open our minds to other possibilities," Jason interjected.

"I totally agree," Anna said, and then she looked down at the dog, which was still staring at her. "What is it Harry? Do you need to go out?" The dog wagged his tail and Anna got up. "I'm sorry, but I need to let Harry out."

I used this as an opportunity to say, "It's getting rather late. I think we should be going."

"There is no need for you to leave," Anna said.

Jason rose to his feet. "Carrie is right. It is getting late."

"Are you sure?"

I nodded and stood up.

Anna walked us to the front door and gave me a warm hug. "Thanks for coming. I hope we can meet again soon."

"Of course. We'll stay in touch," I said, hugging her back.

Jason put his arm around Anna's shoulders and gave her a friendly squeeze. "Call if you need to talk."

"I will."

We left Anna's flat, climbed into Jason's car and he drove me home. As we were approaching my house I spotted a faint light shining through the front room curtains and my heart sunk. Mark was back and I suddenly felt daunted by the prospect of having to face him. Jason noticed it too.

"Do you think your friend has come back early?" he questioned, slowly bringing the car to a stop.

"I think so," I muttered worriedly. "I am not looking forward to this."

Jason pulled off and drove forwards, stopping far enough away not to be seen from the house. He drew me to him and held me for a moment before he asked, "Do you want me to go in with you?"

I shook my head. "I have to deal with this one on my own."

"I'll wait here then."

"No, don't. I'll be all right," I assured him, slowly moving away.

He searched through the glove compartment for something to write on and a pen. He found a scrap of paper, scribbled some numbers on it and handed it to me.

"This is my mobile number. Promise you'll call me the moment there is a problem."

"I promise."

I gave him a kiss on the cheek, opened the door and got out of the car. Anxiously, I walked to the front door of my house. With a deep sigh, I put the key into the lock, and as I did so I suddenly felt a familiar inner warmth spreading throughout my body. I knew instantly that it was some kind of supportive energy to calm me down and help me cope.

Looking up towards the sky, I said quietly, "Thanks, guys," and then I opened the door and stepped inside.

* * *

Mark was sitting on the sofa in the living room flicking television channels, the images flashing dizzily.

"Hi," I said from the doorway.

He glanced in my direction. "Oh, hi, I didn't hear you come in."

"What are you doing home so early?" I asked, taking off my jacket. "I didn't expect you back until Friday."

"The meeting was cancelled," he replied, and then returned to his preoccupation with the television channels.

I retreated to the hall where I slowly hung my jacket on the hook, all the while thinking how best to deal with the situation. Should I talk to Mark now or should I leave it until tomorrow? I was tempted to postpone the inevitable conversation until the following day, but at the same time I knew it would be much better if my feelings were out in the open and the whole unpleasant conversation was behind me. I resolved that I had to find the courage to tell him there and then. Decision made, I walked into the living room and sat down next to Mark on the sofa.

"How did the trip go?" I asked calmly.

Mark flicked to yet another channel. "It was okay."

I tried another question. "So when are you taking over as financial director?"

"Tomorrow."

The conversation was not going very well.

"You are taking the job then?"

Mark continued changing channels absent-mindedly.

"You know I am," he said, totally uninterested.

It was obvious that our exchange was going nowhere, but now I had found the courage to talk to him I was determined to have some kind of conversation whether he liked it or not. I pulled the remote out of his hand and pressed the 'off' button.

"Why the hell did you do that?" he demanded angrily.

"Because I want to talk to you," I said as calmly as I could, "and you have been flicking channels and ignoring me."

"What is it you want to talk about?" he asked impatiently.

I was pleased I had his attention at last.

"I want to talk about us."

"Us?" he asked, as though surprised.

"Yes, us - our relationship."

"It's about my promotion, isn't it? I know you're not very happy about it, but I promise you, nothing will change."

"But that's just it. I want things to change."

He gave a long-suffering sigh. "You know, Carrie, sometimes I don't understand you at all. You have everything any woman could want and you constantly complain."

"Define everything," I challenged him.

"You have a lovely house, you have no financial worries and you have the freedom to do whatever you wish."

It was true that I had all those things, but in my eyes it was far from having everything.

"And I have a fiancé who doesn't care enough for me to listen to my opinions," I said, just to make a point.

"But I do care."

"No, you don't. You accepted the promotion even though you knew very well I was not happy about it. You haven't even bothered to discuss it with me."

"Why would I need to discuss it with you? I simply had to take the job. I could not pass up an opportunity like this."

"Well, it's obvious then that it doesn't matter to you how I feel," I said, and then added, "and you know what? When you were away I finally realised that it never did."

"Now you are being melodramatic," he commented, dismissing the argument.

"You always manage to turn everything around to make me feel unreasonable," I retorted, becoming annoyed.

"You do have a tendency to exaggerate," he said, placing his hand on my knee, "but I still love you."

I found his touch irritating and I pushed his hand away.

"Stop telling me that you love me when you don't mean it!"

He gave me a surprised look. "You need to calm down."

"I am not going to calm down. Don't you understand I am not happy with the way things are between us?"

"What is that supposed to mean?"

I took a deep breath before I said, "It means that I am not sure I want to go ahead with the wedding."

"You can't be serious?" He looked stupefied.

"I am perfectly serious," I said firmly.

"Carrie, if you want me to spend more time with you, I will. There is no need to cancel the wedding."

Why do men have this tendency to conveniently twist everything that is being said to them? It was so irritating.

"I used to want to spend more time with you, but this is not the issue any more."

"Now you have managed to totally confuse me. If you don't want to spend more time with me, why should it matter if I accept the promotion or not?"

"It matters because you chose to ignore my feelings about it," I explained patiently.

"Don't expect me to apologise for wanting a better future for us," Mark snapped. "Now can I go back to watching television in peace?"

He grabbed the remote and switched the set back on, not interested in further argument. His couldn't-care-less attitude infuriated me. I marched across the room and pulled the plug out of the socket.

"Our conversation is far from finished and you are not going to watch television when I want to talk to you."

Mark's eyes flashed with anger. "Switch that television back on!" he demanded brusquely.

I stood my ground. "No!"

He shot to his feet, shoved me out of the way and pushed the plug back into the socket. I was furious and took a few deep breaths to calm myself.

"Okay. You carry on flicking channels if it's so important to you," I said sharply, and left the room.

I knew that was my opportunity to act. I hurried upstairs, opened the drawer of the bedside cabinet, grabbed my engagement ring, and then picked up Mark's pillow and a blanket, and rushed back downstairs. I threw the blanket and the pillow onto the sofa and the ring in his lap.

"The engagement is off, so don't bother coming up to the bedroom!"

Satisfied, I headed for the door.

"Either I sleep in the bedroom or one of us moves out," Mark snapped to my back, and when I turned to face him he added, "and it's not going to be me."

I was not prepared to let him intimidate me like that.

"Well, it won't be me either."

"Should I remind you that I pay the mortgage for this house?" he asked, sounding very sure of himself.

"It's a pity that I am the co-owner then," I shot back.

He laughed. "You couldn't keep up the payments on this house on the money you make from your measly paintings."

"How do you know how much my paintings are worth?" I retorted.

"Judging by the crap you have been painting recently, not very much, if anything at all."

I wasn't quite sure what he meant.

"What exactly are you talking about?"

"I've seen the green face you painted. What sort of rubbish is that?"

I realised that he was referring to the image of an alien face I had painted a few days previously.

"It's not rubbish. It's something you will never have the privilege to understand. Not in this lifetime anyway," I said, and stormed out of the room.

"I am sleeping in the bedroom," he yelled after me.

"No you are not," I yelled back.

As soon as I entered the bedroom I secured the door with a chair. After making sure that the door handle wouldn't move, I lay on the bed trying to compose myself. I was upset and angry, but at the same time I felt great relief that everything was out in the open. I didn't know what would happen next. All I knew was that my relationship with Mark was over.

It wasn't long before Mark came upstairs. He tried to press the door handle and when he realised that it would not move he shook it violently.

"Carrie, let me in!"

I kept still and quiet, praying that the chair would hold. The door shook again and the chair was shaking with it.

"Carrie, damn it, open the bloody door!"

Very quietly, I tiptoed to the door, grabbed hold of the chair and held it with all my might to prevent it from moving. Mark tried to push the door open again, but it would not give, so he ended up kicking it in frustration.

"You'll regret this," he shouted and turned away.

A moment later I heard him going down the stairs. I let go of the chair and flopped onto the floor breathing a huge sigh of relief.

7

The next day, I met Zoe for lunch in the local coffee shop. It was a small, cosy place situated in a quiet side alley off the high street. Zoe was already there when I arrived.

"You look as though you haven't slept all night," Zoe said as soon as I sat down.

"That's because I haven't," I replied. "I had an argument with Mark."

"Over the phone?"

"No, he surprised me by coming back early."

A young waitress with short, spiky hair approached. We quickly ordered salads and teas, and the girl left.

"Tell me what happened," Zoe said. "Did you break the engagement?"

"I threw the ring at him, so I suppose that counts as breaking the engagement," I said, "and I can't tell you how glad I am that I did. He is so bloody annoying, he irritates the hell out of me."

"What did he say?" Zoe pressed.

"I think he expects me to move out of the house," I said with a sigh.

Zoe raised her eyebrows. "Why you?"

"Because he can afford to pay the mortgage and I can't," I explained simply.

"How can he expect you to move out?" Zoe couldn't understand the logic. "It's not as if you have another place to move to."

"Still, I think he might not be generous enough to let me stay."

"To be honest, it doesn't surprise me. He has always struck me as a materialistic and rather selfish bastard."

"I know. How could I have been so blind? He doesn't care where I end up. I thought we could part amicably, but I now know that isn't going to be possible. He is not even prepared to discuss it. I tried to talk to him yesterday, but he either ignores me or twists everything I say."

"It's avoidance," Zoe said wisely. "This way he doesn't have to face the issue."

"I think it's more to do with lack of respect," I responded. "A lot of men don't treat women as equals, and the more arrogant ones believe that a woman's opinion counts for nothing. They can be very manipulative and the woman always ends up confused and often feels guilty for bringing the issue up in the first place. Mark is like that and I would most probably still believe that I am being unreasonable if it wasn't for the fact that I have seen his true face."

Our conversation was interrupted for a moment when the young waitress delivered our teas and salads.

Zoe waited for her to move to another table before she asked, "What do you mean by his true face?" She reached for the salad dressing.

"The way he is inside," I replied. "After all, the physical body is nothing more than an outer shell of the true person."

Zoe stopped pouring dressing over her salad and faced me. "And what was his true face like?"

"Horrible. Really frightening," I said, digging my fork into a piece of cheese on my plate.

"Are you saying that a person can look quite pleasant on the outside and at the same time be ugly inside?"

"Of course. You should know that."

"I always thought that the physical body was a fair manifestation of the true person."

"There are a lot of attractive people who are selfish and arrogant," I said pointedly, "and also there are a lot of not so attractive people who are warm and caring. The way people look means nothing."

"So you've seen Mark's true face and it's ugly. Is that why you decided to break the engagement?"

I nodded. "Seeing his true face opened my eyes to what sort of person he really is. After that it was easy to understand all the arguments and his lack of consideration. It's very sad, but I know he is not going to change."

"I am sure it's for the best. Can you imagine if you married him?"

"I can't, not any more. I don't want to talk to him. I don't want to be in the same room as him," I said, and then added, recalling the unpleasant feeling I had when Mark touched my knee the night before, 'And I can't bear him to touch me."

"It's going to be tricky," Zoe pointed out. "You still live in the same house."

"I know. I've been doing my best to avoid him and it's not easy. This morning I had to wait until he left for work before I felt safe enough to leave the bedroom."

"You know you can always stay with me," Zoe offered understandingly.

"Thank you for the offer, Zoe, but it wouldn't fix anything. It would only be a short-term solution."

"It might be better than living under the same roof with Mark."

"I can't just leave," I reasoned. "It's my house too."

"Well, the offer still stands if you need a place to stay." Zoe lifted her tea cup. "How is the lovely Jason?" she asked, changing the subject.

"He's fine."

"Do you see him a lot?"

"Quite a lot," I said with a timid smile.

"So you are an item?"

"We are close," I said, trying to sound non-committal.

"I am glad."

"Why?"

"Look at it this way. You might be thrown out of your home, but you've got a better man in the bargain."

I smiled. "You always know how to cheer me up."

"But it's true. Jason is gorgeous and you are very lucky," Zoe said, adding, "Vicky thought you made a lovely couple. She keeps asking me to arrange another meeting. What do you say? I know a meeting at your house is out of the question, but we could organise it at my place."

Right now meeting Vicky was not my priority. "I'm sorry, but it really isn't the best time. I've got too many problems to resolve," I said, signalling the waitress for the bill.

"Sure, I understand," Zoe said. "Maybe we can do it later when things calm down."

The waitress brought the bill and Zoe reached for it. "My treat," she said, pulling out her credit card.

Five minutes later, we left the coffee shop and Zoe walked me to my car. "Promise to call me if you need anything," she said.

I realised that she was the second person who cared enough to offer help, so I immediately felt better. Having two supportive friends meant a lot to me.

"I promise, and thanks for being such a good friend," I said, giving her a hug.

We said our goodbyes and I got into my car and drove home.

When I arrived back, the house was empty and peaceful, and it felt like a strange luxury to be alone in it. I flopped onto the sofa, switched on the television and flicked to the news channel.

I quickly discovered that nothing had changed in the world of news. It was grim as usual. The cost of borrowing had risen yet again and up to 2,000 people were feared dead after devastating floods and landslides in Haiti and the Dominican Republic. Bosses had slashed pensions and millions of young people would have to work into their late eighties ...

I didn't want to listen to more depressing stories so I switched off the TV and sat in silence, hugging my knees. My thoughts quickly drifted to Jason and I felt I needed at least to hear his voice. I tried to recall what I had done with the piece of paper containing his mobile number and then remembered that I had put it in my jacket pocket. I rushed to the hall, fished it out, reached for the phone and dialled.

"Hi, it's me," I said brightly when he answered.

"I've tried to reach you several times," Jason said, sounding concerned.

"I had lunch with Zoe."

"How did it go yesterday?"

I sighed, my happy mood disappearing quickly. "It didn't go very well. The whole situation is a little more complicated than I thought."

"Do you want to talk about it?"

"Not really."

"Then I won't pry, but I am here if you need me."

"I know and I appreciate it."

Jason changed the subject. "Anna called me today. She seems very motivated and would like to get more into what we are doing, and she offered her help."

"This means she might be willing to join us in cosmic co-operation?"

"I am sure she will."

"We need to arrange a meeting with her."

"That's not a problem. She wants us to meet one of her friends and she suggested we get together at her place."

"When?"

"How about this evening?" Jason suggested, and then added lightly, "It would give me a chance to see you."

I wanted to see him as well, but talking to people was out of the question.

"Please, Jason, not today. My energies are all over the place. Maybe tomorrow."

"I understand. I'll set it up provisionally for tomorrow evening then," he complied. "By the way, the name of Anna's friend is John Ward and he is a musician."

I concentrated on the name and could feel a great deal of positive energy around John, so I thought there was a lot of potential. I also felt that he was strongly set in his own ways and that he was very proud of his music, especially his own compositions, and would not accept criticism easily. Music was his life and there was not much room for anything else.

"There is potential there," I said shortly.

"Good. Hopefully we'll meet him tomorrow," Jason said, adding, "I want to see you and tomorrow seems like such a long time away."

"I know. I want to see you too, but I am not very good company at the moment."

"Call me if you change your mind."

"I will, definitely," I promised. "If not, I'll see you tomorrow." I clicked off the phone and replaced it in the charger.

It was time to find my inner calmness again, so I opted for yoga to help me balance my energies. I changed into a light blue leotard, made my way to the meditation room and put on some calming music. I began with some simple stretching exercises, moving steadily to more advanced postures, which required a lot of concentration and focus. I was getting to the end of my routine when I heard a key in the front door. Quite involuntarily my body tensed and I didn't dare move.

"Carrie, where are you?" Mark yelled.

Frozen, I sat on my heels with my back straight and my hands on my knees, just waiting. I could hear Mark searching through the house, looking for me, and I knew he would open the door to the meditation room eventually. As expected, the door was flung open.

"Ah, here you are!" he exclaimed, relieved. He was holding a bunch of flowers in his hand. "I finished early so we could spend some time together - quality time. I booked a nice French restaurant for dinner." He extended his hand with the flowers. "Here, a peace offering."

Silently, I took the flowers and put them next to me on the mat.

"Aren't you going to say anything?"

What was I supposed to say? That I did not love him any more? That it was too late? That nothing he did would change the fact that our relationship was over?

I didn't say any of those things. Instead I said, "It would have been nice if you had asked me if I wanted to go out to dinner with you."

"We need to clear the air, so why not do it with the help of a nice meal?" he replied flippantly.

"When will you stop making decisions for me?" I objected sharply.

"Is there any chance of reconciliation if everything I do becomes a problem?"

He sounded aggravated and I did not want to annoy him any further.

"Well, I don't want to go to a restaurant."

"Okay, we won't. I'll cancel the booking," he said, and closed the door.

I sighed resignedly and rose to my feet. Abandoning the flowers on the floor, I left the meditation room and made my way upstairs where I locked myself in the bathroom. I took off my leotard, stepped into the shower and stood under the soothing warmth of the cascading water, trying to collect my thoughts. I realised that deep down I'd always known that it was never going to be easy to break my relationship with Mark. Mark was very sensitive to the opinions of his friends and colleagues. What would they think if they found out that he'd been dumped by his fiancée? Surely, that would only belittle him in their eyes, so he was not going to allow that to happen. He was going to make it as difficult as possible for me to leave. I was dreading the fight, but it seemed that I had to face it whether I liked it or not if I wanted to get away from him.

I spent a long time in the shower, and just as I was stepping out of the cubicle Mark knocked on the door and called, "Are you all right?"

"Yes, I'm fine," I replied, loud enough for him to hear.

"I've cancelled dinner. Come downstairs when you've finished. I've made some coffee for us."

I didn't expect him to be so nice and this confused and unnerved me. Still, nothing had changed and it was over between us, even if Mark refused to accept it, and I had no choice but to tell him again. Wrapping a large towel around my body, I went to the bedroom to dress. I took my time getting dressed and tried to prepare myself mentally for the forthcoming conversation. Not at all sure what to expect, I made my way downstairs to the living room.

Mark was sitting in the middle of the sofa, with a laptop and a pile of papers on the coffee table in front of him. Hearing me approach, he gave me a quick look.

"Your coffee got cold," he informed me, and returned to his laptop

"I can see you brought your work home," I observed, reaching for my mug.

"It was the only way I could leave early," he muttered.

It was obvious he would never give me his full attention.

"I thought you wanted to talk," I said.

"I've got a big problem here," he mumbled, studying some figures intently. "We'll talk in a minute."

As he was so engrossed in his work I left him to it and retreated to the conservatory. I looked around the familiar surroundings and realised that lately I had not spent enough time there. I felt I needed to start painting again and so, putting the mug down, I began tidying up. I sorted out all the canvases and stacked them by the wall, according to size. I threw away the tubes of old paint, and then cleaned all the brushes and dumped the ones that were damaged or overused. I swept the floor and dusted all the surfaces. When all was done I assessed my hard work and was quite pleased with myself. Tomorrow I'll start a new painting, I decided, but now it was time to lay down some new house rules. Full of new determination, I marched back to the living room.

"I want to talk about the house," I stated purposefully.

Mark lifted his head from the papers. "What's there to talk about? The house is as much yours as it is mine."

"You mean half of it is mine?"

"Well, yes ... if you want to put it that way."

"Okay,' I said nonchalantly, "I want the conservatory, meditation room and the spare bedroom upstairs. You can have the use of the living room and the main bedroom. We'll share the bathroom and kitchen."

"What on earth are you talking about?" he asked, his eyes filling with anger.

"As we are no longer a couple, we need to divide the space so we can live together under the same roof until the house is sold," I explained, ignoring his angry look.

"What do you mean, we are no longer a couple?"

"I hope you don't think that bringing some flowers and booking a table in a restaurant mean that our problems have magically disappeared, because they haven't."

"I came home early so we could discuss our problems."

"No, you left the office early so you could do some work at home."

"Carrie, are we going to argue about everything?"

Not wanting to upset him unnecessarily, I replied, "I hope not."

"So what do you want?"

"I want to be able to work here until we decide what to do."

"Of course you can work here."

"Good. Where are you going to sleep tonight?"

"I've got quite a lot of work to do so I'll stay here."

"Goodnight then."

He returned to his computer and I went upstairs and got ready for bed. Once in bed, I read a few pages of a novel and half an hour later switched off the lights and settled down for the night.

A sudden movement of the bed awoke me in the middle of the night, and then quite unexpectedly I felt a cold hand on my breast. Instinctively, I moved away.

"What are you doing?" I mumbled sleepily.

Mark moved closer, throwing his arm across my body.

"I am trying to make love to you."

I pushed him away and sat up. "What is it with you? You don't seem to understand that our relationship is over," I said crossly. "O - v - e - r!"

"You are a selfish bitch!" he spat, getting out of bed.

I was really angry now. "Is that because I don't want to have sex with you?"

He switched on the bedside light. "You are the most unreasonable woman I know and frankly I am not even sure I fancy you any more. You have let yourself go and your body is much too fat for my liking," he said nastily.

"It's just as well we are separating then, isn't it?" I countered.

He pulled a small bag from the top of the wardrobe and started throwing some of his clothes into it.

"I'm going to stay in a hotel for a few days, but I suggest you think long and hard what it is you want. I am not planning on hanging around forever."

His clothes packed, he put on his trousers and threw on a shirt, then sat on the edge of the bed doing up the buttons and putting on his shoes. While he was getting dressed I silently sat on the bed clutching the duvet tightly to myself and waiting for him to go.

When he eventually left the room and I heard the front door being shut I released my hold on the duvet and fell back onto the bed in total relief. He was away and I had a few days to work out what to do. It was more than I had expected.

8

The next morning I awoke with a slight headache and a lot of determination to make the day as productive as possible. It was definitely time to take my life into my own hands and make some positive decisions. It was time to start painting again. Jumping out of bed, I washed and dressed hurriedly and made my way to the kitchen where I had a quick breakfast of toast and marmalade followed by strong black coffee to clear my head.

Ready to face the day ahead, I headed for my studio in the conservatory. I chose a large blank canvas from the pile by the wall and set it on the easel. I stared at it for a while, trying to decide what to paint. A still life was a possibility as there was a good chance it would sell quickly. I could easily put it together from things I had at home. Flowers always sold well, so it could be a composition of wild flowers I could pick in the fields behind the house. Even as I contemplated those options, I knew I wouldn't be happy painting another still life or another composition of flowers. I wanted to paint something more challenging, something I had not painted before. I was still pondering on my dilemma when I saw a very vivid image of a pulsating, colourful sphere with a lot of smaller spheres floating inside. I did not understand the meaning of the image, but I knew straight away that I was expected to paint it.

I sat down on a soft chair, which stood next to the easel, and tried to memorise all the colours and the way the smaller spheres were placed within the bigger one. I could distinguish 12 main colours - light green, black, purple, green, red, carmine, light blue, brown, dark blue, yellow, orange and lemon. Right in the middle of the sphere was a bright white globe, which extended into 12 coloured rays, each of them in a different main colour. At the end of the rays were other smaller spheres, which also had bright white globes in the middle, and each sphere also extended into 12 smaller rays at the end of which were other spheres with bright white globes in the middle. This pattern repeated itself over and over, and every time it was repeated the spheres got smaller and smaller.

The image felt very powerful and I wanted to understand its meaning, so I mentally asked for an explanation. The reply came straight away:

"*The image we've just shown you is a simplified illustration of the cosmos in which you reside. The energy of the Creator is represented by the bright white light and it holds everything within - stars, planets and vast galaxies. The white light breaks into 12 main frequencies, which are represented by 12 rays of different colour. Consequently, the energetic structure of your cosmos and the whole universe is based on the number 12. The energy of the Creator is attached to every frequency much in the same way as in a visible spectrum of light, which you can see through a prism. The prism breaks the white light into a spectrum of colours, but each colour is an integrated part of this light and could not be created without it...*

"*Your planet is a very small part of an embryonic solar system, which operates in an organised manner around a sun. There are 12 planets within each embryonic solar system and they traverse their own orbital patterns surrounded by millions of stars. Each embryonic solar system is a part of a larger solar system. There are 12 embryonic systems within one solar system. There are 12 solar systems within one galaxy, 12 galaxies within one cosmos, 12 cosmoses within one mini universe and 12 mini universes within the whole energetic mass of the universe. Each part of the whole has its own energetic structure, its own time structure and its own space. This universal space is shared by all and it is so vast that it is beyond the human mind's capability to fully comprehend...*

"*Outside your own set of planets there are vast numbers of other planets being mutually dependent upon each other and supported by the energy from the source. The whole of the universe is nothing but a pulsating mass of energy, which constantly changes and expands, and your planet is but a minute part of it...*

"*We have tried to simplify this explanation as much as possible and we hope that it will help you and others to grasp the basic idea of the very complex structure that is the universe."*

When the communication ended I sat still for a while, trying to make a mental picture of it all. My mind kept going back to the colourful sphere I had seen earlier and now I understood why I was expected to paint it. It was a simple illustration of a very complicated energetic structure shown in an easily explainable way.

Full of motivation, I began selecting the colours, for I wanted to paint quickly, while the image was still fresh in my mind. I decided to divide the background into quarters and paint them alternately in two contrasting colours of blue and brown. That way I could paint the white circle in the middle and show light spreading throughout the whole picture by brightening and shading the colours. The picture needed a lot of very precise detail that I knew would take me some time to paint, so I marked the canvas with the basic idea first, then went to the kitchen where I made myself another cup of coffee and sat at the table drawing diagrams and making notes on how to split the colours and in which sequence to paint them.

Back in the studio, I began covering the canvas with the first background colours. I had just finished applying both colours when the phone rang. I picked it up on the fourth ring.

"Hi, babe," Jason said. "Can you talk?"

I couldn't have been happier to hear his voice.

"I can always talk to you."

"Are you busy?"

"Yes, quite busy. I've started a new painting."

"Can you find some time to speak to my friend Martin who is very keen to meet you?" Jason asked, and then he added in much lighter tone, "Keen enough to want to meet you before he goes away tomorrow."

I laughed. "I don't believe he's that keen."

"I promise you he is," Jason continued in a light-hearted tone. "He wants to meet you today and he will be very disappointed if you can't find time to see him."

Suddenly I remembered about our planned meeting with Anna's friend.

"Aren't we supposed to be meeting John today?"

"Unfortunately John can't make it, but Martin can't wait to see you."

"You make him sound more than keen," I said airily, sensing some hidden agenda.

"You could say he is more than keen."

"Then I can't really say no, can I? Why don't you bring him over to my house?"

"What about your house friend?"

"He's not here."

"Great. We'll be with you in half an hour," Jason said finally, and hung up.

I grabbed a clean cloth, soaked it in oil and quickly cleaned the paint marks off my hands. That done, I rushed upstairs to wash and change. It took me a few minutes to choose my clothes before I eventually settled on the new pink skirt and lime silk blouse. I heated up my straightening iron and ran it through my hair, making it shiny and straight. I applied some blusher to my cheeks, a few strokes of mascara to my eyelashes and pearly gloss to my lips. Finally, I pushed diamond studs into my ear lobes and sprayed a few squirts of Dior's Poison around my neckline.

Feeling good, I made my way to the kitchen and brewed some fresh coffee. I placed the coffee pot and three cups on a tray together with a plate of biscuits and some paper napkins, and carried the whole lot into the living room. I was removing the cups from the tray and placing them on the coffee table when the doorbell sounded. I put the last cup down, threw the empty tray on the shelf and went to let Jason and Martin in.

Jason gave me a kiss on the cheek before he introduced his friend.

"This is Martin, the man who couldn't wait to meet you."

Martin smiled in my direction, showing a set of perfectly white teeth. "I am not really an impatient type," he felt it necessary to explain.

Martin was a tall man with thick, sun-bleached hair that fell softly onto his collar. He had blue eyes and healthy-looking, suntanned skin. He was wearing well-fitting jeans and a white linen shirt, the whiteness of which accentuated his golden complexion.

He smiled again. "So you are Carrie." He shook my hand. "Thank you for finding time to see me."

"My pleasure," I said, leading the two men into the living room. "I understand you are going away tomorrow."

"Yes, I travel a lot. Unfortunately it goes with my job."

"What is it that you do?"

"I photograph wildlife."

"How fascinating. Have you photographed anything interesting lately?"

"I took some great pictures of lions and cheetahs in Kenya two weeks ago. Tomorrow I am going to Uganda to photograph chimpanzees, which are always great to capture on film."

"Sounds like a very exciting job," I said, indicating the sofa. "Please sit down."

Martin sat down. "Yes, it's very inspiring."

"Would you like some coffee?" I asked, taking the seat next to Martin while Jason sat in the armchair next to me.

Martin nodded. "Yes, please."

A strong coffee aroma spread around the table as I poured the hot liquid.

"What is the secret of capturing that perfect picture of a wild animal?" I asked conversationally.

"A lot of patience," Martin replied. "Sometimes it takes hours or even days before the perfect opportunity presents itself. Wild animals can be very unpredictable."

I picked up a biscuit. "Have you ever tried making them more co-operative by communicating with them?"

"No not really."

"You should definitely try. Animals are very perceptive, especially chimpanzees. They react to the frequency of your voice. If you are not fearful of them and speak in a calm, controlled tone they will respond to you."

Martin lifted his coffee cup, took a sip and put it down again.

"I am curious about animals being able to pick up the frequency of the human voice. Are you saying that different frequencies carried from human to animal can be read by the animal as information?"

"Yes, and not just human to animal, but human to human as well," I explained. "You can send information in many different forms, but the information is always picked up by the brain as frequency. It can be auditory or visual frequency. Everything that exists is actually energy that vibrates at a specific frequency, and the brain translates the information depending on the frequency of the images or sounds that are being sent out. When it comes to humans, all these frequencies affect our perception and understanding of reality."

"Does that mean that our perception of reality changes just by looking at different images?" Martin questioned.

I nodded. "We lost touch with our inner selves and our super senses have been shut down, so all the information is being absorbed through our physical senses. When we are shown an image, or many images that tell a story, it can easily alter our perception of reality, especially when the words, be it a caption or a spoken word, are used to explain these images. These words are telling us what that reality is. We hardly ever question it, but simply accept it."

"So would you say that our perception of reality can be controlled by images we see on television, for example?"

"Yes, very much so," Jason said, taking over. "Think about it. We watch so-called documentaries and accept all the information as a well-documented fact. Often these programmes voice personal opinions and when the complete story is not known the gaps are filled with speculation. In effect, these programmes are nothing more than someone else's interpretation of the facts, but when the story is backed up by images nobody doubts the authenticity of the information. Viewers simply accept it as factual."

"That's very true," Martin agreed.

"This also applies to everyday news," Jason continued. "News programmes can be very carefully controlled and worded, and because of it they do not allow for an objective opinion. We tend to form an opinion based purely on the interpretation of the story and the images used by the news programme."

"Yes," Martin mused, "this interpretation or misinterpretation of images is very clear when experts analyse images of UFOs, for example."

"The principle is the same," Jason said. "When a so-called expert voices a dismissive opinion about extraterrestrial existence in a television programme or written article, and backs it up with pictures that are interpreted in a dismissive way, the majority of the population will accept the expert's opinion as fact, even though their interpretation of the facts can be very subjective and not necessarily correct."

"You can't dismiss news entirely. We wouldn't know what's happening in the world if it wasn't for the news."

"But do we really know what's happening in the world? Or do we think we know?" Jason challenged.

"I don't know. You tell me."

"I don't know either, but I can tell you one thing: not everything is being reported, and you and I don't have a say in what should be reported and what shouldn't. Whoever decides what to report and how to report it controls the way we view and understand reality."

"From what you are saying, it seems that our perception of reality can be totally controlled by the media," Martin said.

"I would go so far as to say, it is controlled by the media," Jason concluded, picking up a biscuit.

"So what's the solution?" Martin asked, draining his coffee cup.

"We have to learn to reach within for the answers instead of accepting blindly what is fed to us by someone else," I answered.

"You can't deny that some people have greater knowledge of certain subjects than others, and if you don't know enough about the subject you have to rely on the expert's opinion," Martin argued.

"An expert will only accept what he can examine with his physical senses," Jason said. "I haven't come across even one expert who has been able to reach beyond the physical level. Consequently, an expert's opinion is based purely on what he has learned during one lifetime, which must be very limiting when you compare it with the vastness of cosmic knowledge. The trick is to extend your horizons, reach beyond the physical level and try to understand more than what could be confirmed by physical senses, because we all know there is more out there than what we can learn from the so-called experts."

"Still, you learn basic skills like maths, reading or writing from others only because they know something you don't," Martin pointed out.

"That's true, and these skills are very important, but learning them is hardly ever contaminated by another person's opinion, so it does not affect our perception of reality in any way," Jason replied.

Martin smiled. "I'd like to think that this also applies to my published photography," he said, and glanced at his watch. "It's getting late and unfortunately I still have some packing to do, so I need to be going." He stood up. "Can I use your bathroom?"

"Sure. It's at the end of the hall," I directed him, getting up at the same time as Jason.

As Martin disappeared to the bathroom I had a chance to tell Jason about the image of the cosmos I had seen that morning. Jason seemed fascinated and wanted to see the sketch, so we went to the kitchen where it was still lying on the table. We were both bending over the table staring at the sketch when Martin came in.

"I'm sorry Jason, but we have to go," he said.

"Wait a moment," Jason muttered without looking up. "I need to understand this."

"Why don't you stay?" Martin suggested.

Jason turned to him. "I haven't got a car."

"Please stay," I said. "I'll give you a lift home."

"That's settled then," Martin declared, extending his hand to me. "It was a pleasure. We will have to meet up again when I come back."

"I look forward to it," I said with a smile. "Have a nice trip."

"Thank you." He waved goodbye to Jason. "I'll call you when I get back."

"Happy trip," Jason said. "Bring back a lot of great pictures of chimps."

"You carry on with whatever you're doing. I'll let myself out," Martin said, and he headed for the front door.

We returned to the sketch of the cosmos. While we studied it, I explained the basic principles of the energetic structure of the universe and how the pure white light was broken into 12 basic frequencies, and then broken again and again, and how each frequency carried with it the element of the energy of the Creator.

Jason looked up. "So that's why people say that there is a divine spark in everyone."

"Yes," I confirmed, "but the divine spark is not just in everyone, it's in everything around us. Once you realise that everything is connected through this energy, you also realise that it all exists as one, and one aspect of existence automatically affects another."

"Yet everything around us seems to be separating people, and most of them feel that only their little world matters," Jason mused.

"I don't remember if I've told you that there are three basic rules of the universe - knowledge, co-operation and unity. This planet is in chaos because these rules are not followed," I explained. "We have been cut off from the cosmic knowledge and there has been neither co-operation nor unity. Over centuries, many different ideas have been injected into our minds and people have been fighting each other because they believe that their religion or cause is the only one worth following. If people are full of resentment, anger and hate, their religion or cause is a good excuse to express these emotions. Suddenly killings and terror turn into good causes because people fight for their own beliefs or their own god. The world leaders are not much better. They make decisions that lead to even bigger separation because they become egotistical and obsessed with their own power and lose sight of what's important."

"And everything is spinning out of control," Jason concluded.

"It is, but this is necessary for people to realise what they are doing to themselves and the planet. They need to understand that they have to change their ways to save themselves and the planet from destruction."

"I hope it's not going to take too long," Jason said, sitting down on the chair.

"It won't. Time is running out."

"Speaking of the time, how much time do we have before your house friend comes back?" Jason asked, reaching for my hand and pulling me towards him.

I sat on his lap. "He's not coming back for a few days."

"You don't know how good that makes me feel," he said, kissing me softly on the lips and then gently pushing back my hair. "I have a confession to make," he muttered. "I wanted to see you so badly that I ended up persuading Martin to come here today."

I smiled. "I sensed something suspicious was going on when you kept saying how keen he was to meet me."

"He wasn't that keen," Jason admitted. "He wanted to meet you, but as he is travelling tomorrow he would have preferred to meet another time."

"I don't understand. Why drag Martin all the way here when we were going to see each other today anyway?"

Jason pushed my hair back again. "I wasn't sure that we would. The plan was to meet John, and John couldn't make it today."

"So you went to all this trouble just to see me?"

"It wasn't much trouble."

I snuggled closer to him. "Trouble or not, I'm happy you're here."

Jason kissed me again and this time I kissed him back deeply and passionately. The heat of excitement was spreading rapidly inside me as Jason eagerly kissed my neck and then my shoulder.

"I've missed you so badly," he whispered into my ear, whilst undoing the buttons of my top.

The heat in my body intensified tenfold, and then his lips were on my chest, making their way down to my breasts. Suddenly I heard the unexpected sound of a key in the front door. In a flash, as though burned by fire, we shot up and away from each other. Standing next to Jason, I frantically tried to button up my blouse and I was fumbling with the last button when Mark walked in.

He stared at us, taking the whole scene in. "What's going on here?"

I was fully aware that my cheeks were flushed and I looked totally flustered.

"What are you doing back here?" I managed to ask. "You were supposed to stay at the hotel."

"It's just as well I did decide to come back," he said reproachfully.

"What's that supposed to mean?" I asked heatedly.

"Carrie, aren't you going to introduce us?" Jason interjected, sensing the beginning of an argument.

I glanced at Jason and he smiled encouragingly.

"Oh, yes. Mark, this is Jason," I said, making the first introduction.

Jason extended his hand. "Nice to meet you, Mark."

Rudely, Mark ignored the gesture and spoke to me instead. "Are you entertaining other men in my house while I'm away?"

"I don't entertain other men. Jason works for Mr Kaplowski. He came to discuss a painting that I am going to paint for one of Mr Kaplowski's clients," I lied, hoping it sounded plausible.

Mark wasn't to be fooled that easily.

"Is this the way you always discuss business?"

"What do you mean?"

"Your hair looks ruffled and the button across your breasts is undone."

I glanced down and true enough there was a gaping hole where two sides of my blouse had separated. I buttoned up quickly.

"It's not what you think ..." I started, then stopped as I realised I did not need to explain anything to Mark any more.

Mark faced Jason. "You are in my house and I would appreciate it if you left."

I grabbed Jason's hand. "This is also my house and he is not going anywhere."

Mark shot me an angry look. "Carrie, do not test my patience," he said tightly.

Jason managed to catch my eye. "Maybe it's better if I go."

"Absolutely not!" I refused to be bullied by Mark. "You stay right here!" I turned to Mark. "I can entertain anyone I bloody well like and I can discuss business in any way I bloody well wish, and it's none of your bloody business because we are no longer together!"

"We are very much together for as long as you live in this house."

"That's where you're wrong. We are definitely not together," I said firmly, "but I won't leave until the matter of this house is resolved. I refuse to be pushed out onto the street."

Mark's face changed suddenly and I saw a glimpse of the other ugly face.

"You are not in a position to make demands!" he shouted furiously. "You behave like a slut and you deserve nothing better than to be thrown out onto the street!"

Jason placed his hand on my arm. "I think we should leave."

He was right. The whole situation was getting out of hand.

"You are being unreasonable and I don't want to continue with this argument," I said to Mark.

"Why not? I think we should clear the air once and for all," he growled, his face full of hatred. "I certainly don't want you back. You are nothing but a conniving bitch!"

"I am not going to listen to this." I grabbed my handbag and the keys to my parents' house and pulled Jason's arm. "We are leaving."

We took a few steps forwards, but Mark was blocking the doorway.

"Move away!" I demanded, pushing him to one side.

I managed to step through the doorway, but Mark blocked Jason's way.

"Too scared to face the music, pal?" Mark asked cynically.

In response, Jason threw a punch straight into Mark's face and, as he flew backwards, Jason said, "Not scared at all ... buddy."

"Get out of my house!" Mark shouted, blood dripping down his shirt. "Both of you!"

We left the house and walked towards my car.

"Charming individual," Jason remarked.

"I'm sorry. I didn't plan for this to happen."

"Don't worry. We are out of there and I am damned if that bastard is going to spoil the rest of our day."

We got into my car and I started the engine.

"So where are we going to enjoy the rest of this exciting day?" I asked with a smile, determined to push the whole incident to the back of my mind.

"Before we go anywhere we have to organise a place for you to stay," Jason said considerately.

"There's no need as I have the keys to my parents' house."

"That's good. How long can you stay with your parents?"

"I'm not exactly going to stay with them. My parents live in Spain and there is only a woman housekeeper who comes in a few times a week."

Jason looked at me. "You mean the house is empty?"

I nodded with a happy grin.

"And we could spend some time there without being interrupted?"

"I don't know. The housekeeper might walk in unexpectedly," I teased.

Jason smiled. "After the last confrontation I am certainly ready to face the housekeeper."

"My hero," I said, stroking his leg. "You are officially invited to my parents' house to defend my honour."

There was a moment of silence in which Jason stared at me intently, and then he muttered quietly, "I want to make love to you."

I felt a sudden wave of excitement and it was difficult to concentrate on the driving.

"Don't say things like that when I'm driving," I managed to utter.

The lights ahead changed to red and I brought the car to a stop. Jason traced my cheek with the back of his hand.

"I want to spend the night with you," he murmured. "I don't want to wait any longer."

I glanced at him, my heart grew warm and at that moment I wanted nothing more than to spend the night with him.

"That's what I want too."

The lights changed to green and I started the car, bringing us both back to the present. Much more composed, we discussed the evening ahead and decided that Jason should go home to pick up his things and collect his car whilst I went to my parents' house and prepared dinner so it would be ready when he joined me in about an hour.

Happy with the plan, I gave Jason directions to my parents' house and dropped him at the nearest tube station, then drove to the local Marks and Spencer to shop for candles and perhaps some ready-made meals.

* * *

Balancing the shopping in one hand, I unlocked the door to my parents' house with the other, pushed the door open with my knee and headed straight for the kitchen. I unpacked the bags quickly and glanced at my watch. It was nearly 6 o'clock, which gave me roughly half an hour to get everything ready. I switched on the oven and put a bottle of low-alcohol wine in the fridge. While I was waiting for the oven to heat up, I set two places and arranged two large fragranced candles on the dining room table.

Back in the kitchen, I checked the oven. It hadn't reached the required temperature, so I emptied a pack of fresh green salad into a bowl and mixed in some French dressing. That done, I slid a large tomato and basil quiche into the oven, made myself a cup of coffee and sat at the kitchen table waiting for Jason to arrive.

About 15 minutes later the doorbell sounded and I went to open the door. Jason, looking very handsome in linen beige trousers and a crisp white shirt, stood on the doorstep with a sports bag in one hand and a bunch of red roses and a small carrier bag in the other. He stepped inside.

"These are for you," he said, handing me the flowers and the carrier bag.

"Flowers, and a present too? Thank you, sweetie," I said with glee, kissing him on the cheek. "Come with me into the kitchen."

Jason dropped his sports bag on the floor and we went to the kitchen where I searched through the cupboards for a large vase. I found a pearly white one, filled it with water, arranged the flowers and placed it on the worktop. Once the flowers were sorted, I reached into the carrier bag and extracted a small Nokia box.

"A phone?" I asked in surprise.

"Mobile phone," Jason said. "I want you to be able to contact me at any time, anywhere, and especially if you need help."

A mobile phone certainly was a useful thing to have, but it was an additional expense and my financial situation seemed very uncertain at that moment.

"It's a lovely present and I don't want to sound ungrateful, but I am not sure I can afford it."

Jason put his arms around me and we stood facing each other.

"The phone is in my name, so you don't need to worry about the bills."

"You are only a student, so how can you afford to pay my bills?"

"My father gives me a very generous allowance."

"Does he know you are going to use it to pay someone else's phone bills?" I asked, with a smile.

"He doesn't need to know. He has plenty of money." Jason sniffed the strong smell of cooking that had begun to permeate the kitchen. "I think something is burning."

"My God, I'd completely forgotten about the food!"

Grabbing an oven glove, I swung open the oven door and pulled out the burnt quiche. I gave Jason a disappointed look.

"I suppose this is ready to eat, if somewhat overdone."

"I love overdone quiches," Jason said, with an understanding smile.

I smiled back. "Just as well you do, because I can't offer you anything else."

I transferred the quiche onto a large plate, cut off the burnt bits and divided it into four portions. Opening the fridge, I pulled out the bottle of wine and handed it to Jason to carry, then I grabbed the plate with the quiche, and the salad bowl.

"Let's go into the dining room," I said, leading the way.

Jason took his seat at the long side of the table and I sat opposite. While I lit the candles Jason looked around.

"I like this room. Yes, it's very cosy."

My parents' dining room wasn't very big. It adjoined the more spacious living room, and the two rooms were separated by heavy floor-to-ceiling doors. All the dining room furniture was modern and made from good-quality aged oak in a rich golden colour. On one side there was a solid oak sideboard and dresser unit, and on the other an oak buffet with glass doors. The dining table and chairs were also made from oak to match the rest of the furniture. The walls were painted light blue and were decorated with large, colourful pictures framed in gold-leafed wood. The large wall-to-wall window was dressed with heavy cream silk and the same fabric was used for the chair pads. The side lighting was soft and non-intrusive.

I helped myself to a portion of quiche.

"What is your parents' house like?"

"You mean the house I live in?" Jason asked, opening the bottle of wine.

I nodded.

"I live with my father and the house is quite big," Jason said, pouring the wine into our glasses. "There are two very large rooms and a kitchen on the ground floor, three bedrooms on the first floor and two bedrooms and a study on the second. Oh, and there are three bathrooms."

"Where is your bedroom?" I enquired, filling my plate with salad.

"On the second floor. My room is usually messy because nobody ever goes in there," he confessed, and then added lightly, "I promise to tidy it up before you come over."

I smiled at him. "Is that an invitation?"

"Yes, but we have to arrange it when my father's not there."

"Why? I would love to meet your father."

"I don't think you'd like him," Jason said, cutting into his quiche.

I faced him. "Why wouldn't I like him?"

"He isn't an easy person to talk to and neither is my mother."

"Do you see your mother often?" I asked.

"No, we are not that close." Jason sipped some wine. "Are you close to your parents?"

"Not really, but I do love them," I said, lifting my wine glass. "My mother is a very sweet lady and my father is a sensitive soul, although it's often difficult to see his sensitive nature because he tends to live in his own world." I took a sip from my glass. "They are perfectly matched even though they hardly ever agree on anything. When I told them I was splitting up with Mark my mother reacted in a totally different way to my father - she was worried and concerned about my future while he was pleased and happy for me."

"I can totally understand why your father feels that way. Why would anyone want a mean-spirited bastard for a son-in-law?" Jason asked, sounding upset.

"I know Mark can be mean, and I'm sorry."

Jason faced me. "I have no right to say this, but I don't ever want you to go back to him."

"I will never go back to him," I said assuredly. "Even though I will have to live in the same house for a while longer."

"I don't understand why you can't live here."

"My savings are invested in the house I share with him and if I move out now Mark will create every obstacle imaginable to punish me. I will not see my money for years," I explained.

"My gut feeling tells me that he will make your life hell whether you stay or move out."

I had a quick flash of Mark's true face and a shiver ran through me.

"You might be right."

"I know I am and, for what it's worth, I think you should move out."

"I can't as I need to use the studio. I want to finish the painting of the cosmos."

Jason thought for a moment. "There must be a solution. Give me a few days and I might be able to come up with something."

I slid my fingers across the table and reached for his hand.

"Thank you for trying to help."

The mood changed as Jason lifted my hand to his lips and kissed it, looking seductively into my eyes.

"I think it's time for some music," I said, breaking his stare. I walked to the living room and began searching through the CD rack. "Do you like Pavarotti?" I called.

"'I love Pavarotti," Jason called back.

I pushed 'Ti Adoro' into the CD player, chose my favourite track and opened wide the large doors between the rooms, just as the sound of 'Caruso' came through the speakers.

"This is my absolute favourite. Let's dance," I said, taking Jason's hand and pulling him towards me.

"I am really not a good dancer," he tried to object.

"You don't have to be. Just hold me and move with the music."

We slowly began moving to the rhythm of the music. Jason put his arms around my shoulders and I wrapped mine around his waist, and we danced silently, my face resting on his chest, his face pressed into my hair. The music was beautiful and seductive, and suddenly there was an unspoken need to experience our closeness in a different, more physical way. Pavarotti was still singing when Jason pulled me towards the chair. He sat down first then I sat across his lap, facing him, and threw my arms around his neck.

"Why don't we start where we left off?" I murmured.

"Yes, why don't we?" Jason said, as he began undoing the buttons of my blouse, which soon found its way to the floor.

My bra quickly followed. For a moment he looked at my nakedness with his soft, enticing eyes, and then buried his face between my breasts, kissed my bare skin and caressed my nipples with his tongue. I was melting away under the heat of his kisses, but it wasn't enough - I wanted more. I wanted to feel his naked body next to mine. I wanted to lose myself in the sheer delight of making love with him. Grasping his head in my hands, I gazed into his eyes.

"I want us to do this on a large, comfortable bed," I whispered, lifting myself up.

I blew out the candles, took his hand in mine and led him upstairs to the guest room. I switched on a small bedside light.

"Don't speak and don't move," I ordered, and slowly began to unbutton Jason's shirt.

When all the buttons were undone I pushed the fabric off his shoulders and then, kissing his mouth and snuggling my breasts against his chest, I unzipped his trousers. They slid down and he stepped out of them. I gently pushed him onto the bed and pulled his socks and briefs off. He was hard, and for a moment I just stood there looking at him. He was as beautiful as a Renaissance statue: his muscles pronounced and firm, his body masculine and in perfect proportion.

He reached out with his hand. "Come here."

I took his hand, he pulled me onto the bed and then his mouth was on mine, hot and soft, and his naked body was next to mine, my breasts against the warmth of his chest. Our lips were still sealed together as he swiftly removed the rest of my clothes. Totally naked, we touched, kissed and caressed, at first tenderly then more fervently as the fire of our passion intensified.

Ready and eager to make love, Jason turned me on my back and lifted himself up on top of me. I spread and lifted my legs to welcome him and we joined together in the closest and most intimate way possible. He began moving very slowly inside me, and the most exquisite pleasure was building up in my body with his every stroke. Hungry for the final rapture, we found a mutual rhythm and our movement became more hurried and precise, until finally we cried out together and exploded in a shuddering, mind-blowing orgasm.

Totally spent, we lay silently for a while, not moving, and then Jason lifted his head and smiled.

"I think we've just fulfilled the first requirement of our cosmic partnership - and very pleasurable it was too."

I smiled back in total contentment.

A little later we lay side-by-side, staring at each other, Jason's hand caressing my neck.

"You are very beautiful," he said quietly.

I touched his face gently. "You are just as beautiful," I said tenderly.

He pulled me into his arms and we cuddled together.

"We haven't finished our dinner," Jason said after a while. "Shall we go down and finish it?"

This reminded me of the strawberry tart that I had purchased for dessert, which was cooling in the fridge. I lifted my head and looked at him.

"I've got a better idea. We'll eat up here. The quiche was spoiled, so how about something sweet and creamy?"

"Something sweet and creamy sounds good."

"I'll go and get it," I said, jumping out of bed.

I ran downstairs, grabbed the tart and two teaspoons and, balancing it carefully on my hand, I ran back upstairs. I handed Jason a spoon and placed the tart on the bed.

"There are no plates. Just dig in," I said, sticking my spoon in the soft dessert.

Jason filled his spoon with the strawberries and cream, and put it into his mouth. "This is good," he commented. "Really good."

I smiled. "I am doing my best to spoil you."

"Don't ever stop. I like being spoiled."

I kissed him on the tip of his nose. "I promise to spoil you always."

"I am a very lucky guy," Jason said, and then staring into my eyes he added seriously, "and I mean it."

I could feel the familiar sensation of heat building up in my body. Silently, Jason took the spoon out of my hand and put it, together with the rest of the tart, on the bedside table. He then placed his hand on the nape of my neck, pulled my head close to his and kissed me hard on the lips.

"I want to make love to you again," he whispered tenderly.

"Yes, do," I muttered, easing myself down on the bed and pulling him with me.

We made love once more and this time it was more urgent than before and the mutual release came quickly. Afterwards, totally drained, we drifted off to sleep wrapped in each other's arms, peaceful and incredibly content.

9

Jason awakened me with a gentle kiss.

"I have to go," he said quietly.

I opened my eyes and saw him leaning over me, fully dressed.

"What time is it?" I asked sleepily.

"Eight o'clock."

"Where are you going this early?"

"I have an exam at nine."

"When am I going to see you again?"

"I'll try to arrange a meeting with John and let you know."

"Okay, and good luck with your exam."

"Bye, babe, I'll see you later."

He kissed me again and a moment later he had gone. Now fully awake, I lay in bed not quite sure what to do with myself. Now that I was alone in my parents' house I did not want to stay there. All the things around me felt familiar, but nothing belonged to me, so it was a little like staying in a hotel - impersonal and good for a short visit. Besides, I didn't want to waste the full day doing nothing. I wanted to carry on with the painting of the cosmos. I also needed a change of clothes, so the answer was obvious - I had to go back home.

After I had showered and dressed, I tided up the dining room and washed all the dishes. Ready to leave, I reached for my new mobile and dialled my home number. As expected there was no answer. I waited until the answering service picked up the call before I disconnected the line. Just to be on the safe side, I pressed the redial button. Again, no one answered. Satisfied that Mark had left for work, I made my way to the car.

Half an hour later I let myself into my house, my mind buzzing with new decisions. I tossed my handbag onto the hallstand and headed straight to the bedroom where I discarded my dirty clothes and slipped into more comfortable jogging pants and a T-shirt. Securing my hair with an elastic band, I was all set to start work on the painting, but first I had to make some changes in the house.

Picking up the *Yellow Pages*, I searched for security services. I found the number of a local locksmith and called, requesting that someone came over urgently to fit two additional door locks. I was told that no one was available immediately, but a locksmith would be with me at 2 o'clock that afternoon. Satisfied with that, I began moving most of my things from the main bedroom to the guest room. Whatever happened, I was quite determined not to share the bedroom with Mark ever again.

Mission accomplished, I immediately felt better. I made myself a cheese and tomato sandwich and went to the studio. Biting into my sandwich, I stood in front of the large canvas covered with background colours and mentally planned the rest of the painting. By the time I had finished eating, I had a perfectly good idea of how I should paint it. The picture would be very simple, with spheres shown as flat circles and rays as lines of different colours on the background of gradually shaded blues and browns.

I squeezed the required hues onto the palette and began painting, concentrating on the background first. Once that was finished I had a very tricky job to determine where each circle should be placed. The whole picture needed to be very symmetrical and the circles had to be very precise.

I became completely lost in my work and painted until 2 o'clock when the locksmith arrived. An hour later the locks were in place in the meditation room and the guest bedroom. It was an unexpectedly large expense, but one I didn't mind. I was just relieved that it was done.

As soon as the locksmith had left, I returned to my painting and began marking the circles. I was quite engrossed in it when I heard the shrieking sound of my mobile. I picked it up and pressed the 'on' button.

"Hi, babe," Jason said. "What are you up to?"

"I am working on the picture of the cosmos."

"So you're back at home?"

Jason sounded concerned.

"Yes, but don't worry. I've moved all my things from the bedroom and I've had locks put on the doors of the two rooms I am going to use."

"Are you sure that's wise?"

"Moving my things or putting locks on the doors?" I asked.

"Putting locks on the doors," he replied.

"You don't feel I've done the right thing?"

"I don't know," Jason said, hesitantly. "It might aggravate things unnecessarily."

"I had to do it," I reasoned. "Mark's got a nasty habit of sneaking up on people."

"If that's the case, you shouldn't be staying there."

"I have no choice. We've had this conversation before."

"I am far from convinced and I am still concerned."

"Don't be. I'll be all right."

"Okay, it's your call," Jason said and changed the subject. "I've spoken to Anna. John is free this evening and Anna suggested we meet him at her place around seven. She will prepare something to eat."

"Do you want me to meet you there?"

"How about I pick you up some time after six?"

I hesitated. "I'm not sure. Mark might be here."

"Carrie, I don't want him to start controlling our lives."

"You're right. Come over."

"I'll call you on your mobile when I arrive."

"I'll be ready for six-thirty."

"See you then."

* * *

Jason arrived at exactly half past six. I locked the doors to the meditation room and guest room, dropped the keys into my handbag and left the house.

The evening was fresh and pleasantly warm with clear blue skies and a hazy sun, creating a smoky glow in the distance. Jason was leaning against his car with his arms folded across his chest, looking very alluring in his well-fitting jeans, T-shirt and sports jacket. My mind flashed to the previous night when this gorgeous man had kissed me all over, touched me in the most intimate places and filled me with himself, and the memory made my heart soar. Our eyes met and I smiled happily. Jason smiled back. He had a beautiful smile, a smile that lit up his whole face, an irresistibly attractive smile.

"I like the way you look," he said. "Very sexy."

I seemed to have lost the excess weight, so my clothes were more daring than usual. I was wearing a flowery mini skirt, a white fitted shirt with a few buttons open at the top and a short denim jacket. On my feet I wore red high-heeled shoes, showing off my good legs to advantage and making me look more slender. My hair was shiny and full. I had styled it with a side parting and it fell down in large curls below my shoulders.

"That's what a night of passion can do to you," I said, giving him a peck on the cheek.

"Then we must do it more often," he said, grinning lasciviously.

"I think you're right," I said, with a smile.

He grabbed my hand and pulled me to him.

"How could I be wrong? I haven't been able to stop thinking about last night. I haven't been able to stop thinking about you," he whispered, hugging me tightly.

I didn't say anything. I just let him hold me, revelling in his closeness. He kissed the top of my head.

"We'd better go, babe, otherwise we'll be late."

He released me, opened the passenger door and I climbed in. Shutting the door, he walked to the other side of the car and got in. He started the engine, all the while looking at me.

"I am one lucky guy," he said, gently touching my hair.

I smiled at him, feeling very lucky myself and, as I looked at his lovely face, I knew I was falling madly in love with him. My love for him filled my whole being, and I realised that through it I was connecting to a very beautiful and extremely powerful energy, the most beautiful and powerful energy known to man. I knew that, once experienced, this energy had to be nurtured because only through it could I connect directly to the white light.

"I am falling in love with you," I muttered.

Jason stroked my cheek. "I fell in love with you the very first time I saw you."

I moved closer to him and we embraced each other. There was no need for any more words. We simply allowed the love energy to flow between us and join us in a wonderful feeling of belonging and togetherness.

The sudden ringing of Jason's mobile brought us quickly back down to earth. It was Anna checking what time we would arrive. Jason switched off his mobile.

"We must go," he said.

I nodded.

Dropping the phone into his jacket pocket, he put the car into gear and we set off.

We arrived in Richmond 35 minutes later. Jason parked the car and we walked the short distance to Anna's apartment. I pressed the buzzer.

A man answered the door. He was of medium height and his body was solid and heavily built. His pasty complexion was accentuated by bright green eyes and dark brown hair, which was receding at the temples. He looked about 40 and was wearing very traditional clothes: dark trousers and a light blue shirt with a striped tie.

We stepped past him into the hallway and he closed the door. The enticing smell of cooking lingered throughout the apartment and the soft sound of classical music could be heard in the background.

Jason extended his hand in greeting. "You must be John."

The man shook it. "You are Jason, I presume." He turned to me. "And this lovely lady must be Carrie."

"That's me," I said, with a smile.

"Anna is busy in the kitchen, attending to dinner. She has instructed me to entertain you both until dinner is ready," John explained, directing us into the living room.

The living room was sparkling clean and decorated with colourful, fresh flowers. Somewhere in the room incense was burning, filling the air with the soothing fragrance of sandalwood. There were soft drinks and various snacks on the small coffee table.

"Please sit down," John invited, and Jason and I sat down on the sofa. "I hope you like the music," John said, sitting in the armchair by the window. "Beethoven's Piano Sonatas 30 and 31 - very beautiful. Drink?"

I asked for sparkling water and Jason elected to have some fresh orange juice. John poured the drinks and put them in front of us. I lifted my glass of water.

"I've heard that you are a musician," I said to John.

"Yes, I play instruments and write my own compositions," John replied, selecting a few crisps from a green ceramic bowl.

"What instruments do you play?"

"Mainly piano and flute."

"The piano is probably my favourite," I said. "A lot of very beautiful music has been written for the piano."

"That's true," John agreed. "All the best composers have written for the piano. Some pieces have been so well written they are timeless."

I helped myself to some cashew nuts.

"Do you like Chopin? I enjoy listening to his music."

"I do like his music very much. He was a very romantic composer and an absolutely brilliant pianist," John replied.

"I think there is a lot of grace and beauty in his music."

"Yes, and also great originality. His music was very creative and his passionately expressive style completely revolutionised the piano technique. It could easily be said that he is one of the greatest composers of all time."

"Which music do you enjoy playing most?" I asked.

"I've played music written by all the great composers, like Bach, Beethoven, Mozart, Tchaikovsky, Debussy, Liszt and, of course, Chopin, and it's always been a pleasure if not a challenge, but it's never as fulfilling as playing your own material."

"Do you write a lot?"

"Yes and no. I've written two scores for short and not very well-known films, and many small pieces," John said, and then he added with a smile, "I am still waiting to be fully recognised and appreciated."

"I am sure you will be one day."

Anna and her small dog came into the room, interrupting our conversation.

"Hi," she greeted us with a welcoming smile. "I do apologise for leaving John to entertain you. I hope he's looked after you well."

I gave her a pleasant smile. "Very well."

"Good. Grab your drinks and come into the kitchen. Dinner is ready. Harry, get away from under my feet!" she scolded the dog on her way out of the room.

Drinks in hand, we followed Anna and her dog to the kitchen where a large pine table was set with heavy, light blue china, white mats and white napkins rolled neatly inside blue porcelain rings, crystal goblets and silver cutlery with blue handles. A large ceramic dish with a steaming casserole stood in the middle surrounded by three smaller dishes full of fresh butter-glazed vegetables.

We took our seats. Anna sat next to John on one side of the table and Jason and I sat opposite. The dog flopped by Anna's feet.

"It's chicken casserole, in case you're wondering," Anna said. "Please help yourselves."

We began filling our plates with the delicious-smelling food.

"Did you have a chance to talk to John about the current planetary changes?" Anna enquired, passing the dish with potatoes to me.

"No," I replied, transferring some potatoes onto my plate. "We talked mainly about music."

"John is very interested in the changes," Anna said, passing the dish to Jason. "I explained as much as I could to him and I think he was happy with most of the information." She turned to John. "Weren't you?"

"Yes, although I am sure there is still much more I don't know, or understand, for that matter," John replied, with a smile.

"Is there anything specific you would like to know?" I enquired, unfolding my napkin.

John raised his wine glass. "I am a musician, so naturally I would like to learn more about sound," he said, sipping his wine.

"Sound, like everything else in the universe, is just another form of energy." I paused for a second to collect my thoughts before I continued. "We talked about Chopin and about his music being beautiful and graceful, but music can also be discordant and harsh like the current rave music, for instance. If we look at the sound purely from the energy point of view there is an energetic difference between various kinds of music and the difference is the overall frequency of the energy created by the sound, which is not the same as the frequency of the sound itself. Simply speaking, the higher the frequency of the energy created, the more uplifting the sound; the lower the frequency, the more discordant the notes."

"I think I understand that," John said, between mouthfuls.

"It's not easy to compose music that transmits higher energies," I continued. "The great master musicians reached to the higher planes of existence for their inspiration, and their music in turn helps us to connect to those planes, making us feel good when we listen to it. Music is a mixture of different sounds that become one overall energetic frequency, and there could be millions of different combinations, each provoking some kind of reaction in the listener. For example, when the notes are smooth and well harmonised together, music can be calming and comforting or, if they are disharmonious and clashing, it's more likely to be irritating."

"I suspect a good example of this could be the fast, loud and chaotic sound of some of the current commercial recordings," John said.

I nodded.

"I must say I have no time for that kind of music at all," John added. "I find it rather disturbing."

"Yes, it can be disturbing as the entire human energetic system tends to be extremely influenced by sound," I said. "We don't realise just how powerful sound can be. It can easily penetrate deep into our psyche, and when the energetic frequencies are badly harmonised the sound can create all sorts of negative reactions in the listener."

"Would you say that certain sounds can affect human behaviour?" John questioned.

"Very much so," I replied. "Badly harmonised sound is jarring and unsettling, and can produce reactions like anger, fear, anxiety and even depression. These emotions in turn affect human behaviour patterns because they need to be expressed in some way."

"I imagine they do," John said. "It's just as well we have a choice and can choose not to listen to this modern rubbish."

"Quite," Anna agreed. "Although I must say I am puzzled how the sound can produce all these emotions."

"If the music is angry and violent," Jason interjected, "it would be logical to assume that it would increase aggression-related thoughts and emotions."

"But surely we have some control over our reactions?" Anna argued.

"You don't have any control over the frequency of the sound that reaches your brain," I pointed out.

"Maybe not, but I should be able to control my reaction."

"You don't have much control over your reactions when someone is screaming and throwing abuse at you," I explained. "Your reaction could be to become aggressive and angry or you might withdraw into yourself and wallow in self-pity. Either way, you will end up reacting to the frequency of the sound directed towards you. The same applies when a calm person speaks to you in a subdued manner, only this time your brain receives a different signal and your body reacts in a completely different, much more controlled manner. The process is simple. The brain receives a signal in the form of the sound frequency and passes the information to the rest of the body through the nervous system, and the body reacts. Saying that, there would hardly be any reaction if you chose to cover your ears and stop the sound frequency reaching your brain."

"Are you saying that the human mind can be controlled by sound?" Anna asked.

"It can, and it's about time that we realised that," I replied.

"This is rather worrying when you think that most of the young people listen to discordant, jarring music," John said.

"Drugs, sex and noisy, discordant music," Anna commented. "A reflection of our times."

"True, but what about the people who create it?" John asked.

"You can only create at the level you are at yourself," I explained.

"Yes," John mused. "I must say this conversation has opened my mind to a lot of things. I do understand now that I have a certain responsibility when it comes to my compositions, because my music will have an effect on the listener. So my next question is: how do I reach the higher level?"

"By connecting to the higher frequencies of the cosmos and translating those frequencies into well-harmonised sets of notes," I replied.

"Oh, yes, but how do you connect to the higher frequencies?"

"Through calmness and tranquillity; the calmer and more tranquil you are, the higher the overall frequency of your body. The higher the frequency of your body, the higher you can connect. The higher you connect, the better the harmony of the music you compose."

"So there is no such thing as natural talent?"

"Of course there is but, generally speaking, talent is an ability that needs to be developed and perfected. Talent by itself is not enough."

"Talking about special ability," Jason interjected, clearing his plate, "Anna definitely has a special ability to cook delicious food. This meal is superb."

"I am happy you think so," Anna said, pleased. "There is still plenty left. Please help yourselves to more, otherwise it will become dog food."

"We mustn't allow that to happen," Jason remarked, helping himself to more casserole.

The rest of us followed suit. While we ate we continued with our conversation about music, discussing various classical composers, our likes and dislikes, and how each of us had been influenced by different sounds. Eventually, dinner was over and John announced that he had to leave. We said goodbye to him and he departed. Anna cleared the table and made fresh drinks.

"Carrie, what do you think about John?" Anna asked, as soon as she had sat down again.

"I think he is very nice and I hope that our conversation will help him to create better music," I replied.

"I hope so too," Anna said. "I hope he understands that in order to be a better musician he needs to evolve and grow as a person."

"That's true," I agreed, "but remember, not everyone is at the same level. What might seem very simple to understand to you might be impossible for someone else to grasp."

"Why is it so difficult to grasp the basic truth?" asked Anna, sounding puzzled.

"Because our emotions, attachments and old belief systems stand in the way. Also because the inner energy might be too low to reach beyond very basic understanding."

"I seem to be able to connect to everything you say," Anna said, with a pleased smile. "It's as though I have known this already and you are just triggering my memory."

"The knowledge is within you, so it's true that I am only triggering your memory."

"But it seems that not everyone can connect in quite the same way."

"No, not everyone, but you can because you are a highly evolved human being. You are one of us," I said, touching her hand, "and we would like you to join us in cosmic co-operation."

"Of course I will. I consider myself privileged to be asked," Anna said enthusiastically. "What do I need to do?"

"It's very straightforward," I replied. "All you need to do is inwardly commit yourself to the cosmic co-operation. Once you do that, you have made a decision to step into the light, and from that moment on the consciousness will lead you on the journey of knowledge. You will learn through your own experiences, and your understanding will come from within."

"I am totally ready," Anna said. "I feel that at last I have found the divine purpose in life."

"You have," Jason said with a smile. He raised his glass. "Let's drink to our new Family of Light."

We clicked our glasses and it felt really good. It was a small celebration but, nonetheless, a very important one because Jason and I had managed to connect to another like-minded person. This meant that we had increased our energy output tenfold, the energy the planet so desperately needed in the current transition. Also, we all knew that it was the beginning of something much bigger.

We chatted some more and it was nearly 10 o'clock when we left Anna's place and Jason drove me back home. The light in the front room was on, so Jason parked a few metres away from the house.

"Are you sure you want to go in?" he asked, concerned.

"Yes, I am going in," I replied, adamantly. "I am not going to run away."

He drew me close and kissed my forehead.

"Promise to call me the moment he gives you any trouble. I can be here in half an hour."

I nodded in agreement.

He kissed my lips, and then said, "You'd better go, otherwise I will insist that you stay with me."

I badly wanted to stay with him and for a moment I contemplated going to my parents' house, but I quickly rejected that idea, knowing that taking the easy way out would not resolve any of my problems. Moving away, I opened the car door.

"Bye, sweetie, talk to you tomorrow."

"Bye, baby."

I watched Jason drive away and only when he turned the corner did I head for the house. Very quietly, I unlocked the front door and stepped inside. Mark was in the living room, watching television. I took off my shoes and very slowly and carefully tiptoed across the hall towards the staircase. I had managed to climb a few steps when Mark's voice stopped me in my tracks.

"Are you trying to sneak away from me?" he asked reproachfully.

I turned and saw him standing in the living room doorway.

"I didn't want to disturb you," I said calmly.

He wasn't easily fooled.

"Avoiding me isn't going to resolve anything. Why don't you come down those stairs so we can talk like civilised people?"

I sighed resignedly and followed him into the living room.

"What do you want to talk about?"

"Our relationship. What else would I want to talk about?" he asked, sitting down on the sofa and switching off the television set with the remote.

I sighed deeply and sat next to him.

"Our relationship is over."

"Carrie, why do you keep saying that it's over? I am sure we can reconcile our differences if we try. I am willing to change if you only tell me what it is that you want me to change. I give you my word that I'll take everything you say on board."

"It's too late for that."

"It's never too late."

He moved closer and tried to kiss me. I could smell alcohol on his breath, so I turned my head away.

"Don't!"

"I was only trying to kiss you, for God's sake!" he snapped, annoyed.

I moved away from him.

"I don't want you to kiss me. I don't want you to touch me," I said sharply.

His face darkened and the expression in his eyes changed - the ugly man was back.

"Is it because you're fucking someone else?" he asked crudely.

"No, it's not because I'm fucking someone else," I shouted angrily. "It's because I don't like you any more!"

"Is that why you put the lock on the door to the guest room and moved your things from the bedroom? Don't think I haven't noticed."

"If you noticed then you've probably worked out that I am going to sleep in the guest room. I put the lock on the door because I want to make sure you don't sneak up on me when I am asleep."

"Ha, ha, ha," he laughed, mockingly. "So you think you are such a catch." Then he became more serious. "I have a surprise for you, you are nothing but a stupid, unappreciative bitch!"

"I am not going to listen to this."

I turned away and started towards the door.

"Go! Go!" he shouted at my back. "Lock yourself in. See if I care."

As soon as I was sure he could not see me, I hurtled upstairs to the guest room and locked myself in. I sat on the bed feeling numb and wondering what to do. The situation was getting worse and it was more and more apparent that if I wanted to preserve my sanity I needed to move out, but where would I go? My parents' house was the obvious solution, but at the same time it would only represent a roof over my head rather than a home. I needed my own place and at that moment it seemed like a near impossibility. I had no choice; I had to talk to Mark about the money. Having made that decision, I unlocked the door and rushed back downstairs.

"I want to move out," I said, loud enough to be heard over the television noise. "And I need my share of the money from this house."

Mark looked at me. "I am not selling the house. You can forget it."

"Then you'll have to buy me out."

"I'll think about it."

"How long are you going to think about it?" I demanded impatiently.

"As long as it takes," he said, changing the channel. "I'm not in a hurry."

"What is that supposed to mean?"

"Exactly what I said. I am not in a hurry to sell."

"I have some money invested in this house and I need it now!"

He flicked to yet another channel.

"Then I suggest you contact a solicitor."

I realised there was no point discussing it further.

"You know, you are a right bastard!" I said, and left him.

I went back to the guest room and locked the door. Fully dressed, I fell onto the bed and, not knowing what else to do, I lay there for a long time, various scenarios churning in my mind and not one solution in sight, until eventually I fell into a restless, disconcerted sleep.

***

When I awoke the next morning, I was still wearing my day clothes. I glanced at my watch and noted that it was nearly 9 o'clock, late enough for Mark to have left for work. The thought of him brought back all the unpleasant feelings of the previous night and I sunk back into despair, flustered and not sure what to do for the best. Forcing myself, I climbed out of bed, crossed to the window and peered out to check if Mark's car was still parked outside. The car was gone, which meant I was alone in the house and free to do as I pleased.

Unlocking the door, I made my way to the bathroom, undressed and stepped into the shower. For a while, I stood under the cascade of pleasantly warm water, hoping to rinse the stress away. The water was very relaxing and gradually I began to feel better and more prepared to face the day ahead. I washed and, with a towel wrapped around my body, I padded back to the guest room. Dropping the towel onto the bed, I slipped into a pair of sweatpants and a T-shirt, and clipped back my hair. I found my flip-flops under the bed, put them on and went downstairs to the kitchen.

My stomach felt knotted and I couldn't face any food, so I just made myself some milky coffee. With the hot cup in one hand and my mobile phone in the other, I headed for the conservatory to work on my painting, as I was burdened with a strange urgency to finish it as soon as possible.

Approaching the easel, I suddenly stopped in shock. There, right across the canvas, was a large, smudged question mark in bright red oil paint. The only person who could have done it was Mark and, even though I had already stopped expecting that he would be reasonable, I was still appalled that he could be that mean. He had simple-mindedly destroyed all the hard work I had put into my painting and I was infuriated. Why did the bastard have to do that? What was he trying to achieve? If he wanted me out of the house, he was certainly going the right way about it, for I did not want to stay even one more night under the same roof as him.

I grabbed my mobile and dialled Jason's number.

"You'll never guess what that bastard, Mark, has done!" I cried, upset. "The man is despicable. He is mean and horrible, and I hate him!"

"Carrie, please calm down and tell me what has happened," Jason said placidly.

"I can't calm down," I snapped.

"What has he done?" Jason asked patiently.

"The bastard has destroyed my painting of the cosmos, that's what! I am furious," I said nervously, moving away from the damaged canvas. I couldn't look at it any longer, for it was too painful. "It's obvious I can't paint in this house any more. I might as well move out."

"The question is, are you ready to move out?"

"I hoped I wouldn't have to, but now I feel I have no choice, even though I don't exactly know where to go. I can't very well set up a studio in my parents' house," I said, more calmly.

There was a short break in our conversation, and then Jason said, "I might be able to come up with a solution. Give me an hour and I'll call you back."

"Please don't take too long."

"An hour at the most," he promised, and the line went dead.

Totally frustrated, I went into the living room. I dumped the phone on the coffee table, flopped onto the sofa and picked up the previous day's newspaper. Quickly scanning the news section, I noticed a small article about an earthquake that had occurred about 45 miles north of Tehran the previous morning. Thirty-five people were killed and 400 injured. That read, my eyes moved to another small article in the top left-hand corner, which informed the readers that the country's biggest union planned a series of co-ordinated UK-wide strikes by public sector workers in a campaign to defend their pensions. I scanned a few more articles, all equally depressing, and closed the paper, glancing through the front page and the article announcing that last-minute talks were to be held in a bid to avert the planned 24-hour strike on the London Underground and head off travel chaos. The word 'chaos' resonated in my mind. It seemed like the perfect word to describe today's life on Earth.

I folded the newspaper and put it away. I did not have the patience to read any more and I did not have enough optimism to cope with more depressing news. For a moment I sat still and could feel that my energies were all over the place. I knew I needed to do something to calm down and find my equilibrium again. To this end, I decided to do some yoga breathing exercises designed to calm the body.

In the meditation room, I put on some tranquil music and sat on the mat in the lotus position. Closing my eyes, I tried to empty my mind by breathing deeply into my stomach and visualising the movement of energy. With the in-breath I visualised pulling all my scattered energy into my calm inner centre and with the breath out I visualised letting go of all the stress and negativity. Gradually, I began to relax ...

All of a sudden, I could see a ball of very bright white light and could clearly hear some words. I grabbed pen and paper and started writing:

"Nearly all of you have heard the predictions of Earth changes and most of you have taken them with a grain of salt, so we are here to assure you that the changes have begun and they are well and truly on the way. The odd weather patterns, volcanic eruptions, earthquakes, floods and other unusual events will be occurring with ever-increasing intensity as the planet Earth cleanses itself of thousands of years of neglect and abuse, and it will continue to do so for as long as it takes to awaken within people the love and respect that are necessary for its survival. Every single inhabitant of the planet is in some way responsible for the current neglect and exploitation, even if only by being passive and unconcerned. As in a very popular saying, 'What shall you sow, so shall you reap', Planet Earth has began to even out the score. It's time for you to learn from your past mistakes and expand your understanding, to open your eyes to what's happening around you and what's happening to the planet that sustains you. Instead of living in fear of Earth's anger, try to change your ways and work towards the planet's renewal...

"Some of you are too preoccupied with your own concerns and will miss the calling, but we hope that many will respond in a positive way. You have lived for too long in separation. You separated yourselves from the planet that

nourishes you and now it's the time to evolve and unify. It's the time to start communicating with Earth and allow this beautiful planet to teach you how to live in harmony. It's the time to awaken your responsibly to your planet and begin to give back what has been taken away. Those of you who don't understand the importance of this task will isolate yourselves even further and will no longer be able to be sustained by the planet's energies. For those, the future is grim. For all the others, the future will bring light and cosmic understanding, and open the path to the new worlds of the cosmos. It's time to make your choice."

The faint sound of my mobile broke my concentration and I lost the connection. I rushed to the living room and grabbed the phone from the coffee table.

"Hi, babe," Jason said jovially. "I have a solution to your housing problem and I hope you'll approve."

"What's your solution," I asked, moving the phone to the other ear.

"I've spoken to my father and he is perfectly happy for you to move into his parents' house. The house is located roughly five miles from Dorking, which is only a short drive away from where you are now."

"Jason, I can't live with your grandparents!"

"You won't have to, because they don't live there. My father's mother died eight years ago and his father passed away over a year later. The house has been empty for the last seven years and it's all yours."

"I can't afford to rent the whole house," I objected.

"You can because it's not going to cost you anything apart from utility bills."

I wasn't quite sure I'd heard him correctly.

"Are you saying I won't need to pay any rent?"

"Yes, you can live there rent free," Jason confirmed.

"I can't possibly accept it," I said stubbornly.

"Yes, you can. The house has been deteriorating for years. You will be doing my father a big favour by looking after it."

"Is that what he said?"

"Not in so many words, but I know my father," Jason assured me. "He wants this house off his back."

I hesitated. It was probably an ideal solution, but for some reason I couldn't make up my mind.

"I don't know ..."

"Before you decide, I think you should see the place."

"All right," I agreed. "When can I see it?"

"Today. I'll pick you up in 45 minutes."

* * *

An hour later we were driving towards Dorking. The sun was shining and the countryside looked beautiful reflected in its light. We drove through little picturesque villages and open spaces with large fields on either side of the road, looking like patches of different hues of yellows, browns and greens and broken only by an odd cluster of trees here and there. I felt totally uplifted by the lovely views of the English countryside. Planet Earth was truly beautiful, I decided, and it was very important that we did not allow it to be destroyed completely.

We passed Dorking town and about ten minutes later Jason turned into a small country road.

"The house is at the end of this road," he informed me. "It's quite secluded."

A moment later, I spotted the house in the distance. For some reason I expected it to be a small building and I was quite surprised to see a rather large, two-storey extensive structure. The house looked very majestic and I felt a stirring of excitement.

My spirits slumped as soon as we drove closer, however, and I saw the state of the building and the surrounding gardens. The house seemed solidly built, but it looked very neglected, the white paint dirty and chipped in places, exposing the brickwork. There were some slates missing from the roof and others were cracked and had bits broken off. The large windows were covered in dirt and grime, and dark curtains were hanging randomly as though torn away from the rails. The window frames, which were once painted bright yellow, and the front door once bright green, looked dull and dirty, and the paint was peeling off, adding to the overall state of neglect. My father would have had a fit if he could have seen the state of the surrounding gardens. All the bushes and plants were overgrown and the whole garden was covered in weeds. I was beginning to dread what I would find inside.

"I know it doesn't look too great at the moment," Jason said, parking the car, "but with a little work it can be improved."

This was the understatement of the year!

"A little work?" I questioned, raising my eyebrows.

"Well, maybe more than a little," he admitted. "Don't get discouraged until you see the whole place. Come, I'll show you around."

We left the car and headed towards the main entrance. Jason unlocked the front door and I carefully followed him through a dark, wide corridor to the front room.

The room was very spacious with a high decorated ceiling. It was unfurnished apart from two old, dark couches resting against the walls. The walls were covered with dirty yellow wallpaper that was peeling off, and strips of it were hanging down from the ceiling. The windows were large and smudged with grime; in fact everything seemed to be covered in grime and dust.

"It needs a bit of cleaning, then it'll be fine," Jason said, trying to be positive.

I couldn't have disagreed more.

"Where is the kitchen?" I asked, keen to leave the dirty room.

Jason led me to the kitchen, which was located behind the other front room on the left side of the house. As expected, the kitchen was dirty and dilapidated. The units were old and dark, and some of the doors were hanging off the hinges. There was an old cooker and a free-standing fridge, which stood in the corner of the room with its door wide open. The ceramic sink had brown stains from dripping water and needed a good scrub.

"I am not a good cook, but even I can't see myself cooking here," I said, becoming more and more discouraged.

"It'll be a nice big kitchen once we clean and paint it," Jason said, ever the optimist.

"Is the whole house like this?"

"I'm not sure, as I haven't been here for ages. Why don't we go upstairs and see the rest of it?"

Upstairs were three large bedrooms and a bathroom. The large rooms were empty apart from dirty carpets and curtains. The bathroom, like everything else, was in a need of a good clean. There was one more room downstairs and a small toilet, both as bad as the rest of the house.

"What do you think?" Jason asked hopefully.

"It's a big, spacious house, but I can't possibly live here," I answered truthfully.

"Carrie, ever since I suggested this house as a solution the only two words I have heard are 'I can't'," Jason said, frustrated. "I know the house is not in perfect condition, but it's free and with some work it can be turned around. Can you imagine having all this space to yourself? Can you imagine being free and not having to worry about some bastard sneaking up on you when you are asleep?"

He was right, of course, but so much needed to be done and I couldn't possibly do all the work on my own.

"This house needs months of hard work to turn it around," I said pointedly.

"Not if we have help."

"I can't afford to pay for help."

"Here you go again. How about changing it to 'I can'?"

I smiled. "I can listen to your suggestions."

"Good. I've already spoken to Mike, who is a very good decorator by the way, and he is willing to help. He also has friends who will be only too happy to come here and work for a good meal."

"You mean they would all do it for nothing?"

"It's going to cost you the price of a good meal," he said, taking my hand. "Come, I'll show you something."

He led me outside onto a big wooden veranda that extended the full width of the house at the back.

"Wow!" I breathed, stunned by the absolutely breathtaking view of the surrounding countryside.

To our left, all the way to the veranda, was a small forest full of coniferous trees, growing a fair distance apart and creating a beautiful, shaded space with specks of soft sunlight shining through the branches and lighting up the soft carpet of dry needles and cones. Straight ahead, through a wide opening, there were large, open fields, creating an impression of never-ending space. To our right were tall bushes and more trees, enclosing the place and making it very private.

"My grandparents bought the house because of this land," Jason said. "The house is called Woodland and comes with acres of land."

I could imagine myself relaxing outside on the veranda or walking through the forest, and I knew that there was something very special and magical about the place.

"Just before you called I received a message from the Masters about the need to unify with our planet," I said. "It's strange, but it feels like this is the very best place to connect and appreciate the true beauty of this planet. The house itself seems secondary."

Jason faced me. "Does that mean you will move in?"

"There isn't even a bed in this house," I said hesitantly.

"A bed can easily be organised," Jason countered.

"I need other furniture as well."

"We'll find whatever you need."

I was wavering.

"I need help with cleaning."

"I'll help you clean."

I wrapped my arms around him and smiled gratefully.

"You have an answer to everything, don't you?"

"Yes," he said, hugging me. He kissed my ear. "You don't know it yet, but you'll be very happy here."

We stood for a while, snuggling into each other and breathing in the fresh country air. It was very calm and peaceful around us and the only sound that could be heard was the twittering of birds. At that moment I knew, without a shadow of a doubt, that it was the right place for me, and my mind was made up. I lifted my head.

"I want to move here as soon as possible."

Jason smiled. "Is tomorrow soon enough?"

"Tomorrow is fine on the condition that you help with cleaning and organise a nice double bed for us."

He kissed the tip of my nose.

"Consider it done."

I looked straight into his eyes.

"I love you," I said quietly.

"I love you too, babe," he muttered, and kissed my lips tenderly.

Contented, I snuggled closer to him. Life was changing for the better. I had a new home, a gorgeous man at my side and at that point I considered myself very lucky indeed.

10

The following morning, I waited for Mark to leave the house before I ventured out from my room. The plan was set. Jason was hiring a van to help me move all my things to Woodland and I was to do all the packing. We had agreed that Jason would bring the van over around 1 o'clock, so I had only a few hours to collect my things together and pack them.

I had a quick breakfast of cereal and then searched through the cupboards for some bin liners. Equipped with a roll of heavy-duty bags, I headed back to the guest room. I tore a few liners away and neatly folded all my clothes into them. That done, I selected fresh bed linen, towels, pillows and some blankets, and dropped them into more bin bags. Next, I collected all my things from the bathroom and put them in a carryall together with the contents of my dressing table. There were other personal things in the drawer of my bedside cabinet and I pulled it open. As soon as I opened it I realised that the crystal was missing. I sighed deeply in frustration, knowing full well that Mark had taken it. Suspecting he had hidden it somewhere in the house, I began searching for it. I didn't have much time to spare, so I only checked all the obvious hiding places - the crystal was nowhere to be found.

Resigned, I checked the time. It was already after eleven, so I had no choice but to give up the search and return to my packing. I grabbed the bin bags containing my belongings and carried them downstairs. I made a few trips up and down until they were all stacked in the hall and then I went to the garage to look for a large cardboard box. Luckily, I found one and used it to pack some plates, glasses, cutlery, the kettle and various utensils. I left the box in the kitchen and went to the meditation room where I collected all the books and secured them with string. I carried them together with the stereo into the hall and deposited them next to the bags, adding the vacuum cleaner, iron, ironing board and the cleaning materials to the growing pile. As the very last thing, I packed all the painting materials into a small box and placed both next to the stack of canvases I planned to take with me.

I checked the time again. I had half an hour left. Looking at the damaged painting of the cosmos, I realised that the paint was still wet and I could probably save it. Quickly, I fished out a scraping tool from the packed box and carefully began scraping off the red paint. I was removing the last bits of it when I heard the doorbell. I rushed to the door and let Jason in.

"All packed?" he asked.

"Yes, apart from the crystal, which seems to have mysteriously disappeared."

Jason gave me a surprised look. "What do you mean, disappeared?"

"It's not in the drawer. Mark must have taken it."

"It might still be in the house. We must look for it."

"I have looked everywhere I can think of. No luck. If it's here he's hidden it very well."

"We can't leave it with him. We must find it," Jason said worriedly.

"There's no time now," I replied. "We have to take my things to Woodland. You can drop me back here afterwards and I'll have another look."

"In that case you had better leave your car here."

"That's no problem. I will."

Jason looked at the pile of my belongings.

"Is that all?"

"No, there's more stuff in the studio."

"Let's start shifting this lot," he said, lifting a heavy black bag and opening the front door.

One by one, we carried all my things to the back of the van. The damaged painting of the cosmos was the last thing to be put in. Jason laid it very carefully on top of the soft bags and secured it with boxes on either side so it wouldn't move during our journey.

"Are you sure you've got everything?" Jason asked.

"I hope so. I can't think of anything else I should be taking," I replied, and then I thought about Mark's television set. "We could take the television set."

"Television set might be useful," Jason said encouragingly.

I smiled mischievously. "Mark is going to be lost without his television, so let's take it. It'll be a small but very gratifying revenge for taking my crystal."

While Jason carried the set to the van, I had one final look around the house. Perfectly satisfied that I had everything I needed, I locked the door and left.

"Have you got your passport, driving licence, chequebook?" Jason asked, as soon as I climbed into the front seat of the van.

I nodded. All my documents were in my handbag. He started the engine.

"Okay, time to go. We have a lot of work to do," he said, pulling away.

The drive to Woodland took about 25 minutes. Jason parked the van in front of the house and switched off the ignition.

"What's the plan of action?" he asked, facing me.

"I think we should clean and vacuum at least one room before we unload," I said practically.

"How about we clean one of the front rooms?"

"One of the front rooms would be fine," I agreed, reaching for the door handle. "Come on. Let's get whatever we need."

We alighted from the van and walked to the back door. Jason opened it wide.

"Have you managed to sort out the bed?" I asked, looking for the bag with the cleaning materials.

Jason grabbed the vacuum cleaner.

"Yes, it'll be here at four."

"Excellent," I said with a grateful smile.

I found the right bag and we carried all the cleaning stuff to the front door. Jason unlocked it and dumped the vacuum cleaner in the hall, and we carried the rest into the kitchen.

"I hope we can find some large plastic containers here," I said, looking inside the cupboards.

"I think there are some in the shed. I'll go and have a look," Jason said, and disappeared.

I continued searching in the kitchen and making a mental list of the jobs that needed doing in order of priority. First, the cupboards and cooker needed to be scrubbed inside and out, then doors needed to be fixed, worktops bleached and the sink descaled. The fridge was big and in good condition, but it needed to be cleaned and well disinfected. It was disconnected, so I pushed the plug into the socket and switched it on. The light inside didn't come on. I was looking for other switches when Jason came back with a small plastic bowl and a bucket.

"Will these be okay?' he asked.

'Perfect," I said, adding, "I don't think this fridge is working."

"I'll have a look at it later," Jason said, handing me the plastic containers.

I filled them with water, added some detergent and grabbed a bottle of Jiff and some cleaning cloths.

"Which front room are we cleaning?" I asked, handing the bucket to Jason.

"The room next to the kitchen used to be the dining room. The other room used to be the living room. I think it makes sense to clean the living room."

"Okay, let's clean the living room," I agreed, and headed for the front room on the opposite side to the kitchen, Jason following behind. It was the room with the two dark sofas.

"I think we should clean the windows first, then vacuum, then clean the skirting," I suggested, "and these filthy curtains need to be removed."

"I'll take them down," Jason offered, and he climbed onto one of the sofas, reached up to the rail and began unhooking the dirty fabric.

"Try not to shake them too much as they're full of dust," I said, and went to get some bin bags.

We deposited the old curtains into a large bin bag and then

embarked upon washing the two big windows. Jason washed one and I washed the other, using the backs of the sofas for support to reach the higher level. Next we vacuumed the carpet and furniture, and washed the skirting. When all the basic cleaning was finished we brought in all my stuff and piled it up on the floor with the exception of the canvases, which we stacked against the walls.

I checked my watch and discovered that it was already half past three.

"The bed will be here in half an hour," I exclaimed, suddenly concerned that we were running out of time. "We need to clean at least one of the bedrooms before it arrives."

"We'll do what we can," Jason said, reaching for the vacuum cleaner.

Upstairs, I examined all three bedrooms and particularly liked the one overlooking the forest. It was also the biggest of the three.

"This room will be perfect for the master bedroom. What do you think?"

"I agree," Jason replied. "Do you want me to take the curtains down?"

"Yes please, and maybe you could vacuum while I clean the window."

The curtains had been removed, the room vacuumed and most of the grime cleaned from the window when the delivery van arrived. Jason went downstairs to let the delivery men in. They carried a large wooden frame up the winding staircase into the bedroom and put it flat on the floor and then went down to collect the mattress. They brought it up, dropped it on the top of the bed frame and left.

The bed wasn't brand new, but the mattress was firm and clean. I flung myself on top of it and was really surprised how comfortable it was.

"Where did you get this fantastic bed?" I asked Jason.

"It was easy," Jason replied. "It decorated one of the rooms in my father's house."

I lifted my eyes in shock. "You took this bed out of your father's house?"

"It's all right. Nobody will miss it."
"I hope your father knows about it," I said, rising.
"He does and he is happy for you to have it."
"He is? Really?"
Jason nodded.
"Your father is a very generous man. I am beginning to really like him."
"I don't think you'd like him if you met him," Jason said, and checked his watch. "We need to go. I have to return the van."
"Okay. Let's go," I said, heading for the door.

* * *

Half an hour later, Jason stopped the van outside my house.
"I am going to spend about an hour looking for the crystal, then I'll go back to Woodland," I said.
Jason nodded and handed me the house keys.
"I should be back by six."
I gave him a peck on the cheek.
"I'll see you later," I said, and climbed out of the van.
I let myself into the house and stopped in the hall, trying to figure out where Mark could have hidden the crystal. I knew it wasn't in the bedroom because I had checked every possible hiding place there earlier. It was very unlikely that it was hidden in the guest room or bathroom. I figured that if it was in the house it had to be somewhere downstairs, so started my search in the living room. No luck there, so I moved to the kitchen. I searched through every cupboard and corner, but again, no luck. I didn't want to waste any time searching through the conservatory or the meditation room as it didn't make sense for him to hide it there. Instead, I had a quick look in the utility room and garage. I couldn't see it anywhere. Feeling totally discouraged, I scribbled a short note to Mark informing him that I had moved out and leaving him my mobile phone number with the request to call me urgently. Putting the note on the kitchen table, I left the house and made my way to my car.

I started the car and followed the road to Dorking. Ten minutes into my journey I was passing close to Zoe's house, and on the spur of the moment decided to pay her a visit.

Parking outside, I walked to the front door and pressed the doorbell. Nobody responded so I pressed it again. This time I heard the sound of footsteps approaching and a moment later the door opened a crack and Zoe's eyes peered through the narrow gap between the door and the door frame.

"Hi," I said. "Can I come in?"

The door opened wider. Zoe was clad in a white towelling robe and her face was covered in a thick, green beauty mask. She pointed to the mask.

"Can't speak," she mumbled, doing her best not to move her face muscles.

I stepped inside.

"I won't be long and you don't need to speak," I said, following her to the living room. "I popped in because I have some news to share."

"You're not pregnant?" she mumbled, perching on a soft chair.

I sat on the edge of the couch.

"No. The news is that I have left Mark and moved into a different house."

"You moved out?" Zoe exclaimed, despite the restricting effects of the drying clay on her face. "Wait, I need to wash my mask off."

Getting up, she rushed to the bathroom. She came back quickly, her face only partially cleaned, smudges of green still visible around her hairline and ears. She flopped down next to me.

"Tell me what happened," she demanded.

"Mark has been making my life hell and I really have had enough of him and his attitude, so I've moved out," I filled her in briefly.

"I am disappointed. I thought you would come and stay with me."

I touched her hand.

"You're a good friend, Zoe, but I couldn't impose on you like that. I needed to move somewhere where I could set up a studio, and I've found the perfect place."

"Where?"

"I have moved to a very big country house near Dorking. The house needs a lot of work, but the location couldn't be better. It's quite secluded and is surrounded by a beautiful forest and open green fields."

"It sounds great," Zoe said with more enthusiasm. "How did you find it?"

"Actually, I didn't, Jason did ... sort of. It used to belong to his grandparents."

"And nobody lives there?"

"No. The house has been empty for years," I said. "You must come and see it."

"Of course I will," Zoe said, reaching for a piece of paper and a pen. "Give me your address and I'll pop by tomorrow."

Not sure of the Woodland's address, I drew a diagram of how to get there and said, "Mark doesn't know where I'm living, so please don't tell him." I got up. "I have to go. I've got masses of cleaning to do."

Zoe walked me to the door.

"I'll see you tomorrow," she said, pulling on the latch.

I gave her a quick hug.

"Make sure you come," I said, and I headed back to my car.

* * *

Back at Woodland, I let myself in and looked around. Now that I was familiar with the place I could see beyond the dirt and grime. The house was solidly built with brick internal walls and very spacious rooms with high ceilings. Every room had large, tall windows, which filled the house with masses of light. The two front rooms still had the original marble fireplaces and the toilet and bathroom still had the original brass fixtures and hand-painted, multicoloured ceramic tiles. Throughout the house the doors were tall and heavy and had solid brass handles. In the middle of the extensive hall was a wide wooden staircase, which looked quite grand and added a lot of style to the place. The house was, in fact, rather beautiful and I was grateful to have the opportunity to live there.

Without wasting any more time, I picked up a bucket, scouring cream and a bottle of bleach, and made my way to the bathroom. I scrubbed and cleaned until Jason arrived.

"Carrie, come down," he called up the stairs. "I brought some food."

"I'll be down in a minute," I called back.

I pulled off the rubber gloves, washed my hands and hurried downstairs. Jason was in the kitchen and he was holding a brown paper bag. I could smell freshly fried fish.

"Fish. Great."

"I got you a plaice," he said. "I hope that's all right."

"Plaice is fine. I'll get some plates," I said, disappearing into the front room to rummage in the cardboard box for some plates and cutlery.

"I'll wait on the veranda," Jason called after me.

I found some plates and forks, and went outside through the back doorway onto the veranda. Jason was sitting on the wooden steps, which led from the veranda to the back garden, gazing ahead. I sat next to him and followed his gaze to the vast open space that spread out before us, and the warm orange glow in the far distance created by the sun slowly moving towards the horizon. The evening was warm and the air was fresh, scented with the aroma of drying grass and wild flowers.

"This place is magnificent," I said, handing Jason a plate and fork.

"Yes, it is." Jason passed me a hot paper wrapper containing fish and chips. "Have you found the crystal?" he asked.

"Nope," I said, unwrapping the greasy paper, "but I am sure Mark's got it."

Jason transferred his fish onto his plate with a fork.

"How can you be sure?"

"I'm sure because I know that he took it only to upset me and he will keep it as long as he thinks that it's something I care about."

"Then it's very unlikely he'll ever give it back to you," Jason reasoned.

"I don't know, he might. I left him my mobile number and I plan to ask him about it as soon as he calls," I said, adding emphatically, "The only thing I know is that he is not keeping my crystal. Somehow or other I'll get it back from him."

"I hope you will," Jason said, then he changed the subject. "I spoke to Mike. He'll be here tomorrow after lunch. His friend David is coming with him."

"I hope it doesn't mean I have to cook a big fancy dinner," I said, putting a chip into my mouth.

"We'll just heat up some ready-made stuff."

"Only if the oven is working."

"Good point," Jason said. "I'll check it after we've eaten."

It was quite dark by the time we had finished eating. Back in the house, I checked all the lights and discovered that there were no lights in the kitchen, downstairs loo, main hall and one of the rooms upstairs.

"I think I've seen some candles in one of the cupboards," Jason said, and began searching for them. He found a whole pack of them in the cupboard under the sink.

"Good. We've got candles, but what about matches?" I asked.

"It's too dark to look for them now," Jason decided. "I'll drive to the off-licence down the road and get some."

"All right. I'm going upstairs to finish the bathroom."

He gave me a peck on the cheek.

"Happy cleaning," he said with a smile, and headed out.

As soon as he had left, I found the bag containing the bedding in the living room and carried it upstairs into the bedroom. I had made up the bed by the time Jason returned.

"I'm back," he called.

"Could you please check the cooker," I called back. "I shouldn't be too long."

I ran my hands over the duvet to smooth it out and then made my way to the bathroom to finish the cleaning. I washed the sink, scrubbed the loo and washed the floor, and only after I had disinfected everything was I satisfied that the room was clean enough to be used. That done, I went downstairs to the kitchen, which was now properly lit. Jason was examining the back of the fridge, a large toolbox next to him.

"How did you get the lights to work?" I asked, pleased.

"I changed the bulbs. I found some spare ones in one of the drawers."

"Very clever," I said with a smile. "I assume you found all these tools as well."

"Yes, I found them in the shed."

"Very useful. So what is the state of the cooker?"

"The cooker works fine. Just needs cleaning."

I smiled again. "How did I know you were going to say that?"

"Sorry, babe, I know it's a nasty job. I'll help you when I've finished with this fridge," Jason said, and then pointed to a white carrier bag on the worktop.

"I brought some tea bags, sugar and milk."

"Fantastic. I'll make some tea," I said, and went to find mugs and the kettle.

Back in the kitchen, I boiled some water and brewed tea in the mugs. I dropped a teaspoon of sugar into Jason's mug and handed it to him.

"Is the fridge going to work, do you think?"

"I hope so," he replied, sipping the hot liquid.

"I hope so too. It looks like quite a new fridge," I observed.

"It is. My father brought it here a few months ago." He put his mug down and returned to the fridge, checking all the cables.

Sipping my tea, I leant against the worktop, watched him working and marvelled at how resourceful and capable he really was. He appeared to be able to find solutions to most of the problems, and having him around was a blessing. It was great to be with him in the house. We could relax and do whatever we liked without anyone interfering in our lives. It meant total freedom and I couldn't ask for more.

My thoughts were interrupted by a flicker of light inside the fridge as Jason found a loose connection at the back of the box.

"Another ten minutes and it'll be working," he announced.

"While you are doing that I'll clean the sink."

I put my mug down, grabbed a bottle of scouring cream, squeezed a big splodge inside the sink and began scrubbing the grime away.

By 11 o'clock the fridge was fixed, the sink and worktops around it were clean and we were both totally exhausted. There was nothing else we felt capable of doing, so we got washed and went to bed.

I turned off the light, climbed under the duvet and cuddled up to Jason. He kissed the top of my head.

"It's your first night in this house," he muttered. "How do you feel?"

With Jason next to me, the challenge of turning that house around did not seem quite so daunting any more; in fact, in some strange way, I was looking forward to it.

"It feels really good to be here," I said honestly.

"I'm happy to hear it." He kissed the top of my head again. "Let's go to sleep. We've got another busy day tomorrow."

"Goodnight, sweetie."

"Goodnight, babe."

Relaxing in each other's arms, we fell into a restful and contented sleep.

* * *

I half opened my eyes, glimpsed the streams of soft sunlight that had entered the room and realised that it was already morning.

"What time is it?" I mumbled to Jason, who was lying beside me.

Sleepily, Jason checked his watch. "Quarter to nine."

Immediately, my eyes were fully open.

"What time are Mike and David arriving?" I asked.

"They should be here by 2 o'clock," Jason replied, pulling me closer.

"We have to go shopping."

"Shopping can wait," Jason muttered, kissing my face.

I wanted to stay in bed with him, but we had nothing in the house - no food, no drinks, no decorating materials - so unfortunately shopping was the priority.

"No, darling, it can't," I said, giving him a kiss on the lips and getting out of bed. "Come on, get up and get ready."

We washed and dressed, had a quick breakfast of cereal and coffee, and were soon in Jason's car driving towards the nearest shopping area. Our first stop was a DIY store. We spent about half an hour there and ended up buying paints, paint rollers and brushes, various fillers, a few bags of wallpaper glue and packs of different grades of sandpaper. We dropped all the stuff into the boot of the car and drove to a small high street shop, which had a good selection of wallpaper. I looked through all the samples and chose pastel yellow wallpaper for the living room and a two-toned light green design for the dining room. All the decorating materials taken care of, we drove to a supermarket and filled a large trolley to overflowing with different foodstuffs and drinks.

Satisfied that all the shopping was done, we returned to Woodland. Jason parked the car close to the front door and we carried all the food shopping into the kitchen and deposited it on the worktops. I looked at the sad state of the kitchen.

"This kitchen is unusable," I observed with slight panic. "The cooker is filthy, the fridge needs cleaning and the floor is disgusting. How am I supposed to prepare meals in here?"

"You're right, you can't," Jason conceded.

He reached into his jacket pocket, pulled out his mobile and dialled Anna's number. When she answered, he briefly explained the situation to her and asked if she could come over and help with the cleaning. She readily agreed. Jason gave her directions and hung up.

"Anna should be here within the hour."

"Thanks, sweetie," I said gratefully, and then realised that this presented another difficulty. "Where are we all going to eat? With Mike, David and Anna arriving we need some sort of table."

"I could go and get one from Ikea," Jason offered.

Extracting two sandwiches from a shopping bag, I handed one to Jason.

"How are you going to bring it here? Our cars are too small to carry a table."

"I'll borrow Mike's van when he arrives," Jason said, biting into his sandwich.

There was a moment of silence while we ate, and then I said, "When you finish eating could you unload the rest of the stuff, please. I need to start on this fridge."

Jason nodded. "I'll do that and then I'll start sorting out the dining room."

"That'll be great," I said, finishing my sandwich.

As soon as Jason had left, I put on the rubber gloves and started cleaning and disinfecting the fridge. The whole job took the best part of the next hour. I was squatting down in front of the freshly cleaned fridge unpacking some of the groceries when Anna entered the kitchen, followed by her dog.

"Hi," she said in greeting.

Lifting my head, I pushed a strand of hair from my face.

"Hi."

"So this is your new kitchen," Anna said as she scanned the room. "I can see why Jason said you needed a hand."

I placed a large chicken in the fridge.

"I am so grateful you could come. Jason's friends are arriving today to help with redecorating and I am supposed to cook meals for them in this kitchen. I need all the help I can get." The dog came over to me and sniffed. "Hello, Harry," I muttered, stroking him. "You can probably find a lot of very enticing smells here."

"He'll be begging for food. I'd better take him outside," Anna said.

"Let him out through the back door and leave the door open in case he wants to come back in," I advised.

"Harry, come," Anna called, and she left the kitchen, the dog following in her wake.

She was back within minutes. "Harry seems to like your veranda, so I left him there," she said and then added, "What can I do to help?"

"I need to unpack all the groceries, so could you please start cleaning some of the cupboards?" I requested.

Anna walked over to the other side of the kitchen and pushed in one of the broken cupboard doors, trying to close it, but the door wouldn't stay shut.

"We need a man to fix these doors," she declared.

I turned to her. "There are two capable men on the way or you could ask Jason."

"Jason seems very busy in the front room, so we'll probably have to wait for the two capable men to arrive." Anna put on a pair of rubber gloves, filled a bowl with water and began cleaning the units. "I don't know how you feel, but I think these units are too dark and dreary. A lighter colour would immediately brighten up the room."

I ran an appraising look around the kitchen.

"I agree," I said, and examined one of the doors. "These doors are made from solid wood and I'm sure that the dark coating can be easily stripped."

"Let's do it."

Anna sounded enthusiastic.

"It's not a quick job," I warned.

"I know, but it's definitely worth doing. I will do it if you'll let me."

"You've got a shop to run."

"I have a good assistant," Anna replied with a smile. "Besides, I'd much rather be here with you guys."

"If you're sure ..."

"I'd be happy to do it. Really."

I smiled. "Okay. You've got yourself a job."

At this point there was the sound of a car horn outside.

"I think the two capable men have arrived," I said.

Jason came into the kitchen a few minutes later.

"Mike and David are unloading," he announced. "As soon as they finish I'll go to Ikea to get the table."

"Are they staying overnight?" I asked, knowing they had a long drive home.

"I think it's best if they do. They won't be able to do much today as it's nearly 2 o'clock."

"In that case, can you also get a couple of light duvets and some pillows, and perhaps a few large towels, please."

"Sure. Anything else?"

I thought for a moment.

"We need large cooking pans and a roasting tin, a dustbin and a drainer for dishes."

"I'll get what I can. See you both later," he said, and he had gone.

I turned to Anna. "I hope you'll stay for dinner?"

"I'd be happy to."

I picked up a carrier bag full of groceries.

"I am planning to roast a chicken, but to be quite honest I've never managed to get it quite right. Could you help? I wouldn't want to scare the boys off with my cooking."

"Of course I'll help," Anna said reassuringly. "Chicken is my speciality."

Mike entered the kitchen.

"Hi, ladies," he said cheerily, and waited for his friend to emerge from behind the door before introducing him. "This is David, the much-needed painter and decorator."

David was tall and handsome. He had longish blond hair, hazel eyes and a suntanned complexion. His cheeks were high, his jaw square and his teeth white and even. His body was strong and athletic, well-developed muscles protruding through the tight T-shirt he was wearing. He could easily have been mistaken for a sportsman if it wasn't for his rather pasty and dry decorator's hands.

Anna stopped cleaning and smiled.

"I am Anna. Nice to meet you both."

"I am Mike."

"And I am Carrie," I said, completing the introductions. "Would you guys like a drink?"

"Something cold would be nice," Mike said.

"I've got fresh orange juice," I offered.

"Sounds good to me."

"David?"

"Orange juice is fine, thanks."

I poured two glasses of the orange liquid and handed them to Mike and David. Mike drained his glass in one big gulp and put it on the worktop.

"We are ready to start," he announced. "What needs doing?"

"Could one of you help with these doors?" Anna requested, pointing to one of the doors that hung loosely on its hinges.

"I am sure we can fix it," Mike said. "Looks like the screws just need tightening."

"Who is better with a screwdriver?" I asked both men.

They exchanged a questioning look.

"I think that'll be me," Mike said. "David is better at decorating."

"Mike will sort out the kitchen doors," David decided. "I'll start with the redecorating."

I turned to David. "Could you start in the living room?"

"Sure, no problem," David said, agreeably. "Where do you want me to move all the stuff?"

"The plastic bags need to go upstairs to the bedroom. Sofas, canvases, books and the small boxes can be moved into the hall, and the large box needs to come here," I requested.

"Mike, come and give me a hand," David said, and both men left.

Anna followed them with her eyes and then faced me.

"Isn't David dishy?"

I nodded. "Very."

"Have you noticed his muscles?"

"Mmm ... Huge."

"He probably eats a lot," Anna said, with a smile. "We need to make sure there's enough food for dinner."

"There could be a problem," I said lightly. "I only bought one large bird."

"Then the bird needs to be well stuffed," Anna said, and we both burst out laughing.

Mike came back, pushing the large cardboard box in from of him.

"I didn't realise I was so funny," he said jokingly.

Anna scanned him with her eyes.

"Funny? Maybe not, but you're definitely cute," she said with a smile.

"Cute sounds good," Mike responded, and pushed the box close to the wall.

Anna peered into the box.

"You'll be even cuter if you fix the kitchen units. We need to unpack this lot."

"Anything for the nice lady," Mike said, reaching for a screwdriver from the toolbox that stood on the floor by the fridge.

With a big smile on her face, Anna returned to cleaning while I began scrubbing the cooker and Mike concentrated on readjusting of the loose door hinges. We worked in silent harmony for the next hour or so, making impressive progress. Soon the kitchen units were fixed, the cardboard box was unpacked, the cooker was gleaming and the floor had been cleaned and mopped.

"I'll see you ladies later," Mike said, and went to help David with the stripping of the wallpaper in the living room.

Anna and I started dinner, doing all the preparations on the freshly cleaned worktop.

"It would be nice to have a small table here," Anna commented.

"We're strapped for cash at the moment," I said, "but maybe Jason can make one from the wood outside."

Anna stopped scraping a carrot.

"I know someone who loves working with wood. I'll talk to him," she offered.

Things were falling into place quicker than anticipated. So many people were willing to help and the progress within even two days was amazing. I couldn't help but think about the three basic rules of the universe, and specifically about the rule of co-operation. It seemed that when people co-operated together the available energy was multiplied, thus producing astonishing results. A person working alone was limited in what he or she could achieve, but a number of people, all with different abilities but working together towards the same goal, could achieve a lot more. If the motivation of each person involved came from within rather than being fuelled by material or financial gain, the energy was unadulterated and the results were nothing short of remarkable.

"It's amazing how everything falls into place here," I commented.

"It's obviously meant to be," Anna said, dropping the last bit of carrot into a saucepan.

The vegetables were prepared and waiting in the saucepans to be cooked. There was nothing left for us to do until Jason arrived with the roasting tin, so we went outside onto the veranda. I sat on the wooden steps and Anna sat next to me. Harry shuffled over and rested his head on her lap.

"It's very beautiful here," Anna remarked, stroking the dog.

"I think there is something very special about this place, but I am not quite sure what it is," I mused.

"There seems to be so much darkness everywhere around us, but this place is different," Anna observed. "It feels uncontaminated, almost as if it has been spared human interference."

"Yes," I agreed. "That's what it is - no human interference."

"You have to make sure you keep it that way. It will be like a tiny oasis of light in the sea of darkness that our planet has become."

"You are quite right. The planet is totally enveloped in darkness at this time, but things are changing and people like us are here to help penetrate the darkness and low frequencies, and bring in some light."

"It seems like an enormous task," Anna said.

"I know, but we have no choice but to go forwards," I replied. "The process has already started and nothing can stop it now. Each and every person is going to be affected by the current energetic changes in some way, and if someone feels lost and is searching for light we are here to guide them. Planet Earth is changing from the planet of darkness into the planet of light. People who are unable to connect to this light may not be able to survive."

"Does that mean everyone has to make a choice between light and darkness eventually?"

"Yes. The planet's energies are changing with ever-increasing speed, forcing people to reassess what's important and to make choices."

"I think there is a lot of confusion in people," Anna commented.

"That's not surprising, as people's minds have been manipulated for centuries and they are used to others telling them what to do and think. Until they learn to think for themselves they will be forever confused. Various things will be happening around them and their confusion will grow even more if they continue to look to other people for the answers."

"I know what you mean. Everyone has a different theory about things and nobody really knows the correct answer. If you listen to all these different theories you end up more and more mixed up."

Our conversation was interrupted by Zoe, who suddenly appeared on the veranda.

"Hi," she said happily. "Who is that gorgeous hunk in your front room?"

I turned to face her. "I think you are talking about David."

"I hope I am. Who is he?"

"He's a friend of Mike, who's a friend of Jason, and he is here to help with the redecorating." I got up from the steps. "And this is Anna."

Zoe extended her hand to Anna and introduced herself, then she turned to me and said, "Mark is going frantic. He called me six times yesterday demanding that I tell him where you are. Apparently you don't answer your phone."

I realised I had completely forgotten about my phone, which was buried somewhere at the bottom of my handbag.

"I am sure he will call again," I said, not at all sorry to have missed his calls. "What do you think of the house?"

"The place does need a lot of work, but hey, if you can find gorgeous men like David to help you sort it out who cares if it needs masses of work," Zoe said, and then added, looking around, "Oh God, Carrie, all this beautiful space. You are so lucky."

"Yes, I know," I said cheerfully. "I am doubly lucky. I've got this house and a wonderful man as well."

"I hope you're talking about me," Jason said, from the doorway.

I smiled happily. "Of course, who else?" I crossed over to him and threw my arms around his neck. "Did you buy a table?"

He pecked my forehead. "Yes, a dining table with an extension and eight chairs."

"Great," I said, pleased. "What about a roasting tin?"

"I got a big one. It's already in the kitchen," Jason replied. "How much time do I have to put the table together?"

"About two hours."

He kissed my lips and gently removed my arms from around his neck.

"I'd better go and start on it." He waved to Zoe. "Hello, Zoe."

She waved back. "Hi."

"See you all later," he said, and disappeared inside.

"Let's go and roast that chicken," I said to Anna. "Zoe, are you staying for dinner?"

"Is David staying?" Zoe asked with a mischievous smile.

"Yes, he is," I replied.

"Then I will definitely stay."

"I hope you'll help."

"Sure, I'll help."

In the kitchen, there were some Ikea boxes and carrier bags piled up on the floor. We opened them and found plates, glasses, cutlery, various pans, a roasting tin, a set of sharp knives and many different storage containers, plus some tea towels and two pairs of oven gloves.

"All the stuff we need to run an efficient eatery," Anna commented lightly.

Zoe looked confused. "What do you mean? Surely you're not planning to run an eatery here?"

"Sort of," Anna replied with a smile. "We're going to cook meals for the boys."

"Oh, I see. But as much as I'd like to impress one particular boy, I can't say cooking is my forte," Zoe admitted. "Carrie, I think you need to find me something else to do."

"Are you any good at sewing?" Anna asked.

"Quite good actually," Zoe replied. "What sewing do you have in mind?"

"The living room needs a new set of curtains," Anna said, adding Lightly, "You could ask David to help you measure up."

Zoe smiled, quite pleased with the idea.

"Carrie, do you have any fabric I could use?"

I shook my head. "I am afraid not."

"I'll get the fabric tomorrow," Anna offered.

"Fine," Zoe immediately agreed. "Is gorgeous David going to be here tomorrow?"

I smiled. "We'll make sure he is."

"Then, I'll start tomorrow," Zoe declared, "as long as Anna gets the fabric."

"I'll get it first thing tomorrow morning," Anna promised, "but now we need to wash all these plates, cutlery and glasses so we can use them for dinner."

"Zoe, can you help with the washing up?" I asked.

"Why can't Anna do it?" Zoe replied rebelliously.

I looked at her in surprise. "Why do you think Anna should do it?"

"She seems to be much better in the kitchen than I am."

"That's silly. You don't need any special skills to wash a few dishes," I pointed out, "and you promised to help."

"I'd be perfectly happy to help with something else."

"If you're going to help, you have to help with the washing up I'm afraid."

"To be quite honest, I'm not that keen on doing all this washing up."

"Would you be more keen if we asked David to help you?"

Zoe's eyes lit up. "Definitely."

"That means you don't really want to help," I concluded. "You're perfectly happy to leave all the work to us unless David is around so you can make big eyes at him."

Zoe took a moment to think.

"Oh, all right, I'll do the washing up."

"There's no point if you're doing it for all the wrong reasons," I said rationally.

"I'm sorry. I've been acting like a spoilt brat," Zoe responded humbly. "I'll do it because I want to help you."

I smiled and handed her a tea towel. "I'll wash, you dry."

Anna stuffed the chicken with garlic, coated it with oil, sprinkled on mixed herbs, put a few blobs of butter on top and covered it with foil. She dropped the prepared chicken into the roasting tin and carefully placed it into the hot oven.

"One hour and 30 minutes," she announced, and grabbed a tea towel to help Zoe dry the dishes.

We worked in total harmony, and half an hour later all the dishes were washed, dried and stacked neatly on the worktop. Zoe seemed very pleased with herself.

"I'm sorry for being such a pain earlier."

I hugged her. "If you're still coming to work on the curtains tomorrow, I promise no kitchen duty," I said lightly.

Zoe smiled. "It's a deal."

In the dining room the windows and skirting had been cleaned and the carpet had been vacuumed. The new antique stained table and matching chairs had been assembled and stood in the middle of the large floor surface, the chair seats covered with blue and white striped pads. The room was still relatively bare, but it looked more like a proper dining room.

When dinner was ready, Zoe and I set the table and Anna brought the food in.

The men went upstairs to wash and when they returned we took our seats. Jason sat at the head of the table. I took the seat next to him on his right and next to me sat Anna. Mike and David sat opposite us and Zoe placed herself next to David.

I turned to Jason. "Sweetie, could you carve the chicken, please?"

"Sure," Jason said, reaching for the carving knife and fork.

While we were waiting for the chicken to be carved, Zoe looked at David and said, "So where do you live?"

"In Swindon," David replied.

She smiled pleasantly. "Wiltshire? You must have seen a lot of crop circles?"

"Quite a few, yes."

"Have you seen the one on Milk Hill, directly below the White Horse? It looks a bit like a flying bee or some other insect with open wings."

"I've only seen a picture of it."

"It's magnificent, don't you think?" Zoe asked, and smiled again.

David gave her a sexy grin. "Quite amazing."

"The chicken is ready for eating," Jason announced, placing the carving knife and fork on the side of the serving plate. "Please help yourselves."

Zoe helped herself to a few slices of meat and resumed her conversation with David.

"What do you think about crop circles? Do you think they could be hoaxes?"

"Some of them are, for sure," David said, filling his plate with vegetables.

"Some of them are," Jason interjected, "but most of them are too intricate and complex to be dismissed as hoaxes."

"You believe that they are made from outer space?" David asked.

Jason nodded. "There is no other logical explanation," he said, filling his glass with water.

Mike reached for a bowl of carrots. "I must admit I am more inclined to agree with you," he said, putting a spoonful of the vegetable on his plate. "They are getting more complex and it's hard to accept that they are man-made and even harder that they are created by odd weather patterns."

"You must have seen the one that was recently created at Silbury Hill," Zoe said.

"You mean the one with the Ancient Egyptian mosaic in the centre and the symbols from the Mayan Calendar around the rim?"

Zoe nodded.

"I have seen it and it's nothing short of remarkable. The fact that it has been created in two stages adds to the mystery," Mike said. "Do you know that the Mayan Calendar predicted the end of the world in 2012? It's interesting that there is reference to it within this formation. It's as though someone is trying to remind us that time is running short."

"Very spooky," Zoe said. "People talk about the Mayan civilisation. Do you think there have been other civilisations inhabiting this planet before us?"

"Good question," Mike replied. "Do you think there have been other civilisations?"

"I don't know, you tell me," Zoe retorted.

"Of course there have been other civilisations on this planet before ours," Anna said. "I don't understand how so many people have been brainwashed into accepting that the history of this planet goes back only a few thousand years and nothing existed before that."

"It's convenient to ignore the past because we simply have no answers," Jason said.

"And we don't question," I added. "We just accept what is being taught to us by others who essentially are limited in their own knowledge. Fortunately, this will change. The new energies will slowly open our memory banks and we will discover that, in fact, the history of this planet goes back millions of years and that great civilisations have come and gone, and been forgotten."

David reached for his glass of water. "So you too believe that there have been other civilisations on this planet?"

I nodded. "Human legends and mythology talk of one or more technologically advanced civilisations that existed on this planet before the dawn of recorded history. These civilisations equalled or surpassed our own in many ways and there are many examples of this in the fragments of Mayan and Egyptian history we've managed to piece together."

"What I don't understand is why historians have failed to recognise or identify these ancient civilisations if they existed," David said.

"Historians and scientists are looking for concrete physical evidence and it's difficult, if not impossible, to piece together such evidence from a very remote past, especially if it is buried deep in the ground or under the sea," I replied.

"If we believe Plato, a great civilisation was swallowed up by a gigantic cataclysm 9,000 years or so before his time," Mike interjected.

"We might believe him, but orthodox historians will not accept it because they would have to resign themselves to the fact that all their work might possibly be wrong," Jason commented.

"Why argue over it?" Anna joined in. "There is proof of past civilisations. There are physical monuments and structures that have survived like Mayan buildings or the three great pyramids at Giza."

"Egyptologists believe that they were built as the tombs of three pharaohs of the fourth dynasty of Egypt, which dates between 2613 BC and 2494 BC," Mike said. "This doesn't exactly prove the existence of another civilisation."

"We don't know if they were built as tombs," Anna said. "No pharaonic burial has ever been found inside any of the three great pyramids and they contain no inscriptions that would suggest that they were originally built as tombs."

"That's true," Mike agreed. "I go for the theory that they were constructed by astronomers because of their very precise alignment to the true north, south, east and west. You can't get such an accurate alignment without precise observational astronomy."

"Supposedly the pattern of the three great pyramids on the ground is extremely similar to the three belt stars of the constellation of Orion, which might confirm the astronomers' theory," Zoe said.

Jason wasn't happy with this explanation. "Not necessarily."

Zoe and Mike looked at him, waiting for an explanation.

"There is no proof that they were constructed by astronomers, and no proof that they are the product of a very early stage of Egyptian civilisation," he explained. 'But this just shows how little we know. To this day no one knows who built the pyramids and in which epoch they were built. Wouldn't you consider this strange, knowing that the Great Pyramid is the biggest monument that has ever been built on Earth? Granted, it's geometrically and mathematically complicated. Some of the blocks are over 65 feet long and weigh nearly 2,000 tons, and they were lifted and fitted together to the nearest thousandth of an inch. We have no idea how it was done and scientists haven't got a clue either, and yet we are arrogant enough to think that we are the only intelligent beings in the whole universe."

"Maybe we are not the only intelligent beings in the universe," Mike said. "There are theories that the pyramids were built by aliens."

"There are also theories that they are a product of another civilisation," Anna said.

"Either way, we don't know," Jason concluded.

Anna faced me. "Carrie, what do you think?"

"I'm not sure. All I know is that the only way to discover the truth is through direct access to the living library."

"How do you access the living library?" Zoe enquired.

"You do it by raising the frequency of your body and harmonising your energies with the energies of the cosmos."

Zoe lifted her glass. "We should start organising harmonisation sessions," she said, and sipped some water.

"What do you mean by a harmonisation session?" Anna queried.

"Oh, did I say harmonisation? I meant meditation, which when you think about it is exactly the same thing," Zoe said. "Why don't we organise a group meditation outside?" She smiled at David and then added, "It'll be nice to exchange energies and connect to nature."

Everyone agreed that it was a good idea and it was decided that Zoe would organise the meditation session the following day before lunch.

When dinner was finished, the men returned to the living room to tidy up while Zoe, Anna and I cleared the table and carried all the dirty dishes to the kitchen. Anna filled Harry's bowl with the leftovers and took it outside. Zoe and I were left to do the washing up.

"You and Jason seem very close," Zoe commented, picking up a freshly washed plate from the drying rack.

I reached for another dirty plate. "Yes, we are."

"You've been very lucky to have met him before you married that horrid Mark," Zoe said with a touch of jealousy. "I wish I'd met a man half as gorgeous as Jason."

"What about David? Don't you like him?" I asked, putting a clean plate on the drying rack.

"I think he's adorable, but I don't even know if he likes me."

"He seemed quite interested in you during dinner," I said encouragingly.

"He wasn't."

I handed Zoe a wet plate. "I noticed that he smiled a lot in your direction."

"I smiled a lot at him and he smiled back," Zoe said lightly, wiping the plate with the tea towel. "Do you really think he likes me?"

"I'm sure he does."

Zoe smiled mischievously. "I hope you're right because if he doesn't make a move tomorrow I certainly will."

Anna came back and helped us with the rest of the washing up. As soon as the dishes were done, Zoe said her goodbyes and left. Anna stayed long enough to help me to organise the beds and then she also left. There were four of us left in the house. Mike and David settled on the old sofas in the living room and Jason and I made our way upstairs.

Jason went to wash and left me alone in the bedroom. I was sitting on the bed, brushing my hair, when I heard the muffed sound of my mobile. Quickly, I fished it out of my handbag.

"Hello, Mark," I said, knowing it was him.

"At last. Why don't answer your phone?" he asked accusingly.

I sighed. It seemed that he was in the mood for another argument.

"Where are you?"

"I think it's better if you don't know."

"Are you hiding from me?"

"I moved out," I said calmly. "I thought that was what you wanted."

"That's not what I wanted, and you know it."

"Pity, it looks like I've got it all wrong," I said sarcastically, "but while I have you on the phone I want to ask you something."

"Ask away."

"Why did you take my crystal?"

"I told you I didn't want radioactive junk in the bedroom."

"I think you took it because you knew it would upset me."

"Don't be ridiculous."

"I know you by now. You do a lot of things just to upset me."

"You're wrong."

"No, I'm right," I said firmly. "What have you done with the crystal?"

"It's in a safe place."

"I want it back and I also want the money you owe me."

"Why is it that every conversation I have with you eventually leads to money?"

"Because you are holding on to my money and refuse to be fair about it," I snapped. "You just want to be as obstructive as possible."

"Obstructive?" he shouted, upset. "You're the one who left."

"And you're the one who made it impossible for me to stay in the house," I countered.

"If you're talking about your bloody painting, I just wanted to bring you back to your senses."

"What's that supposed to mean?"

"What does it mean? You were painting bloody aliens for God's sake!"

"Since when do you have to approve of what I paint?" I demanded, annoyed.

"I did it out of concern," he said, more calmly.

"You destroyed my work out of concern?" I asked, confused.

"I'm sorry, I didn't want to make you mad," he muttered. "Can you come over so we can talk?"

"What about?"

"About money, what else?"

"You mean you're willing to discuss it fairly?"

"That's exactly what I mean."

"And you're going to return my crystal?"

"Yes, you can have it back."

Against my better judgement I said, "Okay."

"When will you come?"

"I'll call you."

"When?"

"Soon."

"How soon?"

"I don't know. I'll call you when I have some free time."

"I'm not prepared to wait forever."

"You won't have to. Bye," I said, and disconnected the phone.

Agitated, I dropped the phone back into my handbag, climbed into bed and waited impatiently for Jason. I needed him close to feel that everything was all right. I needed him to put his arms around me so I could forget about Mark, money and every other silly problem that occupied my mind. When he eventually came in I lifted the cover and he climbed into bed beside me. I cuddled close to him and rested my head on his shoulder. All of a sudden I saw an image of my mother, but it disappeared quickly.

"I need to call my parents," I muttered, as it suddenly occurred to me that they couldn't contact me and didn't know where I was. "Is it very expensive to call Spain from the mobile?"

"Don't worry about the cost," Jason said, and then added, "I think we should connect the landline anyhow. There is already a BT connection in the house. I'll investigate it tomorrow."

I lifted my head. "Thank you, sweetie," I muttered, lightly touching his lips with mine. "Are you tired?"

"That depends."

I stroked his back. "Too tired to make love?"

"Never too tired to make love."

I kissed his lips tenderly and whispered, "Please make love to me."

"With pleasure," he said, lifting the blanket.

He pulled my nightdress off and sliding down my body softly kissed my bare flesh. I allowed myself to become completely lost in his lingering kisses and tender touch, and I was soon begging for more. We joined together and he made love to me slowly and gently, the exquisite pleasure gradually building up until it came to a peak and exploded in the most wonderful release. Totally spent, I waited for Jason to cover me with the duvet and take me in his arms, as I knew he would.

I quickly fell asleep, blissfully peaceful, curled against his beautiful naked body.

11

I was awakened by a noise, which I was sure had come from downstairs. I cuddled closer to Jason and he opened his eyes.

"Did you hear that noise?" I muttered. "Mike and David must be up already."

"I suppose we need to get up as well."

"Yes," I said, not moving. "I have to feed the workmen."

"And I promised to help them," Jason said. "Who's the first to the bathroom?"

"It'll have to be me," I said, giving Jason a kiss and getting out of bed.

Twenty minutes later I was dressed and ready to start the day. Once downstairs, I popped into the living room where Mike and David were filling various holes and dents in the wall with white filler. Their sheets and blankets were neatly folded away and piled up on their respective sofas, which were moved out of the way and now stood by the window.

"Good morning," I said cheerily. "How was your night?"

Mike looked down from the ladder. "Mine wasn't too bad, but I think David, being the big man that he is, found the sofa a little too small."

"It wasn't too bad," David muttered, mixing more filler.

"Probably it wasn't too good either. I'll try to organise something more comfortable for you next time you're here," I promised. "Any special orders for breakfast?"

"Whatever's going," Mike replied for both of them.

"It'll be something simple."

"Toast and tea will do for me," David said.

"I think I can manage to scramble a few eggs," I said with a smile.

In the kitchen, I put the kettle on then stacked some plates, cups and cutlery on a tray and placed it on the worktop. I cut a loaf of bread into thick slices, scrambled some eggs and brewed a large pot of tea. I carried the whole lot, together with boxes of cereals and a jug of milk, into the dining room and called everyone in.

I had managed to set the table by the time the men came in. They seemed keen to progress with their jobs, so breakfast was eaten quickly without much conversation other than about basic plans for the rest of the day. After breakfast, the men returned to the living room and I was left to clear the table and wash up.

The day was sunny and warm, so after I had finished tidying up I got my exercise mat and went outside to practise yoga. I placed the mat on the wooden surface of the veranda and settled in the lotus position, facing the fields. The air was clean and fresh, and everything around me was very peaceful. I sat motionless for a while, enjoying the natural beauty that surrounded me and the stillness and purity of the land, which gave me a great sense of well-being. Taking a few deep breaths, I tried to connect to the Earth's energies and as I concentrated on the energy flow I heard Amos speaking to me:

"You are currently in a very special part of the planet and it's not by accident that you found yourself there. The area is relatively free from any contamination, and as your group of like-minded people grows, they will have an opportunity to benefit from the energy of the place and learn very different values. Each and every one of you has a choice. You can either respect this small piece of land and benefit from its unadulterated beauty or you can choose to neglect it and miss the opportunity to establish the connection to the planet even if only in a small way. Saying that, it is important that you understand that by respecting and honouring this very special place you channel positive cosmic energies and spread light throughout the whole area. This in turn brings about the rise in surrounding frequencies and creates a change in the whole environment. You think the place is beautiful now. We can assure you that it will be much more beautiful when you learn to connect to this land through the frequency of love, because when you do this the land will respond by supporting you with its own pure energies. Remember, this land should not be allowed to be contaminated by people who show disrespect towards the planet and towards their fellow humans, as any contamination will lower the overall

frequency of the place. We understand that people are not always easy to read, so if in doubt, ask. We know what everyone thinks and feels, and we are always here to advise you."

The communication was interrupted by Harry, who quite unexpectedly appeared by my side and began tugging at my T-shirt. I untangled my legs and stroked the dog. He ran to the door and stood there, wagging his tail enthusiastically and looking at me, as though waiting for me to follow him.

"Okay, I'm coming," I said, and followed him into the house.

Harry led me to the dining room where I found Anna stacking flat packages on the table.

"I think your dog decided that I needed to see you," I said lightly.

"Clever dog. I sent him to look for you," Anna said, tearing some wrapping paper off. "I want you to see the fabric that I bought for the two curtains. I hope you like what I've chosen,"

I touched the silky golden fabric. "It's perfect," I said gratefully.

"I also bought beige cotton lining. I think it will look really nice with the silk."

"It'll look fantastic," I said. "I don't know how to thank you."

"There's no need to thank me. I'm happy to help," Anna said, pushing the packages to the end of the table. "What's the plan for today?"

"I would like to spend the morning outside, so I was thinking about doing some work in the garden, maybe planting some herbs," I said. "How do you feel about helping me?"

"I'd love to."

"Do you know anything about planting herbs?"

"I know that it's too late to plant seeds. It'd be better to plant growing herbs. I think we should go to the garden centre and buy boxes of different herbs ready for planting."

"Good idea. Let's go outside and find the best place to plant them," I said, heading for the front door.

"They will need sunshine and well-drained soil," Anna advised, as we looked around.

I pointed to a small piece of grassed land in front of some shrubs.

"I feel they'll be happy there."

"I'm sure they will," Anna agreed. "We'll just have to trim back the shrubs to create more light on the ground."

"Do you mind doing the trimming?"

"Not at all."

"Cool. You can trim the shrubs and I'll turn the soil," I decided. "Let's check the shed for some gardening tools."

In the shed we found a spade, fork, rake, shears and some gardening gloves. Carrying all the tools, we returned to the chosen patch. I marked out the size of our herb garden and we set to work. While I was removing the stones and other debris, pulling out the weeds and turning over the soil, Anna was cutting back the overgrown shrubs. Two hours later we stopped and assessed the fruits of our labour. We had a perfect patch of dark, soft soil, ready for planting, with neatly cut bushes at the back.

It was time to go to the garden centre and purchase the herbs. Anna wanted to make sure Harry was all right before we left, so we went looking for him. We found him on the veranda lazily lying in his basket. Anna told him to stay there and we made our way to her car.

In the garden centre we headed straight for the area with small plants and herbs. There were many different varieties of herbs, but being practical we settled on the ones we were most likely to use in the kitchen, such as basil, bay, marjoram, parsley, rosemary, dill and thyme.

On our way out, Anna stopped by the garden furniture and insisted on buying a set with garden tables and folding chairs.

"I can't allow you to spend all this money," I said to her.

"You need garden furniture," Anna argued. "Everyone will be happy to spend more time outside and they can't do it if there is nothing to sit on."

At that moment I realised that the house was not going to be exclusively mine. It was to be shared with others and everyone should be able to benefit from the available space.

"I'll let you buy it if you promise to treat the house as your own," I said with a grateful smile.

Anna smiled back. "I already treat it as my own."

Anna paid for two large wooden folding tables and eight folding chairs. We packed our shopping into the boot of her car and headed back to Woodland. When we arrived, Anna drove to the side of the house and parked the car as close as possible to our planting patch. We unloaded all the pots and trays of herbs, and carefully placed them on the ground ready to be planted. All the herbs unloaded, we began to pull out the garden tables and chairs. Anna suggested we should stack them on the veranda, so we grabbed two chairs each and marched with them to the back of the house.

As we climbed onto the veranda, Anna noticed that the dog's basket was empty.

"Where is Harry?" she questioned. "It's not like him to wander off."

"He must be around," I said, resting my chairs against the wall of the house.

Anna added hers, then called, "Harry!" She whistled, then called again, "Harry!"

The dog was nowhere to be seen, so we went into the house to look for him. We entered the front room where Mike and David were papering one of the walls.

"Have you seen Harry?" Anna asked anxiously.

"No," Mike replied.

David shook his head. "Me neither."

"Where the hell has he gone?" Anna wondered aloud.

Jason came in carrying more rolls of wallpaper.

"Have you seen Harry?" Anna asked him.

"I saw him running after your car," Jason informed her. "I called him back, gave him some food and he settled down on the veranda."

"Well, he's not there now," Anna said, sounding really worried. "God only knows where he is."

"Don't worry, we'll find him," Jason reassured her, and he began organising a search party. "Mike and David will look in the forest, I'll look in the fields at the back and you and Carrie can check the front garden and the road."

We all went outside and soon separated, following different

directions and calling the dog's name.

"I should never have left him," Anna fretted, as we searched the front garden. "What if he's got lost or been run over by a car?"

"Please stop worrying,' I said calmly. "I'm sure we'll find him."

Anna wasn't convinced. "He could have followed my car all the way to town."

"Dogs have a very strong sense of smell and they always find their way home," I tried to reassure her.

But Anna was far from reassured. "They also get killed in road accidents."

We followed the country road for about 15 minutes and then decided to check the fields and bushes on either side of the road closer to Woodland. We searched for about an hour, but failed to find Harry. It was pointless to keep searching the same area over and over, so we elected to go back to the house and see if someone else had found him. Mike and David were sitting on the front steps. They shook their heads to let us know they hadn't located the dog. Jason was still in the fields, searching.

Anna was slowly losing hope. "I don't think we'll ever find him," she moaned, wiping a tear from her cheek. "Harry doesn't know this area and he could be anywhere."

I put my arm around her shoulders and squeezed her comfortingly. "Jason might still find him."

Jason returned a short while later, his face forlorn. Anna questioned him with her eyes and he shook his head negatively.

"How could I have been so stupid as to leave him on his own in a strange place?" Anna whined, tears pouring down her face.

At that moment, I spotted a figure of a man in the distance. He was approaching in our direction and seemed to be carrying something furry in his arms.

"Look!" I exclaimed, "I think that man over there has Harry."

As the man came closer, I realised that the furry animal he was holding was covered in blood, and my heart sank. Anna spotted it too.

"Oh no!" she cried in alarm. "He's been hurt."

"Is this your dog?" the man questioned, pointing to the bundle of fur with his chin.

He was wearing well-worn jeans, a brown and white checked shirt, soft hat and Wellington boots, and looked like a local farmer. He had thick, unruly, greying hair, a heavy moustache and soft green eyes. He looked as though he was in his forties.

Anna wiped a tear from her face with the back of her hand. "Yes," she confirmed weakly. "Where did you find him?"

"In a rose bush in my garden," the man replied. "Something must have frightened him and he hid there. He has some cuts and scratches, but otherwise he seems fine."

Gently, Anna took the dog from him, and Harry whimpered.

"Thank you for bringing him back. I hope you didn't have to come a long way," Anna said.

"No, my farm is across the main road," the farmer replied. "Are you new here?"

"Yes," I said. "We moved in last week."

The man looked across the five faces. "How many of you live here?"

"Just two," I replied, not wanting to alarm him. "The other three are friends."

The man nodded. "If you need any eggs or milk, come to my farm and ask for Joe."

"Thank you, Joe," I said pleasantly. "We certainly will."

As soon as Joe had left, I rushed into the house to get some cotton wool and tea tree lotion for cleaning and disinfecting Harry's wounds, and as soon as I found them I hurried back out. Anna was sitting in one of the garden chairs on the veranda with Harry on her lap.

"Look what you've done to yourself, you silly mutt," she muttered tenderly, relieved to have the dog back. "We'll have to clean your wounds, so stay still!"

I soaked a ball of cotton wool in the green liquid and began gently cleaning the blood and scratches on Harry's body, head and ears. Once he was cleaned up he looked much more like himself. He had a few visible scratches on his head, but most of them were hidden beneath his fur.

"I hope he's learnt his lesson and he's not going to run around the countryside any more. Living in the city, the poor mutt doesn't know that a rose bush is spiked with thorns," Anna said, gently stroking her pet.

"We'll have to keep a closer eye on him," I said, closing the bottle of lotion.

There was the sound of a car's horn.

"I think that might be Zoe," I said.

A few minutes later Zoe appeared on the veranda.

"I'm sorry I'm so late. I was planning to leave earlier, but Vicky came over and I couldn't get away ..." She paused when she noticed Harry's scratches. "Gosh, what happened to you, Harry?"

"He ran into a wild rose bush," Anna replied. "The poor thing is still recovering from the shock."

"Silly little thing. Is he going to be all right?"

"He'll be fine."

Satisfied with the answer, Zoe changed the subject.

"I brought my sewing machine with me and I am very keen to start on the curtains. Anna, have you bought the fabric?"

"Yes, it's on the table in the dining room. I also bought some cotton for the lining. I hope you don't mind the extra work."

"I don't mind at all, so long as I get some help." Zoe turned to me. "Carrie, can you spare David to help me with the sewing?"

Anna gave her a strange look. "I thought David was a painter and decorator."

"He seems like a clever boy," Zoe said flippantly. "He can learn another skill."

I smiled. "Somehow, I don't think he'll be too happy to learn sewing."

"Maybe not, but still, I'm sure he'll be useful in other ways."

"Undoubtedly," Anna said.

Zoe checked her watch. "It's nearly 2 o'clock. What about the meditation? Are we going to do it?"

"Not now," I replied. "We need to organise some lunch."

"Haven't you eaten yet?" Zoe seemed surprised.

"No, we spent most of the afternoon searching for Harry."

"With all this excitement I completely forgot about food," Anna admitted. "The boys must be hungry."

"Don't worry. We can quickly prepare something."

"Do you mind if I don't help you?" Zoe asked. "I'd like to start on the curtains."

I gave her a knowing look. "Start on the curtains, or start chatting up David?"

Zoe didn't answer, just smiled mischievously.

"I'll be in the living room," she said, and disappeared into the house.

I turned to Anna. "Let's organise something to eat."

Anna put Harry into his basket and followed me to the kitchen. I opened the fridge and stared at its contents.

"I think we should make some sandwiches," I suggested.

"Best solution," Anna agreed, reaching for a loaf of sliced wholemeal bread while I pulled out cold meat cuts, a big pack of Cheddar cheese and some salad vegetables.

We were busy making sandwiches when Zoe called, "Carrie, come here for a moment. I need you to decide on the length of these curtains."

I dropped the buttering knife onto the cutting board and went into the living room. Zoe was standing on the back of the old sofa, holding the silk fabric against one side of the metal curtain rail. David was helping her by holding the other end of the fabric high up against the wall.

"Do you want the curtains to go all the way down to the floor, or maybe we can cut them shorter and just cover the window?" Zoe enquired, gathering the fabric and pulling it higher to demonstrate the different look.

"Definitely down to the floor," I decided.

"Agreed," Zoe said.

Everything then happened very quickly. Zoe wanted to release the fabric, but it was tangled behind the rail and as she pulled at it she lost her balance and grabbed the metal rail to steady herself. The bracket, which was holding it in place, pulled itself from the wall, leaving Zoe with no support and wobbling unsteadily on the soft back of the sofa. David caught her just in time, but ended up being whacked across his shoulder with the rail.

"Ouch!" he yelled in pain, and nearly dropped her.

"I'm really sorry," Zoe mumbled in shock, as he lowered her to the floor. "I didn't mean to do that."

David let go of her. He massaged his shoulder, his face twisted in pain. "I hope my bones are not broken."

"Why don't you take off your T-shirt and let me have a look?" Zoe suggested, looking concerned.

Carefully, David removed his T-shirt and tossed it onto the sofa.

"You have a nice, strong body, well capable of coping with a small accident like this," Zoe observed.

He looked straight into her eyes. "You think so?"

"I know so." She touched the inflamed spot gently. "Does it hurt?"

He gave her another admiring look. "What do you think?"

She ran her hand over his arm up and down. "I think it's fine."

"Why don't you check it properly?"

"I will. Sit down."

Obediently, he perched on the edge of the sofa.

"I'll be very gentle," Zoe promised. She rested one hand on his shoulder and began slowly rotating his arm with the other. "You'll be pleased to know that nothing is broken."

"Are you sure?" he asked with a sexy smile.

"Positive, but let me do a gentle massage on your shoulder to improve the circulation."

"Sounds like a good idea."

"I'll get my massage table and oils from my car," she said, letting go of his arm.

He grabbed her hand and stopped her from moving away.

"I think that perhaps you owe me a full body massage for all the pain you've caused me."

"You'll miss your lunch."

"No problem. I'll eat later."

They seemed so preoccupied with each other that they had completely forgotten that I was there. Not wanting to interrupt them, I quietly left the room and went back to the kitchen.

"Looks like we've lost two people for lunch," I said to Anna.

Anna gave me an amused look. "Is Zoe monopolising David?"

I nodded. "And he seems very happy to be monopolised. I think a full body massage was on offer."

Anna smiled. "Who would have thought that within minutes curtain sewing could turn into a full body massage?"

I smiled back. "When it comes to men, Zoe can be very resourceful," I said, and reached for my buttering knife.

We finished the sandwiches and took them to the dining room where Jason and Mike were removing the old wallpaper. The door to the living room was closed, so I didn't even bother to call Zoe and David to join us.

"I wonder what those two are up to in the living room?" Mike asked, biting into his sandwich.

"I think Zoe is giving David a massage," I replied.

"Looks like we've lost a worker," Mike commented to Jason with a knowing smile.

Jason wasn't sure. "You think so?"

"What would you prefer, peeling wallpaper off the walls or enjoying a sensual body massage?"

Jason laughed. "Now, that's a difficult question."

"We definitely know what David prefers, so for the time being it's just the two of us."

"Then we'd better get back to work," Jason said, finishing his sandwich.

"Yeah," Mike agreed, switching on the steamer.

"We'll leave you to it," I said.

Anna and I collected the plates and carried them to the kitchen.

"I'll start stripping the kitchen units," Anna decided, depositing the plates into the sink.

"And I'll go and start planting the herbs," I said.

Outside, I stared at the small patch of turned soil and tried to decide how to do the planting. I resolved to avoid straight lines and rigid rows, and began planting randomly, taking care to place the bigger herbs at the back and the smaller ones in front of the patch, and allowing sufficient space between them for growth. When all the herbs were planted, I watered the soil, loosely covered it with wood shavings to keep the moisture in and stood back to admire the final result. My little garden looked pretty neat and I was sure my father would be proud of my efforts.

I was still staring at my accomplishment when Jason came over and hugged me from behind.

"How is my very special gardener?" he muttered, kissing my ear.

I turned around and kissed him on the lips.

"Your very special gardener is rather proud of herself. She planted a lot of herbs that can be used for cooking."

"Very practical," Jason said admiringly. "Talking about the cooking, Anna is stripping the units in the kitchen and the room is full of toxic fumes. How about we order pizza for dinner?"

"You have the best ideas." I removed a piece of wallpaper from his hair. "Who's going to collect the orders and call for a pizza delivery?" I enquired.

"I will," Jason offered.

I gave him another kiss. "Thanks, sweetie."

"What would you like?"

I thought for a moment.

"Small vegetarian pizza with extra cheese, please."

"Vegetarian it is." He brushed some loose hair strands off my face. "I'll see you later," he said, and headed back into the house.

Pleased that I did not have to do any cooking, I spent more time weeding and tiding up the area around the herb garden. I found gardening very relaxing and for the first time I understood why my father had such a passion for it. There was something very satisfying about being in touch with the planet by digging into its soil, planting various living things in it and watching them grow into beautiful plants, flowers and vegetables, knowing that they could only grow because the planet had nourished them with its own energy.

It was nearly 6 o'clock when Anna called me in to see the results of her efforts. She had managed to strip three units and they were now the golden shade of natural wood.

"What do you think?" Anna asked, waving a paintbrush in the direction of the stripped units.

"They look really good," I said, pleased with the result.

"I think we should paint a narrow lime green line around the doors and just finish them with clear vanish," Anna suggested.

"That's a terrific idea," I said excitedly, visualising the final effect. "We should definitely do it."

Anna smiled. "It looks like I've just got myself another job."

"Only if it doesn't interfere with your life," I said.

"The most important part of my life is to be here with you," Anna said.

I hugged her. "I'm very happy you're here and you can stay as long as you like."

She hugged me back with one arm. "Thanks. I appreciate it."

"Do you know what's happening with dinner?" I asked, moving away.

"Jason has already ordered some pizzas. They should be delivered soon."

"Then we need to set the table."

"It's such a nice evening. Let's set it up outside by the forest trees," Anna suggested.

"Okay, I'll go and start on it," I said, and headed towards the veranda.

Outside, I unfolded one of the garden tables, put it on flat ground between the trees and placed the chairs around it. Anna brought out plates, glasses, cutlery and napkins, and we set the table for six and decorated it with leafy tree twigs from the forest.

A delivery man on a scooter with a large box attached to the back arrived with our pizzas and drinks, and we all sat down to eat. Opening the boxes one by one, I cut the food into portions.

Zoe helped herself to a small slice of vegetarian pizza. "I hardly ever eat fast food, but for some reason I knew I would be eating pizza today," she announced cheerfully. She seemed to be in a very good mood.

Mike gave her a strange look. "Maybe that's because Jason was collecting orders for pizzas?"

Zoe was unfazed. "No, I knew it this morning."

"Zoe has a sixth sense," David laughed, pouring coke into his glass. "I only wish she had sensed she would hit me with a curtain rail before it happened."

"I hope you're not making fun of me," Zoe admonished. "For your information, it has been proven that humans have a sixth sense - and that includes me."

"How?" Mike asked, biting into his food. "We've already established that scientists only consider physical evidence and are not interested in exploring the non-physical."

"They managed to prove it by conducting physical tests," Zoe informed him.

"This will be interesting," Mike said, with a touch of sarcasm. "What exactly have they managed to prove?"

"Apparently they carried out more than a thousand experiments and they discovered that people could tell when someone was watching them."

"How?" Mike asked again.

"They put two people into different rooms - let's call them A and B. A could see B on a CCTV monitor and B had no idea that he could be seen. The scientists attached electrodes to B's skin, which showed a reaction every time he was being watched. This proves that somehow he could sense it."

"Remarkable," Mike said, tucking into his pizza. "This might just prove that people can communicate through thought waves."

"Why do we need proof?" Jason joined in. "As soon as people stop concentrating exclusively on the physical reality, they'll discover that they have various so-called psychic abilities. Clairvoyance, telepathy, intuition and premonition have been experienced by many, and they are nothing new. Why are we still looking for scientific proof? Can't we think for ourselves and draw our own obvious conclusions? Do we always have to be told by others what to think or do?"

"It would be nice if scientists confirmed it though," Mike said. "As far as I know, most of them have written off the idea of people having any psychic powers."

Jason lifted his glass of water. "Psychic powers are experienced in a subtle, non-physical way, so how can they be proven by conducting physical experiments?"

"They managed to provide some form of proof," Zoe interjected.

"Not enough for anyone to take any notice," Jason countered.

"Scientists are very limited in their knowledge, as they are only aware of the physical aspect of our senses, so they assume that if you can't see, smell, touch, hear or taste something you are not aware of it," I commented. "This is not quite correct, as we also have five super-senses that send information to our brains using more subtle, non-physical frequencies."

"So this experiment Zoe was talking about proves that we actually have super-senses?" Anna queried.

"Yes. The brain of person A sent out an invisible thought frequency that was picked up by the brain of person B, producing a reaction in his body," I explained. "Our brain constantly picks up non-physical frequencies even though we might not be fully aware of it," I added.

"It's like when you are attracted to someone and that person senses it without you having to say anything," Zoe said, glancing suggestively at David.

David winked at her in acknowledgement and Zoe gave him a small, sexy smile.

Jason noticed the exchange. "How was your massage, David?"

"Very good," David replied.

"I made a special effort to compensate for David's injuries," Zoe said, giving David another seductive smile.

"You'll have to be more careful, Zoe," Mike cautioned teasingly. "You injured a workman and he was out of action all afternoon."

"I'm sure David will catch up next weekend," Zoe said airily.

"Who knows for sure if David will be here next weekend?" Mike commented.

"Won't he?" Zoe gave David a surprised look.

David shrugged nonchalantly.

"Why not?" Zoe asked.

Mike smirked mischievously. "There isn't a bed in this house big enough to accommodate him comfortably."

Zoe quickly came up with the solution. "I have a large, comfortable bed. He can come and sleep at my place."

Jason laughed. "This is one of those offers you just can't refuse, mate," he said to David.

David rubbed his chin thoughtfully. "I think you're right."

"Does that mean you're coming next weekend?" Zoe asked enthusiastically.

"Throw in another massage and I'll be here," David replied, giving her an inviting grin.

"You strike a hard bargain, mister," Zoe said, smiling back, "but I happily agree."

As soon as dinner was over, Zoe, Mike and David departed. Anna helped me to wash the dishes and tidy up, and once she was satisfied that everything was done she picked up Harry and left. Jason was ready to leave as well. He had to go to college the following morning and had decided to spend the night in London. I walked him to the door and he kissed me goodbye.

"Are you going to be all right on your own?" he asked, stroking my hair.

"I hope so," I said, cuddling up to him. "Promise to come back soon."

"I will."

I closed the door behind him and suddenly the house seemed very quiet. I stared at the large space around me and felt an unexpected pang of emptiness. Only a short time ago the place had been full of people and buzzing with activity and laughter, but now, with everyone gone, it seemed cold and unwelcoming. Whatever the house represented, it wasn't enough to give me comfort. Being on my own there made me feel very lonely and the house itself meant nothing apart from the fact that it provided a roof over my head. However beautiful it was, its walls weren't going to fill the emptiness I felt.

Feeling totally miserable, I went upstairs to wash and get ready for bed. Later, as I lay alone in the darkened bedroom, watching shadows on the walls created by the moonlight, I couldn't help but wish that the night would be over soon.

12

The ringing of my mobile awakened me early the following morning, so with one hand I dug the phone out of my handbag and answered it sleepily.

"Hello."

"You said you would call me," Mark grumbled on the other end of the line.

"I was going to call you," I muttered groggily.

"Are you avoiding everyone?"

"Of course I'm not avoiding everyone," I snapped, and then his words registered. "Who else am I supposed to be avoiding?"

"Your father. He called me looking for you."

Something must have happened if my father was looking for me. He very rarely contacted me himself.

"Did he say what he wanted?"

"No, he just asked me to pass the message to you that he had called," Mark replied.

"I have to go," I said urgently, eager to get off the phone and call my parents.

"When can we talk?"

"I don't know."

"Carrie, if you want to see your money, don't brush me off," Mark warned firmly.

"Tomorrow then," I said quickly. "I'll come to the house tomorrow."

"What time?"

"I don't know. Seven, eight …"

"I'll wait for you at seven."

"Okay, I have to go."

I pressed the 'end call' button and I dialled my parents' number in Spain. There was no reply. I couldn't understand why no one was answering and dialled the number again. I waited for ages, listening to the hollow ringing tone, but my call remained unanswered. Where could they be? It didn't surprise me so much that my father wasn't there, but my mother didn't work and was usually at home in the morning. This, of course, didn't mean that she had to be there. For all I knew, she could be in town shopping or visiting friends. I resolved not to panic and would call them again later.

Opening the bedroom window, I took in a few deep breaths of the fresh, crisp, country air. It was another one of those beautiful summer days when the sun was shining brightly and the skies were clear, promising good weather for hours. It was another perfect day to spend outside.

With this thought, I washed, dressed and headed downstairs. Passing through the hall, I caught a glimpse of the wrecked painting of the cosmos, which rested against one of the walls together with many other canvases. I retraced my steps, stopped in front of the damaged canvas and stared at it. I had a very strong feeling that it was important I didn't neglect the painting and did some work on it. My studio, opposite the kitchen, was far from being organised, but the light was good outside and there was nothing to stop me from setting up an easel on the veranda and working there.

That decided, I had a quick breakfast of cereal followed by black coffee, and then carried everything I needed to the veranda and began setting it up. I unfolded the easel in the area that offered the best light, lifted the canvas onto it and searched through the box for suitable brushes and oils to use. Once I had found everything I needed, I was ready to start.

For the next few hours I was totally absorbed in the painting, doing my best to repair the damage. It was a very tricky job and it required a lot of concentration and precision in order to match the exact shades and depth of the existing paint. Eventually, the whole canvas was covered in even colours, which blended nicely together, and I was more than pleased with the end result.

I was making the final corrections when I heard the distinctive sound of Jason's car. Glancing at my watch, I was shocked to discover that it was almost 2 o'clock. I had been so completely absorbed in the painting that I had totally lost track of time. Grabbing a soft cloth, I quickly wiped the paint off my hands, ran down the steps and followed the wide path to the front of the house. The driver's door of Jason's car was open and he seemed to be looking for something in the back.

"Hi," I exclaimed brightly.

"Hi, babe," Jason replied, and as he turned I noticed that he was holding a small fluffy dog. He smiled his gorgeous smile.

"I thought you might be lonely on your own here and brought you a present."

"You brought me a dog?" I asked in surprise.

He stroked the animal. "A very friendly dog."

"I hope it is friendly. Where did you get it from?"

"An old friend of mine who runs an animal rescue centre."

Carefully, I took the small dog from him. It had a long white coat, which felt very soft to the touch. As I held it in my arms, the animal was very quiet and hardly moved. It just stared at me with its big brown eyes as though asking to be accepted. I immediately fell in love with it.

"It's lovely. What's the breed?"

"Tibetan Terrier, and it's a bitch," Jason replied. "I thought it would be nice for Harry to have a female companion."

"She's beautiful." I gave Jason a grateful kiss. "Thank you, darling. That's a really thoughtful present."

"What shall we call her?"

I thought for a moment. "I think it has to be Sally, because it goes very well with Harry," I decided.

Jason ruffled the dog's coat. "Sally suits her nicely."

"How old is she?" I asked, stroking my new pet.

"About 18 months."

"Do you know who her previous owner was?"

"No. I believe she was found abandoned on the street."

Suddenly I felt very protective of Sally.

"I can't believe someone would abandon a cute little dog like this,"

I said, holding her tightly to myself. "People can be so cruel."

"She'll be happy here," Jason said, scratching the animal behind the ear.

"Do you think she's been trained?"

"Probably not, but I was told that she responds to a few commands."

I put Sally down gently. She stood unsurely on her feet and stared up at me.

"Sit!" I commanded.

She sat immediately.

"Good girl." I patted her head. "I'm going to look for Harry's treats," I said to Jason, walking away. "Come!"

Sally followed me into the kitchen where I searched the cupboards for treats. As soon as I found some, Sally fixed me with a pleading stare, her tail wagging in anticipation.

"Sit!" I commanded again.

Obediently, she sat and I gave her a treat. She scoffed it hastily. Her eyes begged for more, so I gave her another one, which disappeared just as quickly.

"No more," I said. "You have to earn it."

Jason came into the kitchen with a small box.

"I bought a new phone for you," he announced, opening the box and extracting a cordless black instrument. "I spoke to BT today and they promised to connect the line by this evening."

"Oh God!" I exclaimed. "I completely forgot to try ringing my parents again. I have to call them urgently!"

Jason gave me a concerned look. "Why? Has something happened?"

"I don't know for sure. My father called Mark yesterday, which is strange as it's usually my mother who makes all the phone calls. I hope she is all right," I added, reaching for my mobile. I pressed the redial button and waited. Again there was no reply. "I just don't know why no one is answering. My mother should be at home."

"Try again," Jason urged.

I pressed the redial button again. The phone rang for a long time before the call was cut off.

"I have no idea why at least one of them can't be contacted and I'm beginning to worry."

"There could be all sorts of reasons why they're not at home," Jason said, trying to be positive. "You just have to keep trying."

"Yes. I'll try again later."

Sally, who sat quietly during my calls, suddenly got up, padded to the back door and stood in front of it as though waiting to be let out.

"I think she might have heard something," I said, walking towards the dog.

Looking out through the glass panels, I saw Anna putting Harry into his basket. I opened the door and Sally ran over to Harry and sniffed around excitedly.

Anna looked at her in surprise. "And who are you?"

"It's Sally," I said from the doorway. "She's my new pet and Harry's companion."

At the mention of his name, Harry gave a loud bark and jumped out of his basket. The dogs sniffed each other, wagged their tails and ran together down the steps into the garden.

"Love at first sight," Anna commented with a smile. "I think it's very unlikely my dog will feel the need to run away again."

There was a moment of silence while we watched the dogs playing happily in the garden. Then they both disappeared from view and Anna turned to me.

"I noticed that you've been working on a new painting. What is it going to be?"

"A simplified illustration of our cosmos," I replied.

Anna looked puzzled. "How can you reduce the vastness of the cosmos to the size of a small canvas?"

"It'll be just a basic illustration of the energetic structure, that's all," I said, and then explained how everything was connected through the frequency of white light, which divided over and over into 12 fundamental frequencies.

"I can see the basic idea," Anna said after I'd finished. "This is going to be an amazing painting. You'll have to hang it in the house when it's finished."

"I'm not sure. The yellow wallpaper in the living room is not the most ideal background for it."

"Then it has to go in the dining room," Anna decided.

"I've already bought wallpaper for the dining room and it's green. Not perfect either."

"Then we have to buy a different one."

I smiled. "Are we going to design the dining room around the painting?"

"Of course," Anna replied without hesitation. "This is not just any old painting."

"What painting?" Jason questioned, coming over with three mugs of tea.

"The painting of the cosmos," I said. "Anna thinks that it should be hung in the dining room."

"Why not in the living room?" Jason asked, handing us a mug each.

"It won't look right on the yellow wallpaper."

"Will it look right on green?"

"No, but as the dining room hasn't been papered yet we can choose a different one and use the green somewhere else," I pointed out.

"Okay, we'll put the redecorating of the dining room on hold for now," Jason agreed.

"It's decided then," Anna said, and we sat down on the steps.

We drank our tea in companionable silence for a while, staring into the far distance and enjoying the stillness and serenity around us.

"What do you say we organise a barbecue?" Jason suggested, breaking the silence.

"A barbecue sounds good to me." Anna sounded enthusiastic. "What do you think, Carrie?"

"Yes, why not," I agreed. "It could be our house-warming party."

"Anna, start making a guest list," Jason instructed, and then turned to me, "What about your parents, babe? Have you managed to contact them yet?"

"Gosh, I must call them," I exclaimed, standing up. "Thanks for reminding me."

I hurried into the house, picked up my mobile and dialled my parents' number in Spain for the tenth time that day. Please, please, answer the phone, I begged inwardly as, for the tenth time, I listened to the hollow ringing tone. No one picked it up. On impulse, I dialled the London number. I was more than surprised when my father answered the phone after the third ring.

"Dad, what are you doing in London?" I exclaimed, mystified. "And where is Mum?"

"I tried to call you ..." Dad responded flatly.

"I know, and I've been trying to call you - in Spain. What's happened?"

"I'm afraid I have some bad news."

I knew it. There was something wrong with Mum. Suddenly, I couldn't breathe and felt as though my heart had slumped all the way down to my stomach. I tried to say something, but words wouldn't come out of my mouth.

"It's your mother. She's ill."

"How ill?" I managed to ask.

"We don't know." Dad replied, sounding dejected. "She's lost a lot of weight, has been suffering from a terrible abdominal pain and she's been bleeding."

The symptoms sounded alarming.

"Has she had any tests done?" I asked numbly.

"She insisted on coming back to England for tests. They are doing them now."

I couldn't think straight. The only thing I knew was that I had to see my mother.

"Which hospital is she in?"

"Charing Cross."

"I'm going to see her," I said urgently, already on my way upstairs to change. "I'll call you later."

Beside myself with worry, I pulled off my working clothes and quickly changed into a clean pair of jeans and a white cotton shirt. I rushed outside to inform Jason and Anna that my mother was sick and I had to go to the hospital.

Jason looked particularly concerned. "Do you want me to come with you?"

I shook my head. My mother didn't know him and now was not the time to introduce them.

"No, it's better if I go on my own."

"I'll be here if you need me," he said, hugging me tightly.

Anna gave me a hug as well. "If there's anything I can do ..."

"Please can you watch Sally for me," I requested.

"Of course I will."

I got into my car and frantically drove to London, breaking all the speed limits. Today of all days I wasn't going to worry about fines and extra points on my licence. I realised I was frantic with worry and was panicking, so I took a few deep breaths to slow my racing heart. It didn't do much good. What if my mother had cancer? What if she died? I couldn't bear to think about it, so I did my best to push those numbing thoughts away and tried to concentrate on the traffic.

I reached Hammersmith in record time, parked close to the hospital, fed the meter and rushed inside. Passing the entrance, I stopped at the information desk and enquired about my mother. I was told that I would find her on the first floor in the radiology department. I thanked the woman behind the desk, hurried to the first floor and followed the signs to radiology, which led me to a large waiting room in the X-ray department. There were some people in the waiting area, awaiting their tests. I couldn't see my mother amongst them. I scanned the whole room and spotted her at the far end lying in a hospital bed.

With trepidation, I made my way towards her. As I got closer I was shocked by her appearance. Her face was pale and gaunt, her eyes hollow and her body appeared skinny and frail. It was obvious that she was very ill.

"Mum, how are you?" I asked weakly, carefully touching her hand.

"I've been better," my mother replied quietly.

I gave her a weak smile. "You'll be all right," I said, with more conviction than I felt. "How long are they keeping you here?"

"A few days, I expect," Mum said. "I assume you've spoken to your father?"

I nodded, and suddenly realised that my father should be by her side.

As though reading my thoughts, Mum said, "Don't blame your father for not being here. I was the one who insisted he went home."

"But why?"

"He hates hospitals," she answered shortly.

My mother could be very stubborn when it came to my father, so I decided to change the subject.

"So what tests have they already done?" I asked.

"All sorts of blood tests and some X-rays," Mum replied. "They're going to do a colonoscopy next."

I squeezed Mum's hand. "It'll be all right," I muttered reassuringly.

There was a small break in our conversation, and then Mum said, "Mark told your father that you've moved out of your house. Is this true?"

"Do we have to talk about it now?" I asked, knowing that the truth would distress her.

Mum nodded. "I'd like to know."

"Yes, I've moved out," I admitted.

"Where to?"

"Into a house near Dorking," I said, adding, "It's a big old house with a lovely garden."

"How can you afford to live in a big house?"

"It's not that expensive actually. The house had been empty for years and the owner wanted someone to move in and look after it," I explained as best I could. "I have some friends who are helping me to do it up."

My mother looked quite concerned. "I don't understand why you had to move out so suddenly."

"Mark and I have drifted apart and it was awkward to live with him under the same roof," I tried to explain. I added, "The new place is really lovely. The house is surrounded by acres of land. It has a large wooden veranda and a lot of original features. You'll love it." I touched Mum's hand. "As soon as you are out of here you must come and see it."

It seemed that Mum had not registered much of what I had said.

"But you have a house. Why move to another?"

"Mark and I don't get on. I couldn't live with him any longer," I reiterated. "I needed my own place."

"What's happened between you and Mark? He said that you were refusing to talk to him, that you were not even willing to discuss your financial arrangements and that you'd moved out without leaving him your new address."

It was far from the truth and I sighed in frustration, but I wasn't going to upset my mother with the details.

"Well, it's not true that I don't want to talk to him. In fact I'm going to see him tomorrow evening."

"That's good," Mum muttered, taking a deep breath. "I get these pains."

She grabbed her stomach with both hands, her face twisted in agony.

"I'll go and get help," I exclaimed in panic, and ran off to look for someone who would know what to do. I found a young nurse who was standing behind a large desk, checking some paperwork.

"My mother's in terrible pain. Can someone please come and help," I demanded urgently.

The nurse looked up. "Where is your mother?" she asked stoically.

I pointed to the bed by the wall. "She's waiting for a colonoscopy."

The nurse checked her paperwork. "She's next in."

"I don't care if she is next or if she has to wait for the rest of the afternoon," I snapped. "She's in pain now and she needs help now."

"There is nothing we can do. She has to wait."

The unconcerned attitude of the woman infuriated me. "What do you mean there is nothing you can do? Isn't this a hospital for heaven's sake?"

She shot me a nasty look. "Your mother has not been diagnosed yet. We can't start giving her medication if we don't know what her condition is."

"You could give her some painkillers."

"We've given her painkillers."

It was pointless talking to the woman, as she obviously wasn't going to help in any way. I rushed back to my mother to see if she was all right. The first thing I noticed was that her face looked even paler than before. She was still clutching her stomach with her hands, clearly still in pain.

Just as my mind was spinning, wondering what else I could do, I heard a voice in my head: *"You can help your mother."*

"What do I need to do?" I asked inwardly, with urgency.

Precise instructions followed:

"Place your left hand on your mother's abdomen and your right hand on her forehead," the voice said. *"You will create a circuit of energy that will help to relax her abdominal muscles. This in turn should relieve the pain, and she may well feel very sleepy once the pain has gone."*

"Mum," I said unsurely. "I'll try to do some healing on you."

"What?" my mother mumbled, her face contorted with pain.

"There is nobody here to help and it's obvious that you are in a lot of pain," I said, holding her hand reassuringly. "I'm going to try to relieve the pain with energy."

"Carrie, you are talking a lot of nonsense," she objected weakly.

"Just lie still," I commanded. "I am going to place my hands on your body and this should help to dissipate the pain." I did the healing for a few minutes and removed my hands. "How is the pain now?"

Some colour had returned to my mother's face.

"I don't know what you've done, but it's nearly gone."

"Good," I said, relieved.

At this point a young male doctor approached my mother's bed. "Unfortunately we are short-staffed today and won't be able to do your colonoscopy, Mrs Simpson," he explained. "Your test has been rescheduled for tomorrow morning. A nurse will take you back to your ward."

As soon as the doctor had departed, Mum looked at me. "You might as well go."

"I don't want to leave you alone in here."

"Really, Carrie, there is no need for you to stay," Mum insisted. "The pain has gone and I feel terribly sleepy. You don't need to stay and watch me sleep. You can come back tomorrow."

"Are you sure?"

"Of course I'm sure. I will probably sleep for the rest of the day."

"You sure you'll be all right?"

"Stop fussing. I'll be fine."

I relented. "What shall I tell Dad?"

"You don't need to tell him anything, just look after him. You know how hopeless he is on his own."

Two nurses came to move the bed.

I leant over and kissed my mother's forehead. "Don't worry about Dad. I'll keep an eye on him. Just concentrate on getting better."

One of the nurses unlocked the wheels and they were ready to push the bed to the lift.

"I'll see you tomorrow," I said, and watched my mother's bed being pushed away.

The moment I left the hospital I reached for my mobile and called my father. When he answered I simply said, "Dad, do you fancy doing a little bit of gardening?"

"Why do you ask?" he questioned, sounding confused.

"I have a huge garden that needs a lot of work and I would really appreciate your help."

"I'd be happy to help, you know that."

"I'm going there now, so I'll pick you up on the way," I said. "Pack an overnight bag."

"I'll wait for you."

I collected Dad 20 minutes later. During our drive to Woodland I told him about my visit to the hospital and about Mum's colonoscopy test being postponed until the following day. I added that she was comfortable and would probably spend the rest of the day sleeping. I also filled him in about Jason, my new pet, Sally, and my new house.

Instinctively, Dad knew that I was much happier. "I'm pleased that things are working out for you," he said, giving me a small smile.

I parked the car in front of the house and turned off the ignition.

"What do you think?" I asked, as we both stared out through the windscreen at the house.

"Very grand," Dad replied.

"Come, I'll introduce you to my friends."

My father followed me into the hall where Jason was standing on the ladder, steaming off the old wallpaper, the floor covered with wet bits that he'd already managed to remove.

I looked up at him. "Jason, come down and meet my father."

Jason climbed down and switched off the steamer. He extended his hand to Dad. "Good evening, sir," he greeted him with a smile. "Pleased to meet you."

Dad shook his hand. "Hello, Jason."

"Anna!" I called down the hall.

Anna came out of the kitchen. "Hi, I didn't realise you were back."

"Meet my Dad," I said.

Anna and Dad shook hands.

"Can I make you a drink?" Anna asked.

"A cup of tea would be lovely, if it's not too much trouble," Dad requested.

Anna smiled. "No trouble at all. I'll put the kettle on."

I turned to my father. "Dad, why don't you go with Anna to the kitchen?"

My father followed Anna and I was left alone with Jason.

"How is your mother?" Jason asked.

"I think she is very ill and nobody seems to know what's wrong with her," I said dismally. "They are still doing tests."

Jason hugged me comfortingly. "Don't worry, babe, I am sure she'll be all right."

"I really hope so," I muttered, getting some strength from him. "Do you mind if Dad sleeps upstairs and we sleep on the sofas?"

"Of course I don't mind."

Dad came over with his tea and I eased myself away from Jason.

"Where are the gardening tools?" Dad asked.

"It's getting late, Dad," I said. "I think maybe you should leave the gardening until tomorrow."

"I don't see why. There's still plenty of daylight left."

I turned to Jason. "Darling, could you show my father all the gardening tools, please. I'll go and help Anna with dinner."

"Come on, sir," Jason said. "We'd better leave the women to their cooking."

My father smiled. "I couldn't agree more. Do you know anything about gardening, Jason?" I heard my father ask as they walked away.

"Not very much, I'm afraid, but I learn quickly."

"Good. You can help me then. Oh, by the way, you can drop the 'sir'. My name is Robert."

"Very well, Robert, and I'd be happy to help."

I smiled to myself, pleased that Dad and Jason seemed to be getting on well together.

13

I was in the kitchen preparing breakfast when I suddenly thought that I ought to call the hospital and enquire what time my mother would be able to receive visitors, and then I could plan the day accordingly. I found the number through directory enquiries, dialled and was transferred to the appropriate ward. The nurse on duty told me that my mother's scheduled tests should be finished by midday and I could visit her at any time in the afternoon.

Just as I hung up Jason walked into the kitchen. "What's for breakfast, babe?" he asked.

"Cereal, soft boiled eggs and fresh fruit," I replied. "The eggs are nearly ready."

The timer went off, so I removed the saucepan from the hot ring, and then carefully fished out the eggs and placed them in two egg cups on the tray.

"Only two eggs?"

"Yes, one for you and one for Dad."

"Aren't you eating with us?"

"No, I've already had some toast for breakfast."

Toast couldn't have sounded like a very nutritious breakfast, because Jason fixed his eyes on me and asked, "Are you all right?"

"I'm fine."

"You look very pale."

"I just need some fresh air." I knew I didn't look my best and it certainly didn't help that I was terribly worried about my mother. "I'm going to take Sally for a walk."

"Good idea."

"Can you take this tray to the dining room, please?" I asked, adding a pot of tea and two mugs to the tray.

"Sure, I'll see you later, babe," Jason said, grabbing the tray and leaving the kitchen.

I went outside to get Sally. Stopping on the veranda I looked around, but I couldn't see her anywhere, so I walked down the steps and called her. Almost immediately she appeared by my side and we set off into the woods.

Walking through the peaceful, undisturbed woodland gave me the opportunity to reflect on things and my thoughts inevitably drifted to my mother and how incredibly frail she looked. I didn't want to admit it to myself, but at the back of my mind I knew that there was always a possibility that my mother could have cancer, and if that was the case there was also the likelihood that I might lose her. My mother and I had never been very close, but I loved her dearly and the thought of losing her was very frightening. I simply couldn't imagine my mother gone and I desperately wanted her to get better. I realised that when it came to my relationship with my mother I had taken a lot of things for granted, and I promised myself never to take anything for granted ever again as life could be so unpredictable and could change very suddenly, leaving us with too many regrets. I knew I had wasted so many opportunities to improve our relationship and I could only hope that she was going to be all right and I would have a chance to make amends.

Sally ran in front of me and stopped, breaking my train of thought. I picked up a stick and threw it ahead for her. She shot after it, caught it in midair and ran back, dropping it at my feet. She stared up at me with her big eyes in anticipation. I grabbed the stick and threw it again. She bolted after it and proudly brought it back. She seemed to enjoy the game and I played it with her until it was time to turn back. On our way back she walked very close to me, and when we reached the house she fussed around me and would not leave my side, as if she could sense my internal turmoil and was making sure that I was not left alone.

"Sally, stop fussing," I said to her eventually, and pointed to my father who was busy pulling weeds out of the ground. "Go and look after that man over there."

She stared up at me, not sure what to do.

"Go! Go!"

This time she ran to my father and obediently sat next to him. I smiled to myself, marvelling at the intelligence of the little dog.

"Dad, keep an eye on Sally for me," I called.

"Don't worry about her," my father called back. "She'll be fine with me."

"Where's Jason?"

"I think he's working in the hall."

"I'll call you when I'm ready to go to the hospital."

Dad nodded and I headed towards the main door. As I looked ahead I spotted a sports car coming towards the house. From a distance it looked like a Mercedes and I definitely did not know anyone who owned one. I shaded my eyes with my hand and stared at it, wondering who it could be. The car drove up and stopped. Both passenger doors opened simultaneously and the first person to emerge was Zoe, followed by a very elegantly dressed Vicky.

"Carrie, darling, I am so happy to see you again," Vicky exclaimed excitedly, giving me a hug. "As soon as I heard that you had moved to a lovely house in the country I insisted on coming to visit." She let go of me and cast her eye over the building. "Looks rather neglected, but once it's restored I am sure it'll be fabulous."

"Hi. Sorry we came unannounced," Zoe muttered, giving me a peck on the cheek. "We won't go inside. Vicky just wanted to see where you live."

"Why don't you show her around?" I suggested. "I'll go and get some drinks."

"Thanks, Carrie. Orange juice would be lovely," Vicky said.

I faced Zoe. "What shall I get you?"

"Some water, please. Sparkling if you've got some," Zoe requested, before turning to Vicky. "Let's go to the back of the house. You simply must see the woods and fields."

"Yes, I must," Vicky said, and she followed Zoe down the path by the side of the house.

I made my way into the house. As I entered, Jason was sanding the walls in the hall with a noisy electric sander, a cloud of white dust filling the air.

"We've got visitors," I shouted over the noise.

"What? I can't hear you," Jason shouted back.

I walked over to the machine and switched it off. The noise immediately died down.

"We've got visitors," I repeated.

Jason removed his dust mask. "Who?"

"Zoe and Vicky," I informed him. "I don't think I'll be able to cope with Vicky today. Can you come and talk to her?"

"Do I have to? I'd rather carry on here."

"Of course you don't have to, but she'll probably ask all sorts of silly questions and I'm not in the mood for answering silly questions."

"Carrie, surely you can talk to Vicky on your own. I don't understand what the problem is."

I stared at him, bewildered. Obviously, my needs were less important than redecorating.

"Okay, you keep sanding the walls because it's obviously very important, and I'll talk to Vicky," I said, and walked off in a huff.

In the kitchen, I filled two glasses with sparkling water and one with orange juice, put them on a tray and carried them outside. Zoe and Vicky were sitting at the garden table, which stood under some tall forest trees a short distance away from the house. I walked over to them, placed the tray on the table and removed the drinks.

Vicky reached for her orange juice. "Thank you, darling." She took a few sips. "These woods are absolutely magnificent, Carrie. You are so lucky to have this gorgeous place."

"The house isn't mine," I said. "I am only renting it."

"Oh, that's a pity," Vicky said, adding with a smile, "but if we believe the Pleiadians, nothing really belongs to us anyway. Interestingly, they also say that the time will come when we realise that all our worldly possessions mean nothing." She drank some juice. "What do you think, Carrie? Do you believe it's possible that in the future we won't care at all for our material possessions?"

"I believe that our values certainly need to change," I replied, trying to make a point. "We are much too attached to the material world. There is so much more to life than our worldly goods, but we don't seem to be interested in discovering more, or simply finding out more, because our minds have been trained to think in a very limited way - the material way."

Vicky looked confused. "I'm not quite sure I understand what you mean."

"It seems that the most important aspects of our existence are material possessions, as if they define our true worth," I said. "People attach great importance to material things. It's as though to possess the best house or the best car or to have the best paid job is the be-all and end-all of our existence. People have become ruthless and calculating to reach these goals. They think nothing of destroying someone's life in pursuit of material gains. It's time these values changed. We can't go on destroying each other just so some of us can have a comfortable, meaningless existence."

"I can't say I agree," Vicky said. "There are a lot of people who work very hard for their money. Surely they have a right to enjoy the fruits of their labour."

"There are also a lot of people who work very hard for very little money and the only thing they know is the constant struggle to make ends meet," I countered. "Do you think they are fulfilled and happy?"

"I am sure they are not," Vicky agreed, sipping her orange, "but they probably don't have the necessary skills to take a bigger responsibility upon themselves."

"Not everyone has to have a big responsibility. People with smaller responsibilities are just as important. There is not even one company or organisation that could function without these people and yet they are often treated with little respect and their hard work is not valued by anyone," I pointed out. "I am not trying to propagate communist ideals, but all I am trying to say is that these people are unmotivated and hardly ever have the opportunity to develop their true potential. They become resentful and bitter. How can that be good?"

"I absolutely agree with you," Zoe said, "but what is the solution?"

"Nothing will change until people learn to respect each other and each other's needs, and until they understand what's truly important."

"And what's that?" Vicky asked.

"They need to understand that we are all a part of the same whole, and what one person does affects another in some way. They also need to understand that only in co-operation and unity can great things be achieved, that material gain shouldn't be the main motivation of achievement, and that things should not be achieved at the expense of others."

"These are big and beautiful words," Vicky said, "but for thousands of years great human beings have tried to influence and change the world, and haven't succeeded."

"This time we don't need great human beings to try to change the world. Everything is changing around us whether we like it or not," I said. "Apart from major changes that are taking place all over the planet, the cosmic energies are also unlocking our awareness. Within that awareness there is knowledge far beyond our current understanding. Once we are able to access this knowledge we'll discover our true identity, which will totally change the way we think. Without this knowledge we are walking blind."

"I hope this is not imminent," Vicky said lightly. "I wouldn't like to think that we are expected to give up our material possessions just yet. I feel quite attached to my little sports car, my Louis Vuitton bags and a lot of other things."

I took a drink of water. "Why are you attached to them?"

"I suppose it's because they make me feel good about myself."

"Surely you as a person are much more important than those things, so you should feel good about yourself with or without them," Zoe said.

"But I am so used to having them that I would feel almost naked if they were suddenly taken away from me."

"When you think about it, it really shouldn't matter," I commented.

"Maybe not, but it does."

"One day you might feel differently," I said.

"Oh, I don't know, perhaps." Vicky was not certain.

"I think that there are more important things in life than having an expensive car or a designer bag," Zoe said. "Like having a loving partner, for example."

Vicky smiled. "Luckily for me, I have both, and my husband is quite generous with his money, so really I have the best of everything."

It was obvious that nothing I had said had penetrated Vicky's brain, so there was no point in continuing with the conversation.

"On a different note," I said, changing the subject. "Zoe, how are the curtains going?"

"One pair has been cut and is ready for sewing," Zoe replied. "I'll start on them next weekend."

"Looks like there is a nice little co-operation going on here," Vicky observed.

"Yes, everyone chips in," Zoe said with a happy smile. "At weekends it's just like one big, happy gathering."

"I must come and contribute," Vicky offered. "I haven't got any special skills, but I could probably help with something like washing up."

Zoe laughed. "Not with those nails."

Vicky examined her perfectly groomed, very long nails. "I agree they might present a problem."

"There you go. No washing up," I said, trying to discourage her, for somehow I couldn't see Vicky doing housework or helping with any other chores.

"I would still like to come. In fact I think I have this Saturday free - evening, that is," Vicky said, inviting herself.

I shot Zoe a questioning look and she shrugged her shoulders.

"If you are sure?"

Vicky had missed our exchange. "Positive."

I checked my watch and it was already after midday.

"I'm sorry, but I have to leave you," I said. "My mother is in hospital and I promised I would visit her."

"I hope it's nothing serious," Vicky said, sounding concerned.

I got up. "No one knows. They are running some tests."

Vicky and Zoe stood up as well.

"You didn't tell me that your mother was ill," Zoe muttered, as we walked towards Vicky's car.

"I didn't know until yesterday."

"How ill is she?"

"Very."

"I'm really sorry. I hope she gets better soon."

"I hope so too."

"I know it's hard, but try not to worry," Zoe consoled, "and especially don't assume the worst. It might be something easily treatable." She gave me a hug. "Please call me if you need anything, otherwise I'll see you at the weekend."

"Bye, Carrie. Thank you for a nice chat," Vicky said, getting into her car.

Zoe climbed into the passenger seat, closed the door and waved to me as Vicky slowly drove off. I waved back and went to get my father

* * *

"The house needs a lot of work," my father commented on the way to the hospital.

"I know, but I have plenty of help," I said, joining the motorway.

"That's good, and I'll help as much as I can in the garden."

I checked the side mirror for traffic. The road was clear and I changed lanes.

"Thanks, Dad. Have you got any suggestions as to how we can improve it?"

"I think the garden is beautiful as it is. It just needs tidying. We can plant some vegetables and flowers to give it more texture and colour if you like."

"I want to keep it as natural as possible, so if we decide to plant vegetables or flowers I would like to be able to grow them organically."

"I agree. A truly beautiful garden is the garden where you pour love into the soil, not pesticides," Dad said. "I suggest we plant some vegetables as they will provide organic food for you. We can also plant a few colourful shrubs and flowers close to the veranda to please the eye."

"Good suggestion," I said, happy with Dad's ideas.

There was a short silence before my father spoke again.

"Jason seems to be rather a nice young man."

"Yes, he is."

"I'm glad that you've found someone as nice as him, and I must say I'm very relieved that you're not going to marry that buffoon, Mark."

"So am I. Frankly, I don't care if I never see him again."

"You don't have to see him, do you?"

"He still owes me money from the house."

"Don't worry about it. Things will sort themselves out."

"I know, Dad. Somehow they always do."

We drove in silence the rest of the way, both preoccupied with our own thoughts. I was thinking about Mum's test results and I was sure my father was worrying about that too. For some reason we both avoided voicing our fears, probably because we had to stay strong for each other.

We arrived in Hammersmith a short time later. I parked the car outside the hospital and put some change in the meter, then we made our way inside and took the lift to the fourth floor. Dad pointed out the door to my mother's room and I slowly opened it. Mum lay motionless in the hospital bed, her eyes closed. Quietly, we approached the bed. Dad gently touched her hand and she opened her eyes.

"How are you, my dear?" Dad asked.

"Not too bad," Mum answered.

"Have they done all the tests?"

She nodded. "They did the colonoscopy this morning and they also did a biopsy."

We all knew that a biopsy meant that the doctors were checking for cancerous cells.

"What did the doctor say?" I asked shakily.

"All I've been told is that my intestines are inflamed and partially blocked by scar tissue, and that they found some small polyps," Mum said. When she saw our worried expressions, she added, "Don't look so alarmed. I haven't exactly been diagnosed with cancer."

"There must be a reason why they did the biopsy," Dad muttered.

"They did it because it's routine, Robert," Mum said bravely.

I squeezed Mum's hand. "When will you get the results?"

"Two to three days," she said, and then, seeing my father's distress, she changed the subject. "I hope Carrie is looking after you?"

"She is, and very well, together with her new boyfriend," Dad said, relieved to talk about something else.

Mum gave me a surprised look. "A new boyfriend? You didn't tell me you had a new boyfriend."

"He's rather nice," Dad interjected. "I'm sure you'll like him."

"Has he got a good job?" Mum asked, always the practical one.

"Not really," I admitted.

"What does he do then?"

"He is studying at university."

"A student?" Mum seemed very dissatisfied with this answer. "How can a student support you?"

"Kate, why is it that you always worry about such unimportant things?" Dad asked, doing his best to defuse the situation.

"Robert, this is important." Mum was adamant.

"Isn't it more important that Carrie is happy?"

"There is no such thing as happiness without financial security," Mum stated.

"Mum, I can assure you I can be happy with just enough money to get by on," I said, trying to put my mother's mind at rest. "Besides, I wasn't happy with Mark, however much money he was earning."

"What about this new house you live in? You said it needed some work. Where are you getting the money to pay for all the renovation?"

It was a reasonable enough question.

"I'm not sure yet," I answered truthfully. "I'll find a solution. I can always sell my paintings and Mark owes me some money."

"But the house is not even yours," Mum pointed out.

"I know, but I can live there as long as I want."

"I suppose we could help as well," Dad offered.

"I can't take money from you," I protested firmly. "Absolutely not."

"Of course we'll help," Mum decided.

Dad patted her hand reassuringly. "Don't worry about Carrie, dear," he said. "I'll make sure she has everything she needs."

The door to the room opened and two nurses walked in.

"I'm sorry, but it's time for Mrs Simpson's X-rays," one of them said, unlocking the bed wheels.

"More X-rays?" Mum complained.

"I'm afraid so," the nurse replied.

I squeezed Mum's hand. "We'll wait here."

"No, please go. I am perfectly all right and there is no need for you to hang around the hospital while I'm having my tests," Mum said resolutely. "Go and enjoy the rest of the day. I'll see you tomorrow," she added as she was wheeled out.

Dad looked unsure, but said, "I think we had better go. She'll only get upset if we stay."

Nodding, I followed him to the lift, which took us to the ground floor, and we left the building.

"Do you need to get anything from your house?" I asked, as soon as we got into the car.

"No, I think I have everything I need."

"Let's drive back then. You can start planting vegetables in my garden."

Forty-five minutes later we arrived at Woodland. I noticed that Anna's Volvo was parked out front, but Jason's car had gone.

"I'll continue in the garden," my father said as we alighted from the car.

He headed towards the shed and I made my way to the house. Opening the front door, I carried on into the kitchen where Anna was applying stripping liquid to one of the doors with a brush.

"Hi," I greeted her. "How are you?"

Anna paused her brushing and faced me. "I'm fine. How is your mother?"

"The doctors found some polyps in her intestines and are checking to see if they are cancerous."

"Oh, Carrie, I am so sorry."

"I know it sounds bad, but I have to stay optimistic."

"Yes, you have to," Anna said understandingly.

"Where is Jason?"

"His sister called and he had to go home. Apparently there was some problem with the house keys. He said he would be back."

I looked around the kitchen. "I can see that you have nearly finished stripping the units."

"Yes, this is the last door and then I am going to start painting the stripes. Would you like to help me? It might take your mind off things."

"I'd love to."

For the rest of the afternoon we were taping the doors with masking strips and painting the gaps between them in lime green. I got so involved in the work that I completely lost track of the time.

"I think we should stop now and start preparing dinner," Anna said, as we finished yet another door.

I glanced at my watch and realised that it was nearly 7 o'clock, which immediately reminded me that I was supposed to meet Mark.

"God, I'd completely forgotten that I'd promised to meet my ex-boyfriend at seven," I said urgently. "Can you prepare something for Dad?"

"Don't worry. You go."

I left Anna to carry on alone and went upstairs to wash and change quickly. Ready, I rushed downstairs and bumped straight into Jason.

"Is everything all right?" I asked briskly, still angry with him for not being supportive earlier.

Jason nodded. "Yeah, my sister lost her house keys and I had to go and rescue her," he explained. "Where are you going?"

"To see Mark."

Jason gave me a dubious look. "Why?"

"Because he asked me to go over to discuss money."

"Can't you discuss money with him over the phone?"

"No, I can't, and I'm already late," I responded, and started for the door.

He caught my arm and stopped me in my tracks. "Don't go."

"You have no right to tell me what to do," I snapped, pulling my arm away. "I don't need a partner to make decisions for me."

"Oh, that's the way it is, is it?"

"Yes, that's exactly the way it is."

His eyes clouded with anger. "Okay, you go and let that bastard abuse you again. What do I care?"

"How do you know he's going to abuse me?" I shot back.

"What else is he going to do? Are you hoping he is going to write a cheque for you just because you've made the effort to go and see him? Not bloody likely!"

At the back of my mind I knew Jason was right, but by then I was furious enough to go and see Mark just to spite him.

"Well, at least I might be able to persuade him to write one, which he has not been prepared to do so far."

"I think you're being a little naive."

"Naive?" I demanded in shock. "You are the one who is being naive."

"There is no point in arguing with you. You have obviously made up your mind."

"Yes, I have."

"Go then, and don't come crying to me if you end up being insulted again."

By now our argument had escalated out of all proportion and we were arguing for the sake of it.

"Don't worry, I won't," I said surlily. "I'll leave you to your redecorating, as it seems so much more important to you."

"Is that what this is all about? Are you angry with me for carrying on with redecorating instead of entertaining scatty Vicky?" Jason asked, as though it had suddenly dawned on him that that could be an issue.

"That, and the fact that you are trying to make decisions for me," I said harshly. "I don't need anyone to make decisions for me, least of all you."

Hurt by my words, he looked at me for a long moment before he said, "I didn't know you felt that way."

"There is a lot you don't know about me. You've hardly walked a hundred miles in my shoes," I said angrily, unable to stop myself.

"Obviously," he agreed sadly.

I checked my watch. It was nearly half past seven.

"I'm late. We'll have to finish this conversation later," I said, and left him staring at me in bewilderment.

* * *

Twenty minutes later I let myself into my old house. Mark was sitting in front of the television, nervously flicking through the channels. I noticed that he had replaced the old set with a new bigger one. I stepped into the room.

"You're late," he complained, turning the sound down.

"Sorry," I apologised, trying to start our conversation on a positive note. "I got held up."

"If I didn't know you any better, I'd assume that you were late on purpose," he said with a smirk, rising.

I thought it was a rather strange statement to make. "Why would I want to do that?"

"Just to piss me off, I suppose."

"Well, I'm here," I said, sitting down on the sofa. "So let's not waste any more time and try to come to some agreement about this house."

"You're not in a hurry, are you?"

"No, not really."

"Then there is no need to rush." He made his way to the bar and poured himself a large whisky. "Would you like a drink?" he offered.

"No, thank you."

"Oh, yeah, I nearly forgot. You don't drink. I hope you don't mind if I do," he said, gulping half of his drink in one go.

Warning bells rang in my head. I decided to press the matter of money.

"Mark, please sit down. We need to discuss our financial situation."

Ignoring me, he knocked back the rest of his whisky and filled the glass again.

"Are you sure you don't want a drink?" he asked, holding up the bottle.

I shook my head. "I don't want anything to drink, thank you."

"Suit yourself." He placed the bottle on the coffee table, sat next to me and gave me an appraising look. "You've lost weight and you look good. In fact you look very ..." He seemed to be looking for the right word, and then came up with, "... appealing." He moved closer and regarded me lustfully.

Feeling distinctly uneasy, I moved away slightly. "Why don't we talk about the money," I suggested with a forced smile. "After all, that's why I'm here."

He drained his glass and poured more whisky into it.

"The money can wait."

All of a sudden I wasn't so sure it had been such a good idea to go there. I thought about leaving, but decided against it, reasoning that it was probably my last chance to reach an amicable agreement with him.

"Mark, you wanted me to come here to discuss money," I said sternly. "So let's discuss it."

It took him a few moments to answer. "What do you think we should do?"

"I think you should have the house revalued, then calculate how much of the equitable value would be my share, based on the amount of my deposit plus my contributions towards the repayment of the mortgage," I proposed. "Does that sound fair?"

"It might sound fair, but it's not really a practical solution," he responded, taking another swig from his glass.

"Then you will have to sell the house."

He was suddenly irritated. "There is no way I am going to sell this house just so you can get your share - no way."

"Okay." I tried to pacify him. "Don't sell it. Pay me off."

He moved closer. "Be nice to me and I'll pay you off."

Alarmed, I moved away. "Mark, stop playing games."

"Darling Carrie, this is not a game," he said seriously, sending a shiver down my spine.

"Don't call me darling!" I snapped.

He leant over and touched my face. "But you are my darling, aren't you?"

I couldn't move farther from him because I had reached the end of the sofa and my back was touching the armrest.

"I am anything but your darling, and if you don't start behaving yourself I am going to leave," I threatened, knowing full well it was pointless.

To my surprise, he stopped pestering me and poured himself another drink instead.

"Okay, let's get back to business." He gulped some whisky. "I am prepared to give you some money on two conditions …"

I didn't like the sound of that. "What conditions?"

"I want you to give me your current address and I want you to go with me to my office party in two weeks, as my fiancé."

His conditions were unacceptable, but I used the opportunity to ask about the crystal.

"I'll think about it. However, I have one condition of my own."

"I'm listening."

"I want my crystal back."

He appeared to be thinking about it and then said, "I am not sure if I should give it to you."

"Then I won't even discuss your conditions."

"Your crystal is in the house, so if I am happy with you I might give it back," he hinted, and took another large swig from his glass.

"Where is it?"

He smiled derisively. "That would be telling too much too soon."

It was obvious that he would want something for it, most likely something I wasn't prepared to give. It was apparent that I had to find another way to get it back.

"I don't like your conditions," I said, returning to our previous conversation.

"You want your money? These are my conditions," he said, slightly slurring his words. "Take it or leave it." Then, quite unexpectedly, he leant over and kissed me on the mouth. "You see, I still care about you."

Angrily pushing him away, I swiftly slipped out from under him and stood up.

"You are crazy!" I exploded. "Totally crazy! If you think I'm giving my address to a crazy person like you, you had better think again!"

"You are being unreasonable, as usual," he muttered in response. "You want something from me, but you are not prepared to compromise. How our relationship has ever had a chance to work I do not know."

I gave him an astounded look. "Our relationship has not worked for various reasons, but my not being able to compromise isn't one of them."

"That's where you're wrong, darling," he said annoyingly, draining his glass.

"Can we go back to discussing money?" I demanded.

"I am tired of discussing money with you. It's always money, money, money," he said, his face twisted in disdain.

"I don't want your bloody money," I said strongly. "All I want is what belongs to me."

"From where I'm standing, nothing belongs to you. It all belongs to me."

God, he really knew how to infuriate me.

"You are one selfish, ruthless bastard," I threw at him.

He laughed. "Funny, I wasn't a ruthless, selfish bastard when I was paying your way."

"That's not the way it was and you know it," I objected sharply, hurt by his words. "I have always contributed fairly, and I paid half the deposit for this house, the deposit you are unwilling even to acknowledge. Come to think of it, selfish and ruthless don't even come close." I started on my way. "My solicitor will be in contact with you."

Mark shot up from the sofa and stood in my way just as I was reaching the front door.

"Where do you think you're going?"

"I am going home," I said, with more control than I actually felt. "There is nothing more to say. You are not prepared to part amicably and I am not prepared to argue over money for the rest of my life."

"I'll give you your money," he mumbled, fumes of alcohol permeating my nostrils, "if you come to my office party."

"No, I won't go to your bloody office party," I said crossly, and tried to move past him.

He blocked my way. "Please, Carrie, it's important to me."

"Well, it's not important to me."

"Why don't we stop fighting? We used to care for each other."

"Indeed, why not?" I said sarcastically. "If you ever decide to give me my money back, contact Zoe."

I reached out and opened the front door. He kicked it shut, shoved me against it and kissed me hard on the mouth.

"You know you care for me …"

I tried to push him away. "Get away, you drunk!" I screamed. "You're hurting me!"

"You know you want me," he mumbled, frantically grasping at my breasts. "We can still make it work."

With all my might, I pushed him away.

"Get it into your thick head that I do not want you! Do you hear? I - do - not - want - you!"

"Oh yes you do."

He grabbed my hair and pressed his lips hard against mine. In utter panic I bit him and his hand flew to his lip.

"You bit me! You bitch!" he spat, and grabbed my elbow.

"Get away from me!" I shouted, wriggling my arm away. "Or I'll report you to the police for sexual harassment!"

That seemed to have the required effect, for he let go of me and lifted both arms in capitulation.

"Okay, okay. Don't get your knickers in a twist."

"Don't you ever, ever touch me again," I warned sternly.

With shaking hands, I opened the door and left the house. I could feel his stare as I walked to my car, but I did not look back. I knew, without any doubt, that the part of my life that involved Mark was very definitely over and it was very unlikely that I would ever step foot in that house again. I realised that I was silly to attach such importance to money, for at the end of the day no amount of money was worth losing self-respect over. Not in my book anyway.

Still shaking, I got into the car, locked all the doors and drove away as fast as I could. I needed to make as great a distance as possible between myself and Mark, and I needed to make it fast.

When I felt safe enough, I slowed down and reflected on the whole horrible day. Apart from my depressing visit to the hospital, I had had my first argument with Jason and then ended up being sexually molested by Mark. I didn't think it could get much worse. In hindsight, my argument with Jason had been so unnecessary and, whether I liked it or not, I had to admit to myself that in this particular instance he was right and I was wrong. How could I have been so pig-headed? I loved Jason with all my heart, and venting my anger at him was definitely not the right way to express my feelings.

What was wrong with me? Why did I have to be so contrary? Why did I have to argue with him instead of discussing it calmly and rationally? He had only tried to protect me and I had stupidly thrown it back in his face. I felt terrible, truly terrible. The last thing I wanted was to cause conflict between us. Conflict always created negative feelings and had nothing to do with true love. It was the fastest road to destroying any relationship, and my relationship with Jason was too special to ruin with pointless arguments. I was the one who started the silly argument, so I should be the one to apologise. I pressed harder on the accelerator in a desperate need to reach Woodland as fast as possible and offer my apology.

I reached the house within minutes and was surprised to see that there were no cars parked on the forecourt. I rushed to the front door and let myself in. The house was very quiet and felt totally deserted. I crossed the hall and looked into the living room. There was no one there. There was no light in the kitchen, so I went upstairs and knocked on the bedroom door.

"Come in," Dad called.

I opened the door. My father was sitting on the bed, his back supported by the headboard, reading a book. Sally was keeping vigil at his side.

"Hi, Dad, where is everyone?"

Dad put the book down on his lap. "Anna had to take Harry to the vet because one of his wounds was infected," he explained. "Jason left just after you. He drove off in a terrible hurry."

"Did he speak to you before he left?"

"He just said goodbye, that's all."

I was more than disappointed that Jason had left without speaking to me. He must have been very upset, which made me feel even worse if that was at all possible.

"Are you all right?" Dad asked, concerned.

"I'm fine," I managed to say. "Have you eaten?"

"Yes. Anna made me some eggs on toast before she left."

"That's good. I'll leave you to your reading," I said, reaching for the door handle. "Do you want me to leave Sally with you?"

"I think she's become quite attached to me, so she might like to stay," Dad said, stroking the dog.

"Goodnight then. I'll see you tomorrow," I said, closing the door.

* * *

Throughout the night I was tossing and turning, half listening for the phone to ring. Every now and then I awoke, realised that Jason was not there and felt dreadfully empty. Early in the morning I felt so restless I had to get up. With nothing else to do, I unfolded my exercise mat on the living room floor and tried to divert my scattered energies by concentrating on some advanced yoga postures.

I spent about half an hour practising various postures, and then sat still in the lotus position with my eyes closed, trying to connect to the calmness around me. My mind kept drifting to Jason and my mother, but I consciously pushed those thoughts away, as I knew that allowing myself to think about either of them would cause me a great deal of anguish. Instead, I tried to think about my love for them and how I could express it more fully. Love was a very special emotion and I felt that our lives would be very empty and meaningless if we could never experience the greatness of love.

As I was pondering about it, I suddenly realised that someone wanted to speak to me and I began listening:

"Everything that exists is energy, which vibrates at millions of different frequencies. Love is the greatest form of energy there is. Love is the frequency of pure white light, which connects all creation within the universe. It is the highest aspect of the Creator. The frequency of love in its purest form is virtually unknown to mankind, as it is so great that the dense physical body would not be able to cope with it. People on your planet have experienced certain aspects of this energy, but they have never experienced its full potential. The energy of pure love is so powerful that it would destroy your current physical body if it ever came into direct contact with it. Your body simply could not channel the high frequency of this energy, just as a small cable could not channel the electricity of very high voltage...

"People on your planet often mistake lust for love. Lust is a very poor expression of love, or rather lust is an emotion far removed from the emotion of love. Love, as you know it, is but a glimpse of the true, unconditional love of the Creator. Your planet has been denied access to this powerful energy for centuries and that's why you have lost your way. Now is the time to reconnect and rebuild it all. Your DNA has been scattered and it's time to pull it all together again, to unlock the data and bring your bodies into the light. Once your bodies begin to channel these higher frequencies you will be able to connect to the higher aspects of the energy of love or, if you prefer, the energy of the Creator. You will be able to experience love you have never been able to experience before and you will realise that this energy is to be shared and needs to be extended to all creation. You will find yourselves intoxicated by this new feeling of love, which will flow through you and totally overwhelm you, and from that, the new beginning will emerge...

"As your planet is moving towards the light and the new beginning, we hope that the understanding of the love energy will help you in comprehending the enormity of this change."

Just before the communication ended, I was shown an image of Planet Earth rising from the thousands of years of darkness and being slowly enveloped in the pure white light. It was a remarkable vision, which carried a lot of promise for the future.

As soon as I opened my eyes, I felt an overwhelming need to speak to Jason. I didn't like the distance between us at all. I badly missed our closeness and desperately wanted everything to go back to the way it was before our argument. Untangling my legs, I reached for my mobile and dialled his number. Almost immediately the answering service picked it up. I left a short message asking him to call, and hung up.

I was folding the mat when Dad came into the room, followed by Sally.

"Are you feeling better today?" he enquired.

"As well as can be expected," I replied, placing the folded mat in the corner of the room, "but don't worry about me, I'll be fine."

"I suppose it would help if Jason was around?" Dad observed.

"Yes, it would," I admitted.

"Why don't you call him?"

"I tried. His phone is switched off."

Dad nodded understandingly. I gave him a peck on the cheek.

"Why don't you go to the dining room while I'll get your breakfast?"

I called Sally and headed for the kitchen where I emptied a can of dog food into Sally's bowl, and then prepared a tray with cereal, toast and coffee for Dad and took it to the dining room. I put it in front of him.

"Would you like anything else?"

"No, that's fine. Aren't you joining me?" Dad asked.

"I'm not hungry," I replied. "I suppose you'll be doing some gardening?"

"I'd like to. What are you going to do?"

"A lot of cleaning."

Dad nodded.

"I'll be upstairs if you need me," I said, and left Dad alone to eat his breakfast.

I knew that sitting around with nothing to do but wait for Jason to call would make me feel really bad. I had to keep occupied and there was plenty of cleaning to do upstairs, so for the next few hours I scrubbed, vacuumed and polished like a woman possessed. When the job was finally done, I flopped onto the bedroom floor, totally exhausted. The eagerly awaited call from Jason hadn't come. It was evident that if I wanted to speak to him I would have to call him myself. I grabbed my mobile and pressed the redial button. Again, my call was redirected to his answering service, so I didn't bother to leave another message. Try as I might, I couldn't understand why he hadn't called me. Was he so mad that he would not contact me for days? I couldn't bear not to see him for days, not to hear his voice for days. I had to do something. I had to go to London and find him, as the waiting was driving me crazy.

Hastily, I changed my clothes and ran outside to speak to my father.

"Dad, we are going to London," I announced urgently.

"Now?"

"Yes, now."

Dad knew better than to ask why.

"I'll just wash my hands," he said, and started towards the house.

I picked up Sally. "We'll wait for you in the car."

Soon we were on our way. The traffic was light and we reached London in 40 minutes. It took another ten minutes to get to Hammersmith where I pulled up outside the hospital. I shifted the gear lever into neutral and left the engine running.

Dad looked at me. "I presume you are not coming to see your mother?"

"I'll see her later," I replied. "I can't leave Sally in the car. It's too hot."

Dad opened the car door. "I'll let you know if there is any news," he said as he got out.

As soon as Dad had shut the door I pulled away from the kerb and joined the traffic. I had no specific plan about where to look for Jason. I didn't know where he lived or where he could be, so I decided that my best option was to find Anna and ask her if she had his address or knew where I could reach him. With this decision in mind, I followed the road to Richmond.

I found her house without any problem. Jumping out of the car, I rushed to the front door and pressed the buzzer. There was no response. "Oh, please, please, open the door," I muttered under my breath. No luck. The door remained firmly closed. As I stood there trying to think where I could find Anna, I suddenly remembered that she used to go horse riding. It was a wild guess, but it was worth a try.

I climbed back into my car and drove into Richmond Park. I parked as close as I could to the stables and made my way to the reception. The same middle-aged receptionist was sitting behind the wooden desk. We exchanged greetings and then I asked about Anna, adding that I desperately needed to speak to her. The woman immediately knew about whom I was talking and informed me that Anna was out in the park and should be back shortly. I thanked her and walked outside.

I waited anxiously for about ten minutes before I saw Anna slowly walking her horse back to the stables. She spotted me as she came closer.

"Carrie, what are you doing here?" she exclaimed in surprise. "Is everything all right?" she asked, dismounting.

"Everything is fine. I just need to find Jason," I replied.

"Give me a few minutes to change and we'll talk." She led her horse into the stables and disappeared behind the building. She re-emerged five minutes later. "Shall we go to Pembroke Lodge for coffee or would you rather go to my place?" she asked.

"Let's stay in the park," I decided, as it was a really nice, hot day with only a small number of downy clouds scattered across the blue summer sky, mildly obstructing the brightness of the sun.

We made our way to Pembroke Lodge Coffee Shop where we ordered coffees and pastries and sat at one of the tables outside overlooking the Thames Valley.

"What's happened?" Anna enquired, stirring sugar into her coffee. "Why are you looking for Jason?"

I poured some milk into my cup. "I'm sure you know that we argued yesterday?"

"All I know is that Jason was rather upset when he left."

"Well, we argued before I went to see my ex-boyfriend, and when I got back Jason had already gone and I didn't have a chance to speak to him. He hasn't called me since, so I suspect he must still be rather cross with me," I explained. "It was a stupid row, which I provoked, and I feel really rotten about the whole thing and want to apologise to him. I've tried ringing his mobile umpteen times, but every time I call the answering service picks it up. Strange as it may sound, but I have no other point of contact. I don't even know where he lives." I took a sip of my coffee. "Anyway, I thought that maybe you knew how I could reach him."

"I have no idea where he lives either, but I might have his home number." Anna rummaged in her white leather handbag and extracted a small Filofax. Opening it, she ran her finger through the alphabet and stopped at the letter J. "Oh, here we are," she said, passing the open notebook to me. "Try to call him."

Fishing my mobile from my bag, I dialled the number. After a few rings a woman answered. She had a pleasant young voice.

"Hi. Could I possibly speak to Jason, please?" I asked, praying he was there.

"I'm sorry, Jason's not here," the woman replied. "In fact he's hardly ever here. You'll probably have more luck ringing his mobile."

"I've tried. I think his phone must be switched off," I said. "Do you know where I could reach him? It's rather urgent.'"

"Unfortunately not. Jason never tells me what he's doing or where he's going. Sorry I can't be of any more help."

"Could you please tell him that Carrie called?" I asked resignedly.

"I will," the woman promised.

We said our goodbyes and hung up.

During my phone call Anna occupied herself by teaching Sally some new tricks. The dog was lifting its paw when I interrupted.

"Anna, who else can I call? Do you know any of his friends who live in London?"

"I'm afraid not."

"Have you got any other ideas where I can find him?"

"University?" she suggested unsurely.

I shook my head. "The university has already closed for the summer holidays."

"Then you'll just have to keep trying his mobile," Anna said, lifting her coffee cup.

Acquiescently, I rang Jason's number yet again and yet again the answering service picked it up. I cut off the phone in total frustration. It was so annoying that the only point of contact I had with my boyfriend was through his mobile and all I could get was some irritating recorded message.

"I don't know what else I can do."

"Just keep trying and he is bound to answer sooner or later," Anna advised.

"I suppose," I said with a resigned sigh. "Looks like it's my time to learn patience," I added, cutting into my Danish pastry.

"Would you like to come back to my place?" Anna asked. "It might help to have some company."

"I can't. I have to go to see my mother - which reminds me, I can't take Sally to the hospital. Could you possibly look after her for me?"

"I'd be happy to." Anna patted the dog affectionately. "Harry is on antibiotics and he's been very miserable. I'm sure he'll appreciate the company."

"I'm sorry, I've been so preoccupied with my own problems that I haven't even asked you how Harry is."

Anna smiled understandingly. "He's all right, but I think it's best if he stays indoors today, just in case."

"So you won't be coming to Woodland?"

Anna shook her head. "Not today," she said, sipping her coffee. She continued, "While we're on the subject of Woodland, do you remember when I mentioned a friend of mine who is good at carpentry?"

I nodded, recalling the conversation.

"Well, his name is George. I spoke to him yesterday and he would very much like to meet you. I thought I would bring him over to Woodland and that way he can see the place and you can both discuss what he could make."

"Definitely. Bring him over."

"Maybe tomorrow if he's free."

"Sure, bring him tomorrow."

We finished our drinks and pastries and walked back to our cars, which were parked side by side in the car park just outside Pembroke Lodge. Anna lifted the back door of her car and Sally, being the friendly dog she was, jumped inside and happily settled by the window.

"Call me if you need to talk," Anna said, opening the side door, "and don't worry about Jason, he'll get in touch. He cares far too much for you not to."

"Thanks," I said, climbing into my car. "See you tomorrow."

I started the engine and drove out of Richmond Park, through Richmond Gate, and then followed the route to Charing Cross Hospital where I spent about an hour with my mother. Mum was still quite weak, but since her colonoscopy she had been put on medication and some colour had already returned to her face, which was promising. However, there was still no diagnosis and the unspoken fear of the dreaded cancer hung in the air. I tried very hard to draw comfort from the fact that Mum looked slightly better and the feeling that she was slowly regaining her strength. Still, after an hour she became tired and sleepy, so I kissed her goodbye and left.

As soon as I walked out of the hospital I made two phone calls. Maybe not surprisingly, the first one was to Jason's mobile. Needless to say, my call was picked up by the recorded answer service again. I left another message and disconnected the line. The second call was to my parents' house. My father answered on the third ring. I told him I was going back to Woodland and asked him if he wanted me to pick him up on my way there. He declined, saying that he had some paperwork to do and preferred to stay in London to attend to it and would come over next time.

It seemed that I would be spending the rest of the day on my own and it was a rather depressing prospect. Where is Jason when I need him? I thought. Well, he wasn't there, but to be fair to him it was entirely my fault and I only had myself to blame. With a deep, resigned sigh, I pushed thoughts about Jason to the back of my mind and instead tried to think of what I could do once I got back to Woodland. There was still a lot of cleaning that needed to be done, but I definitely didn't feel like doing that. I had done nearly three hours of cleaning in the morning and that was enough for one day. I could continue with the painting of the cosmos, but I knew I wouldn't be able to concentrate on it, so that would have to wait. I could paint the remaining stripes on the kitchen units, but decided against it because I felt that it was more important to paint the window frames in the living room in readiness for the curtains. Very quickly, I rejected that idea as well. Frankly, I was too depressed to be able to find enthusiasm to do anything. It was as though all my happy energy had been zapped out of me when Jason left.

I approached the final stretch of the road leading to the house and turned into it. As I cleared the section that was overgrown with trees on both sides, I suddenly spotted Jason's pearl-grey Golf parked on the driveway, and my heart leapt joyously. Swiftly, I parked next to his car and got out.

Jason was casually sitting on the front steps, his wrists crossed and resting on his knees. I walked over to him.

"Hi."

He looked at me and there was no anger in his eyes.

"Hi."

"Why are you sitting here?"

"I left my keys behind."

"Have you been waiting long?"

"About an hour," he replied, getting up. "Where's Sally?"

"I left her with Anna." I fished the house keys out of my bag. "Let's go inside," I said as I unlocked the front door.

Jason followed me into the living room. Dropping my bag on the sofa, I turned to face him.

"I'm really sorry about yesterday. I don't know what possessed me to argue like that. The whole argument was totally unnecessary."

He raised his eyebrows. "I don't know, I've spent a long time thinking about it and I feel it was definitely a lesson worth learning," he said earnestly. "I also feel I should apologise to you."

"No, no, you shouldn't," I objected. "You were right and I was wrong, and it was silly of me to argue."

"I tried to interfere in your life," he said pointedly. "I have no right to do that."

"You had the right to be concerned and I should have listened," I said, stroking his arm. "I'm really sorry that I didn't."

"I was furious with you," he admitted. "I was furious because you didn't seem to understand that the bastard was playing games with you but, as I said, I've done a lot of thinking. I now realise that our relationship should be based on mutual trust and freedom of choice. I should have allowed you to make an error of judgement without making a big issue out of it. I'm sorry. I won't do it again."

"I've done some thinking of my own and I know I was being unreasonable, and I promise that from now on I'll always consider your feelings. I'm truly sorry for upsetting you. I wanted to apologise yesterday, but you left before I had a chance to speak to you."

"I'm sorry."

I smiled. "Do you remember the dialogue from *Love Story*? I think it was something like, 'Love means never having to say you're sorry'."

Jason pulled me close to him and held me tightly.

"To me, love means respecting someone enough to admit your mistakes," he murmured into my ear. "It also means missing someone so much it hurts." He kissed my lips tenderly. "Love means wanting to be with someone so badly that no one else will do."

Melting with his words, I wrapped my arms around him. It was so good to be close to him again, to feel the warmth of his body and smell his now familiar, fresh, masculine scent.

"Did you really miss me?"

"I did - a lot. I couldn't think of anything else but how much I was missing you."

"I think I missed you more," I admitted, cuddling closer to him.

For a while we stood silently, entwined together, just being happy to be close again, and then Jason took my hand and led me upstairs to the bedroom. After he had undressed me, he lifted me up and gently put me on the bed. He watched me with his loving eyes all the while he was taking off his clothes. Naked, he lay next to me and began caressing my body with his hands and lips.

"Oh, babe, I am so very much in love with you," he murmured between kisses.

He was driving me wild with desire. I could feel his hardness pressing against my thigh and I wanted him much closer. I wanted him inside me.

"Please make love to me," I whispered.

As he moved on top of me, I opened my legs and lifted my pelvis to meet his slow, but very definite, thrust. Slowly, he began to move inside me, and then he suddenly stopped and looked at me.

"Don't stop," I begged.

He grabbed hold of my hips and continued with a deeper thrust. I could feel the exquisite pleasure building up, slowly taking over my entire body, until nothing else mattered but to carry the waves to the final release. Two more thrusts and I exploded in a totally overwhelming rapture of ecstasy. The release was so powerful that my body shook in an uncontrollable spasm for some time afterwards and for a moment I lost all sense of reality.

Afterwards, we lay in each other's arms.

"I am taking everything back," I muttered happily. "I think we should argue more often."

He looked straight into my eyes and smiled his gorgeous smile. "Argue or make up?"

I smiled back. "Argue, so we can make up."

"I don't think we've made up yet. I still have a lot more apologising to do," he muttered, placing small, feathery kisses on my neck all the way up to my ear.

He licked my ear while his hands stroked and caressed my flesh. Oh, God, it was bliss, just lying next to him and becoming lost in his every touch, his every caress. Soon, I could feel the exquisite little ripples spreading throughout my whole body, telling me that I was ready to make love again.

"My turn," I said, gently pushing him onto his back.

Climbing on top, I manoeuvred myself astride him, his hardness easily finding its way inside me, and began lifting and lowering my hips, every move sending stronger ripples of pleasure through me. All too quickly I reached the point when I was close to a climax, so I stopped, long enough for the waves to subside, then began to lift and lower my hips again. This time the sensation was deeper, stronger and more beautiful until I could feel it in all my nerve endings, from my head to my toes. Jason was also reaching his peak and, as our energies merged, we both exploded in an uncontrollable, powerful and totally overwhelming orgasm.

Our ecstasy spent, I collapsed next to Jason. Silently, he wrapped me in his arms and I curled up next to him, resting my head on his shoulder. At that moment I realised that I loved him more than life itself. He was my soulmate. He was a beautiful human being, unselfish and understanding, and I was the luckiest girl in the entire universe because he truly loved me. As a result of his love I had changed, or more precisely my outlook on life had changed. I suddenly understood that life was empty without love. Love was the key to it all. Love was the key to happiness, and without love nothing else made sense.

I kissed his gorgeous face. "I love you," I said from the bottom of my heart.

He pulled me closer to him and kissed my forehead. "I love you too, babe." There was a long moment of silence before Jason asked, "How did it go with your ex?"

"He was drunk and quite obnoxious," I replied. "I don't ever want to see him again. In fact I don't think I'll ever want to go to that house again."

Jason stroked my hair. "What about the crystal?"

"Oh my God! I nearly forgot about the crystal. I did ask him about it, of course, but it was pointless. He's not prepared to give it back to me," I said. "All I know is that it's still in the house."

"If it's still in the house we have to go there and find it. The stone is too special to be left with him."

I had to agree. "I have the keys. We can search the place when he's not there."

"I think we should go there tomorrow, just in case he decides to change the locks."

"Okay, sweetie, we'll go tomorrow, first thing in the morning." I stroked his arm. We didn't speak for a short while and then I asked, "Why didn't you answer my calls?"

He moved his head away and gave me a strange look. "What calls?"

"My calls to your mobile," I replied. "I called countless times today. I even left messages."

Jason shot out of bed and grabbed his jacket. He pulled his phone from the inside pocket and checked it.

"Damn! The bloody thing's switched itself off. My mind was so preoccupied with you I didn't even think of checking."

I padded over to him and threw my arms around his neck. "There was me thinking you were trying to avoid me," I said with a smile.

He kissed the tip of my nose. "There was me thinking you didn't call because you were mad at me."

"I'm glad we've got that out of the way," I muttered happily. "I don't know about you, but I'm starving."

"Me too, so let's go downstairs and raid the fridge."

I reached for my dressing gown. "I can rustle up a quick cheese and chicken salad," I suggested, putting it on.

Jason grabbed his trousers. "Sounds good."

Downstairs, Jason settled on the sofa in front of the television while I made my way to the kitchen to prepare a salad. I washed and chopped some salad vegetables and made a mixed salad with grated Cheddar cheese and roast chicken pieces, and arranged it all nicely on two plates. I placed the plates, two glasses and a bottle of sparkling water on a tray and strutted into the living room.

"What's on TV?" I asked, placing the tray on the floor, as there was no table in the room.

Jason pressed a button on the remote control, selecting a channel. "*My Big Fat Greek Wedding*." He pressed another button. "*How Clean Is Your House?*" and again, "*The Bill*", another click, "*EastEnders*."

I handed him a plate. "Let's watch, *My Big Fat Greek Wedding*."

Jason switched back to the first channel and for the next half an hour we watched the film while eating our food and sipping sparkling water. When we had finished eating I lay down on the sofa, snuggling up to Jason and resting my head on his lap. Pretty soon I was fast asleep.

I must have slept for quite some time because when I opened my eyes the film was over and the room was enveloped in darkness with just a flicker of light coming from the television screen.

Jason switched off the television and then gently lifted me up and carried me upstairs to the bedroom.

14

"Babe, wake up."

I opened my eyes and saw the love of my life standing next to the bed, clutching a breakfast tray.

"Wow, is that for me?"

Jason nodded. "A special treat - breakfast in bed."

"Oh, that's really special," I said with a smile, and sat up, resting my back against the headboard.

Jason put the tray on my lap. There was a bowl of Cornflakes, a boiled egg, two slices of buttered toast and a glass of orange juice.

"That's the best I could do," he said.

"I couldn't have done it better myself. Thank you, sweetie."

Jason leant over and kissed the top of my head. "As soon as you're ready, we'll go over to your house to search for the crystal. Enjoy your breakfast."

"Where are you going?"

"I have to finish tidying up all the wood outside. Anna is bringing George over."

"How will she get in if we're not here?" I asked, biting into a slice of toast.

"Good point. We need to leave her a key. I'll call her."

"Maybe Anna can pick up my father on her way. Could you give him a buzz and ask if he would like to come here today, please?"

"Will do," Jason said, and left the room.

Feeling totally spoiled, I returned to my breakfast. When I had finished, I deposited the tray on the floor by the wall and went to the bathroom to wash. I spent about 20 minutes washing, then headed back to the bedroom to look through my clothes, which were mostly still in black plastic bags, for something to wear. I pulled out a pair of stretchy jeans and a soft cotton top, and put them on. Once dressed,

I brushed my hair, arranging it into two neat plaits behind my ears, and applied light pink gloss to my lips. Ready, I headed downstairs to look for Jason. I found him by the shed sorting out planks of wood and stacking them in a pile under an extended part of the roof.

"Do you want me to help you?" I asked.

"No. I've nearly finished," he replied, lifting a large plank and dropping it onto the top of the pile. "Go and lock up. I'll be with you in a few minutes."

"What shall I do with the key?"

He picked up another plank. "Hide it under one of the large stones by the front steps."

I locked the front door, hid the key under the stone and waited for Jason in his car. It wasn't long before he sauntered over and climbed behind the wheel, and then we set off on our mission to recover the crystal.

"Slow down," I instructed, on the approach to my old house. "Mark's car is parked outside."

Jason pulled to a stop. "What time does he usually leave for work?" he asked.

I checked my watch. It was twenty past nine. "He should have left already."

"We'll wait," Jason decided, switching off the ignition. "If he is going to work he should be leaving soon."

We relaxed into our seats and waited. Half an hour later Mark was still in the house and the time seemed to drag on.

"Maybe we should come back tomorrow," I suggested.

Jason wasn't ready to leave. "Let's give it a few more minutes."

Another ten minutes passed and there was no movement, and then, just as we were about to give up, the door opened and Mark stepped out. We ducked down simultaneously and after a few seconds Jason lifted his head slightly.

"Do you think he might recognise my car?"

"I hope not," I replied. "I'm not really looking forward to him finding us here."

We stayed low for a few more minutes, long enough for Mark to get into his car and drive a fair distance away, before Jason raised his head above the dashboard to have a look.

"The coast is clear," he announced.

I sat up and quickly checked the road ahead. Satisfied that Mark's car was nowhere to be seen, I grabbed my house keys from the glove compartment.

"Let's go and start looking, and I don't care if we turn the place upside down. I am not leaving until we find the crystal," I said, and opened the door.

We walked over to the front door. Putting the key in the top lock, I was relieved to discover that it still fitted. The bottom bolt wasn't fastened, so I pushed the door open and we stepped inside.

"I think we should make some sort of plan," Jason suggested, once he had secured the door behind us. "We don't want to waste time looking in places you have already searched."

"True," I agreed.

"Think for a moment. Where is the most likely place he could have hidden the crystal?"

I collected my thoughts. "It's definitely not in the bedroom because I have searched every possible place in there. I don't think it's in the bathroom because there aren't any good hiding places. In fact I don't think it's upstairs," I said. "He thinks that the stone is radioactive, so he has probably hidden it away from the living area."

"Garage?"

"It's a good guess. We might as well start there. Follow me," I said, and headed towards the garage door, which was located at the back of the kitchen.

We entered the garage. The place was badly cluttered since it had been used mainly as a storage space for unused junk. There were various cardboard boxes filled with rubbish and stacked in groups of twos and threes all over the concrete floor. There were assorted tools scattered around, as well as a large number of plastic containers full of nails, screws and other small, unwanted bits and pieces. In between all that there were gardening tools, an old bicycle and a broken vacuum cleaner.

I looked at the whole mess hopelessly. "Any suggestions about where we could start?"

"None whatsoever," Jason replied, clearly at a loss as well.

At that point I heard a noise coming from inside the house.

"Shush …"

I strained my ears to listen. I identified the noise very quickly and it was very definitely the sound of a key being turned in the lock.

"He's back," I said quietly, and pointed to the garage door, which we had stupidly left wide open.

With one quick movement, Jason grabbed my arm and pulled me behind the tallest and biggest stack of cardboard boxes. We crouched down and kept very quiet, hardly daring to breathe at all. I could hear Mark racing around the house. He rushed into the living room, and then upstairs, taking two steps at a time. He spent a few minutes there and then hurried back downstairs and into the living room again. After that he shot across the hall into the kitchen, and then, quite suddenly, the sound of his movement stopped. He must have noticed that the garage door was open because when he began moving again he was very definitely moving in our direction. Once again, there was silence, and I knew that he was only a short distance away, almost certainly standing in the doorway, looking in. We froze, as we couldn't be quite sure he hadn't seen us. After an agonising minute or two he must have decided that there was nothing of interest in the garage and slowly closed the door. We both breathed a sigh of relief.

Still crouching, I faced Jason. "I don't think he'll stay," I whispered.

Jason nodded. "He's probably forgotten something."

"More than likely," I agreed.

We were still behind the boxes, waiting for Mark to leave, when quite unexpectedly I could feel an unusual heat radiating from the box next to me. I put my hand on the cardboard surface to double-check. Yes, there was definitely some kind of heat emanating from that box. Taking Jason's hand, I placed it on the warm spot.

"Can you feel the heat?" I asked quietly.

He nodded. "Yes."

"It could be the crystal."

Jason gave me a winning smile. "I think you might be right."

"Shush," I said, listening. I was sure I'd heard the sound of the front door being opened. "He's leaving."

We waited for the door to shut before we got to our feet.

"Let's look in that box," Jason said urgently, and opened the folded top.

The box was full of all sorts of junk. We searched through it until we found a black refuse bag twisted around a hard circular object. Jason swiftly removed all the junk out of the way and pulled it out of the box. Very carefully, he unfolded the plastic and looked inside.

"Bingo!" he exclaimed happily. "We've got it!"

I peeped inside the bag, at the bottom of which I could see a bright light shining through the clear surface of the crystal.

"This little stone obviously wanted to be found," I commented, marvelling at the way we had come across the right box.

Jason nodded. "It looks like he did us a big favour coming back."

I smiled. "Don't you know that there are no accidents?"

"I can well believe it." Jason pulled the top of the bag together. "I think it's time we got out of here."

We didn't bother to put anything back into the box, just quickly left the house and made our way back to the car.

When we arrived back at Woodland there was only my Mini parked outside, which meant that Anna had not arrived yet. I retrieved the key from under the stone and unlocked the door.

"I'm going upstairs to find a safe place for the crystal," I announced, heading for the stairs with the black bag in my hand.

In the bedroom, I took the crystal out of the bag and gazed at its amazing light for a moment. Straight away, I picked up some information about an earthquake in South America, but I quickly disconnected from it and instead concentrated on the most secure place for the stone. I was moving around the room when I stepped on a loose piece of floorboard. I grabbed the end of the carpet and pulled it away from the floor, then located the loose plank and lifted it up. Underneath, there were wooden beams and in between them was a nice little pocket, which was perfect for the crystal. I wrapped the stone in one of my T-shirts and carefully placed it in the small space, then replaced the piece of floorboard and the carpet.

Satisfied that the crystal was safe, I made my way back downstairs where I found Jason in the living room. He was standing by the window, looking thoughtful.

I crossed over to him and put my arms around his waist. "What are you thinking about?"

He turned and kissed the tip of my nose. "How lucky I am to be living here with you."

"I'm the lucky one," I said with a smile. "I even get breakfast in bed."

Jason grinned. "I would say that's lucky." He touched one of my plaits. "You look really cute with these."

I brushed a strand of hair from his forehead. "You don't look so bad yourself." At that moment I heard a car approaching and looked over his shoulder. "Anna is here."

The car stopped and Anna got out. She opened the back passenger door to release Sally and Harry, who ran to the side of the house and disappeared from view. Then the other passenger door opened and my father climbed out, followed by a middle-aged man who I presumed was Anna's friend, George. Anna seemed to be explaining something to him while my father walked to the back of the car, opened the boot and began unloading some plants. It appeared that the boot was filled with them.

"Let's go and help your father," Jason said, and we headed outside.

"Hiya," I greeted everyone.

Anna turned to me. "Hi." She put her hand on her friend's arm. "This is George," she introduced him.

George was slightly chubby and rather short, but his body frame suited him perfectly. He had a very pleasant, calm face with podgy cheeks and deep blue eyes framed by bushy eyebrows hidden behind gold-rimmed glasses. His hair was light brown with sprinkles of grey at the temples and he was dressed casually in a pair of well-worn jeans and an old light-blue shirt.

"Hello, George," I said with a smile.

"Pleased to meet you," Jason said, extending his hand.

George shook it. "Likewise."

Introductions made, Anna and Jason went to help my father unload and move the rest of the plants, and I was left with George.

"Lovely place," George commented, looking around.

"Yes, it's really nice here. We've been very lucky with the weather this summer and we tend to spend a lot of time outside. Come, I'll show you the rest of the grounds," I said, leading George along the path to the back of the house.

"Wow, this is really beautiful," George marvelled, gazing at the forest and fields ahead.

We walked a little farther.

"Anna told me that you like working with wood."

"I do," George replied, and then he noticed the stack of wood by the shed. "I can see you have plenty of wood here."

"Yes, and I was hoping that it could be used to make some simple furniture for us. The house is practically unfurnished."

"I could certainly make a few nice pieces from this lot."

"We were thinking about something simple," I said. "We can't pay much."

"Oh, don't worry about the money. I'll do it for nothing."

"I don't think it would be fair to expect you to do it for free."

"I'd be happy just to have an opportunity to work here."

"You are most welcome to work here, but are you sure you could do it for nothing?"

"Of course." George smiled. "What good are my skills if they can't be of any use to anyone?"

I smiled back. "They could be of use to someone who can pay you."

"I'd much rather they were of use to someone in greater need," George said. "Do you mind if I have a closer look at the wood?" he asked.

"Not at all."

We walked over to the pile of logs, planks, strips and various other small pieces now stacked neatly together against the shed wall.

George's eyes twinkled as he looked at the whole assortment.

"If you think you might need bigger pieces there are more logs in the forest," I said.

"A carpenter's paradise," George commented with a contented smile.

"I'm not sure. We might be lacking some tools."

"That's not a problem. I'll bring my own."

"You'll probably need some sort of workbench as well?"

George nodded. "I've got one, but it's rather big."

"There's plenty of room outside."

"Can't ask for more," George said, crouching in front of the wood pile. He tapped and rubbed various pieces with his fingers. "Nice and dry. Good for furniture."

"What do you think you can make from it?" I asked.

George looked up. "You tell me what you need and I'll make it."

"Let me think. We need a coffee table for the living room, a small table for the kitchen and we definitely need some storage units," I said, listing our most urgent requirements.

"I can certainly make two tables and a few storage units."

"Anything you can make will be greatly appreciated."

Anna appeared on the veranda carrying a tray. "I've made some tea," she called to us as she descended the steps.

She placed the tray on the garden table, which stood in its usual spot under the trees. She started pouring tea into the small white teacups as we approached. "Sit down, guys," she said, and we took out seats.

Anna passed a plate of biscuits to George. "Have you decided what you're going to make?" she asked.

George took a biscuit. "More or less," he replied.

"George very generously offered to make the furniture for nothing," I said, reaching for the milk jug.

Anna smiled. "George has been very generous ever since his out-of-body experience. He says that the experience has completely changed him."

"That's because it has," George said. "It was the most profound experience of my life. People don't take me seriously when I tell them about it, but I couldn't care less what they think. I know what I saw."

"What did you see?" I asked, sipping my tea.

"Three years ago I was in hospital following a heart attack, drifting in and out of consciousness, and I floated out of my body," George said. "I could see myself lying on the bed and two nurses bending over my body. One was checking my pulse. 'We're losing him! Call the doctor!' one yelled to the other. At that precise moment I saw a very bright white light somewhere in the distance and I remember, as if it were yesterday, that I just wanted to get to that light. I didn't care about leaving my body behind. I didn't care about anything else because I knew I would be safe and that the pain of living would be over. I started floating towards it ..." He paused for a moment, before continuing, "As I was getting closer I suddenly saw a figure who told me that it wasn't my time yet and that I had to go back. In a split second I was back in my body, which was jolting from the electric shock treatment."

"I can understand why this has changed you," I said.

"It has opened my eyes in many respects. I know now that there is life after death. Also, I know that everything that exists is interconnected and if you hurt something or someone you also hurt yourself," George said. "I am grateful for any experiences that life might throw at me because I know that through them I am learning and growing - and I am no longer afraid to live or die."

"Most people doubt that there is more to life than this purely physical existence," Anna commented. "At least you now know differently."

"I've tried to tell people that there is something more, but they are usually very sceptical," George said.

"People tend to be very sceptical when things they can't understand are explained to them by a person without a greater scientific knowledge, as though the only way to reach the truth is through scientific experiments," I said. "However, when it comes to explaining the unexplainable, scientists have the same limitations as anybody else."

"They can't provide scientific proof about life after death or reincarnation, so they reject the whole concept," Anna added. "Still, when you think about it, every known religion teaches about punishment and reward after death, and this is well accepted by most people."

"I think that we all know that there is a force in every physical body that keeps us alive, the force that is no longer with us when we die."

"I certainly know, because I experienced it," George said. "The way I experienced it, the force was me and the body was just a vehicle."

"That makes perfect sense," Anna remarked. "I for one would hate to think that I only had one short life to learn all there is to learn, and would not be given another chance to correct any of my mistakes. When you think about people who have been born handicapped, for example, wouldn't it be horrible just to have one shot at life and end up in a wheelchair? Surely, the whole plan is better than that?"

"There is so much out there," George agreed. "How can we even think that we can learn all there is to learn in one lifetime?"

"There is no way we can," Anna said, reaching for the teapot. She poured more tea for everyone and we chatted some more about reincarnation and out-of-body experiences.

Just before we left the table I asked George, "When do you think you'll be able to start on the furniture?"

"If it's okay with you, I'll come over on Saturday."

"Saturday is absolutely fine."

I said goodbye to Anna and George, and they left, taking both dogs with them as they seemed very unhappy when separated. It was well after 1 o'clock, and considering that nobody had eaten lunch I went to the kitchen to rustle up something for Dad, Jason and myself. Opening the fridge, I stared at its contents and tried to decide what I could cook that wouldn't be too challenging to prepare. There were masses of vegetables in the box, which would only go off if not eaten soon, so I pulled them out and laid them on the worktop. Looking at the whole assortment, I decided to make boiled pasta with roasted courgettes, peppers, mushrooms, onions and fresh pesto sauce. I washed and chopped the vegetables, put them on a baking tray and plonked it into the hot oven. That done, I boiled some pasta. The finished meal was ready in half an hour and it smelled and looked delicious. For someone who had never managed to cook a decent meal before, it was quite an achievement. I carried the food to the dining room and called Dad and Jason. Jason came in a moment later, his face smudged with black dust.

I removed a small smudge with my finger. "What have you been doing? Your face is covered in dust."

"Cleaning the fireplace," he replied, rubbing his cheeks with his hands. He gazed at the food. "Babe, you cooked this?"

"Yes, all on my own," I stated proudly.

"Well done," he said, sitting down at the table.

I sat next to him and we waited for my father, who arrived a few minutes later.

"Food looks good," Dad commented, taking a seat opposite Jason. "I thought you didn't like cooking,"

"I thought so too, but I might become a cook yet," I said lightly.

"Let's try this concoction then," Dad said, and filled his plate with pasta. He tasted some. "Mmm, it's very good."

Jason tried some too. "Excellent."

I smiled, well pleased, and tucked into my own plate of pasta.

As soon as lunch was over Jason said, "I hope you don't mind if I leave you and return to my dirty job of cleaning the fireplace." He got up, pushed his chair under the table and kissed the top of my head. "Thanks, babe, that was really good." He crossed to the living room and I was left with my father.

"How is the gardening going?" I asked.

"Very well. I've nearly finished planting the vegetables."

"Fantastic. We are making progress."

Dad looked around. "The house needs more attention than the garden."

"I know, and luckily a lot of people are willing to help. Of course it would be easier if we could accommodate them here, but the only spare furniture we have are two old sofas."

"I was meaning to give you something and completely forgot," Dad said, pulling out his wallet and extracting a cheque. "Here, use it to buy whatever you need."

I took the small piece of paper from him and looked at it in confusion, for the cheque was blank. There was only my name on it and Dad's signature.

"I don't understand," I said, puzzled.

"I wanted to get some furniture for you, but quite frankly I wouldn't know what to buy," Dad replied. "You can use it to pay for all the things you need."

I stared at the cheque unsurely.

"Don't feel bad about accepting it. That's the least I can do."

The cheque meant I could buy beds and make it possible for more people to stay overnight. It could also buy a wardrobe, which I so desperately needed as I was still living out of black plastic bags.

"Thanks, Dad, this will help a great deal."

"Good," Dad said and rose to his feet. "I'm going to finish planting and then I must ring the hospital to check on your mother."

Dad left the house and I ran into the living room where Jason was still cleaning the fireplace. I waved the cheque in front of his nose.

"Look what I've got," I exclaimed excitedly.

He stared at the cheque, slightly confused. "A blank cheque?"

"Yes, a blank cheque. My father gave it to me so we can buy furniture for the house. Isn't it fantastic?" I crouched next to him and wiped some dust off his face. "We can buy beds for the other bedrooms so more people can stay over."

Jason brightened. "And a wardrobe, so you can unpack your clothes," he said, flopping onto the floor.

I collapsed next to him. "And new sofas for the living room."

"Maybe a table for the kitchen."

"Or a television stand."

"Wait a minute. Let's not get carried away. It's a blank cheque, so maybe we are planning to spend money we don't have."

"Dad said I could buy whatever I needed."

"There must be a limit to how much you can spend," Jason cautioned.

"You're right. I'd better ask Dad just in case," I agreed, "but I'm sure we can buy the beds. If we don't go for expensive furniture we should be able to buy a wardrobe as well."

"How about Ikea?" Jason suggested. "Their stuff is cheap and it can be delivered quickly."

It made perfect sense. "Okay, let's go to Ikea. We can call in at the hospital on the way and you can meet my mother - which reminds me, Dad wanted to ring the hospital. Do you know if the landline has been connected?"

"I'm pretty sure it has." Jason reached for the phone and pressed the button to switch it on. "It's working," he confirmed, and replaced the receiver on the charger.

"I'll tell Dad," I said, rising. "Why don't you go and wash so we can leave soon?" I added before heading out.

I walked over to my father, who was busy planting some lettuce seedlings. "Dad, can you stop for a moment, please? I need to talk to you."

He looked up, his planting trowel poised. "What's the problem?"

"It's about the cheque," I explained. "It would help if you told me how much I can spend."

"I've already told you, spend as much as you need."

"But there is so much that we need. I wouldn't want to spend more than you can afford to give me."

Dad pushed the trowel into the ground and stood up. "Carrie, you are my only daughter and I want to help, so please buy whatever you need and don't worry about the money. I've got enough to pay for all your furniture."

"Thanks, Dad." I gave him a kiss on the cheek. "I love you."

My father wasn't good at showing affection, but he managed a happy grin and said, "Go on, buy whatever you need." He bent forwards and retrieved the trowel.

"Are you going to visit Mum today?" I asked.

He lifted his head and faced me. "I was planning to, but I need to call the hospital first."

"How long do you think it will be before you finish planting?"

"Not long. About 15 minutes."

"Come into the house and use the landline when you've finished," I said, and I left him to his gardening.

Twenty-five minutes later Dad came into the living room where I was vacuuming the carpet around the fireplace. I switched off the vacuum and he made the call to the hospital while I waited anxiously by his side for some news. As he spoke to the nurse on duty, his expression softened and I knew that the news was good. I was only picking up fragments of the whole conversation and I was impatient to know more.

"What is she saying?" I asked eagerly.

Dad waved his hand, signalling for me to wait. Finally, he finished the conversation and put down the receiver.

"The biopsy came back negative," was the first thing he said.

"Oh, thank God," I said with a much-relieved sigh. "Do they know what's wrong?"

Dad nodded. "Your mother has been diagnosed with Crohn's disease."

That left me none the wiser. "What's Crohn's disease?"

"It's an inflammatory bowel disorder that usually extends deep into the lining of the intestinal wall. The bad news is that the disease cannot be cured. The good news is that if your mother responds well to the medication there is a good chance it will go into remission."

"How long does she need to stay in hospital?"

'She's allowed to come home today."

It was such a relief that my mother didn't have a life-threatening disease. However, I was still quite concerned because she seemed so frail and I wasn't sure her body could cope with strong medication. The fact that strong chemicals weaken the body's immune system and nearly always cause bad side effects was enough to make me anxious.

"Do you know how long she has to be on medication?"

"I didn't ask, but I expect for as long as it takes for the disease to go into remission," Dad said, adding, "I know it's not the best news we could have had."

"Yes, but it's still very good news," I responded. "Will you collect

Mum from the hospital?"

"Of course."

'I'm not sure what to do," I muttered hesitantly. "Jason and I were planning to go and see her today."

"I don't think that's such a good idea," Dad remarked. "Your mother is not looking her best. It's probably better if you give her a few days to recuperate. Just drop me at the hospital and you can both visit her next week at home."

"All right," I agreed reluctantly.

Jason came into the room looking immaculate in his beige cotton trousers and a white shirt. I gave him a smile.

"I gather it's good news?" he said.

I nodded. "The biopsy came back negative and my mother is allowed to go home. Dad is collecting her from the hospital today."

"That's really fantastic news," Jason declared, pleased.

"So our plans have changed," I added. "Dad is going to the hospital and we are going to Ikea."

"Are we ready to leave?" Dad asked, impatient to get going.

"I think so," I replied, looking at Jason questioningly.

"I'm ready," he confirmed.

I grabbed my handbag. "Then let's go."

I locked the front door, we made our way to Jason's car and we all headed off to London. When we reached Hammersmith, Jason dropped my father outside the hospital and we carried on to Ikea at Brent Park. We spent close to two hours in the store choosing the furniture. In the end, we decided on one double bed, two single beds, a large wardrobe, two chests of drawers, two sofas, a kitchen table and chairs, and four small stools. We also bought some sheets, pillows, duvets and covers, three very simple bedside lights and a few extra cushions for the sofas.

We arranged for delivery of our purchases on the following Saturday and then, quite exhausted with having done so much shopping, we drove back to Woodland.

15

On Saturday, as it was the weekend, the house began filling up with people. Anna was the first to arrive, with Harry and Sally staring excitedly out of the back window of her car. Getting out of the car, Anna lifted the back door to release them and then called for my help to unload the groceries. The rear seat of her car was overflowing with carrier bags.

"Do we really need all this food?" I asked, picking up one of the bags.

"Of course we do. This place is going to be full of people today and they will all need to be fed," Anna responded adamantly, pulling out yet another heavy bag. "I bought a large, self-basting roasting turkey for dinner. I thought that would be the easiest solution. We can just bung it in the oven and it'll take care of itself."

"Perfect. I'm all for easy solutions."

We carried all the shopping to the kitchen and unpacked most of it straight into the fridge. There was so much food it was quite a job fitting everything in.

"Some of this food could be frozen," I said, squeezing a large pack of cheese in. "The problem is, we don't have a freezer."

"A freezer would certainly be useful. I'll keep it in mind," Anna said, emptying the last carrier bag of its boxes of cereals and placing them in one of the cupboards. "John called me last night. He has composed some new music and would like you to listen to it and tell him what you think. I said he could pop over here this evening. I hope you don't mind."

"I don't mind at all. I like having people around."

All the shopping had been unpacked when Zoe entered the house through the back door, carrying her sewing machine.

"Hi," she said cheerily. "Where can I do my sewing?"

"Why don't you organise yourself in the dining room?" I suggested.

"Cool. I'll see you later," she said, and was gone.

The next person to arrive was George, his van full of tools and various other bits of equipment. Some of it was quite heavy and Jason had to help him carry different items to the back of the house. Once everything had been unloaded, they set up a workbench and a large circular saw in the open space next to the shed. That done, George came into the kitchen and pulled a folded piece of paper out of his back pocket. He unfolded it slowly.

"I've drawn a design for a coffee table," he said, passing it to me. "Have a look and tell me what you think."

I scanned the drawing. The table was rectangular and had what looked like a glass top, which was set in a heavy frame of solid wood. It also had a lower shelf, which was supported by four legs and ran halfway between them and the top.

"It's perfect," I commented with a smile, returning the drawing.

"I'm glad you like it. I'll start on it straight away," he said and departed.

Ten minutes later Mike and David arrived. They carried a pasting table, two ladders, a large bucket and a bag full of various tools and brushes into the living room, and set up for papering the walls.

"I think everyone would like a drink," Anna said, opening the fridge. "Do we have fresh milk? I can't see any."

"Gosh, I totally forgot about milk," I admitted.

"How far is the nearest shop?"

"I'm not sure, a few miles perhaps."

"There is a farm close by," Anna recalled. "Remember Joe?"

"Of course I do. He said if we needed anything to go and see him."

"Well, we need milk, so let's do just that."

Leaving the house, Anna called the dogs and we set off, Harry and Sally running excitedly behind us. We walked down the country road until we reached the T-junction that intersected with the main road. Crossing the main road, we walked about 100 metres before we reached the entrance to Joe's farm. Anna opened a small gate and we stepped into the front courtyard. The courtyard was surrounded by a wooden fence with a wide, low barrier, which opened onto the fields on one side and trees and hedges on the other. To the right there was a brick house with a red tiled roof, bright yellow shutters and a brown front door. Attached to the house was a large, black painted barn with a wooden roof. A small boy was kicking a football about, which bounced off the front wall of the barn. The movement of the ball caught Harry's attention and he ran over and jumped after it. Abashed, the boy froze, not sure what to do.

"Don't worry, he's quite harmless," Anna reassured him. "Harry, come here!"

The boy looked at us sulkily. "What do you want?"

"We're looking for Joe," I said. "Do you know where we can find him?"

The boy dashed to the front door of the farmhouse and flung it open. "Dad!" he screamed. "There's someone to see you."

Joe appeared in the doorway and he recognised us straight away.

"Welcome, welcome," he said in greeting. "How's your dog?"

"Much better, thank you," Anna replied.

"What can I do for you?" he asked, walking towards us.

"We were hoping that you might be able to sell us some milk," Anna said.

Joe gave her a pleasant smile. "You can have as much milk as you want. I will also give you some eggs if you like."

Anna smiled back. "That's very kind of you. Can we have two litres of milk and maybe a dozen eggs then, please?"

"No problem. I'll go and get them for you," Joe said, and he disappeared into the house. He returned a short while later with a carrier bag and passed it to Anna. "Here you go. Enjoy them."

"How much do I owe you?" she asked, reaching into her pocket for her purse.

Joe smiled again. "For a lovely lady like you, it's free of charge."

"Why, thank you, Joe," Anna muttered in surprise.

"You're welcome, and if you need anything else just come over."

"I will," Anna said, and called the dogs.

We started on our way back.

"He likes you," I commented lightly, when we were out of earshot.

"No, he doesn't," Anna responded with a laugh in her voice.

"Yes, he does."

"Okay, he might like me," Anna admitted, "but he has a family and I wouldn't be interested."

"We know he has a son, but we haven't met his wife. He might be divorced for all we know," I remarked. "Just think about all the milk and eggs you can have for free," I added jokingly.

Anna laughed. "Free milk and eggs? That's not exactly what I had in mind."

"Then I think we should invite Joe for tea and find out a little more about him."

She looked at me with smiling eyes. "Are you trying to be a matchmaker?"

"I might be."

"I'm saying nothing."

"You don't have to say anything. I'll invite him."

"Okay, matchmaker!"

When we got back to the house, everyone seemed very busy. Mike and David were papering the walls, Zoe was sewing the curtains and George and Jason were making a coffee table.

Anna sorted out drinks for everyone and then suggested to me, "Why don't we finish the lines on the kitchen units?"

"Good idea," I agreed.

We found the box containing all the materials and Anna measured and taped the lines while I painted them in. We worked steadily until lunchtime when we stopped to prepare food for everyone. Trying to save time, we made an assortment of deep-filled sandwiches and passed them around.

Anna and I took our lunch outside and sat on the steps of the veranda where George and Jason joined us.

"How's the table going?" I asked, biting into my cheese and salad sandwich.

"We're making good progress," George replied.

"Very good progress," Jason declared.. "George is quick and he has a special relationship with wood. It's fascinating to watch him work."

"George loves woodwork," Anna said, "and if you love what you do, it shows in your work. Like Carrie's painting of the cosmos - you can feel the positive energy radiating from it."

George turned me, surprise in his eyes. "Did I hear correctly? You are painting the cosmos?"

I smiled at him. "It sounds very complicated, I know, but it's only a simplified structure of our cosmos, that's all."

"What do you mean by simplified structure?" George asked, stuffing the last bit of sandwich into his mouth.

I picked up a small twig and began drawing circles on the ground, explaining how white light was broken into 12 main frequencies over and over, and how everything was connected through the light and held within a certain aspect of it.

"That's quite amazing. This confirms what I have experienced, that everything that exists is interconnected," George said, fascinated. "How do you know all this?"

"I communicate with other beings from the cosmos and they explain things to me," I explained gently.

"So it's true? It's not my imagination."

"I'm sure you know that it's not your imagination."

"I do, but often when people doubt you, you begin to doubt yourself."

"Never doubt yourself," I said. "Your inner knowledge is your only connection to the truth."

"You are absolutely right," George agreed. "I shouldn't allow other people to cast shadows on what I know to be the truth."

"That's the way to go," Jason said, patting George's knee.

The back door opened and Zoe came outside. "A van from Ikea is here," she announced. "Where can they dump things?"

"I'll deal with it," Jason said, getting up. "Come on, George. We need to sort out the furniture."

"If it's not too big a job, could you put together the kitchen table and some chairs, please?" I requested.

"Will do," Jason replied, and he and George followed Zoe into the house.

Within an hour we had a solid pine table in the kitchen and four matching chairs with rattan seats. Anna and I were sitting opposite each other, pleased with the new addition, when quite unexpectedly a loud voice resonated close by, "Anybody there?"

"Oh no," I said with a resigned sigh.

"Who is it?" Anna asked.

"Zoe's friend," I replied, just as Vicky burst into the kitchen.

"Oh, Carrie, here you are," she exclaimed excitedly. "You are hiding some very handsome men in this house."

"Hi, Vicky," I said, rising. "I wasn't if sure you were coming."

"Darling, I said I would come to help and now I am happy I did - so many nice people here."

"This is my friend, Anna," I introduced.

Anna got up. "Nice to meet you."

Vicky pecked the air next to her cheek. "Lovely to meet you too, Anna." She scanned the kitchen. "Carrie, darling, what can I do to help? Washing up, perhaps?"

It puzzled me how she'd come up with that idea, as there were no dirty dishes lying around anywhere in the kitchen.

"There isn't any washing up to do."

"Maybe there's something else I can do," Vicky offered.

"Would you like to help us with dinner?" Anna suggested.

"I'd be happy to," Vicky said, dropping her Louis Vuitton handbag onto a chair.

Anna pulled some vegetables out of the fridge. "Why don't you start peeling these," she said, handing her a bag of carrots and a peeler.

Vicky took the bag carefully. "Could I have some gloves do you think?"

"Of course you can." Anna reached to the sink for a pair of Marigolds and passed them to Vicky.

Vicky, pulled on the gloves, awkwardly opened the plastic bag and extracted a carrot. She stared at it as though she were not quite sure what she was required to do, then she stared at the peeler for a moment trying to work out how it worked, until finally she began scraping the poor carrot with jerky, uncoordinated movements. Anna and I exchanged looks and it was all we could do not to burst out laughing at Vicky's hopeless attempt to use the peeler.

After a while it was obvious that Vicky didn't have a clue what she was doing, so I said, "Vicky, why don't you go and help Zoe with the curtains?"

"You mean help her with the sewing?"

I nodded.

"I'd like to, but I'm no good at sewing," she confessed, as she gazed at the little stalk that was left of the carrot. "Come to think of it, I'm no good at peeling carrots either."

"Don't worry, I'll peel them," I said. "Just go and have a chat with Zoe."

Vicky dropped the peeler onto the table and removed the rubber gloves. "Just call me if you need any other help," she said, grabbing her handbag.

"Don't worry about helping. Just relax."

As soon as she had left I breathed a sigh of relief.

"Who invited her here?" Anna asked.

"She invited herself," I replied, "to help."

"She's no use in the kitchen."

"I doubt she'll be of any use anywhere else either."

* * *

By 7 o'clock dinner was ready to be served. Anna and I pushed the two garden tables together and set them up under the trees. We carried outside plates, cutlery and hot dishes with freshly cooked food and arranged them on the wooden surface.

John arrived just before seven and we invited him to join us for dinner. There were nine people altogether, but only eight seats, so to accommodate everyone we added another chair that Anna had found in the shed. When everybody was seated, Jason cut the large roast into slices and everyone helped themselves to the succulent meat and butter-glazed vegetables.

Vicky held up the water jug. "Would you like some water?" she asked George, who was sitting next to her.

George raised his empty glass. "Yes, please."

Vicky filled his glass, and then poured some water for herself. "I've heard that you have had an out-of-body experience," she said, replacing the jug on the table.

George nodded and cut into his turkey.

"Sounds very exciting," Vicky continued, loud enough for everyone to hear. "What was it like? Can you tell us about it?"

"There's nothing much to tell," George replied. "Most people know what an out-of-body experience is. Mine was no different."

"I am not sure I know, but I assume you must have felt as if you were outside your body," Vicky said, sipping water.

"He might have felt as if he were outside his body, but that doesn't necessarily mean he was," Mike stated, joining in the conversation. "Who knows exactly what happens when people have these experiences? Nobody has been able to prove that anyone actually leaves their body."

George's fork froze in midair. "I know what I experienced."

"Ah, but the question is not so much what you feel you experienced, but what caused the experience in the first place. It could be something as simple as endorphins in your brain," Mike said, controversial as ever.

"The experience itself is totally detached from the physical brain," George countered.

"How can you be so sure? The brain is a very complicated and misunderstood part of the human anatomy."

"Which makes it easy to attribute an out-of-body experience to some function of the brain, as it can't be proven either way," Jason interjected.

"Near-death experience can be anatomically located within the brain," Mike argued stubbornly. "When the brain is subjected to the sudden and unexplained stress of dying, it actually produces endorphins, which are morphine-like chemicals and could very well generate a near-death experience."

"There is no evidence in medical literature that the stress of dying actually produces significantly greater amounts of endorphins in the brain," George contradicted.

"Why dig into the brain for answers?" Jason asked, backing up George. "Millions of people have left their physical body during a near-death experience and it seems that it's a natural and normal thing that happens to human beings."

John, who was sitting opposite George, stopped eating and faced him. "We do not know for sure if there is life after death. Having had this experience, would you say that there is?"

George nodded. "Undoubtedly. I am totally convinced there is life after death and there is no amount of clinical explanation that will ever convince me otherwise."

"I've heard that people who are born blind can see during a near-death experience," Zoe joined in. "If they are blind, they can't be seeing with their physical eyes."

"Yes, and it's interesting that people who have experienced near-death totally lose the fear of dying," Anna said. "It must be because they know that dying is not the absolute end."

"It's also interesting that all these people report that they can see a bright light," Zoe added, spooning out some carrots from the serving bowl onto her plate. "As far as I know, this is one aspect of the near-death experience that neuroscience hasn't been able to explain."

"If we assume that the near-death experience is the experience that brings our life to an end, there should be total darkness, but instead there is light," Anna observed. "It could almost be said that the opposite is true: by leaving the body we move from darkness into light."

Vicky lifted her head. "Oh, come on, life can't be described as darkness. Life can have so much beauty and light."

At this point I felt I needed to clarify the meaning of light as energy.

"If we assume that light is love, we cannot say that there is a lot of that around, which doesn't mean that we don't experience some form of love, even if it's only a selfish, materialistic kind, or love totally dictated by lust. However, the light or love we are talking about is much more profound. It's experienced unselfishly and is far removed from the darkness that is ever present around us. It penetrates everything with the power of the energy of the Creator. In order to experience this kind of love, we need to change and evolve, and until then we have no choice but to live in ignorance and darkness."

In response, Vicky shot John a derogatory look.

Jason noticed it and responded with, "Vicky has her own ideas about beauty and light."

"I just don't understand why everything has to be so serious," Vicky said in her defence.

"Don't you think that the fact that this planet is heading towards destruction unless people change their ways is serious?" Jason questioned earnestly.

Vicky seemed momentarily put out. "Jason, dear, to be fair, I don't think we were talking about planetary destruction."

"No? Violence, famine, disease, pollution, terrorism, war and weapons of mass destruction are but a few examples of how badly we need to change before it's too late." Jason was in his element.

"I know this planet is far from perfect, but it does not mean there is no hope," Vicky argued.

"That's just it. There is hope. People of this planet have been given a chance to move into the light, but whether they take it or not is up to them."

"I am sure everyone will want to make the right choice."

"No, Vicky, not everyone. Some people are too preoccupied with their own self-importance and too blind to see beyond their own needs."

"Now you're being unfair."

"I don't think I am. I'm just telling it as it is."

"Your comment was addressed to me personally."

"Well, Vicky, it's clear that we totally misunderstand each other."

The argument was getting nowhere, so I decided to intervene.

"I think it's time for dessert," I announced, and began piling up the serving dishes. "Zoe, would you please help me to collect the plates?"

Zoe collected the plates and cutlery, and we took the whole lot to the kitchen and deposited them into the sink. I handed Zoe a stack of dessert plates and grabbed a sponge cake from the worktop, and we carried them outside. Placing the cake on the table, I cut it into nine portions and served a small portion to everyone.

We had nearly finished our dessert when quite suddenly the skies above us darkened and the forest trees were stirred spookily by a growing wind. Within seconds the weather turned and the temperature plummeted by at least ten degrees. Large drops of rain fell through the trees and changed into a very heavy downpour in no time at all.

Jason grabbed his drink. "Quick, run inside!" he shouted, and hotfooted it towards the veranda.

The rest of us quickly ran after him through the back doorway into the house and followed him down the hall into the living room. Everyone was wet, so Jason decided to light the fire. He dropped some wood into the fireplace and lit it with a match. The fire easily took hold and soon the flames were shooting up the chimney, creating a warm golden light. We moved the sofas closer to the fire while David and Mike brought some chairs from the dining room, and we gathered around the welcoming warmth.

Anna called the dogs in and told them to sit by one of the sofas and they obediently settled. She perched on the edge and pulled her cardigan around herself. "John, why don't you play us some of your music," she suggested.

"Yes, John," Vicky said. "It would be lovely to listen to some of your music."

"I'll get my guitar." John went to the hall and returned with a large classical guitar. Sitting down on his chair, he began tuning the instrument. He checked the strings by running his fingers across them a few times. "This is my new composition," he said, strumming some notes. "It doesn't have a title yet."

As he began playing, the music filled the room. The sound was very soft and well harmonised with a lot of smoothly flowing variations. Everyone kept quiet, listening attentively as though hypnotised by the beauty of the soft melody.

When John had finished his piece, he turned to me. "What do you think, Carrie?"

I smiled, pleased that he had taken my advice. "It's very beautiful."

John smiled back. "I'm happy you like it. Shall I play something more lively?"

"Good idea," Anna said. "Play some popular music."

"How about this?" John began strumming John Lennon's, 'Imagine', and then started singing the song in a warm, throaty voice.

The sound was great and not at all what I had expected. I listened to him, mesmerised. After that he sang some more upbeat popular songs and we joined in. Not everyone knew the lyrics or could sing in tune, so it ended up as more of an improvisation than actual singing, but that didn't matter at all as there was a great sense of companionship and a lot of laughter. When John hit the notes of Roberta Flack's, 'Killing Me Softly', nearly everyone messed up the tune and we ended up changing the chorus from 'Killing me softly' to 'Killing softly this song', which produced a great deal of hilarity.

All in all it was a great evening and no one wanted to go home, but eventually, as all good things do, it had to come to an end. It was nearly 11 o'clock when John strummed the last random notes and rose to his feet.

"It's been fun. We must do it again," John said, as the rest of us slowly stood up.

"Most definitely," I agreed.

"It's late. I'd better be going." He gave me a hug. "Thanks for a wonderful meal and evening," he said, picking up his guitar and heading out through the doorway.

Vicky came over to me and kissed the air next to my cheek. "Thank you, darling. I did enjoy myself tremendously."

"I'm glad."

"I'll definitely come over again, but next time I promise to do all the washing up," she said with a smile.

I smiled back. "I'll hold you to that."

"Bye." Vicky waved her hand to everyone and headed out.

Zoe crossed over to me. "I'm stealing a worker from you," she declared with a mischievous smile, shifting her eyes in David's direction. "I'll return him tomorrow."

"Make sure you do."

She gave me a kiss. "It's been great. I'll see you tomorrow." She went over to David, grabbed his hand and they were off.

Mike, George and Anna were staying overnight. It was too late to assemble the Ikea bed frames for them, so the men brought the new mattresses into the living room and laid them on the floor. Anna and I threw some sheets and blankets on them and the beds were ready.

Jason put his arm around my shoulders. "Let's leave them to it," he said, leading me out of the room.

We went upstairs, washed quickly and climbed into bed. Fully contented, I snuggled up to Jason and he stroked my hair. My mind kept going back to the conversation at the dinner table.

"Why were you so brusque with Vicky?"

"I overheard a conversation she had with John and I didn't like what I was hearing."

"What exactly did you hear?"

"She told him that you were trying to make her feel guilty for having a comfortable life, and we both know that's a load of rubbish."

I felt there was more. "What else did she say?"

"That you are just repeating information from the Pleiadians' book and claiming it comes from your own sources."

"But that's just plain silly. Two different sources of information do not exclude it, they verify it," I said, feeling disappointed. "What did John say?"

"He told her that you had given him some very good advice that he probably would not have been able to find in the book."

"That's probably true. How did she respond to that?"

"She said she had found everything you've said to her far from useful and she had decided to be very cautious before accepting any information."

"That woman can't see through her comfort and material possessions," I said, upset. "With that bloody attitude she's not going to be able to open her eyes to different possibilities and she will be forever stuck in the old. Frankly, I don't think she should be coming here any more."

"I agree. You need to talk to Zoe tomorrow," Jason said, and gently kissed the top of my head. "Now, let's go to sleep."

16

Early the following morning, Anna was preparing a cooked breakfast of fried eggs and grilled turkey and chicken sausages, and the inviting smells drew me into the kitchen.

"Hi, how did you sleep last night?" I asked.

"Quite well," she replied.

"That's good." I gazed at the big pan full of freshly fried food. "It looks like you might have to go to Joe's again to get some more eggs."

"I'm not sure I should be accepting free things from him," Anna said, filling a small wicker basket with slices of thickly cut bread.

"Why not? He seems very happy giving them to you free of charge."

"I bet he'll want some kind of payment - eventually."

I picked up a small piece of crust. "I thought you liked him," I said as I popped it into my mouth.

"I do ... sort of."

"He likes you and you sort of like him. I think this might work very well," I said with a knowing smile.

Anna opened one of the top cupboards. "You are really keen for us to get together, aren't you?" she asked, looking at me over her shoulder as she took out some plates.

"I think it would be nice if you had a partner and I like Joe. He has a generous spirit."

Anna smiled, setting the kitchen table. "Okay, I might consider getting some more free groceries from him. We'll see what happens." She crossed to the door and shouted into the hall, "Breakfast's ready."

The men trooped in.

"Smells really good," Jason commented.

"Everything Anna cooks smells good," I said, taking a seat at the table.

Jason squeezed Anna's shoulders appreciatively. "You are a gem.

Maybe you should move in."

Anna gave him a sceptical look.

"I think that while we are redecorating you should definitely move in for the duration," Mike added lightly, taking a seat. "What do you think, George?"

"I'll second that," George said, sitting down next to him.

"You would have to take me and Harry," Anna said lightly.

"As long as Harry doesn't eat all the food you prepare, we don't mind," Jason joked, filling his plate with eggs and sausages.

"I doubt there's any danger of that," Anna replied with a smile, flopping onto the stool between George and Jason. "Harry has a girlfriend now and he's too busy chasing after her. His appetite is not what it used to be."

"Joking aside," Jason said seriously, "now we've got spare beds you are welcome to stay whenever you like."

"Thanks. I'll consider myself invited."

Breakfast passed quickly. Anna and I were clearing the table when Zoe came in. I stopped on my way to the sink with the dirty dishes and looked at her happy face. "You look like the cat who's just caught a canary."

Zoe smiled a very contented smile. "I suppose I am, even if I haven't slept a wink all night."

"Sounds like you've found your match."

"I certainly hope so," Zoe said. "Do you want me to help you with the washing up?"

I nodded. "Who washes? Who dries?"

"I'll wash, you dry," Zoe decided.

"Okay." I deposited the dishes into the sink and reached for a kitchen towel.

"It was such a nice evening yesterday, don't you think?" Zoe asked, filling the sink with water. "Everyone seemed in such high spirits. Even Vicky called this morning to say how much she'd enjoyed it."

"Talking about Vicky," I said. "Jason overheard her talking to John yesterday and what she said wasn't very nice."

"What did she say?" Zoe asked, cleaning a plate with the washing-up brush.

I reached for the clean plate. "I don't really want to repeat what she said, but in essence she doesn't approve of me."

Zoe looked surprised. "She always speaks very highly of you to me."

"Maybe that's because she knows you're my friend."

"Maybe."

"I don't really want the harmony here to be disturbed by her negativity," I said. "I think it's best if she doesn't come here any more."

"I can't tell her not to come," Zoe objected.

"I'm sorry, Zoe, but you're the person who brought her here in the first place."

Zoe turned to me, her hands poised in the sink. "Maybe I brought her here initially, but now she can come on her own and I can't stop her."

"I think she needs to be told that she is no longer welcome here," Anna interjected. "Otherwise she will continue to invite herself."

"And who is going to tell her?" Zoe asked, not at all happy about the possibility that it might have to be her.

"I think it should be you," Anna replied.

"Why me?"

"From the very beginning you've allowed her to manipulate her way into my house and I let her in because you are my friend and you asked me to," I said. "You don't want to upset her by saying no, so you always do what she wants. She can sense your weakness and she is going to use it until you find the strength to say no to her."

Zoe resumed washing up. "I've tried to say no to her so many times, but she doesn't seem to hear it."

"It's probably because when you say no, you don't really mean it."

Zoe didn't respond straight away, as if she was thinking it through, then she said, "I know what you're saying. No means no and I should say it in a firm and assertive way."

I nodded. "Let the fear of upsetting her go."

Zoe sighed resignedly. "Okay, I'll try."

Jason popped his head around the door and met my eyes. "We've finished assembling the wardrobe," he informed me. "You can go and unpack your clothes."

"Thanks, sweetie. I'll do it as soon as I've finished here."

Washing up done, I left Zoe and Anna in the kitchen, and went upstairs to sort out my clothes. I pulled various items out of the big plastic bags. There were evening dresses, pencil skirts, silk blouses and many other formal clothes. I looked at all those clothes and knew that it was very unlikely I would ever wear them again. I separated the evening and more formal clothes from the casual ones, and then selected only a few items from the formal pile and packed the rest ready to be donated to charity.

I was folding the tops and T-shirts I had decided to keep and putting them on a shelf in the wardrobe when Jason entered the bedroom with a very handsome older man. Jason introduced the man as his father. I stared at him momentarily. He was in his mid-forties and had an aura of importance about him, which made him look distinguished as well as attractive. He wore an expensive, well-cut silver-grey suit and a white, thin cotton shirt with the top button casually undone. His hair was dark blond and very neatly cut. He had deep-blue, intelligent-looking eyes and smooth, wrinkle-free skin. He was about six feet tall with a lean, well-proportioned body.

Holding a T-shirt in my hand, I smiled my best smile. "Hi, I'm Carrie," I introduced myself.

"Hello, Carrie. I assume you are the person responsible for keeping Jason away from home?" he asked without a flicker of a smile.

I liked his voice, which was very clear and masculine. I smiled again. "I would prefer to think that Jason stays here of his own free will."

There was a moment of uncomfortable silence.

"Why don't we go downstairs," Jason suggested. "Carrie will make some coffee."

I turned to face Jason. "Could you take your father to the living room, please? I'll bring coffee in a moment."

The two men left. Quickly, I folded the T-shirt I was holding and put it on the shelf in the wardrobe, then gathered all the empty plastic bags and headed for the kitchen. Anna was sorting out the cupboard under the sink. Adding the empty refuse bags to the pile of stuff lying on the floor next to her, I asked, "Have you met Jason's father yet?"

Anna looked up. "No. Is he here?"

I nodded, opening a top cupboard and looking for the coffee. "He has paid us a surprise visit. Do you know if we have any ground coffee?"

"I'm sure we have," Anna said, rising to her feet. She searched through the cupboards and produced a foiled packet. "Freshly ground and still sealed," she announced, handing it to me. "Do you want me to help you?"

"Thanks, but there's no need. You carry on with whatever you were doing."

I opened the packet, put two spoonfuls of richly smelling granules into the coffee maker and switched it on. While the coffee was brewing, I got a tray ready with cups, saucers, fresh cream and sugar. Placing it on the worktop next to the coffee maker, I added some teaspoons and a plate of biscuits. As soon as the coffee had brewed, I lifted the glass pot and put it onto the tray.

"Don't work too hard," I said to Anna, and left the kitchen.

In the living room, Jason and his father sat silently on one of the sofas, an obvious distance between them. As I walked in, I hesitated, not quite sure what to do with the tray as there was still no table. Luckily, Jason came to my rescue and reached for a chair, which he positioned between the two sofas, and I carefully placed the tray on it. He returned to his seat by his father and I sat down on the other sofa, which was positioned at a 90-degree angle to them.

Pouring the hot, dark liquid into the cups, I said, "I apologise for serving coffee on a chair. We're not quite organised yet." I put the pot down. "Any sugar?"

"Two, please," Jason's father requested.

"Cream?"

"No cream, thank you."

I dropped two teaspoons of sugar into one of the cups and handed it to him, and then passed one with no sugar to Jason. A conspicuous tension hung in the air and we sat in silence while I was stirring my coffee.

Sipping his coffee, Jason's father surveyed the room. "It seems you've done a lot of work here. The room looks good."

"It's far from finished, but we're getting there," Jason said. He took a comforting sip of the hot liquid. "So what brings you here?"

"Your sister told me that you are hardly ever at home. I was concerned."

"You could've called me."

"I was in the neighbourhood, so I thought it provided a good opportunity to check up on you."

"I'm a big boy now. Why check up on me?"

"As I said, I was concerned."

"I don't see why you feel the need to be concerned. I've managed to look after myself for years."

"That may be, but since your sister brought your absence to my attention I wanted to make sure you were all right."

Jason shrugged indifferently. "I am all right."

"I know," his father replied. There was a short break in the conversation while he sipped his coffee before he added, "So what are you planning to do in this house?"

"Completely renovate it."

"Renovation takes time. I hope this is not going to be done at the expense of your studies."

"You have never worried about my studies before, so why worry now?" Jason sounded irritated.

His father ignored the belligerent question and said instead, "It's a massive project. Where is the money coming from?"

Jason put down his empty cup. "There is no big cost involved because we have some friends who are helping out and they are perfectly happy to do it for nothing."

"Most of them are here today," I added cordially. "So you can meet them."

"I doubt if my father would be interested in meeting any of my friends," Jason said curtly.

"I'm sure he would be," I said with a smile, and lifted up the pot. "Any more coffee?"

Jason's father drained his cup and held it up for me. "Please."

I topped it up and reached for the plate of biscuits. "Biscuit?"

He took one and placed it on the saucer. "Thank you."

"I expect this house holds a lot of memories for you," I said conversationally, replacing the plate on the tray.

"I suppose it does," he replied, taking a large sip of his coffee. "Not that many good ones, I am afraid."

"My father doesn't like talking about the time he lived here," Jason remarked.

"I'm sorry, I didn't realise," I said apologetically, and changed the subject. "I hope you don't mind that we're changing things in this house."

"Why should I mind? I don't live here any more."

I was slightly confused. "But you still own this place."

Jason's father looked directly at me. "Carrie, it does not matter whether I own this place or not and it matters even less what happens to it. You can paint it black and decorate it with bright red dots and it wouldn't matter one iota to me. I'll never live here anyway."

It was rather surprising that he felt that way. He obviously associated something very unpleasant with the place.

Not sure how else to respond, I smiled and said, "It's a lovely house and we'll look after it as best we can just in case you ever change your mind - and I promise we won't paint it black and red!"

There was a moment of uneasy silence during which he put his cup on the tray. "I think I'd better be going," he said, rising.

Jason and I stood up as well.

"Would you like to meet some of our friends before you go?" I asked.

He checked his watch. "I've got a little spare time."

"Come. We'll introduce you to everyone."

"Do you mind if I leave you to it?" Jason asked. "I have to go and help George to glue the table together."

I shot him a confused look, but said nothing.

"Go ahead. Carrie will look after me," his father said agreeably, but I had a feeling he was rather disappointed.

"I'm sure she will. I'll speak to you later," Jason said, and rushed out.

I smiled resignedly and led his father across the hall into the dining room where Zoe, David and Mike were peeling off the remnants of the old yellow wallpaper. I made the introductions and explained to Jason's father about our plans to decorate the room in a light beige and sky blue colour scheme. He didn't comment, just nodded approvingly. From the dining room we moved on to the kitchen and I introduced him to Anna. I spent a few minutes telling him how we had stripped the old varnish from all the units to make the whole room lighter and added that we planned to change the wall colour from green to white. He acknowledged this with another silent nod and we walked outside through the back doorway. I led him down the veranda steps towards the shed where George and Jason were working on the coffee table, and used the opportunity to introduce him to George.

Jason's father admired the perfectly flat blocks of dark wood, which were very neatly inserted into the corners of the much lighter beautifully finished frame. "Where have you learned to match and finish wood so well?" he asked George.

George smiled. "Love of the wood is my teacher."

Jason's father touched the perfect joint. "For what it's worth, I think you are doing a fantastic job."

"Thank you, sir," George said, pleased.

Jason and George returned to their woodwork and we moved on, cutting across the back garden towards the vegetable patch.

"We've done quite a bit of work in the garden," I explained. "Here we're cultivating organic vegetables. They've only just been planted and need to grow before they can be eaten, but that shouldn't take too long." I indicated the herb garden. "Over there we're growing herbs that we use in our cooking. I don't think we're going to plant anything else, apart from some flowers by the veranda. We want to leave the rest of the garden as natural as possible."

Jason's father seemed to relax a little. "I must say I'm impressed with what you've managed to achieve so far."

"It's amazing, I know. We are very lucky that there are so many people who are willing to help. I think it's because this place is so beautiful and we are all very keen to spend time here."

"I'm glad this place can be of use to someone."

We walked in silence for a while, and then I asked if he would like to stay for lunch.

"Thank you for the invitation, but unfortunately I have to get back to London," he replied with a slight smile.

"Maybe some other time then?"

"Maybe."

We approached his silver Mercedes and stood awkwardly for a moment before I asked, "Shall I call Jason?"

"No, there is no need."

He fished his car keys out of his trouser pocket and clicked the remote.

I held out my hand. "Thank you coming and thank you for allowing me to live here," I said gratefully.

He shook it. "It's probably been the best decision I've ever made," he said, and opened the car door. "Thank you for the tour. It was quite educational."

"I'm really glad I've had an opportunity to meet you. Please do come again."

"We'll see," he said, and climbed into the car.

I stood there watching him drive away, thinking that he was really rather nice and that I would like to get to know him better. His car cleared the corner and I was just about to turn and walk back into the house when I spotted Joe in the distance, carrying what appeared to be a large cardboard box.

"Hi, Joe, how are you?" I asked when he came closer.

"Fine thanks," he replied. "I hope you don't mind me coming over."

"Not at all. You're very welcome."

"Is your friend about? I've brought her some fresh poultry."

"You mean Anna?"

"I'm not sure of her name. She's the one who owns the dog that got caught in my rosebush," he explained awkwardly.

"That's Anna. Wait here, I'll go and get her," I said, and rushed into the kitchen where Anna was busy scrubbing the old tiles behind the hob. "You've got a visitor," I announced cheerily.

She turned and looked at me in bewilderment. "A visitor?"

I nodded. "He's brought some fresh poultry for you, and is waiting outside."

"A visitor who brings gifts? It must be my lucky day," Anna responded with a pleased smile. "I suppose I'd better go and say hello." She pulled her rubber gloves off and deposited them on the edge of the sink. "Can you think of an easy lunch while I am away?" she asked, and disappeared.

I peered into the fridge and quickly decided to make cheese and pickle baguettes with some fresh salad. Taking out the salad vegetables, I sliced some tomatoes and washed the lettuce. I opened a pack of thickly sliced Cheddar cheese and a jar of sweet pickle. I was cutting the French stick into portions when Anna returned with the box in her hands.

"Joe brought far too many chickens," she said, dropping the box onto the table. "I told him we needed a freezer to store them. Luckily, he has a spare one he can give us. I offered to pay for it, but he adamantly refused to accept any money. He is going to bring it over, but I am not sure if I should be accepting all these free gifts. This business of him giving me free stuff worries me."

I looked at her and saw real concern in her eyes. "I don't understand why the attention of a generous man is so worrying?"

"It's worrying because I have no idea what this is leading to."

"He is only trying to be nice to you."

"I don't know anything about him and the whole situation is making me feel uncomfortable."

"You know that he likes you. You know that he has a good heart, otherwise why would he look for the owner of a stray dog?" I said.

"He's also not bad looking," I added.

"You're probably right and I'm being silly," Anna conceded.

"Just give it a chance," I advised, "and stop worrying. It's not like you have to have a relationship with him if you don't want to."

Anna gave me a questioning look. "You think I'm overreacting?"

I nodded.

"All right, I'll give it a chance."

"Good. Now, could you help me to finish lunch, please?"

Anna gazed at the long slices of French stick. "Sandwiches again?"

"Why not? Everyone loves our sandwiches."

We filled each baguette with cheese, pickle and salad, and put them on seven individual plates. Anna took four into the dining room and I carried the remaining ones outside, together with some drinks.

"Lunch," I announced to George and Jason. "Where do you want to eat?"

George seemed very preoccupied with the gluing of some wooden strips. "Can you leave mine here, please? I have to finish this before the glue dries up."

Jason extracted one plate and one small bottle of water from me, and placed them on the workbench. "Can I leave you to it?" he asked.

"No problem. You go and have your lunch."

Jason placed his hand on my elbow. "Come on, babe, let's sit down." He led me to the veranda and we sat on the steps.

I handed him a bottle of water. "Your father left without you saying goodbye to him. I think he was disappointed."

Jason unscrewed the bottle. "I doubt it. My father doesn't expect a goodbye from me every time I see him," he said, taking a swig of water.

"Maybe I got it wrong."

"More than likely. My father doesn't care much about me."

"I don't agree. He came here out of concern for you, so that shows he cares," I said pointedly, biting into my baguette.

"Carrie, my father and I do not get on. I don't know why he came here and I doubt it was because he was concerned about me. I have been away for days before and he hasn't even noticed I wasn't there."

Jason acted as though it were all unimportant, but I knew differently. I could see that the estrangement from his father wasn't easy for him.

"I am sure he does care, but maybe he doesn't know how to show it," I said gently. "Do you know what happened here that makes him dislike this place so much?"

Jason took another swig from his bottle. "As far as I know, my grandfather was very cold and indifferent towards my father because he believed he was the product of some affair my grandmother had had with one of his friends. He felt betrayed and there was a lot of hatred in the house because of it," he explained. "Still, I don't understand why my father would behave in exactly the same way towards his own son."

"Maybe it's because he doesn't know how to be any other way."

"Love and indifference don't go together though," Jason reasoned, tucking into his sandwich. "If my father loves me, why is he so indifferent towards me?"

"One doesn't necessarily exclude the other," I replied. "Your father's indifference doesn't mean he doesn't love you. It might simply mean that he doesn't know how to show his love for you."

Jason sighed. "I don't know."

"Think about it. You went to your father and asked him if a friend of yours who desperately needed a place to stay could live in this house. This place had been empty for years because it was too painful for your father to acknowledge that it existed, and he wanted to wipe it out of his memory and never hear about it again. Despite all this, he still said yes, because you asked him. He overcame his strong resentment towards Woodland today to come here and see if you were all right. It wasn't easy for him, but his love for you was stronger than the years of bitterness. I bet that if you look back you'll find that he has never refused you anything."

Jason thought for a moment. "You are right. He always gives me anything I want."

"I think that's his way of showing that he cares."

"Maybe. I've never thought about it like that. I've always thought he gave me things out of guilt."

"He gives you things because he wants you to love him."

"I do love him in a strange kind of way."

"Have you ever told him that you love him?"

Jason shook his head. "No, not in so many words."

"Next time you see him, try telling him. You'll probably find that doing so will totally change your relationship with him."

"You think?"

'I'm sure it will."

We stopped our conversation because we could both hear the growing sound of a rattling motor engine that seemed to be coming from somewhere at the front of the house.

"What do you think that is?" I asked.

"I have no idea. Let's go and see," Jason said, rising.

Together, we walked along the side path to the front of the house where Joe was manoeuvring a tractor with a small trailer between the parked cars. He stopped it close to the main entrance and jumped out of the small cabin.

"I brought the freezer," he announced.

"Thanks, Joe, that's very kind of you," I said, and walked closer to see a dirty metal box that was resting on the trailer. "I assume that's it?"

Joe nodded.

"Does it work?"

"Yes, it works very well. It just needs cleaning," Joe replied, adding, "I'll need some help to take it off the trailer."

"I'll help you," Jason volunteered.

Joe turned to me. "Do you want us to carry it inside?"

'Yes please, into the kitchen. I'll open the door for you," I said, and rushed to the front door.

Joe released the back flap of the trailer and it dropped open. He pushed the freezer to the edge, and then he and Jason lifted it off the trailer, Jason holding one end of the box and Joe the other. They carried it through the front doorway as I held the door open for them. Once they had passed through, I closed the door and followed them into the kitchen.

Anna, who was busy at the sink washing the dishes, turned and looked at the freezer. "Oh, hi, Joe, I didn't expect it today."

Joe eased his end of the metal box down onto the floor. "You said you didn't have room in the fridge," he said as Jason let the other end go. "I thought it would be bad to let all those chickens go to waste."

"Yes, it would be." Anna grabbed a kitchen towel and began drying her hands.

Joe stared at her. "Anything else you need, just ask."

She faced him. "Anything?"

"Anything."

She smiled. "You insist on spoiling me."

Joe smiled back. "As far as I'm concerned, a lovely lady like you deserves to be spoiled."

"What about your wife? Doesn't she mind that you are spoiling other ladies?" Anna asked.

"As she's left me for another man I doubt that she does," Joe replied, and they exchanged flirtatious glances.

"Where do you want us to put this freezer, babe?" Jason asked.

I pointed to an empty corner. "Could you push it over there, please."

Jason grabbed the top edge of the freezer. "Come on, Joe, let's shift this thing."

"Right."

Joe grabbed the other side of the box and began pulling it while Jason pushed it. In no time at all, the freezer had been positioned in the designated corner.

"I need to go and help George, so I'll leave you to it," Jason said, and headed out.

Joe gazed at Anna. "Well, I'd better be going then."

Anna smiled at him. "Thanks for the freezer."

"I'm only around the corner if you need anything."

"I'll remember that."

"Well, I hope I'll see you soon. Bye."

"Bye, Joe."

As soon as Joe had left I smiled at Anna. "Was I right or was I right? I told you he liked you."

"You were right," Anna admitted. "And you might be pleased to know that I quite like him too," she added.

"I am more than pleased." I glanced at the cardboard box on the table. "Are the chickens still in that box?"

Anna nodded. "There was no room in the fridge for them.'"

"It's just as well Joe delivered the freezer today then."

We both looked at the dirty freezer box and then at each other.

"Needs a good scrub," Anna said.

"A bloody good scrub," I agreed, and we both reached for rubber gloves and cleaning cloths.

* * *

The evening was fresh and warm with the smell of summer in the air, and Jason invited everyone to the local pub for dinner. The pub was called The Royal Oak and was situated about a mile from the house.

Anna called the dogs in, we locked them in the kitchen and then we made our way outside where everyone was waiting.

"I think we're ready to leave," Jason said.

Anna walked to her car. "It looks like I'm on my own."

"Why don't you invite Joe to join us," I suggested.

"Yes, do," Jason encouraged.

"I'll stop on the way and ask him." Anna opened the car door.

"Do you know how to get to the pub?" Jason asked.

"No, but I'm sure Joe does," Anna replied, and climbed in.

We piled into our respective cars and drove out in convoy, Jason leading the way. As we reached the first intersection we took a left turn. Joe's farm was about 100 metres down the road, and Anna stopped outside while the rest of us carried on to the pub.

The Royal Oak was a light-coloured brick building with a charcoal slate tiled roof, surrounded by a well-kept green garden of mowed grass, random growing trees and some wild bushes, which provided nice cover from the nearby road. On the grass were six large wooden tables with solid benches on either side attached securely to the heavy wooden base. The place was still relatively empty and most of them were vacant. We chose one in a nice quiet spot at the far end of the garden and sat around it. Anna and Joe arrived sometime later. "Sorry for taking so long but Joe had to arrange a babysitter," Anna siad while Joe quickly organised two chairs and placed them alongside each other at one of the short ends of the table.

"I'll go and get some menus," Zoe announced, and sauntered inside the building.

She emerged with a pile of plastic-covered, colourful sheets printed on both sides, and handed them out. We studied them for a while and when everyone was ready Jason and Mike collected the orders and disappeared inside the pub. They returned shortly afterwards with trays full of drinks, which they passed around.

Jason reached for his mug of low-alcohol ale. "I would like to use this opportunity to thank you all for your hard work, which has been greatly appreciated," he said. "I hope you can see how much can be achieved if we all work together. With our combined skills we are transforming the house. George is a great carpenter, David a great decorator and I am what you might call a jack of all trades. Zoe is good at sewing, Anna is the greatest cook, and with Carrie's help she makes sure that we are all fed. All things considered, I think we make a great team." He held his beer aloft. "Cheers," he added, and took a big swig.

"Cheers!" Everyone raised their drinks in a toast.

"I never would have guessed I'd be appreciated for my sewing," Zoe commented laughingly.

David smiled at her. "I appreciate you for much more than that."

"You do?"

"You're quite a decorator, for a start," he said, his tone light.

Zoe smacked his arm playfully. "Don't make fun of me."

"Zoe, you'd better watch him," Mike interjected jokingly. "He told me in confidence that your decorating skills leave a lot to be desired."

"Thanks, mate. Next time remind me not to tell you anything in confidence," David said good-humouredly.

"I get the message," Zoe said. "Carrie, you'd better find me something else to do next weekend. I refuse to help these two spoiled brats. I've been slaving all day trying to help them and that's the thanks I get."

David put his arm around her and pulled her to him. "You can slave for me any day. I've loved having you around," he said seriously.

"You have?" Zoe asked, gazing into his eyes.

"Sure. I like spending time with you whatever we do."

Zoe kissed his cheek. "You are such a sweet man."

"And you are the sweetest girl," David replied, and squeezed her tight.

Zoe smiled a very happy smile. "I think we are a very suitable pair, don't you?"

"Yes, we most definitely are, sweetheart."

At that point the food was delivered by two young men, and placed quickly and efficiently in front of everyone. As we tucked in, the atmosphere at the table was relaxed and sociable. There was a lot of friendly banter, jokes and laughter.

"What is it that you farm, Joe?" Mike asked, cutting into his roast chicken.

Joe sipped his beer. "Mostly wheat and corn."

"Have you had any mysterious circles in your crop yet?"

"No, not yet."

"What do you think they are?"

"I'm not sure. All I know is that I couldn't make them with a combine, let alone with a board and a piece of string," Joe said, spearing a chip with his fork.

"Many farmers say these formations are destroying their crops. Would you mind if a circle appeared in yours?"

"Why should I mind? They aren't done maliciously. There must be a good reason why they appear."

"You seem like a generous man," Mike said lightly. "I hear you've donated a box of chickens and a freezer too."

"I don't know about generous. I was just trying to impress a very nice lady," Joe admitted with a meaningful smile in Anna's direction.

"No doubt the lady has been impressed," Mike commented.

"Anna, were you impressed?" Zoe wanted to know.

"How could I not have been? It was all given to me from the heart,'" Anna replied, and smiled at Joe.

Mike laughed. "How times have changed. It used to be jewels that impressed a lady and now it's chickens!"

"Don't knock chickens, Mike," Zoe said. "When you're hungry you can't eat jewels."

"Never a truer word has been spoken," Anna said, squeezing Joe's hand reassuringly.

The sun was setting and the outside lights were switched on, illuminating the garden with a dimmed yellow glow, and the dinner was nearly over. Our table had been cleared and there were only a few half-full glasses left.

Jason drained his. "So, who's coming to help next weekend?"

"I'll be here," Mike announced.

"Me too," David said.

"And me," Zoe confirmed, gazing lovingly at David.

"You can count me in," George added.

"I'll definitely be here," Anna said, turning to Joe. "What about you, Joe? Would you like to spend next weekend with us?"

"Is that an invitation?" Joe seemed unsure.

"If you feel you need to be invited, then it's an invitation," Anna replied.

"Then I'll be happy to join you."

"Good. This means we'll all meet again next weekend," Jason said, rising.

The rest of us stood up as well and we walked slowly in a group to the car park where we separated and climbed into our five different cars and set off on our journeys back home.

Anna slowed down by Jason's car and lowered her side window. "I'll follow you," she said. "I'm going to collect the dogs."

We arrived at Woodland ten minutes later. Jason went inside and I waited for Anna to park. I waved to Joe, who was sitting in the passenger seat. Anna got out of her car and we walked into the house.

"Things seem to be moving on with Joe," I commented lightly.

"Yes, they are. He invited me to his place for a drink and I accepted." Anna opened the kitchen door and called the dogs. They both ran happily into the hall. "Wish me luck. I'll see you tomorrow," she said and headed for the front door, the dogs following.

Anna left and the house suddenly seemed very quiet and still. I checked that all the doors were locked and made my way upstairs. Jason was in the bathroom, so I waited for him to come out before I went to wash myself. Feeling tired, I washed quickly and soon joined Jason in bed. We snuggled up to each other and within minutes we were fast asleep.

17

At the break of dawn I was quite unexpectedly awakened by a voice resonating in my head. I lay motionless, listening. The voice was telling me that Jason and I were expected to prepare ourselves to join our partners on a cosmic journey that would last a few weeks. I was advised that we needed to plan the timing of the journey very carefully and make proper arrangements to allow for our absence.

When the message had ended I sat up on the edge of the bed and gently shook Jason's arm to wake him up.

"What's up?" he mumbled.

"Wake up. I need to talk to you."

He half opened his eyes. "I'm listening."

"I've just received an important message. We've been invited to join Amos and Elia on their ship for a cosmic journey."

Fully awake now, Jason stared at me as though not comprehending. "Are you sure you heard correctly?"

I nodded.

"Wait a minute ... Amos is talking to me now." I listened for a moment. "He is confirming that he would like us to join him on his ship for an intergalactic journey. He says that it's time for human entrance into the family of galactic civilisations and that it's time for the inhabitants of Earth to reclaim the right to be a part of the cosmos, the right that was taken away from them centuries ago."

Jason sat up beside me. "This is unbelievable. How long is this trip going to take?" he asked excitedly.

I passed the question on to Amos and waited for his reply, which came almost instantly.

"He can't give us the precise time because the time spans within different parts of the cosmos are different to those on Earth. He's estimating that it will take a few weeks of Earth time."

Jason's excitement was quickly replaced by concern. "But we can't just leave everything for weeks?"

"Of course we can. People have been known to go on long holidays."

"It will take some planning."

"So let's start planning."

"How much time do we have?"

I passed Jason's query on to Amos and repeated the reply.

"As much as we need. Amos will wait for us to tell him when we are ready."

"Okay, let's think about it rationally," Jason said. "The first thing we need to do is to find someone to look after the house while we're away."

"Anna might be able to keep an eye on the house."

"If she can't, what are our other options?"

I couldn't come up with any other solution.

"I'm sure we'll find someone," I said, trying to be positive.

"I hope we will, but whatever happens I think we should secure this place."

"What do you mean by securing it?"

"This house doesn't belong to us. It belongs to my father and he will not be very happy if he finds out that we have left it with strangers. He might decide he wants it back."

That was bad news.

"Even if I'm renting it?"

'Well, you're not really renting it, are you?' Jason pointed out.

"That's true," I had to agree. "So what are you suggesting we should do?"

"I'll talk to my father and try to persuade him to sign it over to me. He hates this place, so hopefully he will agree. You will need to talk to Anna. I'm concerned that she might not want the responsibility."

"She doesn't have to move here," I reasoned. "It would be enough if she kept an eye on the place and came here once or twice a week."

"Ideally she should be here every weekend so the work can continue," Jason replied. "If there is no one here, people will stop coming and the place will be left to rot as before."

"We'll only be away for a few weeks. I'm sure we can find a way to keep things as they are. I'll talk to Anna today," I said, adding, "I think we should let everyone know that we are going away."

Jason faced me. "What do you suggest we tell them?"

"I would like to tell them the truth, but I doubt they'll be able to cope with it. We'll have to tell them we've decided to take a long holiday."

Jason grinned, suddenly realising the enormity of what was happening. "Babe, are we really going on a ship to travel through space?"

I grinned too. "Yes, we are."

"I can't believe it! This must be the best day of my life!" he said animatedly. "It can't get any better."

"Oh yes, it can," I said, falling back onto the bed and pulling him with me.

"Thinking again, maybe it can," he agreed, kissing me on the lips and undoing the buttons of my nightshirt.

* * *

We had breakfast together, then Jason left to see his father and I sat alone in the kitchen, trying to decide what to do. I thought of finishing the painting of the cosmos, but I was feeling too unsettled. My life had taken a very unexpected turn and it was all so unbelievable and exciting I found it difficult to concentrate on anything, but at the same time I didn't want to waste the morning doing nothing. Rising, I went to the living room, unfolded my yoga mat and placed it on the floor. I put on some calming music and lay down on my back, closed my eyes and dedicated the next half an hour to total relaxation.

Much more composed, after my repose, I set up an easel in the back room and began working on the nearly finished painting of the cosmos. I painted the last few circles and then spent some time making corrections to shapes and lines, and four hours later the painting was finally completed. Pleased with my efforts, I carefully lifted it off the easel and carried it upstairs into one of the empty bedrooms where I propped it up against the wall to dry. That done, I went back downstairs to make myself some well-deserved coffee. I was pouring hot water into a mug when the back door opened and Anna walked in.

"Hi," she said, tossing her handbag onto a chair.

"Hi. Coffee?"

"Please."

I fixed another mug of coffee and handed it to her. "I'm glad you're here because I need to talk to you about something very important," I said, reaching for my drink. "Let's sit down."

Anna moved a chair and sat at the kitchen table. I sat next to her.

"What I am going to tell you might sound unusual or even improbable," I began tentatively, nursing my mug in my hands.

"Improbable?" Anna asked with obvious curiosity.

"Something very unusual happened last night ..." I paused, unsure how best to tell her.

Anna had a worried look on her face. "Yes?"

I decided to be straightforward. "Last night I received a message from one of our cosmic partners. It appears that being in cosmic co-operation means our work is as much on the planet as it is in the cosmos, and Jason and I were invited to join our cosmic partners on one of the ships."

I stopped and looked for Anna's reaction. Her expression had changed from worry to bewilderment.

"Do you mean that you are going to be taken away on a ship?"

I nodded and took a sip of my coffee.

"When?"

"As soon as we are ready."

Anna looked concerned.

"It's an amazing opportunity for us," I said.

"I realise that, but what about this place?"

"We must make sure the house is not left unattended. Jason and I were hoping that you might be able to look after it while we are away."

"Carrie, people come to Woodland because you and Jason are here. They won't come to work on the house if you leave," Anna said. "What will you tell them?"

"Obviously we can't tell them the truth," I replied. "I think it'll be best if we tell them that we are going away on a long holiday."

"Do you know how long you will be away?"

"Hopefully it won't be for too long, a few weeks perhaps."

"I suppose nothing much would change if it's only a few weeks. I could certainly look after the place for a short time, in fact I would be happy to do it."

I touched her hand across the table. "Thanks. It means a lot. This house is very important and I would feel terrible if we had to leave it abandoned." I noticed that she hadn't touched her drink. "Why aren't you drinking your coffee?"

"Oh, I completely forgot about it. I suppose I'm in some kind of shock," Anna replied. "Shock in a good sense, but I just feel sad that you are leaving me behind."

"Don't feel sad. One day you'll go as well," I said reassuringly. "Everyone who is in cosmic co-operation will eventually travel on the ships. By joining into cosmic co-operation you automatically become a member of the cosmic Family of Light and it's only a matter of time before you'll be requested to work in the cosmos as well as on the planet."

"This sounds absolutely fantastic. It gives me so much hope for the future," Anna said. "Is there anything else you want me to do besides look after the house?" she enquired.

"Yes, there is one other thing. I know Sally is practically your dog now, but could you look after her for me?"

"Of course I will."

"You don't need to be here all the time, but it would be great if you could spend weekends here so people can still come and benefit from this place," I said. "If you stay here during the week you'll probably find this place rather lonely."

"I'm not too concerned about that. Joe would be only too happy to keep me company."

I gave her a curious look. "How did it go yesterday?"

"We spent a long time chatting and I discovered a lot of things about him - nice things."

"Do you think it might lead to something more?"

"Possibly."

"I am happy you like him."

"So am I, especially now that you are going away. It's nice to know I won't be left on my own."

"We're not leaving you. We'll be back in a few weeks."

"I know, but this place will be very empty without you."

There was the sound of a key in the front door lock and a moment later Jason entered the kitchen.

"I'm glad you're both here," he said, pulling a chair out and sitting down between us. "I've got some exciting news."

"I don't think I can cope with any more exciting news today," Anna said, smiling.

Jason looked from me to Anna and back. "I assume you two have had a chat?"

"Yes, we did," I replied. "Anna has agreed to look after the place while we are away."

"Thank you so much, Anna. You can't imagine how much this means to us. This house is so important, not just for us, but for everyone who is willing to work for the cosmic good. People who come here can learn co-operation and unity, and the tranquillity helps them to think independently and reassess everything. Admittedly, it's only a start, but nevertheless it's a very important start and we would feel really bad if we left and nobody carried on the work we have started here."

"I do understand," Anna said. "This place has become like my second home and being here is very important to me."

"We feel exactly the same way," Jason said with a smile. "Now, I said I had some exciting news and that is that my father was so impressed with everything we've done here that he has agreed to sign the house over to me."

"That's fantastic," Anna and I chimed together.

"It's better than fantastic," Jason said excitedly. "It means that this place can now be fully dedicated to the Family of Light."

"I like the sound of that," Anna muttered with a smile. "I promise to look after it as if it were my own."

"How long will it be before the place is officially yours?" I asked Jason.

"Not long. The papers should be ready to sign within days."

"So all the immediate problems have been solved and it looks like we might be able to leave in a week."

"We need to organise a proper send-off," Anna said, adding as an afterthought, "I know what we can do. Remember when we were talking about organising a barbecue?"

Jason and I nodded.

"Why don't we organise it for this weekend? We can invite everybody and it will give you an opportunity to say goodbye."

"That's a great idea," I agreed readily.

Jason seemed happy with the suggestion as well. "Let's do it."

"I don't want you two to do a thing," Anna said bossily. "I'll organise the whole party."

"Let me at least buy the barbecue," Jason offered.

"I will, if you promise to buy a very big one," Anna said with a smile.

"That's an easy promise to keep," I observed lightly. "You have to make it more challenging for him."

"Hey, now," Jason objected. "I am not up to big challenges."

Anna appeared to be thinking. "Can you imagine having a large brick barbecue outside? We could just drop stuff onto the grill and feed a lot of people without having to slave in the kitchen for hours."

"I'm all for that," I said. "What about you, sweetie?"

"I don't have a clue how to build a brick barbecue," Jason protested.

"I thought you were a jack of all trades," I teased. "Surely, you can build a simple barbecue."

"I've seen a pile of bricks outside Joe's barn," Anna added lightly. "I am pretty sure he won't mind parting with them."

"I'll give it my best shot," Jason relented, "but don't expect miracles."

"Who expects miracles?" Anna and I asked in unison.

"You two are like a couple of parrots," Jason said, and we all laughed.

"I'll miss you guys," Anna muttered.

"We'll miss you too," Jason and I said together.

"We are three of a kind," Anna said laughingly.

"Yes, we certainly are," I agreed with a smile.

* * *

Later that day, Jason and I drove to Barnes to pay a visit to my parents. We stopped at an Interflora florist on the way so Jason could get a large, expertly arranged bouquet of flowers for my mother.

He was clutching an impressive bunch of yellow roses and pink lilies as we reached the front door of my parents' house.

"How do I look?" he asked, adjusting his shirt collar nervously.

"Very handsome," I said, pressing the buzzer. "I'm sure my mother will approve."

The door opened and we faced my father. I smiled. "Hi Dad."

"Good afternoon, Robert," Jason said pleasantly.

"Good afternoon. Come in, come in," Dad invited, and we followed him down the hall.

As we entered the living room my mother stood up from her armchair to greet us. I was pleased to see that she looked much better. Her pasty complexion had been replaced by a healthy rosy colour, she had lost the dark circles under her eyes and her previously emaciated-looking frame had gained some weight. Her face was made-up and her hair was freshly washed and styled. She was nicely dressed in a cream silk blouse and brown skirt.

I walked over and gave her a hug and kiss. "Hi, Mum, how are you?"

"Getting better," she replied.

"You are looking well," I said, glancing in Jason's direction. "This is my friend, Jason."

Jason flashed his gorgeous smile. "Pleased to meet you." He held out the bunch of flowers. "These are for you, Mrs Simpson."

Mum smiled back at him. "Thank you, they are lovely. Please call me Kate," she said appreciatively, and passed them to my father. "Robert, dear, could you put them in some water, please?"

"Can I offer you anything?" Dad asked on his way to the kitchen. "Tea perhaps?"

"Tea would be lovely," I said.

"Please sit down," Mum invited.

Jason and I flopped onto the large soft sofa and my mother returned to her seat in one of the armchairs.

I gazed at the array of medicine bottles that stood on the side table next to where my mother was sitting. "Are you taking all those drugs?" I asked, concerned.

My mother glanced to her side. "Yes."

"How are you feeling on them?"

"As well as can be expected. The inflammation has gone down and I can hold my food down now without that horrible, crampy abdominal pain I had, but I do get nauseous and I also tend to get bad headaches."

"What are you taking?"

"Mainly steroids and antibiotics, and I also take something called immunosuppressive agents."

"No wonder you get nausea and headaches. You are taking very strong chemical substances and, as much as they help to alleviate the symptoms of your condition, they also do some damage to your body."

"I imagine they do, my dear. Still, I have to take them and I don't really have any choice."

"You should only take these drugs for a short period of time to relieve the symptoms," I said. "After that you should look into alternative therapies."

"Carrie, I know you mean well, but you are not a doctor," Mum responded. "How can you possibly know how to treat Crohn's disease?"

"Of course I'm not a doctor, but I do know that the drugs you are taking are strong enough to damage your immune system, so in effect you are treating one problem and creating another. If your immune system gets too weak your body won't be able to heal itself, so it's important that you try to control the symptoms with less damaging remedies." I reached into my bag and pulled out a book on nutritional healing. "I brought this book for you. You need to look through it. There is plenty of information on how to heal your condition with vitamins, minerals, herbs and food supplements," I said, handing it to her.

"Thank you, dear," Mum said. She glanced at the book and then put it to one side. "My priority is to get better, so for the time being I have to follow doctor's orders."

"At least promise me that you'll look into other methods of treatment. Very often they work very well," I insisted.

Dad entered the room with the tea tray. "I'll make sure she does," he said, placing the tray on the coffee table.

I caught his eye. "Promise?"

"I promise. I want your mother to get better."

"You are making me better, dear," Mum said, patting his hand. "You've been doing so much for me I practically don't have to lift a finger. I am getting terribly spoiled in my old age."

"That's the least I can do. After all, you've been looking after me for years," Dad said with a smile, taking a seat in the other armchair. He faced me. "Your mother needs to recuperate properly and we've decided it would be preferable if we go back to Spain where the weather is so much warmer than here."

I wasn't surprised by their decision. "How soon are you planning to go?"

"I booked the flights for next Sunday," Dad replied. "I'm sorry I won't be able to finish the work in your garden."

"That's all right, Dad. The garden is lovely as it is."

"Must be quite unusual, as your father can't stop talking about it," Mum said lightly. "He says it's wild, but quite beautiful."

"It is beautiful. You have to come and see it before you leave."

"Why don't you invite your parents to our barbecue party?" Jason suggested.

"Yes, definitely. Come to our barbecue on Saturday," I said.

Mum shot a questioning look at my father. "What do you think, Robert?"

"I think you should certainly see the place, but it's some distance away and we don't have a car."

"I would be very happy to come over to collect you and drive you there," Jason offered.

"In that case we'll definitely come," Mum decided, and reached for the teapot. "Tea?"

Jason smiled. "Yes, please."

"So what do you study?" she asked, filling one of the cups.

"The history of art," he replied.

Mum moved the cup in front of him. "I understand you both live in your father's house?"

"Yes."

"I am sure you appreciate that because we live abroad I tend to be quite concerned about my daughter," Mum said, pouring tea into the rest of the cups.

"That's perfectly understandable."

"I would feel much less concerned if I knew that you were serious about her."

"Mum!" I admonished.

Jason shot me a pacifying look. "It's all right. Yes, I am very serious about your daughter."

"Carrie wasn't happy in her last relationship," Mum felt it necessary to add. "I would hate to see her unhappy again."

"I don't understand why you worry, Kate. She seems very happy to me," Dad intervened. "As for her previous relationship, any woman would be unhappy with that moron, Mark. He had nothing to offer anyone."

"You never liked him," Mum muttered.

"No I didn't, because he wasn't an easy person to like," Dad retorted.

Mum faced me. "Did you get any money from him?"

I shook my head. "Not yet."

"Why not?" Mum asked, sounding surprised.

"He's decided not to sell the house, so we haven't come to an agreement," I replied.

"Is he planning to pay you off?"

"I don't know. I haven't managed to get any answers from him yet."

"I hope you've contacted a solicitor?"

"No, I haven't. I don't have enough money to cover a solicitor's fees."

"Why don't you see your father's solicitor and we'll settle the bill?" Mum suggested. She didn't wait for me to reply, just said to my father, "Robert, could you call Mr Barker and arrange an appointment, please? I want to make sure that this is dealt with before we leave for Spain."

"I'll get his number," Dad said, as he got up and headed out of the room. He returned a few minutes later. "Mr Barker will see you on Friday at four," he informed me, handing me a piece of paper. "Here is his address and phone number in case you need to change the appointment."

"Thanks, Dad," I said, dropping the note into my handbag.

"Make sure you go," Mum said, rising. "I am beginning to feel tired, so I hope you don't mind if I go and lie down." She came over to me and kissed the top of my head. "I'll see you on Saturday." She then turned to Jason. "Goodbye, Jason. Thank you for coming."

"I think we should be going," I said, as soon as Mum had left the room.

Dad walked us to the front door.

"Jason will pick you up on Saturday," I said, giving him a goodbye kiss.

Dad nodded. "Just let us know what time he's coming."

"I'll call you."

* * *

The following morning, Jason and I got up early to get started on all the things that needed to be done before our departure. We were in the kitchen finishing our breakfast of poached eggs on toast when Anna walked in.

"Hi. How are you two this morning?" she enquired cheerily, hanging her handbag on the back of the empty chair.

"Fine," I replied. "Would you like some coffee?"

"I'd love some, but don't bother getting up. I'll get it myself." She grabbed a jar of instant coffee, dropped a spoonful into a mug and filled it with hot water. With the mug in her hand, she joined us at the table. "I popped into Joe's on my way here to ask him about the bricks," she said, sipping the hot liquid. "He is happy to part with them and he will load them onto his trailer and bring them over around lunchtime. He is free this afternoon and can stay to help."

"In that case I'd better go and get a grill," Jason said, getting up. He picked up his dirty plate and dropped it into the sink.

"Joe said you will need some mortar to bond the bricks together," Anna added. She reached behind for her handbag and handed Jason her car keys. "Take my car as it has more room in the back."

"Thanks. I'll see you both later," he said, and left.

We finished our coffee, cleared the table and did the washing up. When the kitchen was spotlessly clean I suggested that perhaps we should go and decide which room we could convert into Anna's bedroom.

Upstairs, I opened the door to one of the smaller bedrooms where the painting of the cosmos was propped by the wall.

"Oh, you've finished it!" Anna exclaimed when she saw it. She stood silently in front of the canvas, admiring it. "It's absolutely beautiful," she commented quietly.

"You really like it?"

She nodded. "Yes, I do."

"Do you remember when you suggested decorating the dining room to accommodate this painting?" I asked. "I was thinking that perhaps you could make it your project while we are away."

"That's a terrific idea, but it means the room will be decorated to my taste."

"Your taste is great and I can't think of anyone better for the job," I said with an encouraging smile.

Anna smiled back. "Then I'll definitely do it."

"Good. Now, let's decide on your bedroom."

There were two rooms from which to choose, both in need of refurbishment. The room we were in overlooked the front courtyard, which made for a very uninspiring view. On the good side it was the larger of the two rooms, but it required a lot of work to put it right. My eyes wandered, trying to assess roughly how much time we would need to decorate it when I noticed a big wet stain that had spread in one of the corners of the ceiling.

"This room is no good. The roof is leaking," I said worriedly. "It'll be costly to repair, which of course is a problem."

Anna followed my gaze. "It's quite a big leak. This should be repaired as soon as possible before the whole wall is destroyed," she commented.

"I know, and we'll have to find a solution soon. Let's check the other room."

We moved on to the second bedroom, which was situated at the other end of the hall.

Anna walked to the window. "I like the view," she said, staring at the open countryside spreading out below.

I joined her at the window. "Yes, it's really nice. Obviously it has to be this one then."

Anna looked around. "We would need to redecorate it."

"Yes, and we need to do it quickly."

"How about we start on it straight away? We can begin by removing this dirty old wallpaper."

"Good idea."

"I'll go and get the steamer," Anna said enthusiastically, and rushed downstairs. She returned very quickly with the steamer, folded steps and a scraping tool. She handed the tool to me and connected the steamer to the mains. "I'll steam, you scrape," she suggested.

We worked until 12.30 p.m. when Jason came back with a large, hooded, stainless steel barbecue grill and bags of dry mortar mix.

Anna made some sandwiches and we sat outside on the veranda steps sharing them and waiting for Joe to arrive. Around 1.15 p.m. we heard the now familiar sound of his tractor, so all three of us strode to the front of the house to help him unload the bricks. One by one we carried them to the edge of the garden on the right side of the property and laid them in a pile next to some shrubs. When all the bricks had been lifted off the trailer, Anna and I returned upstairs to carry on with the work in the bedroom, leaving Jason and Joe to start on the brick construction for the barbecue.

By the evening everyone was tired and hungry. Anna prepared a quick dinner of pasta and mushroom sauce, and we sat at the kitchen table to eat.

"Joe, can you come tomorrow and help me to lay the bricks?" Jason asked, tucking into his pasta.

Joe reached for his glass of water. "I could come in the afternoon, but I will have to bring my boy with me."

"Sure, bring him over," Jason said. "He can help us to lay some bricks."

"I doubt it. He doesn't seem to be interested in much except his football," Joe said sadly. "He used to be a nice little boy, but since his mother abandoned him he has become rather difficult and unsociable."

"Well, he won't be able to play with his football here," Jason said, "but hopefully we can interest him in something else."

"I sincerely hope you can. I have tried and failed."

"Bring him over. I am sure he'll be fine."

Soon after dinner Joe got into his tractor and drove off. Anna, Jason and I took the dogs for a walk in the woods. The sun was slowly setting and the last light of day covered the trees in a misty evening glow.

Our conversation turned to Joe's son. "The boy must be quite angry at his mother for leaving him," Anna remarked.

"I know exactly how he feels," Jason commented, speaking from experience. "Unloved and rejected."

"I will never understand why some people reject their own

children," Anna said wistfully. "I would do anything to be able to have a child, but unfortunately it's not meant to be."

"You don't know. If things work out with Joe you can become a stepmother to his son," I remarked.

"I like Joe, but his son sounds like quite a handful."

"He is only a small boy. He probably just needs to know that someone cares for him."

"Joe does care for him."

"I'm sure he does, but the boy obviously feels very lonely and needs more than Joe can give him."

"I don't know. It's such a commitment. It wouldn't be right to get close to the child and then, if things didn't work out, abandon him like his mother did."

"Anna, you have to learn to trust your instincts," I said. "Every experience in life is a lesson worth learning. Stop analysing everything. You should start making decisions based on your instincts, not on assumptions."

"It might sound easy, but it's not," Anna replied.

"It's not that difficult either. Don't try to anticipate the future. At best it's only speculation as to how things will work out and this confuses the mind. It's impossible to make the right decision when your mind is confused like that."

Anna thought for a moment and then said, "You are right. No more assumptions."

Turning back, we walked in silence for a while.

"Tomorrow, I would like to start on the bedroom early, so there's hardly any point in my driving back to London," Anna said, breaking the silence.

Jason put his arm around her shoulders and gave her a friendly squeeze. "Why don't you stay until Monday?"

"I'd love to, but I have to be in London on Friday," Anna replied. "I have an appointment with my accountant that I can't break."

"At least stay until Friday," I said.

"You sure you don't mind?"

"Of course we don't. You are part of this household and you are always welcome here," Jason said.

"Thanks, you two are like my close family and I love you both."

Jason gave her another squeeze. "We love you too."

18

By Friday the outdoor barbecue had been built and was standing majestically in a quiet area of the garden partially surrounded by shrubs. It was a big construction of neatly laid red bricks with a shiny stainless steel grill, which sat in the middle of an extensive top surface. The idea to build it had been a great one and everyone was very pleased with the final result, especially Jason. Anna's room was nearly finished as well. The ceiling was freshly painted with white matt emulsion and the walls were covered with stripy cream wallpaper.

It was nearly 3 p.m. and I was alone in the house, getting ready for my appointment with my parents' solicitor, Mr Barker. In the morning Anna had left for the meeting with her accountant, taking the dogs with her, and Jason had left just after lunch to meet his father to finalise the transfer of the house.

I slipped into a navy pencil skirt and pale yellow cotton shirt, added a necklace of semi-precious stones and brushed my hair back, securing it with a large, flat clip. After applying a touch of gloss to my lips, I slid my feet into a pair of navy court shoes, grabbed the file containing all the documents and made my way to the car.

Mr Barker's office was located in West London and it took me the best part of an hour to get there. I gave my name to the receptionist and was ushered into a spacious room where Mr Barker sat behind a large mahogany desk, looking very formal in his dark suit, white shirt and dark tie. He indicated a soft chair opposite and I sat down.

He looked at me from over the rim of his spectacles. "How can I help you?" he asked stoically.

"I hope you can help me," I started, and then explained the situation concerning the co-purchase of the house with my ex-partner and my difficulty in recovering my investment. I added that

I was going away and needed someone to act on my behalf. Mr Barker agreed to take the case and assured me that the matter would be dealt with during my absence. He requested that I sign the power of attorney, which I did without hesitation.

I reached for the folder. "These are all my documents," I said, handing the file over to him.

He placed the folder on his desk and covered it with his hands, indicating that the meeting was over. "I'll keep in touch."

Feeling as though a heavy weight had been lifted off my shoulders, I left Mr Barker's office, got into my car and drove back to Woodland. I entered the empty house, wandered through to the kitchen and made myself a cup of coffee. Carrying the hot mug of coffee, I went upstairs to the bedroom. Sipping the hot liquid, I stood in front of the window admiring the view of the wood spreading wildly below, and reflecting on the fact that soon I was going to leave it all behind and travel into the complete unknown. With a sense of anticipation, I realised that my life was going to change dramatically and nothing would ever be the same again, and this realisation left me with a strange feeling of emptiness and wishing I could hold on to my current life for a little while longer.

My thoughts were interrupted by the sound of a key in the front door.

"Carrie, where are you?" Jason called from the hall.

"Upstairs in the bedroom," I called back.

He rushed upstairs, taking two steps at a time.

"How did it go?" I asked.

He came over and wrapped his arms around me. "It went very well," he said, kissing me on the lips, "and to celebrate, I am taking you out to dinner. I've booked a table in a very nice restaurant."

"What brought this on?"

"The realisation that very soon our lives are going to change irrevocably and nothing will ever be the same again," he said and kissed me again. "So tonight I want us to forget about everything else and spend a last very normal evening together."

"That's funny, as I was thinking exactly the same thing."

Jason smiled. "Great minds think alike." He checked his watch. "We've got about an hour, so you need to get ready."

"It won't take me long to get ready. I just need a quick shower and a change of clothes." I gave him a peck on the cheek and headed for the bathroom.

After my shower, I covered my body in a dressing gown and went back to the bedroom to get dressed. Jason had already changed into a golden brown summer suit and white cotton shirt. He looked absolutely gorgeous and for a moment I just stood there staring at him.

"You look so handsome in a suit," I said eventually. "You make me feel bad as I have given all my evening clothes away."

"I thought about it and I got you something else." He reached behind the bed and produced a designer carrier bag with a large maroon satin bow. "I hope you like it," he said, handing it to me.

I looked at the bag in surprise. "This looks expensive."

"Nothing is too expensive tonight. Open it."

I pulled the end of the ribbon, undoing the large bow, and peered inside the bag. There, covered in light pink tissue paper was emerald green fabric, which looked like silk chiffon. Slowly, I pulled it out.

"Wow!" I said excitedly, dropping the bag onto the bed and unfolding a full-skirted dress with fitted bodice, long V-neck and mid-length narrow sleeves. "It's very beautiful. Thank you, sweetie. I've never had anything as beautiful as this before. I am going to feel very special tonight." I gave him a kiss. "You go downstairs while I dress. I want it to be a surprise.'"

Jason left and I began to get ready. I styled my hair with straightening irons, applied a small amount of make-up to my eyes and face and then covered my lips with coral-pink lipstick. Choosing my best plain silk underwear, I put it on and sprayed Dior's Poison around my neckline and onto my wrists. That done, I slipped into the silk dress and stood in front of the mirror. The dress fitted me perfectly and looked gorgeous, but it needed some jewellery. Rummaging through my drawers, I found the diamond and emerald necklace Mark had given me for my birthday. I took it out of its box and held it against my skin. The necklace complemented the dress very well, but as I looked at it I was reminded of Mark and I knew it would be wrong to wear it. I put it back in the box, feeling certain I would never wear it again. I found some small diamond studs and put them on instead. To complete the look, I chose a pair of caramel high-heeled sandals and a small caramel evening bag. Slipping my feet into the shoes, I walked slowly downstairs, feeling like a million dollars.

I gave a twirl. "Taa - ra!"

Jason grinned happily. "You look stunning."

I grinned back. "I feel stunning." I walked over to him and stared into his eyes. "I love you," I said quietly, stroking his hair.

He touched my cheek gently. "I love you too, babe."

"I think we should be going," I muttered, taking his arm.

"Yes, we should,' he agreed, and led me outside to his car.

He held the door open for me and I got in, carefully holding up the skirt of my dress. When I was comfortably seated he closed the door, walked around to the other side of the car and climbed in. He started the engine and we set off to London.

Jason and I reached Knightsbridge 50 minutes later and, after parking the car in one of the side streets, we walked a short distance to a small restaurant located at the back of Brompton Road.

The place looked very cosy with dimmed spotlights, warm candlelight at the tables and romantic music in the background. It was fitted out with solid dark wood tables and brown leather chairs, which were well separated and offered a substantial degree of privacy. As we entered, we were greeted by a smart black-suited man who appeared to be the restaurant manager. He politely checked our booking, picked up two large red leather-bound menus and led us to a quiet table at the back of the room. Once we were seated, he swiftly handed us the menus, lit the table candles and departed.

A short while later a waiter appeared to take our order. He scribbled the order on his small pad and he departed too. Within minutes he brought our drinks and not long after he began serving the food. For the next hour we ate the delicious food and talked quietly, completely absorbed in our private conversation and totally oblivious to our surroundings. Eventually we finished the main course and the waiter cleared the table and brought our desserts.

I touched Jason's hand across the table. "Thank you for this evening, sweetie. In fact, thank you for everything, but mainly for making me so very happy."

He lifted my hand to his lips and kissed it gently. "You know I'll do anything for you."

I nodded.

He looked straight into my eyes. "You have given me a lot and everything has been given freely, expecting nothing in return, which makes me want to give you as much as I possibly can and more. My life has been enriched and changed, for you have taught me how to look at things differently ..." He paused for a moment before continuing. "When I went to see my father today, all I could see was a very unhappy human being and all I wanted to do was to make my peace with him. We talked and said things to each other we would never have said if it weren't for you. You helped me to understand that my father cares for me and you opened my eyes to the fact that I love him, and I told him as much. For the first time in my life, my father told me that he was proud of me. He was proud because we took an old, dark, cold house and managed to make it warm, friendly, welcoming and liveable again. The resentment my father has felt towards the place during his whole life evaporated during his one visit because he could see hope for a better future." He reached into his inside pocket, took out an envelope and handed it to me. "Here, open it."

Slowly, I opened the envelope, pulled out a set of official-looking papers and examined them. They were the deeds to Woodland and they were issued in our joint names. Bewildered, I stared at Jason questioningly.

Jason just smiled and said, "It wasn't difficult to persuade my father to transfer the house to both of us. He knows how much I care for you and he also knows how special you are."

"But I can't accept it," I protested.

"Why? The deeds are in both our names, but you and I know that the house really belongs to many other people."

I knew exactly what he meant.

"You're right. We can never think of Woodland as exclusively ours. The house will always be sad and empty unless it is filled with people," I said, gazing into his eyes. "Without you being there the place would be very lonely for me, and don't think that you haven't taught me anything, because you have. You've taught me the difference between a loving person and a mean person. You've taught me how to be happy and how to take chances. Without your encouragement there would not be a house full of people. Without your love I couldn't have grown in the way I have." I gave him a loving smile. "And thank you again for organising this evening for us and for making me feel so very special tonight."

"You are very special to me," Jason muttered, squeezing my hand.

"And you are more than special to me," I said quietly.

We looked at each other and smiled, knowing we wanted to be away from the restaurant, to be on our own far away from everyone and everything. Jason signalled the waiter for the bill.

The waiter came over and looked at our untouched desserts. "Anything wrong with the food?" he asked.

"No, it looks delicious and I am sure it tastes delicious too," I replied with a smile.

His eyes showed surprise. "But you haven't touched it."

"It's no reflection on the food," Jason said. "You see, this is a very exciting evening for us - a kind of celebration."

"That's nice to hear. What are you celebrating, sir?"

"You would not believe it if we told you that we have been invited to travel on a spaceship and that tonight we are saying goodbye to our old life."

The waiter gave us a very strange look and we both laughed.

"Only kidding." Jason changed tack, seeing the waiter's confusion.

The waiter offered a relieved smile. "I'll go and get the bill, sir," he said, and walked off.

Jason paid and we left the restaurant, got into the car and drove back to Woodland.

We entered the house and walked into the semi-dark living room, which was illuminated only by the light of the full moon shining in the sky above the windows. Jason managed to find the 'Ti Adoro' CD and put it on, and as the beautiful sound of Caruso filled the room he pulled me close and we slowly began moving to the rhythm of the music.

"Do you remember when we danced for the very first time?" he asked quietly.

"Of course I remember. How could I forget?"

"It was a very special night," he said, lifting my chin with his index finger.

"Yes and tonight is no different," I replied, staring into his eyes.

He lowered his head and our lips touched. The kiss was tender and erotic, and desire spread throughout my body like a bush fire. The music was still playing when I took his hand and led him upstairs.

We undressed each other urgently, fell into bed and made the most beautiful and tender love, the love that engulfed us with a strong, unquenchable need for each other and fused our energies so completely that we nearly lost all sense of being and became one. It was as though by fusing our energies so totally we were connecting to something much greater than either of us had ever experienced before, as well as connecting to a wonderful new beginning.

Eventually, we came down to earth and lay cuddled together, not wanting to separate, even for a second. It wasn't long before we both fell into a very tranquil and easy sleep.

* * *

Early in the morning, when the first rays of sunshine filtered into the room, I was awakened by a surge of energy that shot through me like a strong current. I was aware of Amos trying to communicate a message concerning our departure.

I touched Jason's arm. "Wake up, sweetie. Amos wants to speak to us."

Jason opened his eyes and I related the information to him exactly as I heard it:

"The star gate will open an hour before midnight. Our ship will land behind your current dwelling. Please be ready to travel at midnight your time. You don't need to take anything with you. There has been a special apartment prepared on the ship, which has been designed in such a way as to make human travel as comfortable as possible and where you will find everything you might need. We are looking forward to welcoming you on board and rejoice at this opportunity to travel with you through space. Please do not fear anything and, above all, stay calm. Farewell for now."

When the message ended, I needed Jason's closeness and cuddled up to him.

"So it's tonight," he said quietly.

"Yes," I muttered. "It feels so strange."

Jason stroked my hair. "It'll be all right."

Now that our journey was imminent, I couldn't help but feel slightly apprehensive.

"I doubt if I would be courageous enough to face it on my own," I admitted.

"I'm glad you are courageous enough to face it with me," he replied.

"With you I'll go anywhere. I'll even go on a spaceship," I muttered, "but you must promise not to abandon me."

He kissed my head. "I'll never abandon you. We are in this together."

After that we lay silently for a while, preoccupied with our own thoughts, trying to comprehend fully that within a short space of time we would travel through space and see different worlds, worlds that we couldn't even imagine at present.

Eventually, Jason said, "I think we should get up, babe. We've got a busy day ahead."

"You're right." I gave him a kiss and climbed out of bed.

We washed, dressed and made our way down to the kitchen. I brewed some fresh coffee and we sat at the kitchen table.

"I'm not really hungry," I said. "Are you?"

"No, not really." Jason turned to me. "Is this really happening?"

"Yes, and as exciting as it is we have things to do and a party to attend, and we have to do our best to carry on as normal. Instead of thinking about the enormity of it all, why don't we make some kind of plan for today?"

"Okay, let's make a plan."

"I think our first priority is to make sure that Anna's room is finished," I said. "There's not that much to do, but the carpet still needs to be cleaned, the window frame needs to be painted and the furniture has to be assembled. Maybe George can put a few shelves up for her."

Jason nodded. "I'll ask him as soon as he arrives."

"That will probably take the best part of the day and then we have to prepare everything for the party, and don't forget that you have to collect my parents."

"What time should I collect them?"

"The party starts at six, so I think you should be there around five."

"First things first. I'll go to the hire shop and hire a carpet cleaner," Jason decided. He drained his cup and stood up. "Why don't you call your parents and tell them to be ready for five," he added, and gave me a kiss. "I shouldn't be too long."

I finished my coffee and made the call. I was putting my mobile down when Anna arrived carrying a big cardboard box.

"What have you brought?" I asked.

"Food for the barbecue," she replied, dropping the box onto the kitchen table. She pulled out a few packages of meat, put them into the fridge and returned to the box, rummaging inside.

"Anna, can you stop this for a moment, please?" I said. "I'd like to talk to you."

Her hand froze in midair and she faced me. "You are leaving," she guessed.

"Yes, we'll be leaving tonight," I confirmed.

"Tonight?"

I nodded. "After the party, but can we try to carry on as normal until then?"

"It's not going to be easy, but we can certainly try," Anna said, and returned to her box. "We need to take some chickens out of the freezer."

"I'll get them," I offered, lifting the top lid of the freezer. I pulled out three frozen chickens and put them on the draining board and then walked over to Anna. "Let me help you with that lot."

We were still unpacking the food when Mike and David arrived, and a few minutes later Zoe showed up. She had brought two Marks and Spencer carrier bags full of food.

"Where can I put these?"

"Just put them on the worktop for now," I replied.

"I've spoken to Vicky," Zoe said, taking out boxes of gourmet hors d'oeuvres and stacking them on the worktop. "Carrie, you'll be pleased with me," she added with a small, proud smile. "I told her straight that no one was expected to show up here unless they were invited and that included her."

"How did she respond?" Anna wanted to know.

"At first she looked at me blankly as though not comprehending, and then she said that she understood and she definitely would not be coming over unless she was invited. To be honest, I really can't say I'm sorry," Zoe said, dropping a few more boxes onto the worktop. "I noticed a new construction in the garden. What exactly is it?"

"It's a barbecue," I replied. "Jason and Joe built it especially for tonight's party."

"Looks impressive," Zoe commented. "What time is the party starting?"

"Six o'clock."

"Is there anything I can do to help?"

I turned to face her. "You could do some sewing."

"Sure, no problem. What sewing do you want me to do?"

"We need curtains for one of the bedrooms upstairs." I opened a kitchen drawer and searched for a tape measure. When I found it, I said, "Let's go and measure the window. Hopefully we have enough fabric left."

"Anna, are you coming?" Zoe asked.

"Yes," Anna answered, and followed us out of the kitchen.

We headed upstairs to Anna's room and measured the window, and then we measured the reminder of the gold fabric.

"There'll be enough for a pair of short curtains," Zoe decided.

"It would be great if you could sew them today," I said.

"I'll do my best. Whose room is this going to be?"

"Anna's."

"How come Anna's got her own room?" Zoe questioned, sounding surprised.

Anna and I exchanged glances, and I wasn't quite sure what to say.

"I need the room because I'm going to be spending more time here," Anna replied for me.

"I should have known," Zoe exclaimed. "It's Joe, isn't it? You have a thing for Joe!"

"Maybe." Anna was vague.

"You have. Admit it."

Anna smiled. "I'm admitting nothing."

"Anna, there is no need to be so secretive about it. There is nothing wrong with fancying an attractive man," Zoe said, and grabbed the fabric. "I suppose I'd better go and start on these curtains. With Joe around you'll definitely need them." She was on her way out when she bumped into Jason and George. "Oh, hi guys."

"Hi, Zoe," Jason said. "Where are you off to?"

"Me? Need you ask?" she stated, raising her hand with the fabric.

"More sewing?"

"Yeah, more sewing. See you all later," she said, and was gone.

Jason faced Anna. "Hi Anna. George is going to put some shelves up for you here." He pointed to one of the walls. "About two or three on this wall. What do you think, George?"

"I think it'll look good," George agreed.

"While George is doing that, maybe Anna and I can paint the window," I suggested.

"Cool. You do that and I'll clean the carpet and assemble the furniture," Jason said. "Let's get to work."

Miraculously, by 5 o'clock Anna's room was finished. It looked really inviting and bright with its light blue carpet, cream walls and a white gloss window frame. Resting against one wall was a double antique-stained pine bed, which was covered with crisp, white cotton linen and a mix of small, decorative cushions in white, beige and light blue, which were neatly arranged by the headboard. Next to it there was an antique-stained chest of drawers with a dressing mirror on the top surface and a small lamp. There was also a soft chair covered in thick, flowery beige fabric. Anna was very pleased with the final result.

We only had an hour left to set everything up for the party. George helped us to carry the kitchen table outside. We placed it close to the barbecue and Anna threw a white cloth over it. We used it for all the ready-to-eat food. There were bowls of fresh salad, plates full of hors d'oeuvres and an assortment of other snacks. The top of the barbecue, on either side of the grill, was utilised for all the food that required cooking. There were packs of various meats, pieces of marinated chicken, kebabs, burgers and several dishes with freshly cut vegetables. The garden tables, which were pushed together and stood next to the kitchen table, were used for plates, cutlery, glasses, small bottles of soft drinks and cans of beer. George set up a stereo on the veranda and put on some easy listening music, which sounded throughout the garden, creating a festive atmosphere.

When everything was ready, Anna and I went upstairs to change. Anna changed into a nice grey evening dress, which she had brought with her. The dress fitted nicely and showed off her figure to full advantage. She decorated it with three long strings of pearls and put a nice pearly clip in her hair. I dressed in a pair of dark fitted trousers, knee-high boots and a white shirt open all the way to my breasts and tied in a knot at the waist. I added diamond earrings and left my hair to fall down loosely around my shoulders.

Ready, we went outside to wait for the first guests to arrive. We were standing in front of the house chatting when we spotted Joe with his son, Thomas, coming down the country lane. They were both clad in their best attire - clean well-ironed shirts, dark trousers with straight creases running down the legs and dark, shiny shoes.

"Good evening, ladies," Joe said, as they approached. "May I say you both look lovely this evening."

Anna gave him a pleasant smile. "Thank you, Joe."

Thomas rushed over to Anna. "Can I play with Harry and Sally?"

Anna put her arm around his shoulders. "Of course you can, but how about you help me to put some charcoal in the barbecue first?"

"Is that going to be fun?" Thomas asked, not quite sure if it was a good idea.

"A lot of fun," Anna assured him. "We'll play a very clever game to find out who can put more charcoal in the barbecue on the count of ten."

"Okay," Thomas agreed happily, "but I'll go first."

"I'll tell you what," Anna said, leading him away. "You go first and then the person who wins goes first again."

"I bet I'll win every time."

"You are a clever little boy, so I'm sure you will."

Joe had a big, happy smile on his face. "Anna's definitely got the magic touch. The transformation in my boy is nothing short of amazing."

"Joe, there is no transformation," I said. "You can see your son as he really is."

"I haven't seen him this happy for a long time - if ever." Joe faced me. "And you know what, I couldn't be happier."

Other guests started to appear. The first to arrive was John, and then Martin with his girlfriend. A short time later, Jason's father pulled up in his Mercedes and lastly Jason arrived with my parents.

I asked Jason to look after the guests and took Mum on a tour of the house together with Dad, who decided to join us.

Mum looked out through the master bedroom window. "What a beautiful place," she marvelled, impressed.

"I told you it was beautiful," Dad said. "Now you can see for yourself that it's all for the best."

Mum turned away from the window and faced my father. "Robert, how can you say it's for the best when this is only a temporary roof over her head?" she asked, pointedly.

"No, it's not," I said, putting the record straight. "As of yesterday, I own half of this place."

Mum gave me a puzzled look. "What do you mean you own half of it?"

"I do. Jason's father signed half over to me."

Mum looked at me in total bewilderment.

"It's true, he did," I confirmed.

"He must be a very generous man," Mum commented, still not quite believing.

"He is, and Dad is right, it's all turned out for the best. I have my own place without a mortgage and Mr Barker is going to negotiate a settlement with Mark for me, so you see I am much better off and you have no excuse to worry about me any more."

Mum patted my arm. "I know I didn't want you to leave Mark, but now I am glad you did. I think it's time I stopped telling you what to do."

I gave her a quick hug. "You know I'll always appreciate your advice, but you need to understand that I have to start making my own decisions, even if some of them are not going to be good ones."

Mum smiled. "Let's hope you'll make mostly good ones."

"I wouldn't worry on that score," Dad said. "She's made quite a few good ones recently."

"I won't argue with that," Mum agreed.

Suddenly I realised I had to speak to Jason's father. "Can we go downstairs? I need to find Jason's father and thank him for the house."

"You haven't thanked him yet?" Mum asked in surprise.

I shook my head. "Not yet."

"Go and find him," Mum said. "There is no need for us to rush."

"Dad, take Mum to the back garden," I said, trying to make sure that my mother didn't overexert herself. "There are some chairs out there."

"You go. I'll look after your mother," Dad replied, waving me off.

I went outside through the back doorway and glanced around. I could see Mike, David and Zoe sitting in the woods, chatting and drinking beer. John, George and Joe stood together by the veranda laughing at each other's jokes, and little Thomas was playing with the dogs nearby. I walked down the steps and scanned the garden looking for Jason's father. I spotted him standing alone by the shed, nursing a glass of water in his hand and staring at the nearly finished coffee table. I walked over.

"It's very pretty, isn't it?"

He glanced at me. "Yes, quite beautiful," he replied, and his gaze returned to the table.

There was a moment of uncomfortable silence.

"I wanted to thank you for the house …" He didn't respond, so I carried on. "You can't even imagine how grateful I am. It was so generous of you to give it to me and to be quite honest I can't even find the right words to express how I feel. The only thing I can say is that I haven't met anyone as generous as you in my entire life, and that's saying something."

Jason's father looked around. "I hated this place with a passion, but I suppose I've always known that it would eventually belong to Jason," he said, and then faced me. "When it comes to my generosity, you are mistaken. Jason practically insisted that you share the ownership of this place, so it wasn't entirely my decision."

"But you could have refused," I pointed out.

"And alienate my son for the rest of my life?" he said with a small smile. "I am sure you understand that that was never an option."

"Your generosity is quite evident in your love for your son," I said, "and no, I wasn't mistaken. You are a very generous man."

He gave me a bigger smile and the sadness, which had been in his eyes before, was no longer there. "Jason said that there was something remarkable about you and, strangely enough, I didn't have any trouble believing him."

"Thank you. That is the nicest thing that anybody has ever said to me. After all, you don't know me at all."

"Let's just say that there is something in your eyes, something I find easy to trust."

It was my turn to smile. "You are much too nice to me. I promise I'll do my best not to disappoint you."

"I'm sure you won't."

"Thank you again for the house. I'll look after it in the best way I can."

"I know you will."

"Enjoy the party," I said, and walked away, looking for Jason.

I found him on the veranda, searching through CDs.

"Could you please look after your father," I said. "He seems rather lonely. Maybe you can introduce him to my parents."

"Good idea."

I patted his arm. "I'll see how the cooking is going."

I made my way to Anna who was busy watching over the barbecue.

"How long before the food is ready?" I asked.

"This lot is ready," she replied, using large metal tongs to turn a piece of marinated chicken. "You can call everyone to come over here."

"Will do." I turned to go and bumped straight into Martin. "Oh hi. How was your trip to Uganda?"

"Really good."

"Did you manage to get any nice pictures of animals?"

"Yes, I got some great pictures of chimpanzees and I had an opportunity to communicate with them, which was absolutely fantastic."

"How did you communicate?" I asked curiously.

"I went to a sanctuary where a keeper was trying to reunite a baby chimpanzee with its mother. It wasn't going very well, as every time the mother tried to approach the baby the little chimp ran away to the keeper. The mother was getting quite distressed and jumped around the cage making loud, wild noises, so I asked the keeper to let me have a go. At first the baby was very unsure and kept a safe distance from me. I started talking to her very quietly and calmly, and eventually she became more trusting and allowed me to hold her. I talked very quietly and calmly to the mother before I let the baby free. For a moment they just stared at each other without making a sound and then all of a sudden the mother moved forwards and the baby didn't run away. It actually ended up snuggling into the mother in a very trusting way. It was quite an experience."

"I can imagine," I said. "So you enjoyed your trip?"

"Very much so."

"Where are you going next?"

"I'm not sure. I would like to work more with chimpanzees if I can. They are such amazing animals," Martin replied, and glanced at the fare. "The food looks good."

"Anna is a great cook. Have you been introduced?"

"Briefly," Martin replied.

"You're a wildlife photographer, aren't you?" Anna asked, turning some vegetables on the grill.

Martin nodded. "Yes, I am."

Anna smiled. "I know it's not really wildlife photography, but maybe you could take some pictures of our dogs."

"Sure, but unfortunately I haven't brought my camera with me."

"You are welcome to come again," I invited.

"I definitely will," Martin replied. "Maybe next weekend."

"Do you have any other skills besides photography?" Anna asked with another smile. "We need all the help we can get to renovate this house."

Martin laughed. "I am very good at painting walls, as it happens."

"Great. There is quite a bit of painting to be done," Anna said, and reached for a plate. "What can I offer you?"

"The food looks so good I think I'll try a little of everything, and can I have two chicken kebabs on another plate, please?" Martin requested.

I left them to it and went to inform everyone that the food was ready.

By 8 o'clock everyone had eaten. We all gathered by the veranda and it was time to announce that we were leaving. Jason walked over to the stereo and switched off the music, and I joined him on the veranda.

"We have some news to share with you," Jason said loudly. "And it's not that Carrie and I are getting married," he added with a smile. "However, the news is about Carrie and myself ..." He paused for a few seconds. "The news is that we've decided to go away."

Nobody spoke, but just stared at us in shocked silence.

"We are not going away forever," Jason continued, "but we will be away for a few weeks. We hate the thought of leaving this place even for a few weeks, as it has grown so much since we moved in here and we are hoping that all the work can continue during our absence. Anna has agreed to look after the place for us and cook all the meals for everyone who can spare the time to come here and help."

Zoe shot me a critical look. I looked away and caught my mother's eyes, which were just as condemning, so I ended up dropping my head and staring at the wooden floor of the veranda.

"Where are you going?" Mike asked.

"Travelling," Jason replied. "We are taking a well-deserved break."

"But how can you just leave?" Zoe complained. "We all come here because you are here and now you are leaving us."

"It's only for a few weeks," Jason replied patiently. "We'll be back before you can sew another set of curtains."

"You know that's not true." Zoe looked miserable.

David put his arm around her waist. "I'll be here," he said, trying to reassure her.

She looked up at him and managed a smile. "I suppose with you being here there's still a good reason to come."

"I'll be here as well," Mike said.

"I am planning to continue as well," George declared.

'And I will definitely be here," Anna confirmed. "Let's face it, all of us love spending time here and we shouldn't just stop coming because Carrie and Jason have decided to take a break."

Little Thomas pulled at Anna's dress and she looked down. "Are they taking the dogs with them," he asked.

"Of course not," Anna replied.

"Can I come and play with them?"

Anna shot a look in Joe's direction. "Only if your father comes with you."

Thomas turned to his father. "Dad, will you come with me?"

Joe ruffled his hair. "Wild horses wouldn't stop me."

Anna smiled happily. "Jason, switch the music back on and let's continue with the party," she said. "Would anyone like a drink?"

While Anna collected orders for drinks, Zoe came over to me. "Why didn't you tell me?" she questioned accusingly.

"I'm sorry, Zoe. We only decided to go away in the last few days," I replied.

Zoe looked disappointed. "You told Anna. You even prepared a room for her."

"Anna didn't know until very recently," I tried to explain, "and her room has been redecorated very quickly."

"I thought I was your friend," Zoe sulked.

I hugged her. "You are my friend."

"You'd better come back soon, you hear?"

"I'll be back before you know it."

My mother was next. "What is this about you going away? You are just settling here. I think it's very irresponsible of you to leave all these strangers to look after the place."

"Mum, you promised you would let me make my own decisions," I reminded her.

"I think I said it in haste," she said, sounding as though she wanted to take her promise back.

"Kate, you have to let it go," Dad intervened. "We had an opportunity to go and live abroad and we took it, leaving Carrie behind. She's been coping very well on her own. If she wants to go travelling and she had found a trustworthy person to look after this place, let her. Don't try to make her feel guilty as though she is doing something wrong. When else is she going to be able to travel? When she is our age?"

"I suppose you're right," Mum admitted reluctantly.

"You know I'm right. You can't constantly interfere in Carrie's life. You have to let her make her own mistakes."

"But that's just it, I don't want her to make any mistakes," Mum argued.

"She'll make them whether you want it or not. That's the way life is."

"Mum," I interrupted. "I love you dearly and I'd hate to disappoint you, but you have to trust me when I tell you that this is a trip of a lifetime and I couldn't have made any other decision, and certainly not just to please you."

Mum faced me. "A trip of a lifetime, you say?"

"Yes, Mum. This is definitely going to be a trip of a lifetime."

"In that case, go with my blessing."

I gave her a kiss. "Thanks, Mum. That means a lot to me."

Soon, it was 10 o'clock and Jason and I we were fully aware that time was running out, so we decided to draw the party to a close on the pretext that we were leaving the following day and needed a good rest before departure. Within half an hour most of the guests had departed. Mike, George and Anna were staying overnight.

While Mike and George helped Jason to tidy up, I took Anna upstairs to our bedroom. Opening the drawer, I pulled out the box containing the diamond and emerald necklace.

"I've got this piece of jewellery that I suspect is worth quite a lot," I said, handing it to her. "Could you please sell it and use the money to repair the roof?"

Anna opened the box and stared at the sparkling necklace. "Are you sure you want to sell it? I could look after it for you until you come back."

"No, please sell it. I don't want to keep it. It only brings back bad memories," I said decisively. "I've got something else to give you," I added, lifting the carpet and the plank of wood, and reaching for the crystal. "This is very precious and I want you to look after it for me while I'm away."

Anna looked at the crystal curiously. "What exactly is it?"

"It's a very unusual stone. When you hold it you can connect to any part of the planet and you get all sorts of information." I passed the crystal to her. "Try it. Just hold it and tell me what you feel."

Anna concentrated for a moment. "I can feel that there is terrible flooding somewhere on the planet. I think it's in Bangladesh. The water is coming from under the ground and is covering a huge area of land." She looked at me. "And the water levels continue to rise ... Is it really happening?"

"I believe so."

"But this is such a major disaster and nothing has been reported."

"I think you will find that a lot of things are not being reported."

"Why?"

"To avoid panic, I suppose."

"But this crystal ..." Anna asked, totally baffled. "How does it work?"

"The crystal is a part of the planet, so through its energy you can connect to the planet itself," I explained.

"Are you sure you want to leave it with me?"

I nodded. "Just make sure it's safe," I said, and hugged her. "I'll miss you."

"I'll miss you too," Anna said sadly.

Jason entered the room and seeing Anna's sad face pulled her to him and held her silently.

After a while she pulled away, her eyes tearful. "I'd better go. You need to get ready."

"We'll see you soon," Jason muttered.

She nodded and crossed to the door. "Have a safe trip, guys," she said and left the room, closing the door behind her.

We changed into comfortable clothing and lay on top of the bed, holding each other.

"How are you feeling?" I asked.

"Apprehensive," Jason admitted.

"Me too."

"We'll have to go soon."

"I know."

We didn't say any more until it was time to leave.

* * *

At about quarter to midnight we tiptoed downstairs into the

kitchen, and then through the back doorway onto the veranda. Jason took my hand and led me down the steps and along the path leading to the open fields, the moon illuminating our way.

Sally, sensing that we were leaving, ran after us. We stopped.

"Sally," I said to her. "You have to go back and look after Anna for me." She stood there, staring at me, but when we began walking again she didn't follow us.

Within minutes we reached the large, open field spreading across the valley at the back of the house. It wasn't long before I could hear the familiar humming sound and spotted the flickering lights of the ship, which was slowly descending until it finally stopped, hovering above the ground.

"It's happening," Jason whispered, squeezing my hand.

"It is," I replied, holding onto him firmly.

"A huge adventure is awaiting us," Jason declared, sounding positive.

I tried to stay focused. "Yes, and we mustn't fear anything."

"No, there is nothing to fear," Jason said reassuringly.

We stood rooted to the spot while the ship landed. Slowly, the door opened and flooded the ship with light.

I heard the invitation to come on board and said to Jason, "They are waiting for us."

"Let's go and let the true adventure begin," Jason said, and holding hands tightly we began climbing towards the open door, eventually becoming enveloped in the light.